CW00347210

The
Traveling Man

To Emma,

love from,

Jane Harvey-Berrick

Jane Harvey-Berrick

♡

18.4.15

HB

HARVEY
BERRICK
PUBLISHING

The Traveling Man

Copyright © 2015 Jane Harvey-Berrick

Editing by Kirsten Olsen and Trina Miciotta
Cover Design by Hang Le

First published in 2015
ISBN 9780992924621

Harvey Berrick Publishing

Cover photograph by Michael Anthony Downs
Cover model, Tyler Gattuso

The Traveling Man

Jane Harvey-Berrick

iv

DEDICATION

To Libby.
My friend who has travelled life's bumpy road with
humour and wisdom.

ACKNOWLEDGMENTS

To Kirsten Olsen, editor, de-Britisher, friend, and sharer of twins, whose patience is legendary, and talents even greater.

To Trina Miciotta for being the third wheel on our tricycle, and for her unfailing study and knowledge of the hottest models.

To Hang Le for her stunning cover work and never-ending creativity. And she's just so lovely and patient. And did I mention creative?

To Michael Anthony Downs for being so generous with his time and talents.

To Sheena Lumsden, for all her work behind the scenes, ably supported by Jade Donaldson.

To Love Between the Sheets for arranging my blog tour.

Several gals have been kind enough to let me take their names in vain for this story: Gina Sanders, Tonya Bass Allen, Lisa Matheson Sylva, Beverly Cindy, Lulu Astor, Mirelle Christopher, Rhonda Koppenhaver—thank you all!

I'd also like to thank Audrey Thunder, Dorota Wrobel, Dina Eidinger, Bella Bookaholic, Lelyana Taufik, Nikki Costello, Gabri Canova and Gina Bookley for research photos, pimping and never-failing support.

For lovely messages that make me smile, Ana Kristina Rabacca, Marie Mason, Clare Norton, Abril and Daniel, Jenny Angell, Celia Ottway, Lisa Ashmore, Gitte Doherty and Jenny Aspinall.

A. Meredith Walters, Roger Hurn, Monica Robinson, Devon Hartford, Gillian Griffin, Sawyer Bennett, Kirsty Moseley, LH Cosworth, Penny Reid, Karina Halle, Lex Martin, Jules Barnard and the wonderful Ker Dukey, friends who share the writer's lonely path!

The Stalking Angels: Sheena, Aud, Dina, Bella, Shirley Wilkinson, Cori Pitts, Dorota Wróbel, Barbara Murray, Emma Darch-Harris, Kandace Milostan, Kelsey Burns, Lelyana Taufik, MJ Fryer, Hang (MJ), Gwen Jacobs, Kirsten Papi, Trina, Sarah Bookhooked, Sasha Cameron, Rosarita Reader, Jacqueline Showdog, Remy Grey, Ashley Snaith, Kandace Lovesbooks, Jo Webb, Carly Grey, Jen Berg, Carol Sales, Meagan Burgad, Andrea Lopez, Paola Cortes, Kelly O'Connor, Gabri Canova, Whairigail Adam, Julie Redpath, Jade Donaldson, Sharon Mills, Rhonda Koppenhaver, Emma Wynne-Williams, Ellen Totten, Nicola Barton, Lovey Anna Leavell, Stacia Lynette, L. e. Chamberlain, Lisa G. Murray Ziegler, Drizinha Dri, Aime Metzner G, Terra Chastain, Andrea Jackson, Brunihna Mazzali Belissimo, Sarah Lintott, Natalie Townson, Elle Christopher, Nancy Saunders Meyhoeffer, Mary Dunne, Fuñny Souisa, Erin Spencer, Caroline Yamashita, and Luiza.

For their support and encouragement, I'd also like to thank…

The Book Bloggers
Aestas Book Blog
Badass Bloggettes
Between the Sheets
Books and Beyond Fifty Shades
FMR Book Grind
Hopeless Romantics
Kelly's Kindle Confessions
Kelsey's Korner Blog
Love Between the Sheets
Maryse Book Blog
Natasha is a Book Junkie
No BS Book Review
Perusing Princesses
Shh Mom's Reading
The Smut Club
The Southern Book Belles
The Sub Club Books
Swoon Worthy Books
Totally Booked

And the Fanfic readers who were there from the start.

Other Jane Harvey-Berrick Titles

The Education of Sebastian
The Education of Caroline
The New Samurai
Exposure
Dangerous to Know & Love
The Dark Detective
At Your Beck & Call
Summer of Seventeen
Lifers
Dazzled
The Traveling Woman (*not yet published*)

CONTENTS

PROLOGUE

I was ordinary. Nice.

He was extraordinary. And he wasn't always nice.

But he was beautiful.

Handsome was too small a word for his smooth golden skin, stretched across sharp cheekbones and strong chin; eyes the color of the sea before a storm, the expression questioning, vulnerable; lips soft and pliant, rose-kissed; his body hard, sculpted, dangerous...

He could breathe fire, he could eat flames, but the word 'love' burned on his lips.

I was on the journey before I even knew our story had started.

Funny the way things work out.

PART ONE: BEGINNINGS

CHAPTER 1
MY TENTH BIRTHDAY

Two eyes, black as buttons, were watching me. The figure in the darkness crooked a finger. *Come here*, the gesture said. I took a step forward into the shadows.

"What are you doing?"

"Hiding," said the boy.

"Why?"

His smile was mischievous and I should have known better. Perhaps I did. But when I was ten, I didn't care.

"I want to show you something," he said. "Or are you too chicken?"

I was definitely chicken, and I already knew that he was going to get me into trouble…

My parents hadn't wanted to go to the carnival, but it was my birthday, so I was allowed to choose how we were going to spend the day.

My older sister, Jennifer, wanted to go ice-skating at the indoor rink in Minneapolis. But I hated ice-skating because I couldn't do it, and I didn't like being in the city much either. Usually Jennifer got her way, but because it was my day, for once I was allowed to choose—and I chose the carnival.

The posters announcing that the carnival was coming went up just after the Fourth of July and two weeks before my birthday. I knew right away that's what I wanted to do on *my* day.

To me, the carnival promised a world of magic. I'd never been anywhere in my life, never even left Minnesota. But carnie people, they had homes with wheels and could go wherever they wanted. They weren't stuck in a small town, dreaming of the world beyond.

When I told my family what I wanted to do, Dad snapped his newspaper over the breakfast table and gave me *The Look*. We were all petrified of *The Look* and would do anything to avoid it and the wrath that usually followed—even Mom.

"The carnival is full of people who want you to waste all your money on silly games, just so you can win a $2 stuffed toy. Is that what you want for your birthday, Aimee? Your birthday money wasted? You might as well throw it away."

I couldn't meet his eyes and I shook my head wordlessly. Because I did want to go to the carnival: desperately. But when silent tears tracked down my cheeks, Mom wrapped me in her arms, and I buried my face in her softness, smelling cinnamon and something lemony, a scent that always made me feel safe.

"Don't worry," she said, "we'll go to the carnival."

I was shocked. It was the first time I'd ever seen her stand up to my father. I was ten.

The carnival had never come to our small town before, but then Mr. Peterson up and died, which was very selfish of him, or so said the ladies of the town guild, because his high school drop-out son rented the field to the carnies, and all sorts of unsavory people were going to swarm into our nice, quiet town and paint it red.

I rather liked the sound of that: all those dull, concrete buildings and ugly malls painted as red as Madonna's lipstick. Until Mom told me it was a metaphor. Our elderly neighbor, Mrs. Flock, lived for gossip and drama, and she told everyone that if the carnies came, the streets would run with blood. I asked Mom if that was another metaphor, and Mrs. Flock said, "Not necessarily."

She made it sound like the townsfolk were Colonel Custer and the Seventh Cavalry, and a thousand million Sioux were going to come swarming over the horizon. I couldn't wait. *Finally,* something exciting was going to happen.

And then, the day before my birthday, they arrived.

It was a Friday towards the end of July, and the air shimmered with summer heat, even the flies were drugged and lazy. I was sitting under my tree with a book when the ground began to hum. I watched with awe as the road outside our house growled and rumbled. I imagined bronzed horsemen sweeping down with their black hair flying and the pounding of the horses hooves. I was only mildly disappointed when a stream of massive sixteen-wheelers roared past in a cloud of diesel and dirt.

I ran to watch them, ignoring the grit that flew up, making my eyes water and covered my clothes in a layer of fine red dust.

My blood felt hotter in my veins and I clenched my fists in excitement.

They were here!

The huge trucks poured into Mr. Peterson's field and I wanted to run down the street and watch, but Mom came out and caught my wrist.

"You mustn't go over there by yourself, Aimee," she said, her voice low and urgent. "It's not safe."

That made me want to go even more, but I was a good girl and used to listening to my mother. So I didn't go, no matter how badly I wanted to.

Instead, I climbed as high as I could into the bitternut hickory tree in the front yard, scraping my knees on the granite-gray bark that looked like scales. The leaves were still green and would stay that color until September, when the first cold front rolled in. It was a useful place to hide when I didn't want to be found, which was quite often.

The dust swirled like smoke and a knot twisted my stomach. I screwed up my face and peered into the red cloud, my greedy eyes feeding on the distant scene. Tinny music drifted on the scalded air and the monstrous trucks disgorged the rides piece by piece, wrestling the hot metal into fantastical shapes.

The only one I could make out at this distance was the Ferris wheel. It rose up like the skeleton of a mythical beast, promising a new world and distant horizons from the highest point—so much higher than my old hickory tree. My ten-year old self was filled with hopes and dreams.

"Aimee, get your butt down here! Mom's looking for you."

I scowled through the leaves. Jennifer had found me.

"What does she want?" I yelled.

But Jennifer had already kicked my book into the long grass and headed back inside.

I took one last look at Camelot rising toward the Minnesota sun, and slid down the tree, shoving my dirty hands in the pockets of my shorts.

That night when I went to bed, my limbs twitched with

anticipation. I could hardly hold my excitement inside. *They* were there, just across the field—carnie people. If I breathed in hard enough, maybe I could catch the scent of hotdogs in the still air, and imagine the sugary sweetness of cotton candy gluing my long hair to my lips.

I was old enough to know that magic didn't exist, and young enough to hope that I was wrong. I was sure that if magic belonged anywhere in the world, it was living and breathing right across the road in Mr. Peterson's field.

I pushed my thin sheet to the end of the bed and knelt on the mattress, elbows propped on the windowsill. Pink and yellow lights flashed a gaudy warning: *danger, blink-blink, blink-blink*.

When I woke the next morning, the first thing I did was stare out the window at the Ferris wheel, stark and still in the bright white sky. I relaxed a fraction. I'd been so afraid that they'd vanish in the night, gone like fairy dust. Maybe I did believe in a magic—just a little.

"Happy birthday, baby girl!" sang Mom, bustling into the room to rain blueberry-scented kisses onto my squirming face.

"Mom!" I shrieked and laughed, ducking her extravagant hug.

"Someone's getting pancakes for breakfast!" she smiled, her eyes crinkling with happiness.

Too much pleasure was rigorously policed in our house and doled out like cough medicine; pancakes were the Shangri La of breakfasts, only permitted on birthdays and holidays. Mom loved pancakes as much as I did. At times like this, it was me and Mom against the world.

I raced downstairs, crashing into the kitchen table, my fork hovering over the stack of golden goodness, waiting for permission to eat.

Dad glanced up over his newspaper and wished me a happy birthday. I gazed at him nervously, thanked him, and looked away.

Jennifer thundered down the stairs behind me, forgetting that she was 13 and learning to be cool.

"Enjoy!" laughed Mom, smiling as we swooped in like vultures, shoveling pancakes onto our plates and drowning them in syrup.

Mom helped herself, too, and the three of us inhaled a gazillion calories, buzzing with excitement and a sugar high that would last all morning. Until I came crashing back to earth, with Jennifer's demand that we go skating in the city.

My gratitude to Mom wavered over the years, but that day, that very special birthday, she was on my side.

"No, Jennifer; it's Aimee's birthday, so we're going to the carnival. You'll enjoy it."

Dad pressed his lips together, his disapproval louder than a yell. My eyes dropped to my empty plate, hiding the smile that threatened to break out.

After breakfast, time seemed to slow down, then spin backwards, loop around a few times and crawl across the face of the kitchen clock, mocking me every second as the blue hands stuttered and hesitated.

I had new books to read. Gifts for my birthday from Mom and Dad—although I doubt he even knew what Mom had chosen—but every part of me longed to be in Mr. Peterson's field, investigating the mysteries that I was sure were hidden among the bumper cars and carousels.

"It doesn't even open until 2 o'clock," reassured my mom.

Bad tempered and sulky, I flung out of the house, climbing my tree and looking longingly into the distance.

I couldn't tell you why the carnival lured me with its sticky fingers and bright, whirling colors, except to say that it was *different*, and that excited me. I'd only read about 'different' in books, never experienced it for myself. Perhaps it was a case of be careful what you wish for.

Finally, after an anxious lunch where I could barely swallow my salad, it was time to go.

As we prepared to walk the 200 yards to Mr. Peterson's field, we passed my father's new Mercedes. He frowned, wiping a finger through the red film that coated the hood, and my heart sank. Jennifer met my eyes, knowing what I was thinking, because his expression meant that she'd be washing the roof tomorrow, being tall enough to reach it without standing on an upturned bucket, unlike me. I'd be left to wash the hubcaps then polish them to a blinding brightness.

I pushed the unwelcome thought away: that was tomorrow, and right now I was here.

On the way to the carnival, I had to hold Mom's hand. My father's steps were slow and measured, each one shouting his disapproval. I tugged at Mom's hand, desperately trying to hurry her along as we made our way to the entrance.

"I don't see how they can justify charging $20 each for this," Dad muttered, already irritated by the carnie in the ticket booth.

He was arguing about the entrance fee for the four of us. He had no intention of going on any of the rides, and I doubted Mom would either. He thought it was a waste of money. I agreed. I wanted to tell him not to pay the money and that I'd be fine with just my sister for company, but my tongue stuck to the roof of my mouth and the words wouldn't come out, which was pretty much what always happened when I thought about disagreeing with Dad.

My eyes were pleading and I think I saw a shadow of sympathy in the carnie's eyes.

"Creating magic don't come cheap," he said to Dad.

My eyes widened: was there real magic here after all?

Dad snorted and I think he would have replied, but Mom begged quietly, "Adam, please."

The carnie's eyes narrowed, but he didn't say anything else, simply handing each of us a wristband to prove that we'd paid. Besides, there were already people pressing in behind us, eager to spend their money to enter the hallowed grounds.

If I'd had my way, I'd have run helter-skelter up and down the midway, spending my money on every gaudy game that caught my eye, but Mom insisted that we walk along, examining everything, working out which sideshow stalls we would try, in an orderly fashion.

I wanted to scream—it wasn't supposed to be orderly; it was supposed to be chaotic and loud; it was supposed to be fun.

Jennifer was looking at a display of cheap cowboy hats, her eyes fixed on a candy-pink one with a silver star pinned to the front. I knew she wanted that hat badly, but it would be hard work to convince Mom why she 'needed' it.

As they argued, Dad's eyes full of boredom and disdain, that's when I saw him—the boy, watching me.

I stepped into the shadows.

"I want to show you something," he said. "Or are you too chicken?"

I looked over my shoulder at Mom and Jennifer and my father.

"I'll come," I said, putting my hands on my hips, "but it had better be good."

He held back the tarp and I wriggled inside, the heat matting my hair to my face and sweat making my scalp itch.

"Where are we going?" I asked, peering through the gloom as the tarp dropped back in place and shadows filled my eyes.

But all I could hear was the boy's footsteps, further away now.

"Come on, chicken!" he laughed.

I blinked rapidly, my eyes adjusting to the darkness, and I stumbled after him.

When we finally emerged into daylight again, I could see that his eyes were really a strange light gray edged with dark blue. I'd never seen anything like them before. I stared for several seconds before he blinked.

I gazed around: we were far away from the midway, and the noise was a mumble and mutter of confused sound.

"Where are we?" I said.

"Away from the rubes," he replied.

I didn't know what a rube was, and I was fairly sure I didn't want to be one, but then he grabbed my hand and we ran across the brown grass.

Suddenly I realized where he had taken me. I could see the metal frames that were hidden behind the colorful frontage, the strings working the puppets, you might say, and I instantly deflated. I wanted to cry. I came to the carnival wanting the magic of it all. Believing, albeit foolishly, in the illusion that was laid out before my eyes. Instead this strange boy had revealed to me the proverbial card up the sleeve. The rabbit in the darn hat!

I opened my mouth to yell at him, but he smiled, showing a dimple in his right cheek, and put his finger to his lips.

"You'll have to be quiet," he said. "Mr. Albert doesn't like loud noises."

"Who's Mr. Albert?"

"You'll see."

I followed him, noticing for the first time that his jeans were torn at both knees and that his t-shirt was too big and too dirty. He pushed his crooked bangs out of his face and threw me that mischievous look again.

We were standing outside one of the hulking RVs that were the carnies' homes.

"What's your name?" I asked suddenly.

The boy paused, his hand hovering over the door handle.

"Kes," he said at last.

My nose wrinkled. "That's a funny name."

He shrugged. "I know. What's yours?"

"Aimee. Pleased to meet you."

I cringed immediately, knowing that it was the sort of thing Mom would say.

Kes grinned and scratched his narrow chest, pushing a finger through a hole in his t-shirt. Then he pulled the door open and stepped inside.

"Aimee, meet Mr. Albert."

I didn't see him at first. He sat so still, that my eyes drifted past him, but then he bared his teeth and hissed at me.

I gasped and jumped backwards.

"It's alright," said Kes, wrapping his long fingers around my hand. "He won't hurt you—he just doesn't know you yet."

He took a step forward, towing me behind him, then dropped my hand.

"Hey, Mr. Albert," he said softly, reaching out slowly.

"It's a monkey!" I breathed, my eyes wide with wonder.

Kes nodded. "He's a tufted capuchin from Venezuela."

He reached out and the tiny creature leapt into his arms, cuddling against Kes, and wrapping thin arms around his neck.

"Shouldn't he be called "Senor Alberto?" I said.

Kes burst out laughing. I hadn't meant to be funny, but it seemed to happen all the time at school. I didn't mind it too much today because Mr. Albert pulled a face and reached out to touch my hair. He tugged it gently then started chattering away at me.

"He likes you," Kes said confidently. "Do you want to hold him?"

"I don't know. I've never held a monkey before."

Kes smirked at me, and I lifted my chin.

"Alright then."

"You have to ask him," said Kes.

I thought he was teasing me again, but his face was serious, his dimple nowhere to be seen. I looked back at the monkey who was watching me warily.

"Mr. Albert," I said, "would you like me to hold you?"

The monkey chattered and screeched, and my hands trembled as I held them out. But then, quite suddenly, he jumped into my arms, as light as a cat, his long tail wrapping around my wrist.

I squealed and Mr. Albert pulled my hair, a little harder this time.

Kes frowned. "I told you—he doesn't like loud noises."

"Sorry," I whispered. "Sorry, Mr. Albert."

Kes beamed at me. "He likes it when you talk to him."

I stroked the monkey's soft fur, smiling as he jabbered softly in my ear.

His face was that of a little old man's, but his eyes were round and bright. I stared at his tiny fingers and leathery palms, feeling his warm dry paw on my arm. His expression was so knowing, I felt as if he could see every dream I'd ever had. I wondered if he was a magic monkey. Here, in this place, it felt like magic was possible.

Kes watched me, a smile tugging at his pink lips. I smiled back shyly, not used to being studied so intently.

"Can I see inside?" I asked, changing the direction of his gaze.

Kes frowned. "There's not much to see."

"Well, show me your bedroom."

He pulled a face. "I can't. It's in the main part of the RV. There's only one bedroom and that's Grandpa's. Mine's a pullout under the table."

"Oh," I said, not sure what to say.

"If it's hot, I sleep outside."

"I've never done that," I admitted.

Kes looked puzzled. "Why not?"

I shrugged. I'd never even camped in the backyard. I couldn't imagine my father doing something so undignified.

There was a gulf between Kes's world and mine—and for some reason the thought made me sad.

"We could take Mr. Albert for a walk," Kes suggested suddenly.

"Is that allowed?"

Kes lifted a shoulder, so I wasn't sure if that meant yes or no. I followed him out of the RV, Mr. Albert clinging to me, his dark eyes unblinking, lips pulled back in a wide grin.

It was only slightly less stifling outside, and my clothes were sticking to me. I wiped my forehead with my fist and blew my hair out of my face.

"You're kind of skinny, aren't you?" Kes observed. "How old are you?"

My cheeks flushed a dull red. "I'm ten," I snapped. "How old are you?"

"Eleven next birthday," Kes replied, grinning.

"That's the same age as me then," I pointed out.

He shrugged again.

"Come on," he said with a quick grin. "Let's go to the coconut stand. Mr. Albert likes coconuts."

"I've never had one," I admitted.

Kes squinted at me. "You've never had a coconut?"

"That's not weird," I said stoutly. "I don't know anyone who's had a fresh coconut."

As we walked toward the midway, several of the carnies called out to Kes. He waved but didn't stop, weaving his way under the guide ropes and past the canvas tents until we were at the back of the coconut stand. He zipped in under the tarp and snagged a coconut that had rolled to the floor.

I heard someone yelling and Kes ran out laughing, a large hairy coconut clutched to his chest.

"Come on!" he said, looking over his shoulder and beaming at me with pride as the tarp shook and quivered as if something very large was trying to get through.

We ran laughing, Mr. Albert clinging to my shoulders like a furry backpack, his paws holding my hair like reins.

Finally, we stopped in the shade of the Ghost Train, our backs to the faded outline of ghouls.

Kes expertly cracked open the coconut on a tent peg and showed me how to suck out the milk as it dribbled down his chin and stained his t-shirt. Then he wiped his hand across his mouth and passed the coconut to me.

I'd never tasted anything quite like it—sweet and sour, all at the same time.

Mr. Albert pulled my hair harder.

"Ow!"

Kes laughed. "He wants some, too."

Mr. Albert slipped down to the dirt and greedily drank the rest of the milk. Then Kes split the coconut shell into pieces and showed me how to scrape off the meat with my teeth. It was much nicer than the milk, and I gorged myself on the sweet flesh.

Sighing contentedly, I rubbed my tummy and lay down, staring out at the shimmering heat and flawless sky. Kes lay next to me, and we listened to Mr. Albert chattering to himself.

"What's it like living in a carnival?" I asked, my voice distant and sleepy.

"I dunno. What's it like living in a house?" he replied.

"Haven't you ever lived in a house?"

"During our winter break, we have a log cabin by Arcata Bay," he said. "But it's not like a house."

I thought about that, what it must be like traveling all the time, always moving, never staying.

"You must have seen loads of places," I sighed.

Kes shrugged. "Yeah, I guess."

"What was your favorite?"

His forehead wrinkled.

"I liked Carhenge. That's in Nebraska."

"Car what?"

"It's this huge wheat field, and all these cars have been planted in a circle and stuck in the ground. They've even got a '62 Cadillac. And they're all painted gray to make them look like they're made of stone.

I frowned, trying to imagine it, then realization struck.

"Oh, like Stonehenge?"

Kes shrugged. "I don't know what that is."

I smiled. "Anyway, I thought you were going to say the Grand Canyon or something like that."

"Yeah, that was cool, too."

Kes had been to Chicago and Las Vegas, walked through Times Square and had swam in both the Atlantic and the Pacific Ocean. Everywhere I mentioned, he had a story of something amazing. Yes, it sounded magical.

"Where do you go to school?" I said at last, grasping for something ordinary that at least would sound familiar.

"I don't."

His answer shocked me. "Not at all?"

"Nope. You can't learn anything in school."

"That's silly!"

"No, it isn't!" he shot back. "I know everything about the carnival, and that's all I need to know."

Getting an education was like the Holy Grail in my house. We were hardly ever allowed to take a day off sick, only if we had a temperature that was sky high or we looked as pathetic as a skinned squirrel, and Mom knew that the teacher would send us home anyway.

Kes's voice lowered. "I've never been to school," he admitted shyly. "I don't like books. Yeah, I hate books."

"How can you not like books?" I squeaked, gaping at him.

I could imagine hating *a* book, but I couldn't imagine anyone ever saying that they hated *all* books.

"There must be some books that you like?" I tried again.

Kes pulled a face and shook his head.

"What about 'The Hobbit'?" I asked, mentioning my current favorite.

"Never heard of that," he said. "What's a hobbit?"

"I'll read it to you," I said, my voice filled with confidence.

I was good at reading—it was the only thing I did well, as far as my parents were concerned. But thinking of that made me realize that Mom and Dad would be looking for me.

"I'd better get back now," I sighed.

Kes looked disappointed.

"But it's been the best birthday ever!"

He blinked a couple of times. "It's your birthday today?"

"Yes, that's why I wanted to go to the carnival. It's my birthday treat."

"If you come back tomorrow, I'll show you loads of other cool stuff," Kes offered.

I chewed a fingernail while I thought about it.

"I'd like to, but I don't know if Mom and Dad will let me." I sighed. "But I'll be able to see you from my bedroom window. I'll wave, even though you won't know I'm doing it."

Kes frowned. "You live in that white house on the road?"

"That's right!" I said surprised.

"I've seen it. It has a big ole hickory tree in the garden."

I grinned at him. "I climb that tree every day. I hide there when I don't want anyone to find me."

Kes grinned back and I knew I'd shared a secret with him, just like he'd shared Mr. Albert with me.

"Come on," he said. "I'll take you to your mom and dad."

We wandered along the midway, and I held my head up proudly as every eye swung in our direction, people doing a double-take when they spotted Mr. Albert. I loved it and I hated it. Kes was unaffected, sauntering along with his hands in his pockets, calling greetings to the other carnies.

When I saw my father, I froze. His face was red with anger, and a purple vein throbbed in his forehead. Worse still, he was talking to the Sheriff, pointing a finger in his face and shouting.

"Is that your old man?" Kes asked.

I nodded, my stomach threatening to spew up coconut.

Mom saw me first, and she cried out, running toward me. But before she could touch me, her trembling hand clutched her throat and she shrieked.

"What is that thing?!"

Mr. Albert objected to the noise and bared his teeth at her, yammering loudly and spitting, his small face wrinkled with fury.

Dad and the Sheriff ran toward me, and I was afraid they'd shoot Mr. Albert, but Kes calmly unfolded the little monkey from my waist and swung him up onto his back, grinning the whole time.

His smile died when a hard-faced carnie strode toward him and grabbed his upper arm, spinning him around.

"What are you doing messing with a townie girl?" he snapped. "And you've got work to do."

"Just wanted to show Mr. Albert to her, Grandpa," Kes said sullenly.

The man's lips thinned further; he plucked Mr. Albert away with one hand and casually backhanded Kes with the other, knocking him to the ground.

I stood there, stunned. I'd never seen anyone get hit before. In my house, the punches were always verbal.

Kes wiped away a trickle of blood from his lip and pushed himself to his feet.

"You alright, Miss Aimee?" asked Sheriff Smith kindly. "That boy hurt you at all? He … touch you … or anything?"

"No!" I said sharply. "He showed me Mr. Albert and we ate a coconut. He was nice to me. When I said I had to get back, he took me here right away."

The Sheriff and my Mom exchanged looks, but my father's expression told me I was in big trouble. No one seemed to care that Kes had a split lip, and that made me mad.

"You're all being really mean to him," I cried, my own lips trembling. "It was the best birthday ever until you all spoiled it!"

Jennifer gaped at me in admiration, and it was only then that I noticed she was wearing the pink cowboy hat.

"Come along now, Aimee," said Mom. "Time to go."

I sighed and wiped my hands on my shorts, determined to show better manners than the adults.

"Bye, Mr. Albert. Bye, Kes. Thank you for inviting me to your, um, home."

Kes grinned at me, seeming to forget that he was still bleeding.

"Bye, Aimee. Happy birthday!"

His grandpa dragged him away by the collar of his t-shirt, holding him so tightly, Kes's feet barely touched the cracked ground.

"Do we have to go home now?" whined Jennifer. "I wanted to see the rodeo show."

I stared at her in surprise—I knew that was a danged lie. Then she winked at me and my breath stuttered in shock. Jennifer *never* did anything nice for me, but she had today. I grinned back at her, then ducked my head as Mom gazed at her suspiciously.

"Aimee doesn't deserve to see the show," Dad snapped.

"I expect she was led astray by that boy," Mom replied blandly.

That wasn't even the smallest bit true, not really, but I held my tongue, because this way I'd get to see the show.

Mom held my hand so tightly she was in danger of twisting it right off. At least that's what it felt like.

We followed the crowd toward a field behind the towering Ferris wheel, where four tiers of ramshackle bleachers were arranged in a U-shape. Slowly, they began to fill with people who seemed happy and carefree.

Dad led us to a set of four seats at the furthest point away from the popcorn-snacking hordes.

I wished I had some cotton candy or a hotdog to eat, but I knew there was no chance of that now. But I was content to see the show.

The sun was at the back of our necks, slowing cooking us like hogs on a roasting spit. Jennifer was so pink that her freckles seemed to be three dimensional, and Dad's nose looked like all it needed was some barbecue sauce. Mom said I took after my Grandmother Luiza. I shared her straight brown hair and olive complexion. The kids at school called me The Mexican or Chippewa when our teacher, Mrs. Oioli wasn't around. I didn't care; I imagined carrying a tomahawk to school in my backpack and casually getting it out at lunch break. That would stop the comments, I was sure.

But I wasn't immune to the heat that sizzled around us, scorching the grass to a dull brown so even the air smelled like burnt paper.

But then the mournful cry of a bugle cut through the drowsing crowd, and we all sat up, stiff with expectation.

A pony galloped into the arena carrying a cowboy. Either he was very young or very short; I couldn't tell because his face was covered by a bandana. Two more ponies followed, ridden by men wearing sheriffs badges, their mounts weaving around like barrel-racers, pretending to chase the young cowboy. I could see their flanks heaving, their nostrils wide and their ears forward. I didn't know much about horses, but these ones looked as excited as I felt.

The sheriffs and cowboy careered around the arena, jumping on and off the ponies with the same ease that I'd walk down the stairs, so casual, but so daring.

Every time it looked like they'd catch the little cowboy, he dodged out of their grasping hands, leaping to the side, vaulting over the saddle as the pony zigzagged, following instructions I couldn't see. The crowd's ooh's and ah's, gasps and laughter rippled around. I was on the edge of my seat, watching the ponies dance and the cowboy's incredible acrobatics.

With a final show of bravado, the cowboy leapt to his feet, so he was balancing on the pony's racing back, then he somersaulted off, losing his hat and his bandana slipping.

I saw Kes's dimple and wide smile, and I couldn't help jumping to my feet and shouting my delight along with the rest of the crowd.

By then he was already 'my Kes'.

CHAPTER 2
THE BOY IN THE HICKORY TREE

Tap.

Pause.

Tap.

I looked up from the book propped on my pillow and scowled at the window.

Tap.

This time I saw a tiny stone bounce off the glass and tumble down. I sat up, surprise and excitement rushing through me.

When I crawled across my mattress and opened the window, staring at me from twenty feet away, hidden by the thick leaves of my hickory tree was Kes, grinning and waving.

I waved back, then gasped as he ran lightly along the slender branches and launched himself through my window, just at the moment when I thought he was sure to fall.

He landed cat-like on the floor, then stood up, brushing leaves and dirt onto my rug.

My mouth dropped open, feeling as if my world had slipped out of focus. Boys didn't just jump through my window.

Kes stuffed his hands in his pockets and raised his eyebrows. Maybe he was waiting for a round of applause. Maybe I was waiting for him to disappear in a puff of smoke, because I was certain he couldn't be real.

I poked him with my finger and he flinched, a flash of anger darkening his slate-gray eyes.

"Why did you poke me?"

"Why did you jump through my window?"

His lips slid over his teeth and he seemed uncomfortable.

"I wanted to see you," he said at last. "And you didn't come around yesterday. I like your room."

I squinted, trying to see my room through his eyes. It wasn't large and I didn't have my own TV like a lot of kids at school. It was decorated with posters of boy bands from magazines that Jennifer read, and I didn't think it was anything special, but Kes's eyes had found the one thing in my room that I was proud of: he was staring transfixed at my bookshelf.

"Have you read all those books?"

His voice sounded awed.

"Sure! These are my favorites."

I pulled out 'The Hobbit' and handed it to him. He took it as reluctantly as if I'd handed him a snake. He slid a grubby finger between two pages and peeked inside.

"It doesn't have any pictures," he said, his voice disappointed.

"It doesn't need any. It paints pictures with words."

Kes frowned at me and shook his head. "I don't like books," he said stubbornly.

"You'll like this one," I insisted.

I made myself comfortable on the bed and Kes sat down next to me, his eyes wary as I began to read.

Lost in the story, it was several minutes before I realized that Kes was still staring at me.

"What?" I said, annoyed and uncomfortable.

"You read really good," he mumbled.

I frowned at him, waiting for the slur hidden in the compliment, but his eyes had dropped to his fraying jeans.

"Thank you," I said after a long pause.

"I can't," he said. "I can't read."

He glanced up at me quickly as his cheeks stained red.

I didn't know what to say. I'd never met anyone who couldn't read; even the kindergarteners at my school seemed to know some words.

"Not at all?"

He shook his head.

"I tried to learn once, but I couldn't. I guess I'm too dumb."

"I don't think you're dumb," I said with certainty. "You can do loads of stuff that I can't. You're amazing."

Kes gave me his shy smile again and my heart was captured from that moment. I didn't know it then; I didn't understand what it meant, but whenever I looked at him, my skin felt warm, like my own personal sun was shining just for me.

"Do you want to go see Mr. Albert?" he asked, changing the

subject, his eyes now bright and happy.

Disappointment was bitter when I replied, "I can't."

He frowned, staring at me as he tested my answer. "Did you get in trouble?"

Had he already forgotten that we were both in trouble and his own grandpa knocked seven bells out of him?

I nodded.

"Are you grounded?"

"Yes," I sighed. "For the rest of my life, I think."

Kes laughed quietly, his eyes glittering with devilry.

"Let's go anyway. I'll help you."

I looked at him doubtfully. I'd been allowed to go to church the day before, but I was supposed to stay in my room for the next few days as a punishment for disappearing at the carnival.

Kes could sense my resistance was weak—as it always would be when it came to anything he wanted to do—and over the years, it was a weakness that he plundered ruthlessly.

"I shouldn't," I whispered.

He waited, smiling at me the whole time, his eyebrows raised in challenge.

"Okay, I'll go."

He grinned widely, then sprang onto the windowsill and held out his hand toward me.

I shook my head rapidly.

"I can't do that!"

"I'll help you," he encouraged eagerly. "I won't drop you. Well, I will, but you'll be really close to the ground by then, so you can just roll."

I'd never 'just rolled' anywhere in my life, not even during gym class, which was easily my worst subject in school. But Kes's challenging expression took me prisoner and wouldn't let go.

Taking a deep breath, I stuffed my copy of 'The Hobbit' in one back pocket, and 'The Lion, the Witch and the Wardrobe' in the other, on the grounds that if I landed on my butt, the additional padding would help. Even though the pockets were large, I still had to squish the thick books to make them fit, and I was thankful that I was wearing a pair of Jennifer's old cargo shorts that were a little baggy on me. I must have looked a very odd shape.

Of course, if I'd have been thinking clearly, I'd have chosen

'Lord of the Rings' instead. All those extra words ought to be useful for something.

I crawled across the bed and edged out so I was sitting on the windowsill, my heels drumming nervously on the wooden cladding outside. Kes's arm was warm against my side, and when he gripped my hands, his palms were rough and dry.

"You're shaking!" he said, his voice curling up at the end in surprise.

"Of course I am, jackass!" I snapped.

He laughed lightly. "Hold on tight, Aimee."

His skinny arms, sticking out of his shoulders like two twigs, were a lot stronger than they looked, and soon I was dangling 12 feet above the ground. Kes leaned out so far, I was afraid he'd come tumbling after me.

He was holding me tightly, and my fingers had gone white.

"Ready?" he whispered.

I stared at the ground, certain that I was going to die and be smeared all over Mom's petunias like a particularly messy PB&J sandwich.

"Don't forget to bend your knees," Kes said cheerfully. "Three, two, one…"

And then he dropped me.

I squealed, thudding down onto the hard-packed earth, the breath whistling out of my lungs as I lay on my back, gulping for air like a fish.

I barely heard the soft thump as Kes landed next to me, standing with his hands on his hips, grinning down. Then he pulled me up, still coughing and gasping, and we ran zigzag toward the shelter of the hickory tree.

"Not bad, Aimee," he laughed, planting a friendly noogie on my head.

I batted his hands away.

"If I'm going to learn to jump out of windows, you have to learn to read," I said breathlessly.

His expression darkened.

"Chicken?" I asked, resting my hands on my hips and jutting my chin out.

He didn't answer, instead gripping my hand and heading for the road at a fast jog.

Once we were out of sight and in the safety of the street, he let go, shoving his hands into his pockets again and whistling a tune I didn't recognize.

My heart began to beat faster as we neared the carnival entrance, an arch decorated with balloons, and I could hear the shriek of people rushing down the rollercoaster and the crash of the bumper cars knocking against each other.

Kes nodded casually at the carnie taking money at the entrance.

"Got yourself a girlfriend, Kestrel?" he said, laughing widely so I could see dark gaps where his teeth should have been.

Kes shocked me by cussing, but the man just laughed some more. Sure, I'd heard language like that before from high schoolers, I just hadn't expected to hear it said in front of an adult. Since he'd saved me from my wicked parents who'd locked me in my lonely tower, I'd thought of Kes as my prince. When I came to know him better, I changed my mind, thinking of him instead as a dark lord. But that came later.

I could see him watching me out of the corner of his eye, waiting for me to comment on his dirty mouth or the fact that the man had called me Kes's girlfriend, but I wasn't going to give him the satisfaction.

"Kestrel? Is that really your name?"

Kes sighed. "Yeah, but I don't really like being called that. My brother's name is Falcon, but everyone calls him Con. No one thinks that's weird, because it's short for Connor, too. My name really sucks."

"I like it," I said, nodding firmly so he knew I was serious. "It's different."

Kes narrowed his eyes. "Bullshit," he muttered, but his tone was hesitant as if he really hoped that I meant what I said.

"I wouldn't say it if I didn't think it," I said, softer now. "Anyway, it suits you."

And it did. There was a quickness, a sharpness about his movements that reminded me of a bird of prey, and he saw everything, his keen eyes missing nothing.

He side-eyed me again, but then I saw him smile to himself. It was his private smile, one that he didn't share very often, one that I felt was mine alone.

That magical afternoon, we knocked over targets with baseballs, fished for prizes in a pond, ate hotdogs so spicy that my tongue nearly shriveled, rode every ride, played every game, and never paid a dime. We shot ducks in a row, threw balls into a net to win prizes, and rode on the bumper cars three times. Once, Kes even let me drive, his expression magnanimous until I slammed us into a bunch of cars as hard as I could. Then he held on tightly and grinned at me as I smiled proudly.

Kes even stole a couple of cans of soda when a female carnie had her back turned. She caught me staring at the empty space where the cans had been, then saw Kes smirking at her.

"You little booger!" she yelled, and reached out to grab him.

He danced away, still grinning, and winked at her.

Then he ran off down the midway and I had no choice but to run with him.

He finally flopped down in the same place as Saturday, our backs against the wooden skin of the Ghost Train, the rattle of cars and happy screams a constant percussive accompaniment.

Kes passed me a soda, and I pressed the can to my face, enjoying the cool slide of the aluminum against my overheated cheeks.

I was sensible and let the can rest for a while before I tried to open it, but Kes aimed his right at me and soaked me with a sticky stream of cola. I screeched and lashed out, sending the can flying, covering his t-shirt.

I stared at him, a little afraid he might yell at me, but his grin was even wider.

"Nice punch, slugger!"

I felt inordinately proud of his compliment, no matter how misplaced.

He wiped his face with his t-shirt then yanked it off and tossed it onto the ground. I couldn't do the same thing, so I had to sit feeling hot and sticky. But the books were digging into my butt, so I pulled them out and stacked them next to me.

Kes's eyebrows popped up.

"Why'd you bring those?"

My cheeks pinked as I admitted that they helped break my fall.

Kes burst out laughing, holding his ribs as he rolled on the ground. I pouted crossly. It wasn't *that* funny.

Eventually, realizing that laughing by yourself is a lonesome sport, Kes rolled onto his stomach, his dimpled grin coaxing a smile from me.

"Alright," I sighed, "it was *quite* funny."

"Read me some more about that hobbit?" he said, phrasing

his words like a puzzle he had to solve.

I grinned back at him, rubbing my dirty hands against my shorts, because books were precious and I didn't want to soil the creamy pages.

Kes rested his chin in his hands as he gazed up at me, spellbound by the words I conjured in front of him. It occurred to me that I had found magic at the carnival after all, just not in the places that I'd been looking.

After a while, my throat felt dry and sandpapery, and as I'd drank all of my soda, I had to stop.

Kes was lying on his back, his eyes closed, his chest and back coated with red dust and speckled with blades of bent grass.

"You read really good," he said again, as my voice cracked and rustled to the end of the chapter.

I could hear the longing in his voice.

"I can teach you, if you like," I offered.

He opened one eye, his expression skeptical, then he shook his head.

"Cluck! Cluck! Chicken," I crowed and flapped my arms.

He shot up, anger pulling his eyebrows together.

"Am not!" he hissed.

I grinned at him, then smoothed a patch of earth over, making a clean surface to write on. Slowly, I dragged my fingers in the dirt and scratched the letters for him to see, sounding them out as I wrote.

"K.e.s. See? The first letter is sharp and prickly like it sounds, and the 'S' is just like a snake, hissing and squirming."

Kes's eyes lit up. "That makes sense," he said grudgingly.

"And the 'e' is like a knot that ties the two sounds together."

I got him to write in the dirt, copying the shapes I made.

His letters were wobbly and uneven, and the 'S' was backward, but it spelled 'Kes'.

"I wrote my name," he said, and his voice wobbled like his word.

I nodded solemnly. "Yes, you did. You're not dumb."

His eyelashes slanted down and I knew he was hiding tears. He sniffed a few times, then risked a glance at me.

"Thanks, Aimee."

"You're welcome, Kes."

We both heard his name being called at the same time, and I cowered as his grandpa came stomping up. He stopped suddenly when he saw us, a flurry of confused expressions rippling across his face.

"You again," he said flatly, staring at me.

I gulped and tried to make myself look as small and insignificant as possible. Kes crossed his arms and stood in front of me, and although his head hung down and he couldn't look his grandpa in the eye, I felt like he was protecting me.

His grandpa's gaze crawled over me, pausing at the books, then hesitating again at Kes's name scrawled in the red dirt. When I dared to look up, he was staring right at me, his cold stony eyes the exact same color as Kes's.

"Your folks know you're here?"

I bit my lip and shook my head slowly.

"Okay," he said, his gaze sliding again to our dust-writing. "Time for the show."

Kes nodded, his shoulders slumping with relief.

I stuffed my books back in my pockets and trailed after them. No one had invited me, but I wasn't leaving until they shooed me away. I was grateful that Mom ignored me most of the time, unless I was hungry or made too much noise. So with a bit of luck, she wouldn't check my room. At least, I hoped not.

As I trotted along the midway, trying to keep up with their long strides, I realized that Kes and his grandpa were some sort of carnie royalty. His grandpa was greeted as 'Dono' or 'Donohue' which I supposed was their surname. He scared me, with his sharp bitter eyes, and fierce tattoos that covered his arms—I couldn't think of him as 'Grandpa'.

The greetings shouted at Dono and Kes were respectful, if more colorful than I was used to. I felt almost accepted as I strutted along beside them, my head held high. I was Kes's girlfriend, and I wanted everyone to know it. I just hoped he didn't try to kiss me—I didn't like him *that* much. Not yet.

I followed them around to a small corral behind the mini bleachers, where three ponies stood in the shade of a tarp. I could smell warm hay and hot horseflesh as they snorted and stamped, tossing their tidy manes, and eyeing me warily.

Kes reached out and stroked the nose of the pony nearest to us. He was a pretty Palomino, his chestnut coat glossy, white socks not yet stained red by the dust. Enough people around here rode horses so I knew a bit about them, but I'd never been horseback riding myself.

"This is Jacob Jones," said Kes, running his hands along the pony's flank, laughing as the whiskery nose tried to push into his pocket. "You get your apple after the show," Kes admonished him gently.

"You won't bite me, will you, Mr. Jones?" I asked nervously.

Kes snickered. "You don't have to call him 'mister'."

"It's polite," I said, undeterred. "We've never met before."

Jacob Jones seemed to agree, tossing his head proudly. I reached out and patted him carefully, smiling as the pony's ears twitched with pleasure and he made soft snuffling sounds.

We were interrupted by an older boy, whose lanky frame had just teetered over the edge of adolescence, awkward and condescending at the same time.

"Who's this?" he asked stiffly, his angry gray eyes fixed on mine.

Kes stuck out his lip and frowned, but didn't answer.

The boy sneered at him. "Rubes aren't allowed back here; you know the rules."

"Grandpa said it was okay," Kes spat back.

That wasn't technically true, but I wasn't going to argue.

I saw an expression of surprise wipe the anger from the boy's face, but then he frowned again and shrugged his shoulders.

"Whatever. You have to get changed for the show."

Muttering and grumbling to himself, Kes kicked off his tattered sneakers and dropped his pants where he stood.

I gasped and turned my back. The other boy laughed out loud.

"Your girlfriend is shy, Kestrel."

"Don't call me that, *Falcon*," he huffed.

So this was Kes's brother. He was good-looking, but arrogant, as if everything was a bad smell under his nose. I decided I didn't like him; he was mean.

"Anyway, she's not my girlfriend, she's just Aimee."

Oh, that stung. I felt the same sort of pain as if he'd slapped me. I didn't realize that he was protecting me from his brother's teasing, so the hurt settled inside me, hard and indigestible.

When I threw a haughty look at Kes, his expression was apologetic, but he didn't say he was sorry—Kes never apologized. Ever.

He pulled on his cowboy costume of newish jeans and fancy Western shirt, then tied a red bandana around his face and plopped a black Stetson on top of his head, squishing his hair in one direction and spiking it up in the other.

Con pinned on his Sheriff's badge and strapped a pistol to his hip. I hoped it wasn't real, but it definitely looked it. The second 'Sheriff' was Dono, and that surprised me.

"You can wait over there," he said, pointing a thick finger at the entrance to the small arena as he mounted the largest of the ponies.

I was excited to see the show up close, but I didn't want to let him know that. I nodded crisply and marched off, so I didn't see the smile that made his mustache twitch.

I jumped when the bugle call was blasted out right next to my ear. A small man was standing beside me, laughing at the pained expression on my face. And when I say a small man, I mean really small.

Shocked, I took in his thick neck and large head, my eyes traveling down to his broad shoulders and muscled arms that seemed too long for his barrel-shaped body. He gave an impression of compact strength, while at the same time being an inch or two shorter than me.

It was hard to tell how old he was because although his face was a cobweb of wrinkles, his hair was thick and black, and his eyes were bright and alert like a robin.

"So, you're Kes's girl," he said, his high-pitched voice amused but not unkind.

I squared my shoulders and looked him in the eye. "No, I'm not. I'm Aimee."

He grinned at me, his teeth very white in his dark face. "Hello, Aimee-not-Kes's-girl. Back to see the show already?"

I must have looked surprised because he pointed to the corner of the bleachers where I'd sat two days before.

"You were here with your family." He grinned at me again. "And now you're here with Kes."

"I'm just here," I said, not sure why I felt defensive.

Maybe it was because Kes had been so dismissive of me. I hoped that if I ignored him, the strange little man would leave me alone.

But then I heard a chattering behind me and Mr. Albert jumped onto my back, winding his paws into my long hair and rubbing his face into my neck.

"Well, lookee there! I never seen him do that before. He

must like you."

I couldn't help smiling. "He's my friend," I said proudly.

The little man edged closer, his face inches from mine. "You've been sprinkled with fairy dust, missy. The carnival is in your blood now."

To be honest, he was creeping me out a little bit and I hugged Mr. Albert a little too tightly, making him squawk and tug my hair.

I turned my eyes back to Kes, a habit that was already as natural as breathing. He was standing on the back of his galloping pony, balanced on his toes, his knees flexing to the rhythm. Then he leaped into the air, landing on the back of Con's pony. The crowd cheered; then both boys stood up, using each other to balance, and together they jumped back onto Kes's pony, moving with a synchronicity that was stunning to see and spoke of long hours of practice.

Their final showstopper was to perform a series of somersaults while they raced their ponies around barrels and over small jumps. I gasped as Kes cartwheeled off his pony, landing with perfect balance in the center of the arena to take his bow. As Jacob Jones raced around, Kes swung a leg across him again, and they galloped past me at full speed, hooves kicking up enough dust to make me cough.

Kes was dripping with sweat, rubbing a filthy hand across his forehead and fanning himself with his hat.

"What did you think?" he asked.

"You were amazing!" I gushed. "That was way more tricks than you did on Saturday."

He nodded and used his shirtsleeve to mop his glowing face.

"Yeah, Jakey was off his feed on Saturday, so I took it easy on him. He sometimes gets like that when he's been cooped up in a trailer the day before. He's okay now."

"Do you like traveling all the time? It must be amazing seeing new stuff."

Kes shrugged. "Yeah, I guess. I don't really know. We move around a lot."

I followed him as he led his pony in slow circles, helping to cool him down.

"I have to take care of Jakey now, but I could show you the Ghost Train later if you like."

I nodded enthusiastically, then watched as he did his chores.

"Who's the funny guy with the bugle?" I asked.

Even though Kes had his back to me, I could tell that he'd gone stiff.

"That's Ollo, and he's not funny."

I was quiet for a moment. "I didn't mean anything by it," I said at last, "I've just never seen anyone like him before. He reminded me of a character in 'The Hobbit'."

"You mean a dwarf," said Kes, turning to stare at me.

My face was scarlet and I looked down. "I guess," I said quietly.

Kes sighed. "He's one of us."

I wasn't sure what to make of that, but I nodded like I did. Then I asked the question that had been burning on my lips.

"Where are your parents?"

Kes scowled. "You're really nosy."

I bit my lip and looked down. "You already know all about my parents, you've met them," I reminded him.

"Mine aren't around," he said shortly.

I didn't know what he meant. Were they dead, or living somewhere else? If they'd died, he'd say so, wouldn't he? I hoped he'd tell me at some point, because I didn't think I was brave enough to ask again.

I had to wait impatiently while Kes took care of Jakey, and it seemed like forever before he was satisfied that the pony was sufficiently cooled. I was impressed by how thorough he was, especially since he had such a carefree attitude to everything else. We walked further away from the carnival, and in the distance I could see Con walking the other two ponies.

After about 20 minutes, Kes led Jakey back to the patch of shade by the tarp, sponged him down with lukewarm water, letting him drink from the bucket. Just as I thought we could finally enjoy the Ghost Train, Con came back with the other two ponies and made it clear that Kes had to take care of them, as well.

Kes shot his brother a look, but didn't argue.

This time I helped him, so besides being hot and sweaty, I smelled of horse, too. In other words, I stunk, but I didn't care.

Kes didn't thank me for helping him; he seemed to take it for granted that I would. Maybe I should have been annoyed.

Once all the ponies were settled with hay, we were free to go. Kes stripped off his Western shirt and dunked it in the bucket of water that the ponies had been drinking from. Then he swung it over the fence, leaving it to dry. I guess that his laundry was done.

We wandered along to the Ghost Train, and every now and then, his warm skin would brush against my arm, giving me goose bumps.

At the Ghost Train, Kes walked to the front of the line casually, smirking at the annoyed shouts of the people waiting.

The carnie working the ride winked at him, and bowed us into the first car as if we were royalty. I was embarrassed and happy all at the same time, even more so when Kes casually slung his arm around me and squished me into his skinny chest. I pushed away from him and scowled, a move which made the carnie laugh and Kes's cheeks redden.

I liked him, but I wasn't having any of that!

Ten seconds later, I changed my mind. The ride was kind of silly, with dummies jumping out and someone dressed in a Halloween mask leering at us, but it scared me silly, and I was more than happy to burrow into Kes's warm skin and shriek every time a cobweb brushed across my hair or back.

It was a long three minutes, and I couldn't wait to get into daylight again. Kes was grinning at me, a very superior masculine smile on his face, that made his dimple pop. I'd see a lot more of that expression in the years that followed.

As the light began to fade from the sky and the heat dwindled enough to make it bearable, Kes led me back to his trailer and made messy sandwiches for me and Mr. Albert. Con was stretched out in the shade of the RV, studying what looked like a math book.

"He can read?" I whispered.

Kes shrugged and looked down. "Yeah, Con's really smart. He wants to go to college."

I heard the pain and resignation in his voice, and it made me more determined than ever to help him if I could—if he'd let me.

I was about to suggest getting my book out again when Dono came back.

"Time to get you home, young lady," he said.

I glanced nervously at Kes, but I could tell by the look on his face that he wasn't going to argue.

Sighing, I stood up and helplessly brushed the dirt from my

clothes. I looked a mess, and Mom would be fit to be tied when she saw me.

"And you, Kes," ordered Dono. "You've got some explaining to do. Put a shirt on and wash your face."

Kes looked like he was about to say something, but then changed his mind. Con watched us curiously as I shifted from foot to foot, his grandpa's stare making me squirm.

When Kes was ready, we walked solemnly toward an ancient looking truck, then drove the 200 yards to my house.

Mom was opening the door before the engine died. In the silence that followed, I could hear it popping as it cooled.

"I believe this is yours, ma'am," Dono said, nodding at me.

Mom was flustered.

"Where have you been, Aimee? I've been going out of my mind! I was going to call your father."

An icy shiver trickled down my spine.

"Sorry, Mom," I choked out. "I just wanted … I wanted…"

What had I wanted? I couldn't even put it into words. Taste the forbidden? Leave my safe little cocoon to experience something different? I wasn't sure.

Kes stood there, his hands shoved deep into his pockets, his handsome face surly. Every fiber in his body screamed that he'd rather walk across hot coals than stand in front of my mom.

"Well," she said breathlessly. "You're home now, that's all that matters. Anything could have happened to you and…"

"No, ma'am," Dono interrupted. "Nothing will happen to Aimee while she's with my boy, I can promise you that."

He threw a hard look at Kes, who shuffled his feet impatiently.

"It seems like these two have become friends," Dono went on. "Your girl has been helping Kes with his reading. You could say that he's missed out on some schooling—it seems innocent enough to me."

I knew that he was sending Mom a message, I just wasn't sure what it was.

"I see," said Mom, although she still looked puzzled.

"If Miss Aimee wants to visit us again, she'll be looked after, ma'am. In fact, she'd be very welcome."

There was no way Mom could be immune to Dono's surprisingly beautiful manners. You could be a mass murderer, but as long as you spoke nicely and were polite, you'd be welcome in Mom's home. I guess that was the southerner in her; at least, that's what Dad always said.

"I see," Mom said again. "Well, thank you for bringing her home, Mr…?"

"Donahue," he supplied. "Nathanael Donahue."

"Well, Mr. Donahue, Kes, I thank you for taking such good care of Aimee. I surely appreciate that."

Dono nodded and turned to leave. Kes followed and then looked over his shoulder and grinned.

That dimple was going to be the death of me.

Mom didn't have the heart to tell Dad about my jaunt, so it remained our secret. Jennifer had gone to stay with a friend, so no one else knew that I spent the rest of the week with Kes.

Each day I read him another chapter from 'The Hobbit' and then we'd spend some time practicing letters. Kes got easily frustrated and I had to be super patient and give him a time-out when he shouted at me. Sometimes I needed a time-out, too, because he'd make me mad enough to spit.

Mr. Albert used to join our study sessions, sitting in my lap or playing with my hair, chattering quietly.

Then Kes would have to go do his show, and I'd sit in the front row, pleased as punch to see his acrobatics and hear the roar of the crowd.

Some old hypocrites had done their best to whip up trouble, blaming the carnies for everything from a pick pocketing in town to a bad harvest, and a bunch of them got riled up enough to head over to the carnival with the intention of having it shut down.

Everyone—meaning Mom and Dad—expected a fight, and Mom's fingers hovered over 911, but later Kes told me that Dono calmed everything down and showed them the permits, and the townsmen went away with their tails between their legs.

I didn't entirely trust Dono, and I hadn't forgotten that he'd given Kes a fat lip, but I had to concede that he was wily enough to outsmart pretty much everyone, including those old hymn-singing biddies, like Mrs. Flock.

I was pleased about that. The two hours I spent in church every Sunday morning seemed long enough to build my own ark, sail it around the world, and still be back for the homily.

But time was running out in a very real way, and soon the

carnies would be packing up and moving on to the next town. I was dreading it.

On our last night, Kes took me up in the Ferris wheel. I don't know why, but we'd both been avoiding it, like it was a giant period at the end of our two-week sentence. But tonight, that was where we headed.

Kes had finished his final show and the ponies were cleaned up. We both smelled of horse and sweat and hay and sunshine. We walked down the midway, the backs of our hands brushing together, we were so close, and even though we were surrounded by people, it felt like we two were the last in the whole world.

Kes caught my elbow and hauled me to the head of the line, ignoring the angry stares that bounced off his bony back.

"Ike, we need a bucket for ourselves," he said.

The carnie smiled shrewdly. He was only a few years older than Jennifer and probably should have still been in high school. He was thin and slightly stooped, but the muscles in his forearms were corded, giving him a wiry, dangerous appearance.

I took a step closer to Kes, uncomfortable with the carnie's eyes studying me from tip to toe.

"You want me to stop it when it gets to the top, Kes? Give you time to … do whatever?"

I felt my cheeks flush at the insinuation, but Kes just looked at him levelly.

"You want me to tell Grandpa you said that? You know she's protected."

I didn't know what he meant, but the carnie did, because he backed off instantly.

"Just messin' with you, Kes. Didn't mean nothin' by it."

As we climbed in, Ike clicked the safety bar into place and pulled a lever. The bucket shuddered and swung, and I held on tightly. We rose a few feet, then stopped as the next group were loaded in.

Slowly, we rose upwards, and at last I could see the whole carnival laid out beneath me. Happy sounds drifted up on the still air and the lights glittered like jewels. I could see our house, I could see my hickory tree, and I could see the town in the distance, dark and sullen compared to the bright lights surrounding me.

Behind us, the sun was sinking in a stunning display of pinks and purples, reds and yellows, the shadows slowly lengthening.

"It's beautiful," I breathed. "I wish I'd come up here before."

Kes shrugged. "I come up here every night after you've gone home."

My breath stuttered and that pebble of disappointment rolled around in my stomach.

"Oh," I said, my broad vocabulary reduced to a single syllable.

Kes turned his head to look at me, and for once his smile was gentle.

"I can see your house from here," he said. "I can see your tree and your bedroom window. Nobody bothers me up here, so that's when I think of you."

"Oh," I said again, but this time a smile was in the sound.

"I've never had a real friend before," Kes said, his eyes searching out the edges of the horizon. "I didn't know I was missing anything."

I heard what he wasn't saying, at least I think I did. "I'll miss you, too."

His eyes fell to my clasped hands and he plucked them apart, his palms rough and dry as he held my fingers.

"I'll come back next year."

"I'll wait for you," I said sadly. "I could write you?"

Kes pulled a face and looked down. "I don't read good enough for that."

"I could send you a picture postcard," I offered gently. "And I'll sign my name so you know it's from me."

He smiled brightly, his dimple deepening.

"Can I kiss you?" he asked, softly as if he was sure I'd say no.

I took a deep breath. My first kiss was going to be at the top of a Ferris wheel. I'd never heard of anything more romantic.

"Okay," I said, wiping my mouth with my sleeve.

Kes leaned in and I felt his dry lips press against my cheek.

I turned to stare at him and he was grinning, looking inordinately proud of himself.

We held hands for the rest of the ride, and I'd never been happier.

If life truly is about balance, then I should have expected the misery that followed Kes's departure.

I watched, distraught, as the rides that I'd once thought monstrous, were broken down into humiliated lumps of metal. Canvas and tarps were folded and rolled and stacked away. Jacob Jones and the other ponies were loaded into a trailer.

Mr. Albert clung to me, pushing his head into my neck and gripping my hair tightly.

"He'll miss you," said Kes.

I nodded, because I was afraid that if I spoke, I'd start to cry. And I didn't want to be a girl in front of Kes.

Con sat in the cab of the RV, his feet on the dashboard, reading a book. He didn't even look up as Kes climbed in and settled Mr. Albert on his knee.

"Bye," I said, my voice cracked and hoarse.

Kes smiled tightly, torn between being cool and wanting to say goodbye. Even then I could read the mix of emotions he tried so hard to hide.

He waved quickly then fixed his eyes on the road ahead. Dono nodded once and gunned the engine.

The cavalcade exited the field one at a time in a blast of diesel fumes, and I could pretend that it was the grit in my eyes that made me cry.

I watched as the huge trucks disappeared into the distance. When I turned to look behind me, Mr. Peterson's field was battered and barren. Holes from tent pegs cracked the dry earth, and wide dusty tracks marked where the midway had been. Scraps of litter nestled in the few remaining stalks of grass, and a couple of empty bottles glinted dully in the sunshine.

I had two weeks of memories that shone as insubstantial as my dreams, and fifty long weeks to wait for my life to start again.

I sat on the grass and cried.

The last days of summer crept by slowly. For everyone else, like Jennifer and my friends from school, summer raced past with dizzying speed, but to me it seemed to drag and stumble, and all the color had been leeched out of the world. I couldn't bear to read 'The Hobbit' anymore, so I stuffed it to the back of my bookshelf, a candy wrapper marking the last page that I'd read aloud to Kes.

I badgered Mom until she took me into town to buy a postcard to send him. I knew he wouldn't get it for months, not until they went to their winter ground, but I wanted to write it.

I sat for ages, wondering what to put, uncertain how much Kes would be able to read.

In the end, I kept it simple and short.

Next year we'll finish our book.
Love, Aimee.

I hoped he'd understand.

It was Spring before I got a reply. There was no message, just a beautifully drawn picture of a small creature with large, furry feet—our hobbit. My address had been written with such a heavy hand that the postcard looked as though it had been engraved. That was one clue that Kes had written it himself, the other was that some of the letters were the wrong way around.

Dad sneered when he saw it, muttering under his breath, cruel words that I didn't want to hear. Mom didn't look very pleased either, but Jennifer gave me a sympathetic glance, then went back to reading her magazine.

But to me, it was the most precious thing that I possessed.

Next summer couldn't come soon enough.

CHAPTER 3
FANNING THE FLAMES

My perch at the top of the hickory tree had grown uncomfortable two hours ago, but I hadn't moved. The bark dug into my bare legs, and my toes were numb. I was hot and thirsty, and my eyes were sore from staring toward the sun. Sweat streaked my face, and my hair clung to my scalp in clumps, and still I didn't move.

In a few days, I would be 11, and yesterday the posters had gone up around town—the carnival was coming.

The Right Reverend Shaw spoke half-heartedly about the evils of gambling, which included throwing a ring around the neck of plastic duck to win a prize, a comment that had me rolling my eyes in church. I half expected to be struck down, but when God gave me a pass, I decided that He must like the carnival, too, because of all the smiles it brought to town.

I thought Mrs. Flock had put him up to it, but Jennifer thought that the boring as all heck Right Reverend Shaw had gotten the idea all by himself because he didn't like fun. I didn't care and didn't listen.

But my heart beat faster every time I thought about seeing Kes again. Had he changed? Did he think I'd changed? And since I was starting Junior High in the Fall and all my girlfriends were talking about the cute older boys we were sure to meet, I wondered if Kes would look at me the way boys looked at Gina Sanders who'd been wearing a training bra for a year.

There was nothing special about me. I was an average student, and my body was still thin and childlike. My parents called me pretty. The boys at school called me pretty average. It was a surprise to everyone, most of all me, when *he* noticed me last summer.

We'd been friends, at least I think we had. The uncertainty made me feel as if my stomach was trying to climb out my throat. I swallowed it back and pinned my eyes to the horizon, squinting into the sun.

Was that a cloud? A slight smudge of darkness? I couldn't be certain. I waited, tension threatening to send my body into a cramp.

A sudden flash of light made me blink. The sun was reflecting off something bright and shiny, something like a windshield. And I knew—they were coming.

Minutes later, the heavy rumble of trucks shook the ground and I squealed with excitement. They roared past in a cloud of smoke and fumes, shaking the tree as if a tiny tornado had swept through the yard.

Soon, Mr. Peterson's field had disappeared under a film of red dirt as the earth blossomed beneath the heavy tires.

I ran from van to truck, truck to trailer, asking the same question, "Where's Kes?"

And then I found him, leaning nonchalantly against the side of his RV, talking to two other boys.

His hair was longer, shaggier, and I think he'd grown a couple of inches, but he was the same.

"Kes!" I called, waving wildly.

He turned towards me, his eyes widening for a second and a pleased smile curling his lips, but then he raised one shoulder in a casual shrug.

"Hey," he said.

I skidded to a halt. A whole year of wishing and wanting and waiting and all I got was 'hey'? My heart sank. I wanted to cry, but I wouldn't give him the satisfaction.

I slowed to a walk, trying to swallow the breathlessness of running.

"I've come to see Mr. Albert," I said, lying as carelessly as I could.

A shadow of emotion crossed his face, then he hooked a thumb at the RV behind us, not even bothering to speak.

Dragging my feet with disappointment, burning with resentment and pain, I tapped lightly on the metal door and heard Mr. Albert's shriek.

I opened the door and the little monkey leapt into my arms.

"At least *you* haven't forgotten me," I whispered, stroking his warm, soft fur.

He wrapped long fingers around my neck, then tugged on my hair.

"I'm taking Mr. Albert for a walk," I called over my shoulder, pretending that I didn't care whether Kes followed me or not.

I'd expected our reunion to be awkward, and I'd expected to be nervous; I *hadn't* expected to be so casually dismissed. I couldn't help hating Kes just a little. I wanted to hate him a lot, but I couldn't do it.

It was only a few minutes before I felt a prickle on the back of my neck and I turned to see Kes following me, his hands in his pockets, a cocky smile on his face.

"Hey," he said again.

I ignored him, walking faster, losing myself in the chaos as the carnival slowly bloomed across the dusty field.

"I have to go unload Jakey and the others," he said.

"So, go!" I snapped. "I'm not stopping you."

He grabbed my arm and Mr. Albert hissed, not appreciating being jerked to a halt.

"Are you mad at me?" he asked, his raised eyebrows fighting the anxiety I could see on his face.

"Yes," I said honestly. "You're a jerk. You acted like you didn't want me there when you were talking to your *friends*." I emphasized the word harshly. "I won't hold you up."

He rubbed the back of his neck, looking sheepish and defensive at the same time.

"I liked your postcard," he said at last.

I immediately melted.

"I liked yours, too."

He grinned at me, and that darned dimple popped out. I'd already forgiven him.

The following year I turned 12. It was also the year that Kes taught me how to breathe fire.

It was stupidly dangerous and my parents would have died of shock if they'd known. And I think Dono would have skinned Kes alive, but by the time he found out, I'd already learned the basics.

I was sitting next to Kes as we made s'mores in the campfire, drowsy from sunshine and happiness, my knees pulled up to my chest, listening to him talk with the other carnie boys. When I first met him, it had only been Kes and Con traveling with the carnival, but now there were three more kids. They were nearer Con's age than ours and I would have described them as rough, but they were friendly enough. And even though Kes was the youngest, it was clear that he was the leader.

Unlike Kes and Con, the other boys didn't have an 'act'; they were just there with their parents and helped out on the sideshows and stalls.

Con was in the RV studying, so it was left to Kes to describe the new act. He watched me from the corner of his eyes, his smug smile lazy and contented.

"Tell her about it, Kes," said Zachary, a tall, thin serious-looking boy of about 16 or 17.

"Maybe she should just see it," Kes replied coolly.

"I'm sitting right here!" I said, poking Kes with my finger, not at all appreciating being talked about like I wasn't there.

He'd already let me see past his cool public persona, so I wasn't falling for that again. Then he grinned, showing me the smile that I was certain was only for me.

"All right, but you'll scream like a girl."

I wasn't sure what he meant, but I rolled my eyes anyway. "I *am* a girl, dummy!"

"You sure?" he said nastily, eyeing my skinny body in a way that definitely wasn't complimentary.

My cheeks heated immediately as the other boys laughed. Part of me was furious, part of me was hurt, and a small but restless part of me knew that I'd brought it on myself—Kes hated anyone calling him dumb, and I knew the reason for that. But still, he didn't have to lash out.

It was a pattern that would be repeated many times over the years.

I stood abruptly.

"I'm going home."

Kes barely glanced at me, and it was Zachary who got to his feet.

"I'll walk you home, kid."

I nodded and strode off through the parking area and along the midway.

We were silent for several minutes as I gulped and sniffed, forcing the tears away.

"He's an asshole," Zachary said quietly.

I sniffed harder and picked up the pace.

"He's been really excited to see you again."

I glanced at Zachary out of the corner of my eye. "Doesn't seem like it."

Zachary sucked his teeth, then spit at the ground.

"It's a guy thing."

"Whatever," I said from between gritted teeth.

Zachary was silent. I guess he'd said everything he wanted to say.

When we arrived at my house, he shuffled his feet.

"Nice place."

"Thank you."

"So…" he hesitated. "See you tomorrow?"

I shook my head, and he sighed.

"Okay, see ya, Aimee."

"Thanks for walking me," I called after him.

He smiled quickly then disappeared into the dark.

Mom was waiting for me in the kitchen. I thanked my lucky stars that Dad was watching TV in the living room, because I really didn't want to see the condescending look he was sure to give me, because I was congenitally unable to hide how I felt.

Mom looked up from her magazine, but her smile slipped when she saw me.

"Everything okay?"

I flung myself into a chair.

"Boys are dumb," I said, choosing that word deliberately even though Kes wasn't there to hear it.

"What did he do?" Mom sighed.

I shrugged my shoulders. "Pretended like he didn't care if I was there or not. And he was kind of mean."

Mom made a grab for the first part of my sentence.

"How do you know he was pretending?"

It was hard to explain, because when I thought about it, all Kes had said to me was, "You'll scream like a girl."

"That's what it felt like," I answered uneasily. "And his friend said he'd been excited to see me."

"So what went wrong?"

"He was a jerk."

I mashed my lips together, refusing to paint my humiliation in brighter colors.

Mom fixed things in her usual way by giving me a freshly baked cookie and a glass of milk.

Shortly after that, I went to bed. My curtains were open and the stars were a glittering feast in the darkness. The weight of disappointment pinned me to the mattress and I let a few tears trickle down my cheeks before I resolved to forget all about Kes.

Of course, it didn't work out like that, because some time in the night a soft thud woke me up, and a warm palm clamped down over my mouth. My scream threatened to choke me, but then Kes's grinning face loomed out of the night.

I shoved his hand away.

"Get off!"

He grinned and hopped up onto the end of my bed, sitting Indian-style.

"Told you you'd scream like a girl," he snickered.

"And I told you that I *am* a girl. Dummy."

I knew that was a low blow, but I was too angry to care.

Kes scowled. "I'm not a dummy."

"You are when you pretend you don't want to see me and act all cool in front of your friends. You were *mean*," I stated, folding my arms across my chest.

His expression softened, but the apology I was waiting for never came. "I'm not a dummy," he said again.

We stared at each other, his eyes holding their secrets.

I sighed, remembering how much I'd missed him.

"You don't treat friends like that," I explained. "I'd been looking forward to seeing you all year and then … well, you were mean."

"Will you come and see my act tomorrow?" he said, his voice grudging and sullen, as if asking that small favor was almost more than he could bear.

"Do you want me to?" I pushed.

He nodded, but wouldn't look at me.

I sighed again. "Fine, I'll be there, but you'd better not be a jerk."

He laughed quietly, and I could see the white gleam of his quick smile.

"See you tomorrow," he said.

Then he swung himself out of the window and landed on the ground with almost no sound at all.

I would have doubted that he'd been there at all … except

for the fact I was smiling.

Mom's face showed her confusion over breakfast. She'd expected a sulky, sleep-deprived daughter; instead I was suppressing a private smile and itching to get out of the house.

Dad had left for a sales conference early that morning, so we were all much more relaxed than usual. Which was why Mom just sighed and shook her head when I said I was going to the carnival and would be gone all day.

She tossed me an apple as I squirmed to get away. "In case you want to eat something healthy," she said, shaking her head.

As if.

I walked down the dusty road quickly, smiling when I saw the poster advertising the carnival. My bare legs were coated with a fine red film, but I didn't care. I couldn't see Kes at first, so I collected Mr. Albert and spoiled Jacob Jones with my unwanted apple. I was sure he'd enjoy it much more than me anyway.

Eventually, I found Kes helping set up a small tent draped with colorful scarves. This time he grinned and waved me over, introducing me to the hatchet-faced woman carnie who eyed me coolly.

"This is Madame Cindy, but you can call her Bev."

I smiled shyly and gave a limp little half wave.

"She's a fortuneteller," Kes added, his dimple making a quick appearance before he hid his smile.

I must have looked doubtful because Madame Cindy raised her eyebrows and pursed her lips.

"You don't believe in the Fates, girl? You think you are immune to their perverse laws?"

I had no idea what she was talking about, but her intense stare made me take a hesitant step back.

Kes snorted. "The rubes love it."

Madame Cindy frowned at him. "You shouldn't mock, Kestrel, the Fates are listening and they hear your scorn."

Kes rolled his eyes and grabbed my hand, towing me away. When I glanced over my shoulder, Madame Cindy was still staring after us.

"She's scary," I whispered, even though she couldn't possibly hear me from that distance.

Kes shrugged. "I don't really believe all that stuff, but she's a really good guesser. Anyway, she's Grandpa's *friend*."

The way he said it had an odd inflection and I narrowed my eyes as my feet shuddered to a halt. "You mean, like a *girl*friend?"

Kes shrugged and looked away.

"How do you know?"

He pulled a face. "I just know."

I was shocked to think that someone who was a grandpa could have a girlfriend.

"But … he's really *old*," I scoffed.

Kes shot me a look. "Yeah, he's nearly 60, and that's kind of ancient. But I don't say anything so he doesn't give me a hard time about you and…"

His words trailed off and I wondered what else he was going to say. He shook the thought away and we sat down in our old spot beside the Ghost Train.

Kes stretched out and closed his eyes, his face peaceful.

I stared at him for a moment, then peeled Mr. Albert off my back and lay down next to him so our hands were nearly touching.

"Have you been practicing?" I asked finally.

Kes turned his head and cracked an eyelid.

"Practicing what?"

"Your reading and writing," I said, trying not to sound irritated. What else could I have meant?

"Ah, not so much," Kes admitted. "It's boring without you."

I sat up quickly. "Then we'd better get started," I said.

Kes looked at me, and I suspected that his reluctance was more pretend than real, otherwise we wouldn't be hiding out behind the Ghost Train.

I took him through the basics again, disappointed that he'd forgotten a lot of what I'd taught him the last two summers, but he could still write my name and address as well as his own, and he was proud of that.

Then I made the mistake of showing him a book I'd brought with me that I thought would help him.

He took one look at the pictures and tossed it into the dirt.

"That's for babies!" he growled.

I twisted my lips to the side, realizing I'd just insulted him. But I wasn't going to apologize for trying to help him either. I twisted my lips to the side, realizing I'd just insulted him. But I wasn't going to apologize for trying to help him either. Instead, I pulled out my ratty book. We'd finished 'The Hobbit' the previous year and had gotten halfway through the first 'Harry Potter' as well, so I just began reading from where we'd left off.

We broke off when my throat started aching and my stomach rumbled loudly.

Kes laughed and sprang to his feet as if his legs were made of springs not flesh and bone like everyone else. He pulled me up and Mr. Albert climbed my body, his very own jungle gym.

When we got to the RV, Con was there, sitting outside in a deckchair. I hadn't seen him clearly the night before and I was stunned to see how much he'd changed. In the space of a year, he'd gone from being a boy to a man. Instead of the lanky adolescent of the year before, hard muscles and thick shoulders pushed against his torn t-shirt.

The only thing that hadn't changed was that he had a book propped up on his knees. When he saw me, he raised his eyebrows in surprise.

"Oh, it's you."

"Hey," I said, glad that Mr. Albert took that moment to jump down, so we both had something else to look at.

Kes walked into the RV and I heard him rummaging through the tiny kitchen, then he tossed me a bag of chips through the window.

"Get one for me, squirt," Con shouted.

Kes muttered under his breath, but threw a bag of corn chips at his brother's head.

Con laughed and caught it easily. "Temper temper, little brother. You don't want to give your girlfriend the wrong idea about you."

I didn't like Con, but I loved hearing him call me Kes's girlfriend.

After that, he ignored us, and it was only when the sky began to drag toward the west, that Con stretched and unwound his long body from the deckchair.

"Time to get ready for the show, Kes," he said, yawning.

Excitement filled me, and Kes's expression brightened.

"You'll really like it," he said, his gray eyes silvery in the failing light.

Kes and Con disappeared into the RV to get ready. I was going to take Mr. Albert with me to the makeshift arena, but Kes stopped me.

"He has to stay inside for this," he said, pulling Mr. Albert into his arms.

"Why? He always used to sit with me."

Kes smiled. "He doesn't like it anymore. You'll see."

Disappointed, I slouched off to the bleachers. I didn't like sitting by myself. It felt weird, and I could see people giving me sidelong glances as the seats began to fill with families and groups of teenagers.

I stared at my hands, pretending to be very interested in my ragged nails. Then I felt someone gently touch my arm. I looked up to see the dwarf Ollo smiling at me.

I put my hands over my ears, and Ollo looked at me in surprise.

"For when you blow the bugle," I said.

His eyes scrunched in a smile and he laughed.

"I don't do that now," he chuckled. "We've got a new act. Didn't Kes tell you?"

"Well, he said it was new, but I haven't seen it yet."

Ollo smiled. "Aw, he wanted it to be a surprise—that's cute. It's all his idea; he's got a real talent for showmanship. He could go far."

I wasn't sure what Ollo meant. How far could anyone go in a carnival that traveled around small towns in the mid-West? But I didn't say that.

Ollo winked at me, then went off to take his position at the entrance to the arena. He plopped down on the ground behind a set of small tom-toms and began to play. The sound of a steady drumbeat filled the air, and I shivered at the primal sound.

The murmur of the crowd dropped away, and we all gasped when Kes exploded into the arena riding at a gallop. Kes was barefoot and wearing jeans, but that was all. No costume, no bandana, no shirt, no hat. Instead he was carrying a flaming torch in each hand, controlling Jacob Jones with just the lightest pressure of his knees. My jaw dropped, and a sigh rose up from the crowd as the red and yellow flames flickered brightly against the darkening sky.

Con followed, carrying a single torch, similarly dressed. I heard two high school girls sitting behind me giggle, and I rolled my eyes.

Kes slid his leg across the neck of his galloping pony and

leapt to the ground. I nearly jumped out of my seat when he brought one of torches up to his face and a huge flame shot from his mouth.

Then Con tossed him the third burning torch and Kes started to juggle with them. I could barely watch, and saw most of the act from between my fingers. But I was so proud of him, too. He couldn't spell and he barely knew the alphabet, but he could hold a crowd transfixed.

Dono galloped in wearing a leather vest, then threw a fourth torch to Kes. I felt sick with fright as the flames seemed to engulf his hands. I knew they hadn't, but gosh, it sure looked like it! The torches flew into the air as Kes juggled them expertly. Then he tossed a torch to Dono and one to Con as he leapt back onto Jacob Jones. I could almost feel the heat of the flames as Kes galloped past; the roar of the crowd, the steady beating of the drum—it was raw and real, too much and not enough.

At the end of the show, all three members of the family stood in the center of the arena to take their bows. The crowd gasped and I screamed as Kes swallowed the flames of a single torch. As one, people rose up, stamping their feet, clapping and cheering. The applause rolled around the arena as first Kes, then Con and finally Dono, jumped onto the backs of their galloping ponies and shot out of the ring.

I raced after them and saw Kes toss the last three torches into a water barrel. I threw myself at him, babbling incoherently as my fingers slipped on his sweat-slick skin.

"You were amazing!" I shrieked loud enough to make him wince.

His grin said it all.

"Where … how … who taught you to do that?"

Kes jerked his chin at Ollo who winked at me.

"I want to learn," I whispered in Kes's ear. "Teach me."

At first he looked shocked, and then he nodded minutely.

"Don't tell anyone," he said.

I don't know what made me say it and I was terrified when Kes agreed, but I wasn't backing down either.

It turns out that there's a trick to being a fire-breather—it's more like being a fire *blower*.

"Just don't breathe in," Kes said, his expression serious and worried.

I'd never seen a worried Kes before, so that made me even more nervous.

"You don't have to do this, Aimee," he continued, a small quake in his voice.

I shook my head. I couldn't say anything because my mouth was full of lighter fuel.

Kes had schooled me for two hours in the correct angle to hold the torch, the amount of fuel to hold in my mouth, and the way I needed to spit it onto the flames. He'd checked and rechecked the direction of the faint breeze, shifting me with his strong fingers to the exact place he deemed suitable. He'd also insisted on soaking my clothes and hair in water before he let me try, and my face and arms were smeared with a protective gel.

"Okay," he said at last, his voice resigned when he could see that I wasn't going to back out. "I'll count down to one, and then you blow out. Just *don't breathe in!*"

He'd said it like a gazillion times, but I listened because I was terrified of my eyebrows going up in smoke … or worse.

Even though he'd given me a pair of thick leather flame-proof gloves to wear, Kes didn't even trust me to hold the torch myself, which was just as well because my hands were shaking so badly.

"Three, two, one … blow!"

I blew as hard as I could, toppling backward when a three-foot flame appeared to shoot out of mouth.

I yelled and coughed as I swallowed a trickle of lighter fuel.

Kes immediately tossed the torch into a water barrel and passed me a can of soda.

When he saw that I was unharmed, his face split with a huge grin.

"Wow, you did good, Aimee! That was awesome!"

I took a gulp of soda, rinsing my mouth in the sugary drink before I spit onto the ground.

My eyes were watering as I glanced up at him. The look of pride on his face was worth the effort.

"Can you teach me to do the other bit, you know, to be a fire *eater?*"

"No way, Aimee," he laughed. "It's too dangerous. But I can teach you to juggle. Without the flames."

When he smiled at me, still shaking his head, his eyes were soft.

I felt like I'd live a thousand deaths to see that look again.

I never did learn to juggle.

The next day, we broke our pattern of lazy lessons behind the Ghost Train. Dono was going into town to talk to the mayor about permits—I guess people were causing trouble again—and we decided to take a ride with him. Con was going, too, on his way to study at the library.

I didn't like Con much, but I had to admire how dedicated he was. Kes said it was because he couldn't wait to get away from the carnival. Looking at Con's perpetual frown, I thought he was probably right.

Kes and I decided we'd spend some of my birthday money and share a milkshake at the diner. Unfortunately Camilla Palmer was there, one of the meanest girls I've ever met. She was sitting in a booth at the front where everyone could see her, with her entourage of sheep-like followers. I hated them, and they didn't know I existed. Guess that made us even.

I stopped Kes as he was about to walk inside.

"I think we should go somewhere else," I whispered, edging to the side so they wouldn't notice me.

Kes glanced across and his expression darkened.

"You don't want to be seen with me," he said, his voice hard.

"It's not that! They're mean—I know they'll say horrible stuff."

Kes just looked at me stony-faced, his arms crossed over his torn t-shirt.

"Fine," I sighed, "but don't say I didn't warn you."

And he was partly right, too; I was afraid of what Camilla and her pack would say to me when we were back at school. There was no way I'd admit that to Kes. I didn't want him to think I was a coward, even though I was.

He opened the door and shouldered his way inside. I followed, keeping my head down. I hoped he'd choose a booth at the back, but that wasn't Kes's way. He took a stool at the counter in full view of the whole diner. I scuttled up behind and sat next to him, pretending to study the menu that I already knew by heart.

"Oh my God!" Camilla screeched. "It's Lamey Aimee wearing her thrift store clothes." And then she laughed like a drain.

My heart clenched anxiously. It seemed as though Camilla

did know who I was after all. Worse still, she had a horrible nickname for me. My cheeks were bright red and I felt tears prick my eyes.

Kes nudged me.

"Is that why you didn't want to come in here?"

"I told you she was mean," I said, dodging his question.

Then Camilla noticed who I was with and she laughed again loudly. "Looks like Lamey Aimee has a boyfriend. Talk about scraping the bottom of the barrel."

I didn't know if she meant me or Kes, not that it mattered, because he jumped off his stool and stalked over to Camilla's booth.

They got really quiet then. Kes could be pretty intimidating when he wanted to; he carried an air of recklessness that said to hell with the consequences, and right then he was scaring the pants off of those girls. I wondered what he was going to do.

"You've got a mean mouth," he said flatly.

Camilla looked at him uncertainly, and one of her friends whispered, "He's one of those carnie boys."

Camilla wrinkled her nose. "I wondered what the smell was."

Kes didn't say a word. He just picked up the dirty plate from their table, still smeared with ketchup, and mashed it all over Camilla's white tank top.

She squealed and jumped up. "You've ruined my shirt! You'll pay for that!"

Kes grinned. "Nah, you just need to wash it."

Then he flung a glass of coke over her, leaving her shocked and dripping. Everyone turned to stare as Camilla screeched.

Kes stood with his hands on his hips laughing at her. Then he turned to me and winked. God, I wish I'd had the nerve to do something like that—I just knew Camilla would take it out on me once we were back in school. Maybe if I showed her my fire-breathing she'd leave me alone. Maybe.

As before, time passed too quickly. Kes and I spent every day together, and every evening I went to see his show.

When Mom spoke to Dad on the phone and told him how I was spending my time and with whom, I heard her say some harsh words about "that white trash boy", a phrase that made my cheeks burn hotter than my attempt at fire-breathing. But Dad was out of town again, so I tried not to pay too much attention.

I didn't tell Kes what had been said, but I didn't have to—he knew what townspeople called the carnies. He'd heard it in every town he ever visited. A lot of people said that they ripped you off and stole your money if you didn't keep a close eye on them. It seemed so unfair.

Mom and Dad didn't know that I'd overheard them, but they wouldn't have cared anyway. If they had their secrets, I certainly had mine, because every night, when they'd gone to bed, Kes would jump in my window and we'd talk and talk and talk, carrying on the conversation that had been running all day.

It was so innocent, and if Kes liked to kiss my cheek before he left at dawn, well, that was our business.

"I'm really going to miss this," I said as we sat together on my bed, our last night together.

Kes sighed. "Me, too."

The year before, I'd tentatively suggested to Kes that we stay in touch by email but he'd immediately blown that idea out of the water. I decided to try again now. I got the same response.

"But you don't have to write much," I tried to convince him. "You could just send me photos. That would be cool."

"No," he said adamantly.

Then he scratched his thumb over his eyebrow, a gesture that meant he was nervous.

"I'll be 13 in December. Grandpa says I can have a cell phone for my birthday. Sometimes he says stuff like that and it doesn't happen, but if I get one, can I call you sometimes?"

"Seriously?! You'll have your own phone! That's awesome, I'm so jealous. Jennifer didn't get her own cell until she was 14, so I've got awhile before I'll get my own." I frowned. "I'll give you my number here, but…"

"But what?"

"Mom and Dad are weird about about me getting calls."

He sneered at me. "You mean they'll be weird if you get calls from me?"

I winced, peering up at him from under my lashes. "Well, yes. Probably. But if you phone on a Sunday evening about 7 o'clock, that's when they watch TV together."

"Yeah, whatever," he said.

I knew his feelings were hurt, but it was the best I could do.

"I really hope you call," I said lamely.

When I woke up the next morning, he'd already gone.

CHAPTER 4
EVERYTHING CHANGES

It was a week after New Year's when the phone rang one Sunday evening.

It had been a month since Kes's birthday and I'd almost given up hope that he'd call. Maybe he'd lost my number. Maybe Dono hadn't gotten him a cell phone after all. Maybe he didn't want to talk to me. Maybe, maybe, maybe. I hated not knowing.

I'd sent him a card for Thanksgiving, another for his birthday, and yet another for Christmas, but I never heard back, not even a postcard. But then that night, he called.

Dad told Mom that the phone was ringing. Mom told Jennifer to answer it, and Jennifer yelled that I was nearer. Grudgingly, I put down my book and picked up the phone: caller unknown.

"Hello?"

"Aimee?"

"Oh Em Gee! Kes, is that you?"

His laughter crackled down the line. "Yeah, it's me."

"How are you? Where are you? What are you doing right now? It's so good to hear from you!"

"I'm [*hiss*] and we're [*crackle*] so maybe…"

And then the call cut off. I waited impatiently for him to call back. As I shivered in the cold hall, praying silently, Mom shouted from the living room.

"Who was it, Aimee?"

"I'm not sure," I lied. "The call got dropped and it was all crackley."

"They'll call back if it's important," she said.

He didn't, but a week later I got a postcard. Kes had drawn a picture of himself shooting a cell phone with a bow and arrow. I laughed out loud then ran upstairs to hide it.

It's hard to explain what those two weeks every summer meant to me. I lived for them, I breathed for them, and the rest of my life seemed to be spent waiting. Of course, I went to school and I had girlfriends—no boyfriends because I was still skinny and hadn't really gotten any boobs yet. Not that I would have been interested; none of the boys in school could measure up to my colorful carnie boy.

Unsurprisingly, Camilla hated my guts and went out of her way to pick on me. But I discovered that all I had to say to her was, "Do you want fries with that?" and it shut her up.

It didn't stop her doing mean stuff like leaving horrible notes in my locker, or getting the other kids to refuse to talk to me, but I could live with that.

And every summer I had my precious two weeks.

The year I turned 13, Con left to go to college at Northwestern, which really impressed me. But he didn't even stay to work the summer season. Kes told me he got a job as a waiter in the city, instead. I knew that hurt Kes and Dono, although neither of them said anything to me. They'd had to bring in a couple of older guys who did a cowboy/target shooting/knife-throwing act, and that year I got to be the target, which made me scream and almost disgrace myself. But the highlight was always Kes's riding, fire-eating and flame-juggling—it was captivating, magical.

Each year Kes seemed to grow taller and broader and more handsome. By the time we were 14, Kes's eyes wandered when pretty girls walked past, and his voice cracked and squeaked like a broken toy. But 14 turned to 15, and 15 turned to 16, and it was still me that he spent his time with. I just didn't know what he did the other fifty weeks of the year. I wasn't sure I wanted to.

And I wasn't the only one who noticed that he'd changed. The summer I turned 16, Camilla plotted her revenge.

Jennifer was full of stories about how amazing college was: how awesome her roommate was; how fabulous the professors were; how incredible the campus was; how cool Minneapolis was to live in. I couldn't help thinking that with a year of college under her belt she'd have been more creative with her adjectives. She said I was being a bitch (true), and that I was jealous of her (also true), and that I wished I had her life (not true).

But I'd started thinking about college, too, even though it was a way off. Specifically, I was interested in being an elementary teacher, specializing in dyslexia. I'd figured out the root of Kes's reading problems years ago. Without trying to raise his suspicions, I'd quietly started testing the extent of his disability. From what I could figure out, he was at the extreme end of the spectrum, to the point where I'd say he was severely dyslexic.

He'd confuse even simple words like 'cat' and 'cot', refused point blank to read aloud, and would have to read a short paragraph several times to get the gist of it. When I made him read, or rather when he could be persuaded to sit down and try to read, he'd use his finger to follow along the lines, and I could see that he'd miss some words entirely and skip around the page. He hated it, and it made him bad tempered and moody.

He wasn't great with numbers either, especially long ones, but there was nothing wrong with his mental math, and he was faster at doing sums in his head than I was. He wasn't too bad at reading maps either; he said maps were like pictures, so he had no problem interpreting them, although long place names baffled him, but his sense of direction was phenomenal, and because he'd traveled so much, his US geography was way better than mine, a fact he enjoyed rather too much. I didn't mind, because I knew how hard book-learning was for him.

I wished I knew more about Kes's problems so I could help him better, but he hated admitting to any weakness. My dream was to teach and help kids like Kes. But how did that dream fit in with a future where Kes still traveled with the carnival? I couldn't answer that question.

I saw the carnival posters go up two weeks after the Fourth, and I knew I would see him again soon. I studied myself in the bathroom's full length mirror, hoping that *this* year he'd look at me the way he looked at those other girls.

My boobs had finally made a late arrival and I was wearing real, grown-up bras. Jennifer helped me experiment with makeup, although I felt more confident sticking to the basics: some sparkly eye-shadow and mascara, with a strawberry-flavored lip-gloss that I chose for Kes, because he mentioned once that he loved strawberries but hardly ever had them. I hoped that he'd want to kiss me—a lot.

I was also hoping that this year we'd progress from kisses on the cheek. I didn't want him to look at me like his sister, and my feelings were very far from thinking of him as a brother.

I'd thought of Kes as my boyfriend since we were ten years old. Now that I'd been 16 for a whole day, I was ready to take things further. Not all the way, not yet, but I definitely wanted more. And if boys were as dumb as Jennifer said, I was going to have to show Kes how I felt, tell him with words, not wait for him to work it out. The thought was nerve wracking.

My sixteenth birthday had felt like a huge anticlimax. I'd gotten a ton of books, which was great, and Jennifer had bought me some cute clothes, but I really hoped my parents would spring for a cell phone. They hadn't—again—and my baby-sitting money wasn't enough to pay for one either.

So my hopes for a memorable summer were pinned on the arrival of the carnival—and Kes.

I waited all day. The heat of late July cracked the sky and sucked the air from the land. Near the lakes, the buzz of mosquitoes was loud and most people had screens across their windows to keep them out.

I'd already gone to bed when I heard the carnival's sixteen-wheelers rumbling down the road. I sat up and crawled to the window, watching the headlights flash by, wondering which RV was Kes's, and wondering if he was thinking of me.

I left my window open all night, just in case, but he never came.

When I woke up the next morning, tired and bad tempered from hours of painful anticipation, my feelings were complicated and tightly knotted. But when I looked out and saw the Ferris wheel's skeleton stark against the white heat of the summer sky, I smiled.

The carnies must have worked through the night to get up the majority of the tents and sideshows.

Some of the townspeople thought that carnies were shirkers, but nothing could have been further from the truth. It was a hard life, breeding hard people, although I could see that Kes loved it. I couldn't imagine how he'd fit into a normal world. The thought made me shiver, because I couldn't imagine how I'd fit into his world, either.

I forced myself into a more positive frame of mind, determined not to show how anxious I was feeling. I'd already laid out the clothes I was going to wear: some bootylicious jean shorts and a pale blue tank top that revealed my bellybutton when I stretched my arms. I planned to stretch them a lot around Kes.

I also had my favorite push-up bra trimmed in pale pink lace, and with matching panties. I wasn't sure how lucky Kes was going to get, but I couldn't wait to find out.

I swiped the mascara wand through my lashes and brushed on some gold eye shadow that really suited my olive complexion.

Jennifer grinned at me when I came down to breakfast and gave me a thumbs up. She knew how much this meant to me, and despite our constant bickering, we'd gotten pretty close.

I slipped out before Mom could catch me, sending up a prayer of thanks that for the past few years, the carnival had arrived on a Thursday night, meaning that my father was already at work. There was no way the outfit would have passed his morality test.

I got my first wolf-whistle when I sauntered to the entrance arch. A carnie who must have been in his twenties and was covered in tattoos up to his neck, grinned at me.

"We're not open yet, princess. But you can come back and see me later."

I gave him a haughty stare. "Actually, I'm looking for Kes."

He gave a throaty laugh. "Aren't they all? Take a number and get in line."

His words made my stomach churn, but I refused to let him see how it affected me.

"Whatever," I said, tossing my long hair over my shoulder. "But he's expecting me and so is Grandpa Donohue, so unless you want to get in trouble, you'd better let me through."

His eyebrows shot up, and then he bowed from the waist and waved me inside.

"After you, princess."

I marched past him, feeling my cheeks heating up when he whistled again, then laughed wildly.

Over the years, I'd learned that there was a fierce hierarchy for positioning the carnies' motorhomes. Dono had the top spot, which was at the furthest end from the noise and smells of the rides, although it may also have been because he was the only person traveling with animals, but I didn't think that was the main reason.

I saw Ollo first, who whistled and grinned, but was wrestling with the layout for the bumper cars, so I waved and walked on.

I thought I saw Zachary at one point, but I couldn't be sure.

When I found Kes, he wasn't alone. A girl with wild red hair that streamed in riotous spirals down her back was leaning all over him, her breasts almost mashed against his chest. I tried to read Kes's expression: he seemed neither happy nor annoyed, just being super cool Kes, gazing into the distance.

I swallowed, a warm feeling crawling up my belly as I stared at him. He'd grown taller. Not as tall as Dono yet, but nearly as tall as my father. His shoulders were wider and I could see his biceps pushing through his ragged t-shirt, but he was still on the thin side, wiry, I guess. He looked stunning, like he should be in a boy band—you know, the bad one that makes all the parents fear for their daughters' virginity.

I watched him out of the corner of my eye as I turned to study the competition. I had to admit it wasn't looking good. The girl was taller than me and wore a low cut tank top that showcased a lot of cleavage. Her boobs were no better than mine, I decided—there was just more of them on show. So whereas I looked safe, nice you might say, she looked dangerous. Her arms were covered in colorful tattoos, her ears pierced five or six times each, and she had silver rings through her lip and eyebrow. Her face was hard, but beautiful, even caked in makeup.

I guessed she was maybe two or three years older than me, it was hard to tell.

As if she felt my gaze on her, she swung toward me, her eyes blazing.

"No rubes back here!" she yelled. "Get the fuck out!"

I was shocked that a complete stranger would speak to me like that. I froze, my eyes darting to Kes. He turned to look at me, his frown of annoyance changing to a warm smile.

"Chill, Sorcha," he muttered. "The shrimp's a friend."

I wanted to laugh. I wanted to cry. He was pleased to see me, but so dismissive. I stood there with my mouth hanging open. And then I was in Kes's arms, breathing in the scent of sweat and soap and something like fresh hay that was so familiar.

"Hey, kid! How you doing?" he said, as he led me away.

His voice had deepened. No longer childlike, it was a light, pleasant tenor.

"Don't call me kid!" I snapped, punching his shoulder.

He laughed and rubbed the spot where I'd hit him. His dimple popped out and I wished I'd hit him harder—then kissed him better.

"Okay, not a kid," he smiled, but then I watched his eyes darken as they drifted down my body, pausing at my chest, then doing a slow sweep along my legs and hips. "No, not a kid," he said again, and this time his voice was gruffer.

"Kes!" the girl yelled after him. "We have to practice the new routine."

Oh God, that harlot was part of his act? *And* she had a cool name. Yep, it was official—I hated her. It was also clear that it was mutual.

Kes didn't even bother to answer, and that gave me bittersweet satisfaction.

Without even discussing it, we both headed to the Ghost Train and I squatted down on the short, prickly grass, leaning back on my elbows, giving him the best view of my legs and chest. And yes, he looked. Then he smiled to himself and gracefully sank to the ground, sitting Indian style.

We grinned at each other, a pleasure that was almost nothing to do with raging teenage hormones.

"How've you been, Aimee? You look good."

His voice was a little wistful. Ah, *there* he was; *my* Kes."

"Okay," I said. "School has been kind of sucky, and I've missed you."

"What's up with school? I thought you liked that shit?"

"I did, I do. I mean…"

"But?"

"You remember that girl Camilla?"

Kes rolled his eyes and laughed lightly. "Yeah, definitely memorable."

"Well, she's kind of been a bitch ever since."

Kes frowned. "But that shit was years ago."

This time it was my turn to roll my eyes.

"You don't know girls very well if you think that she'd ever forget something like that—or forgive it."

He scowled.

"She's still giving you a hard time?"

I didn't want to sound too pathetic, so I played it down.

"Yeah, but nothing I can't handle."

His face was dark with anger, but I didn't want to discuss my problems. I had two weeks to be happy—I was darn well going to make the most of them.

"What have you been up to?" I said brightly. "Sounds like you've got a new act?"

Kes grinned, his eyes sliding to mine. "Jealous?"

I huffed a little, but then admitted the truth. "Yes, I'm jealous."

His gaze softened. "You don't need to be," he said softly. "Sorcha's just a friend."

"That's what you call me," I said, stupid tears making my eyes prickle.

Kes shook his head slowly. "No, you're my girl."

I blinked rapidly. My heart was going a mile a minute, I was so excited and nervous. I looked up at him, wanting to seem calm, trying to control the huge smile that was threatening to break out.

"Really?"

"You know me better than anyone, Aimee."

But to be honest, that wasn't saying much. He was so closed-off when it came to how he felt about things. He'd never spoken about his parents, and I had no idea what his hopes and dreams were for the future—or whether I fit into those plans. But I'd never thought he was a liar either, so maybe I had to trust him.

That sounded dangerous: trust the boy I saw for just two weeks a year with my fragile heart? I knew it was a mistake. Unfortunately it was one I'd already made years ago.

He reached out and brushed his thumb along my bottom lip.

"You're my girl, Aimee. No one else."

Then he leaned forward and pressed his lips against mine. It wasn't hesitant and it wasn't demanding; it was what I'd been waiting for, and it was perfect.

Without any need to think, my arms wrapped around his neck and pulled him closer. He unwound his long legs until he was hovering over me, his body resting full length against mine.

A sound between a moan and a growl rumbled at the back of his throat, and I opened my mouth, giving and taking my first ever full-blooded, heart-pounding, open-mouthed kiss, tongues thrusting and tangling wildly.

He tasted sweet like soda and something else I couldn't put a name to.

Our kiss was sloppy and we clashed teeth which made me jerk back, but Kes just took it as an opportunity to kiss and lick my neck. It was the most amazing sensation as pinpricks of heat broke out across my body.

I moaned softly and I felt the pulse jump in his neck, his heart thudding against his ribs. My body arched up to meet him, and I could feel a bulge in his jeans pushing against my thigh. For a fraction of a second, I was off balance and unsure, but then I reached down and rubbed my hand along it.

Kes growled and bit my throat, his teeth sinking into the tender flesh at the base of my neck. When his hands slid up from my waist and under my t-shirt, I pulled away.

This was going much faster than I was ready for. I loved it; God, it felt amazing! But I was worried that Kes would want to take it even further, and I definitely wasn't ready for that—not out here, in the open.

He lifted his head, staring down into my eyes.

"I guess we should stop," he said, regret fighting with the lust that made his eyes glitter.

"I guess we should," I said, my voice weak.

He rolled off me and lay back on the grass, one hand over his eyes, the other resting on his flat stomach.

The silence stretched out until it became uncomfortable.

"That was…" I began, not sure how to finish the sentence.

Kes propped himself up on one elbow to look at me.

"Hot," he said, grinning.

I laughed with relief. "Oh, definitely! I'm burning up here!"

He leaned closer. "Burning … or wet?"

I slapped his arm and laughed again. "Both," I admitted shyly.

"Oh shit," Kes sighed, then adjusted himself not very discreetly.

I couldn't help watching, I really couldn't.

It was my first experience of the male member. I felt proud that I'd done *that* to him. It was thrilling to find that I could provoke such a raw, masculine response. We weren't children anymore, but our bodies were eager to make decisions that our brains knew were dangerous. Maybe that was just me. It was certainly hard to keep my rational brain awake when I felt drugged by his kisses and desire.

I flopped back, letting my breathing slow and the wild passion return to a low simmer.

I swallowed several times, then turned my head to look at him.

"Kes, what do you think will happen to us? I miss you so much when you're away."

He sighed and his eyes closed.

"Do you ever think about the future?" I went on.

"Yeah, sometimes."

"Well, what do you want to do?"

"What do you mean? I want to do this." He was irritated.

"Is that all?"

He bristled immediately and I knew I'd said the wrong thing.

"What's wrong with it?" he snapped.

"I didn't say there was anything wrong with it!" My voice was defensive.

He looked like he was debating whether or not to be annoyed, but then his eyes closed again.

"No, you never have," he conceded. "That's why you're different from all the other townie girls."

I was silent for a moment.

"Do you remember the day we met?"

He laughed lightly. "Of course! I was supposed to be mucking out the horsebox, but I didn't want to do it, so I was hiding from Dono. I was watching all the rubes and then I saw you."

I smiled at the memory. "Why did you speak to me?"

He shook his head. "I don't know. You just looked so excited. You were tugging at your mom's hand and she wouldn't let you go. You looked like you wanted to go running down the midway, but she was hanging on tight."

"I thought I was going to see magic," I admitted. "You know, real magic."

Kes snorted with amusement.

"It's not funny!" I laughed. "Anyway, I did find magic."

Kes turned his head toward me, frowning.

"What do you mean?"

"It was so exciting, seeing the carnival appear in Mr. Peterson's field overnight. It had been a boring patch of grass, and then there was a whole city of canvas and colorful lights. It seemed like someone had waved a magic wand or something."

Kes groaned. "Seriously? Have you any idea how hard it is to get the show ready? We've usually driven all day to get here, then as soon as we arrive we have to set up. It takes the whole fucking night: your hands are raw from pulling on tent ropes, and your stomach's growling like a bitch because you haven't got time to stop and eat; and the next day you've got to fucking smile while you stick a broom in your ass and sweep the floor!"

I was laughing so hard at his description that it made me snort.

"Well, you took me to meet Mr. Albert—you were a real life carnie with a monkey. That seemed like magic."

He grinned. "Yeah, that's the point. Gotta keep the illusion."

I chewed on my next question for a minute before asking it.

"I don't want us to be an illusion," I said. "I think about you all the time—do you ever think about me?"

He didn't answer immediately and my heart sank.

But then he sat up, brushing grass from his hair.

"Yeah, I do."

I sat up, too, watching his face.

"You make that sound like a bad thing?"

He gave a small smile. "No, but…"

"But what?"

He sighed. "Aimee, you're smart and beautiful and…"

"Wait! You think I'm beautiful?"

Kes smiled softly. "Yeah, I always have. Even more so now."

"Wow!"

My heart, lead-filled a moment ago, now felt incredibly light.

But Kes's smile seemed sadder. "You'll do amazing things," he said. "I know it."

"So will you," I insisted. "You already have!"

He looked down, twisting his long fingers together before shredding some blades of grass.

"You're going to love the new show," he said, his voice wistful.

"Does it have knife-throwing in it?" I teased. "Do you throw knives at Sorcha? Because I'd be totally up for seeing that!"

He laughed in surprise and leaned in to kiss me on the cheek. "Feisty girl." Then he stood up in one smooth, feline movement. "Come on, let's go see Mr. Albert. Dono wants to say hi, too."

I frowned and bit my lip. "Your grandpa scares me."

Kes smiled. "Yeah, he scares most people, so don't worry about it. He likes you."

"Really?"

"Yeah. Why are you surprised?"

"I don't know. He never seems that happy to see me."

Kes grinned. "If he didn't like you, he wouldn't let you hang around with us."

"Well, okay then, I guess. By the way, why do you call him 'Dono' now?"

Kes's cheeks looked flushed when I glanced at him, and he ran his thumb over his eyebrow.

"It sounded babyish to keep calling him 'Grandpa'. I dunno. Is that weird?"

"I guess not if he doesn't mind."

Kes laughed. "I never asked him—I just started doing it. He hasn't said anything so it must be okay."

"I bet he has a way of letting you know if he's mad."

"I've got the bruises to prove it," he laughed.

I gasped and stared. "Does he still hit you?"

Kes shrugged. "Only when I've fucked up."

"But … but … it's wrong! He shouldn't hit you."

Kes was amused. "I know where the line is, Aimee. It's my fault if I step over it. Don't worry about it."

I must have looked mad, because he quickly changed the subject.

"How's your sister, um, Jennifer?"

"She's in school at Minneapolis, and I really miss her when she's away."

Kes pulled a face. "Fucking college."

I knew how he felt about anything to do with education, but it made me sad.

"Do you ever hear from Con?"

Kes shrugged. "Yeah. He came back, I mean home, to Arcata, last New Year's. He's pre-med. He wants to be a doctor."

There was a mixture of pride and something darker in his words. I knew Kes still thought of himself as dumb, and his brother's achievements seemed to compound that view.

I planted my feet and put my hands on my hips, having to look up to meet his eyes.

"Kestrel Donohue, you are the most amazing boy I have

ever met, so you stop that right now!"

Kes looked taken aback. "I could never do what he does."

"No, and neither could I. But there are very few people in the world who can do what you do either."

Kes frowned. "When he's a doctor, he's going to be able to save lives."

I shook my head impatiently.

"We need doctors, of course we do. But what you do—you make people happy. When you're in front of a crowd, nobody can think about their problems or their worries or anything else. You have a gift, Kes, an amazing wonderful gift. It's special, just like you."

I whispered those last words.

Kes stared, his eyes stunned, then he pulled me against his chest, his lips crushing mine so fiercely that I knew they'd be bruised. I didn't care.

"Say you mean it!" he hissed against my mouth.

"I do!" I cried. "I do mean it!"

He kissed me harder, his hands gripping my hips painfully.

Until we were interrupted.

"Oh my God, look at you two," laughed Sorcha loudly. "How sweet is that? You'd better watch out, Kes, or you'll be putting up a picket fence and buying a minivan any day now."

She sniggered at her own joke, making a choking motion.

"Fuck off, Sorcha," Kes said, as if he didn't care if she lived or died.

"Yeah, what he said," I murmured, caring only that I was in his arms and he was looking at me like he'd never let go.

She grunted and stalked off—not that I noticed.

"Please tell me you've never kissed her," I said to Kes. "Or anything else."

He gave an embarrassed laugh. "No way! She's slept with half the guys here—my dick would probably fall off."

"That would be a shame," I purred, rubbing against him.

I had no idea where this new, brazen version of myself had come from, but I liked it. Apparently Kes did, too, because he started running his hands up and down my back until he was cupping my ass and pulling me against his growing erection.

I think at that moment I'd have let him do anything he wanted, but then he stopped and blew out a long breath. His eyes were wild and I could tell it was taking every ounce of restraint for him to stop. Honestly, the want and need inside him scared me a little.

He swallowed several times, and I saw the storm in his eyes die back.

"Come on," he croaked, "let's go get a soda. Mr. Albert will be happy to see you."

Dono was sitting outside the RV with Mr. Albert in his lap, talking quietly to Madame Cindy. I realized it was the first time that I hadn't seen Dono in motion. I think Kes got his restlessness from him.

Mr. Albert shrieked when he saw me and leapt into my arms. Dono's mustache twitched, and he nodded.

"Hello, Mr. Donohue," I said politely, still nervous despite the years I'd known him. "Madame Cindy."

"Hello, Aimee," she responded comfortably. "Good to see you again, darlin'. Good to know you'll take care of our boy," and she pointed at Kes with her chin.

I had no idea what she meant about 'taking care' of him. I'd never met anyone who was more capable of looking after themselves. I smiled politely and sat on the ground, concentrating on cuddling Mr. Albert who was chattering happily and tugging my hair.

Kes just rolled his eyes, but made sure that Madame Cindy couldn't see him. He went inside the RV and passed me a cold soda.

It felt strange sitting there with the people who made up his family. We'd never really done that before. It felt like things were changing between us.

"Why don't you give her that present you've got hid, boy?" Dono said out of the blue.

Kes's cheeks flamed red as my gaze ping-ponged between him and his grandpa.

"You got me a present?" I asked, pleased but a little bewildered.

Kes's blush spread down his neck and even the tips of his ears looked like they were on fire.

He threw Dono an angry look, muttering under his breath. Then he ducked back inside the RV and came out holding something in a plastic bag. He wouldn't meet my gaze and went striding off.

Madame Cindy smiled. "Better go after him, darlin'."

Mr. Albert made little chirruping noises, but didn't try to come with me.

I followed Kes, jogging to keep up.

"Hey, wait!"

Kes was grumbling to himself, but his flushed cheeks seemed to be returning to normal.

"Fuck's sake! I hate having no privacy," he bitched. "Let's go into town."

"That's hardly private," I pointed out.

"No, but it's away from here!"

"We don't have a car."

He eyed me warily. "I could take the truck. I have my permit."

I crossed my arms.

He shrugged. "Dono lets me drive all of the time."

"That's because he's sitting up front with you!" I pointed out.

I really liked the idea of being alone with Kes, but I wasn't sure driving illegally was the best idea he'd ever had.

Then I saw Zachary walking toward us.

"Hey, Aimee! I thought I saw you earlier. How are you?"

"Good, thanks," I said, smiling at him.

"What are you guys up to?" he asked, raising an eyebrow as Kes scowled.

"Oh, just hanging out, you know. We were thinking about going into town," I said casually.

"I was just heading that way if you need a ride," Zachary offered.

I could tell Kes was going to tell him no, so I got my answer in first.

"That would be great! Thanks, Zachary."

I wasn't sure what Kes's problem was with Zach, but it was an uncomfortable journey into town.

Zachary had graduated to being second in charge of the Ferris wheel these days, something that seemed to require a good knowledge of engineering as well as several Health & Safety qualifications. Talking about the tests Zach had to take irritated Kes even further. I tried to change the subject several times, but Zach was proud of his achievements and eager to talk about them. I learned far more about the International Association of Amusement Parks regulations than I ever wanted or needed to know.

When Zachary let us out of his truck, saying our ride back would be in a couple of hours, Kes's mood was sour. I could feel his threatening glare, even though his eyes were hidden behind some fake Aviator shades that made him look really hot.

But first I needed to address the elephant in the room that Zachary's talk of tests had introduced.

"You know, they allow extra time for tests if you're dyslexic," I began tentatively. "Sometimes they'll even let someone read out the questions for you and…"

"I don't want to talk about it," he bit out.

I would have liked to say more, something to soothe and reassure him that I didn't think he was stupid, because I could tell he was thinking it.

Instead, I smiled as steadily as I could. "So, now we're in the heaving metropolis of Fairmont, what do you want to do?"

Some of the tension left his shoulders, although I could see that his fists were still tightly clenched.

"Where's good to eat?" he said at last.

"There's the diner, or Perkins do great pancakes?"

Finally, Kes smiled. "Pancakes sound great."

As we strolled along the street, he slung his arm around my shoulder. He'd never done that before.

I squinted up at him, wishing I'd thought to bring sunglasses. "Is this a date?"

I swear his cheeks looked warm as he glanced down at me.

"Do you want it to be?"

"Yes, please," I said shyly.

"Then it's a date," he said, looking ridiculously pleased.

My overwhelmed heart gave a happy lurch. I was with the hottest guy I'd ever met and he was happy to be on a date with me. It was every teen dream I'd ever had come true.

I debated whether I felt brave enough to hook my arm around his waist, or even tuck my hand in the back pocket of his jeans.

I settled for his waist, feeling the firm flesh under my fingers as he grinned at me.

At Perkins, we were shown to a table, and Kes tossed me the menu, resting his arms along the back of the booth.

"What's good?" he said.

I wondered how many times he'd used this method as a way

of deflecting attention from the fact that he could barely read. The thought saddened me.

"Well, we could go traditional, blueberry with maple syrup, or their Griddle Greats is pretty good—buttermilk pancakes, Belgian waffles and French toast with syrup."

I didn't care that it was breakfast time, or maybe brunch: I wanted sugar.

"Let's do that—one of each, then I get to try both."

I huffed a little, not meaning it at all. "Fine, but 50/50 or it's no deal."

Kes grinned, his even teeth white against his perennially tan face.

"Sure!"

I wasn't certain I believed him.

Our server sauntered over, devouring Kes with her eyes. To my dismay, it was one of Camilla's cronies. She barely registered that I was there; her eyes were all over my boyfriend.

"Can I help you folks?" she asked in a syrupy sweet voice.

"We'll take one order of the blueberry pancakes, one of the Griddle Greats, and two Mr. Pibbs. That's all. Thanks, Lauren."

She blinked as she looked at me, recognition making her frown.

"Oh, Lamey ... I didn't see you sitting there."

Kes narrowed his eyes, his body coiled as if he was about to leap up. I laid my hand on his arm, and watched with pleasure as Lauren's eyes got wider.

Kes was onto my game, grinning as he casually slid his arm around my shoulders and pulled me against his body. Then he brushed a soft kiss against my lips before he looked up at Lauren and winked.

Lauren's lip curled into a sneer as she walked away, and Kes's gaze softened as he stared at me.

"Is she one of them?"

I nodded unhappily.

He didn't say any more, but I got the feeling he was plotting something.

"Hey," I said, desperate to break the sudden dip in his mood, "I believe you have a present for me."

His smile lit up his eyes and I swooned a little inside.

"Uh, yeah. It's not much, but…" and he pushed the plastic bag toward me.

When I pulled the small box out of the bag, I began to smile.

"You got me a cell phone?"

He rubbed his neck. "I thought we could talk, you know, when I'm gone. You said your parents wouldn't pay for one, so I thought … it's not expensive or anything, but I put thirty bucks on it to get you started."

I leaned across the table and kissed his soft lips.

"I love it," I whispered.

"Good," he said, looking relieved.

Our date went by too fast. I loved having his company all to myself. I loved how easily we talked and joked together. I loved the person he was when we were like this. I wanted more of it, but as always, the clock was ticking.

I felt as if I'd met my soulmate, but he was always being taken away from me. Life was so unfair. But at least we could talk to each other now. That was something.

After we finished our pancakes, we had to hurry. At least Kes wasn't in a foul mood with Zachary anymore.

Back at the carnival, I watched Kes preparing for his act. He made sure Jacob Jones and the other ponies were warmed up, then he went into a huddle with Sorcha and the two guys that I hadn't met yet. Sorcha rested her hand on his shoulder as he talked, but I don't think he even noticed. His focus was unwavering and I could see how much this meant to him.

Ollo came over while I was perched in the bleachers, watching.

"Hey, Aimee! Good to see you again, girl."

"You, too, Ollo. How are you?"

He laughed, coughing slightly. "Ah, getting old," he said, shaking his head. "That's why I've got to pass on all my tricks to Kes."

"Like knife-throwing?" I questioned, blanching as Kes pulled out a set of brightly polished steel throwing knives.

Ollo nodded. "It takes even more skill than fire-eating, although you wouldn't guess it. Anything with fire always gets the audience going, but then you'd know that, wouldn't you?"

I pretended I didn't have a clue what he was talking about. We both knew that Kes wasn't supposed to have taught me any of the fire-breathing skills.

Ollo smiled and looked back at Kes who was throwing knives onto a wooden board, forming a bristling cordon around

Sorcha. I couldn't help hoping he'd miss, just a tiny bit.

"He's not interested in her," Ollo said, patting my knee.

I sighed and offered him a weak smile. "I know, he told me. But he sees her all year; I only get him for two weeks."

"Not for winter break," Ollo corrected me. "But yes, it's tough not being with the person you love."

I tried to hide my shock. I'd never dared say the L word to myself, let alone share it with anyone else. I spent fifty weeks of the year trying to keep my emotions tightly tethered. Maybe that's why everything seemed so intense now.

"You can't hide it," Ollo said quietly. "And neither can he. You'll work it out. You just gotta have a little faith."

"Faith in what, Ollo? Because sometimes it's just so hard."

"Faith that you're meant to be together," he said, nodding to emphasize his point.

"How do you know?" I begged.

"How do you know you love our wild Kestrel?" he asked.

I shook my head. "I just know."

"Then there's your answer."

He patted my knee again and went to take up his position on the drums. I was even more confused after our conversation.

71

CHAPTER 5
RISING STAR

After their rehearsal, Sorcha left to change into her costume, and Kes came to find me.

"What did you think?" he asked.

"Wow! That's the short answer. Just wow! You were amazing! You could be on TV or in Vegas with an act like that. It's…" I was almost lost for words. "It's like magic!"

His grin was huge. "You really think so?"

"Definitely!"

Kes's expression became determined. "I want to make this work," he said fiercely.

I was a little taken aback. "What do you mean?"

He pressed his lips together. "Carnivals are dying out, Aimee. How much longer can we go on trekking from one small town to the next?"

"But … but the carnival's been getting bigger and better every year?"

Kes sighed. "I've heard Dono talking to Madame Cindy about how it's not making any money. He's always worried about the price of gas; permits are harder to get and take longer and the Health & Safety regs are killing us; we've got Safe Haven to pay for … I mean Arcata. Forget it. People want to get on an airplane and travel to Disneyworld and go on the big rides. Small carnivals like us, we're dying. The good acts are being picked up by people like Cirque du Soleil." He looked down. "A guy came to see me after one of the shows."

I gaped at him. "Cirque du Soleil want your act? But that's awesome!"

"I can't go," he said.

"What? Why not?"

"Dono," he said simply.

"But … he wouldn't want to hold you back?"

"This is his life," Kes said quietly. "If I left him, I don't think he'd carry on." He shrugged. "And anyway, they didn't want the horses—they don't do animal acts. But I'd have to be 18 anyway. The guy backed off when he found out I'm 16." Kes smirked at me. "Guess I look older."

As he continued to stare, his smile slipped away, and the hunger that had been simmering inside blazed to life.

I licked my lips, my stomach clenching and my blood flaming to match his.

When Kes leaned in to kiss me, every thought rushed away—until the bitch Sorcha interrupted us *again*.

"The rubes are lining up," she said, sneering at me on the word 'rube'. "Twenty minutes till show time."

Kes sighed against my lips. "I'd better get ready. Stay for the show?"

"I wouldn't miss it," I said honestly.

Kes's 'costume' hadn't changed much in the last couple of years. He was still barefoot and bare chested, but this time, Sorcha was hanging over him, covering his face with ghostly white powder and circling his eyes with thick black liner. Then she painted what looked like ivy growing up from his neck to his temple. The effect was surprisingly eerie, and I reluctantly had to admit that she was doing a great job.

Sorcha's costume was Bride of Frankenstein meets Caspar. She was wearing a skimpy bra top that looked two sizes too small, and a floaty chiffon skirt that made her legs seem to go on forever. I hated her.

Her makeup matched Kes's and they looked like a perfectly ghoulish but beautiful couple.

I could see why the Cirque du Soleil agent had been surprised by Kes's age. He looked like a man; Sorcha was all woman, and I looked like a little girl.

When the drumbeat started, the small arena stilled, a few whispers rippling around the ring. And then Kes galloped out holding two flaming torches, with Sorcha riding behind him, clinging to his waist.

My jealousy was so bitter that I wanted to throw up, but the audience clapped and whistled.

She slid gracefully to the ground, her bare feet sinking into the sawdust. Her focus was on Kes as he galloped around her. He hung from Jakey's neck as he planted one torch to Sorcha's left and the second to her right, so her wild hair seemed to catch fire. The two other guys galloped into the ring, each tossing a lit torch to Kes. They were dressed head to toe in black, a contrast to Kes's bare skin that made them appear threatening.

And then the show began. Kes stood on Jakey's racing back briefly, then leapt to the ground.

He juggled the flaming torches, ran, jumped, and somersaulted onto and from Jakey's back again and again, always fluid, always in motion. I held my breath until my head spun. He wasn't born for an office or a desk job; he was born to thrill, to make you gasp, to stop you in your tracks so you'd have to ask, *how did he do that?*

Sixty minutes later, the audience was on their feet, stamping and yelling. I was almost afraid that the bleachers would collapse. Kes's body glistened with sweat and his chest and stomach heaved, but the look on his face—he'd found his own little slice of heaven. I was proud of him, and I was on my feet, too. Heavy envy made me dig my fingernails into the palms of my hands until they stung, because Kes scooped Sorcha into his arms and tossed her onto Jacob Jones before leaping up behind her and riding out of the ring.

"Oh my God! He is so hot!" shrieked a girl sitting behind me.

"You'll never guess who I saw him with in town this afternoon," said a familiar voice. "411 alert—Lamey Aimee!"

"You're kidding me."

The hairs on the back of my neck rose as I recognized the screeching: Lauren and Camilla.

"Totally!" Lauren continued. "And they looked pretty cozy."

Camilla laughed coldly. "There's no way a girl like Lamey can keep a guy like him satisfied, if you know what I mean."

They all laughed and a warm flush rose up my cheeks.

"Well, duh!" laughed Lauren. "That little virgin wouldn't know what to do with a stud like that. But it's obvious he's banging that hooch from the show. It's too funny! Lamey Aimee has a carnie boyfriend!"

"Not for long," said Camilla. "Just watch me."

They all laughed, like it was the funniest thing they'd ever heard.

I wanted to stand up and shout that he was mine, but instead I slid further into my seat and hoped that they wouldn't see me. Then I cursed myself for being so pathetic.

As soon as they left, I hurried to the RV.

Hooch-face was there, cleaning off Kes's makeup, and they were both laughing. My heart fluttered and something inside me felt like it died. I had to get a grip on this horrible jealousy—but how do you stop the monster that whispers and cackles, telling you that you're second choice, second best?

I tried to smile, but I probably looked like I'd swallowed something bad. I forced myself to plaster on my game face.

"You guys were amazing out there. The makeup was really great, Sorcha."

See? I could rise above my petty jealousy.

But the skanky bitch ignored me.

Kes turned to smile. "Thanks, Aimee. Sorcha did a great job—as usual."

My smile turned into a grimace as she grabbed his chin so he had to face her again.

"Keep still," she snapped.

I wanted to die when he winked at her.

"Kes, I have to go now," I said, my voice sick.

"Really?" he said, sounding disappointed. "I thought we could hang out some more."

"I'm kind of tired," I lied.

"Probably past her bedtime," Sorcha sniggered.

Kes laughed and his eyes glittered. "Yeah, probably."

"Okay, so ... see ya," I said faintly.

I walked away, not wanting to watch them share any more smiles. But then my new phone buzzed in my pocket, and I jumped.

The message said:

* Leaf ur wind open *

I wanted to stay awake, but lack of sleep the night before and the sheer turmoil of every possible emotion during the day had worn me out. I jerked awake when I heard a soft thud on my bedroom floor.

"Kes?"

I don't know why I said that—nobody else had ever climbed

through my window in the middle of the night.

He didn't speak as he crawled up the mattress. I could smell soap and hay, so I knew that he'd showered, then bedded the ponies down for the night.

Kes never asked if he could kiss me, he just took what he wanted, what he knew I'd give him. His lips were warm and firm as he searched for my mouth, kissing up my neck and across my cheeks. I ran my hands along his spine and I heard the breath catch in his throat.

When he yanked his damp t-shirt over his head, I drowned in the feeling of his silky skin and hard muscle under my fingers.

His kisses became deeper, an edge of impatience in them that made my blood catch fire.

His hands roamed under my t-shirt, and I hissed with shock and pleasure as he squeezed my breast with one hand and tugged at my panties with the other.

"Kes, we have to stop," I moaned against his throat.

"Why?" he whispered, before his teeth fastened over my nipple.

I was finding it hard to remember the reasons, because his hands, his breath, the heat of his skin, it made my body sing.

He unzipped his pants, then grabbed my hand and pushed it inside his jeans.

"Touch me!" he hissed.

Shocked but not scared, I wrapped my fingers around his hard cock, surprised by the heat pulsing in my hand. I squeezed tentatively and Kes moaned, a long, feral groan of pleasure. I pumped him a couple of times and he buried his face in my neck, his body shuddering.

"Oh shit!" he gasped, and then he came all over my hand.

I was so stunned, I almost giggled, but I managed to keep my mouth shut.

Kes rolled onto his back and flung one arm across his beautiful face, breathing hard.

I wasn't sure what I was supposed to do, but my hand felt all sticky and gross. So I groped on my table for a tissue and cleaned myself up, wondering if I should, I don't know, dab his dick or something. In the end, I decided to leave it to him.

Now he was peaceful, I could appreciate the hard planes of his chest and stomach in the moonlight, the body that was almost a man, his beautiful face that still had a little of the round softness of a child. And he was here, in my bed. I felt calm and excited, like I could fly to the moon or float away on an ocean of bliss.

Slowly, Kes peeled his arm away from his face and turned to look at me.

"You didn't come, did you?"

"No, but that's okay."

He frowned and scrubbed his hands over his eyes, the moon's pale light softening the hardness I sometimes saw in his eyes.

"The girl's supposed to come first," he sighed.

I immediately felt like I must be defective in some way. Was that how it was supposed to happen? I wasn't even entirely sure I'd ever had an orgasm. I touched myself, sometimes, and it felt nice, but that was all.

"Um, sorry," I said nervously.

Kes chuckled. "Jeez, Aimee! That's not what I meant! It was amazing to feel your hands on me."

"Don't you do it all the time? I thought boys were always…"

Kes eyed me thoughtfully. "What makes you think that?"

I laughed, more than a little embarrassed. "One of the girls at school—she says her brother … well, anyway…"

Kes grinned and kissed the crook of my elbow, which I thought was adorable.

"I don't do it as much as I'd like. There's no privacy. I get like three minutes max in the shower. And that's not usually enough to rub one out *and* wash. Dono's on my case about wasting water the whole time because it's a pain if the tank runs out."

"That was less than three minutes," I pointed out.

Kes looked a bit embarrassed. "Only because it was you touching me."

That made me smile.

Then without any hint of self-consciousness, he kicked off his jeans so he was completely naked, and pulled me against his chest, kissing me senseless.

I could feel he was already hard again. Did that mean he wanted me to give him another hand job? I reached down to stroke him and he groaned, then pushed my hand away and started kissing up my neck, his breath hot against my shivering body.

"No, I want to see if I can make you come."

"Oh, okay. You don't have to if you don't want to."

He paused in his kissing, then looked me in the eye.

"Oh yeah, I really want to."

"Have you…" I hesitated, not certain I wanted him to answer my question.

"Have I what?" he murmured as he made his way down my chest to my breasts.

"Um, with another girl?"

He paused, his mouth around my breast, and then pulled away with a soft pop.

"I've done some stuff," he admitted grudgingly.

"Oh."

I could hear the disappointment in my tone, so I was darn sure he could, too.

"I haven't gone all the way," he said quietly.

"Well, what have you done?" I asked, my voice brittle.

He sighed. "Just fooled around, you know?"

"Not really," I snapped. "I haven't even kissed another boy."

"Aimee…"

"It doesn't matter," I said, even though it did.

Maybe it was irrational, but it hurt to hear him say that there had been other girls. Maybe he climbed into their bedrooms, too. Maybe he…

"It didn't mean anything."

His sharp words interrupted my increasingly lurid imaginings.

"Sure," I said, trying and failing to keep the ache out of my voice.

"Look," he said, his voice rising with anger. "The guy's supposed to know what to do!"

"So, that's your excuse for going with some skank?" I said disbelievingly.

I was stupid. I was naïve. We'd been dating officially for just a few hours. I wanted to kick myself, but I couldn't stop my stupid mouth from voicing every insecurity I'd ever had.

"Jesus! I haven't, okay?!"

When I spoke again, my voice was small. "Really?"

"No!"

He hesitated, and I could see the moonlight reflected in his eyes as he stared up at the ceiling.

"This one time…" He paused, glancing at me quickly. "A girl

sucked me off. But that was all."

Tears prickled behind my eyes. "When did that happen?"

"Does it matter?" he snapped. When I didn't reply, he eventually relented. "A few months back."

"Was it Sorcha?"

He laughed humorlessly. "No. Just some girl."

I swallowed and plucked at the sheet so I didn't have to look at him.

"Am I … am I just some girl?"

His body jerked and then he pulled me into his arms so I was lying across his chest again.

"No! God, no. You're my friend, Aimee. You're … different, special."

That wasn't exactly what I needed to hear. But it would have to do.

I snuggled into his bare chest some more. "I like that you're a virgin, too," I said.

A surprised laugh rattled out of him.

"Yeah? Even though I don't know what the fuck I'm doing?"

"We can figure it out," I said. "Although I've got a rough idea of how it all fits together."

He laughed softly. "God, you're something else, Aimee."

"Have you only just noticed?" I asked, a smile in my voice.

"No," he said, his voice serious. "I've always known that."

"Good."

His lips brushed across my shoulder.

"I could try to get you off then?"

I rolled my eyes—it seemed like such a guy thing to say when we were having a romantic moment.

"I'm kind of tired now and I'm really comfortable. Maybe tomorrow?"

"Okay."

I could hear the disappointment in his voice, but he didn't try to push me.

We lay together peacefully, one of Kes's hands around my waist, the other stroking my arm. As I lay on his chest, I listened to the strong, steady beat of his heart. It was reassuring.

I jolted awake and stared in shock at the clock on my bedside table. Sun was pouring in the window, and Kes's beautiful eyes were blinking at me in confusion. Then I heard Mom calling up the stairs.

"Aimee, bring your laundry down, will you? I'm going to do a wash in a minute. Aimee?"

"Answer your mother," came my father's angry voice.

"Holy shit!" I gasped, leaping out of bed and looking around me wildly.

Kes sat up, his eyes wide.

And yet even with the seriousness of the situation, I couldn't help the hot glance as my eyes slid down his beautiful naked body.

"Coming, Mom!" I yelled, tearing my eyes away and pulling on a pair of shorts.

Kes grinned at me as he stood and let the sheet fall away. I couldn't help looking, and my eyes nearly fell out of my head when I caught an eyeful of what I guessed must be the legendary morning wood. His dick seemed larger in daylight, and I wasn't sure how that was even possible—I hadn't been able to get my fingers all the way around him last night.

He dragged on his jeans and stuffed his dick in his pants, wincing slightly. We both searched for his t-shirt as Mom yelled at me again.

"Where the fuck are my sneakers?" he muttered.

I found one under the bed and he found the second tangled up in the sheets. I had no idea how that happened.

"See you later?" he whispered.

I nodded furiously, shooing him with my hands.

But he grabbed my waist and kissed me dizzy before he winked and launched himself out of the window.

I nearly had a heart attack. He hadn't even bothered with the tree—he just jumped right out of the window. I gasped and ran to look, but he was already sprinting to the safety of the hickory tree. He turned once, waved, and then jogged toward the carnival field.

As quickly as I could, I gathered an armful of dirty clothes and ran down the stairs, nearly tripping over Jennifer. She blocked my path as I tried to pass her.

"We need to talk!" she hissed.

I had a horrible feeling I knew what the topic was going to be.

I stuffed my clothes in the washing machine, and probably

gave myself an ulcer trying to act normal while we all sat around the breakfast table. Breakfasts were the worst meal of the day because Dad insisted that we all eat together, like some Norman Rockwell family. I mean really, like, "Please, would you pass the jelly?", "May I have a second glass of juice?"

I didn't know if he believed in the illusion, but it was a façade we were all expected to keep up. The falseness grated on me more each year.

Recently, Dad had taken up golf, becoming almost fanatical about it. I think we all breathed a sigh of relief because it meant he was out of the house all day each Saturday.

But I couldn't avoid Jennifer. She kept throwing me searching looks, so I wasn't surprised when she followed me up to my room after breakfast.

I sat on the bed, arms folded, and waited for the inquisition.

"Kes stayed last night," she said flatly. "I know, because I saw him leave about five minutes before breakfast."

I wondered if I could get away with saying that he'd only just arrived and I wouldn't let him in, but the look on Jennifer's face told me it wasn't worth lying.

"Yes, he did," I said at last.

She seemed a little taken aback that I hadn't tried to deny it.

"So, you're sleeping with him?"

"Obviously," I said, raising one eyebrow.

"Obviously," she snapped back. "You're having sex with him!"

I blushed to the roots of my hair, then shook my head. "No," I whispered.

Her voice softened considerably. "Are you going to?"

"I think so," I nodded, my voice a whisper.

She blinked rapidly. "Wow!"

I glanced up at her. She didn't seem angry.

"You're not mad at me?"

Jennifer frowned. "Why would I be mad at you?"

"You don't think I'm a slut or anything?"

She shook her head. "No, of course not. You've been crazy about that boy since you were a kid. But..."

"But what?"

"He'll be leaving again in two weeks."

"I know," I said miserably.

"Are you sure you want to do this?"

81

She didn't sound like she was being judgmental, but I could read between the lines.

"Yes and no. I want to, but I'm nervous, too. I know it's going to hurt, isn't it?"

Jennifer seemed embarrassed. "That's what I hear."

It was my turn to look surprised. "I thought you and Luke…?"

"Ha well, no, we didn't. We fooled around, but I wanted to wait."

"Is that why you guys broke up?"

"Yes! What a jerk! Can you believe it? He thought just because we'd been dating for a few months that I should put out!"

"I always thought he sounded like a jerk," I giggled, enjoying the shared moment.

"You were right," she admitted. "But are you right about Kes? I don't mean to be a bitch, but he seems like the kind of guy who'd be a total player. He could have a girl in every town for all you know."

I sighed and studied my fingernails. "He says he doesn't. He hasn't even slept with anyone else."

"And you believe that?" Jennifer interrupted.

"I trust him," I said forcefully. "And besides, he bought me my own cell phone so we can talk every night."

Jennifer's skeptical look softened to a smile. "Oh, that's really sweet! Maybe I'm wrong about him."

"I don't know how it's going to work out," I admitted. "They have winter break for ten weeks every year in California. Maybe I could fly out there and visit…"

Jennifer shook her head. "Dad would never go for that, and I'm not sure Mom would either."

Hearing her confirm it made my eyes tear up again. "I don't know what to do," I said. "I love him."

Jennifer sighed. "I can see that."

"Honestly, I'm not sure if I'm ready to take the next step, but he is. And if I make him wait another year, what's to say he won't find someone else?"

"Jeez, Aimee! If he can't keep it in his pants until you're ready, what basis is that for a relationship?"

"But that's the point!" I cried. "We *can't* have a relationship! You said it yourself. I get him for two weeks a year, period. But it's two whole years before I can leave home and go to college, and even then he'll still be traveling all over. I've thought about it and thought about it and I don't see how it can *ever* work. So if all we get is now, then I'll take it. This way, he'll always be my first time and I'll always be his—and he'll always be a part of me."

The tears began to flow, and Jennifer wrapped her arms around me. She hugged and hugged and wouldn't let go.

"Be careful," she whispered.

Fate was against us. Screw that! Kes was moody and difficult, brilliant and beautiful. He scared me and he protected me. He could be incredibly hurtful and incredibly thoughtful. He wasn't perfect, but he was perfect for me. He challenged me, he took me out of my safe little box and showed me the world could be magnificent. He was everything I wasn't, but somehow, together, there was a synergy, an alignment, something that just made sense, no matter how crazy it seemed to anyone else.

All these thoughts whirled around in my head while I showered. I imagined his hands sliding over my skin, his hands kneading my breasts, his hands teaching me what my body could do, and just the thought of it made my skin flush from top to toe.

And for two weeks, he was mine. Two weeks, and tonight.

I dressed carefully, but there was nothing overt. If he wanted low cut clothes and cleavage and sex appeal, there was Sorcha for that. But he hadn't chosen her, he'd chosen me. Somehow, this beautiful, baffling boy wanted me.

I felt calm as I walked down the street to the carnival field. I passed the same carnie as the day before. Instead of giving me a hard time, he just winked and waved me inside.

But when I found Kes, he surprised me again. He was shirtless, which seemed to be the norm for him these days, and he was wearing a bandana over his hair, presumably to stop sweat dripping into his eyes. That wasn't what surprised me. I was used to seeing Kes hot and sweaty: working with the ponies, mucking out the trailer, practicing in the ring, but today he was bent over the hood of Dono's truck, wrestling with something in the engine.

The muscles tensed in his arms, and he cursed as a wrench went flying from his hand.

"Good morning to you, too!"

He stood up quickly and hit the back of his head against the hood.

"Ow! Fuck!" he yelped.

I couldn't help giggling.

He turned around, a rueful smile on his face.

"Don't tell me you're a mechanic, too!" I said.

"Okay, I won't."

"Seriously, do you know what you're doing?"

He grinned. "Pretty much. Older model engines are fairly simple."

I cocked my head to one side and smiled at him. "You never cease to amaze me."

His smile grew even larger. "Come here," he whispered.

"No way!" I laughed, dancing out of reach. "Your hands are covered in grease."

He wiggled his fingers, and I squealed as he took a step forward. But Dono interrupted us.

"There's a bottle of GoJo in the glove box," he said pointedly.

Kes threw me a mischievous look and raised his eyebrows, but he didn't argue with his grandpa, and went to clean his hands.

Dono sank into a deckchair and waved at the empty seat next to him. I perched on it nervously as Dono continued to stare at me.

"Kes is a good boy," he said quietly. "Treat him right."

My mouth fell open. I'd spent so much time questioning whether Kes was right for me, it had never occurred that anyone would ask if I was right for Kes.

"I will, sir. I promise."

He nodded. "No need to call me sir."

Kes returned wiping his hands on a rag. His eyes narrowed, and I wondered how much of the conversation he'd caught. He opened his mouth to speak, but Sorcha interrupted him. I was getting sick of her sudden entrances.

"We made the local paper, Kestrel," she said, draping an arm around his neck and glaring at me.

I didn't even pretend to like her, and I hated that she used Kes's full name. I'd decided only I was allowed to do that. But I don't think Kes liked it either, because he shrugged free from her and looked at the page she pointed to.

He smiled. "Yeah, great photo. That should bring in the crowds tonight."

"Freakin' A!" Sorcha crowed. "But read the last paragraph."

Kes tensed instantly and Dono looked like he was going to say something, but I reacted without thinking. I snatched the newspaper out of Sorcha's hand, scanning the story.

I caught Kes's eye, seeing the flash of relief and gratitude. That was all the thanks I needed.

Sorcha was pissed.

"What's your fucking problem?"

"Shut up," I said casually. "I'm reading."

She started to say something else, but Dono quelled her with a look.

"Wow, Kes, this is amazing. It says, 'An outstanding theatrical experience that set this jaded reviewer's excitement-meter at 100. Totally unexpected in a small town carnival, it was fun, furious, sexy and sensational. You won't see a better show this side of Vegas. Young Kes Donohue is a rising star and one to watch. See him now and you can say you saw him before he was famous.'"

I took a stuttering breath before I jumped up and down, squealing loudly.

Kes looked stunned and Dono merely nodded.

"Better get the spare seats set up for tonight, boy."

I swear that underneath his bushy mustache Dono was smiling.

"Oh, it mentioned you, too, *Sheila*," I smirked.

Sorcha's face colored and she stalked away.

"What was all that about?" laughed Kes.

"They got her name wrong," I grinned. "Poor Sheila."

"You're evil," he murmured, pulling me into a hug and kissing me in full view of his grandpa.

"Seats, Kes!" snapped Dono.

After that, it was every carnie to the arena to put up a fourth side of bleachers. They didn't usually need so many seats, but Dono was hoping the publicity would bring in more customers.

Everyone was so busy that I was put in charge of the ponies' warm-up. Kes thrust Jacob Jones' reins into my hand, along with the other two ponies, and I started walking them around the field to get them loosened up.

"Trot them, Aimee!" yelled a hot and sweaty Kes from the top of the bleachers' scaffolding.

Muttering under my breath, I broke into a jog, towing the ornery animals after me. They didn't want to be running in the hot sunshine anymore than I did, and soon all four of us were bad tempered and sweaty.

"Don't tire them out!" Kes yelled, and I may have mumbled something very rude under my breath.

Sometimes there were two shows scheduled on a Saturday, depending on how busy it was. Wet weather killed off the whole carnival, but there wasn't much chance of that today. The shows were usually slightly different, too: the afternoon show was more family friendly; and the evening show as dusk fell, that had the more dangerous, edgy tricks. The newspaper reporter had evidently seen the evening show, so Kes and Dono debated on how much of the darker material they should include.

But soon it was clear that a third show was going to be needed.

The tattooed carnie who usually ran the gate jogged over to Dono.

"Boss, I've sold out both shows already and they're still coming. What do you want to do?"

Dono glanced up at Kes, his gaze questioning.

"I'm up for it," Kes stated.

Dono nodded. "Do it."

Kes slid down from the scaffolding, like some sort of sexy fireman, barely even looking at what he was doing. I had to grit my teeth as he dropped the thirty feet to the ground in a few seconds.

The day was brutal. By the end of the second performance, the ponies were lathered with sweat and Sorcha looked like she needed to be wrung out. Jesse and Blake, the two guys who rode with Kes, had abandoned their black shirts after the first show.

But because Kes was the focus, he'd had the bulk of the work. He looked exhausted and had suffered a slight burn on his left hand because of a mistimed throw from Sorcha. To be fair, I could see that she felt really bad about it, cooing over him, and rubbing his shoulder. What that had to do with a burn on his hand, I had no idea. I marched over with the First Aid kit, made sure his skin was clean, then covered it with an anti biotic gel and a thin sheet of saran wrap to protect it.

Sorcha threw me a look. I would have said something, but Kes definitely didn't need the aggravation of two girls bickering.

When he stood up to give the ponies their cool down, I pushed him back into his seat.

"You need a rest," I said. "I'll walk Jacob Jones and the others."

He started to protest.

"Look," I said forcefully, "you're tired already and you can't afford any more mistakes tonight. Take. A. Rest."

He grinned tiredly, his mouth twisting up in a lopsided smile.

"I kind of like you bossy."

"Good," I said. "Get used to it."

I gathered up the reins and walked the three ponies in a slow circle. Mr. Albert joined me, riding on Jacob Jones and chattering away.

I was surprised when several people came over to talk to me, assuming that I was with the carnival. I'd lived in this town my whole life, but suddenly I felt like I belonged.

I answered their questions confidently, only faltering when a little boy asked me how long it took to learn to breathe fire. His mother looked horrified, so I lectured him about how it took years and wasn't something he should try at home, ever. The hypocrite in me was surely going to burn in Hell, but his mom looked grateful and quickly dragged him away.

Lots of girls my age and older were hanging around, too, hoping for a glimpse of Kes. I may have let Jacob Jones tread on their toes as I strolled past, but one bolder girl thrust a piece of paper in my hand.

"The guy without the shirt—give him my number."

My jaw dropped, and I stared at her in amazement as she winked at me and walked away. A cold feeling trickled through me. Was this how it was for Kes? Girls throwing themselves at him everywhere he went?

But then I drew back my shoulders and ordered myself to woman-up. If Kes wanted a casual hookup, he could easily have had it by now. If he just wanted sex on tap, he could have that with Sorcha. But he didn't: he wanted me.

The third show went even better and the crowd was wild. Kes gave it everything, and even Sorcha stayed focused. People cheered and stamped so hard the bleachers shook and trembled. Kes and the guys had to return three times for an encore, and

Sorcha smiled so much, I thought her jaw was going to cramp.

Finally, Kes shook his head and gave up. His fans wanted him, but he was done.

Sweat poured from his body, so that the makeup was just a smear of black eyeliner giving him a scary Marilyn Manson appearance. His chest was heaving and his legs shook as he slid down from Jacob Jones.

I took the reins from him and quietly walked the three ponies, whose heads were heavy and hanging dejectedly. After twenty minutes, Dono came to find me and together we sponged them down and settled them for the night.

"The boy's tuckered out," Dono said, his lips barely moving as he spoke, as if every word were precious and he was afraid he'd lose one if he spoke carelessly. "He's grateful for everything you've done today. He won't say it, but he is."

I wasn't sure how to respond, so I just nodded and gave him a small smile.

When I walked back to the RV, Kes was asleep in one of the deckchairs, his lips slightly parted, the flush of his exertion fading from his cheeks, leaving him looking uncharacteristically peaceful, and very young.

Sorcha was watching him, too, but I got the impression that she was really waiting for me. She sashayed over and planted her hands on her hips.

Her makeup was smeared in streaks and her hair was a tangled mess, but she still looked amazing. I really, really hated her.

"Another ten days, we'll be gone," she said, her tone conversational. "You think he wants you, but he doesn't—not really. You're all the things he's never had: house, family, regular life. But that's not his reality and it never will be." Her eyes pinned me. "He wasn't born for a cage, surely even you can see that. He'll never leave the carnival, he loves this life."

"He loves me, too," I murmured, any fight I had, leaking out of my voice.

Sorcha shrugged as she turned and walked away. "For now, but I'll be the one to pick up the pieces."

I hated that witch. I hated her like I'd never hated anyone, not even Camilla fucking Palmer, not even my father. It felt as if Sorcha's words had cursed us, and I would never ever forgive her for telling me the truth.

CHAPTER 6
HOLDING BACK THE TIDE

Since it was late, Zachary offered to walk me home. I felt a little awkward accepting his help because I wasn't sure if Kes would like it.

"You're quiet," Zachary said. "I guess you're tired; it's been a long day for all of us. It was good, though."

I nodded, but didn't answer.

I could see him watching me from the corner of his eye.

"Did you guys have a fight?" he asked.

"No!" I snapped. "Why would you say that?"

"Sorry," he mumbled. "You can tell me it's none of my business … but you seem kind of upset."

I sighed. "I'm sorry, too. I didn't mean to bite your head off. It's nothing really."

"It must be something to make you look like your dog just died."

I gave him a thin smile.

"Just some stuff Sorcha said."

He laughed roughly. "Don't listen to her. She's been hitting on Kes ever since she joined the carnie this Spring."

"He said she'd slept with half the guys here?"

I flushed when I realized Zachary could be one of her harem. Could girls have harems?

"Yeah, nearly that many," he chuckled. "I'm not one of them in case you were wondering—she's not my type … and she's not Kes's type either. She'd like to be—you saw him out there tonight. He shines so bright, he's going to be a star. She's not dumb, she can see that and she wants a part of it."

"Maybe, maybe not, but she'll be there when I'm not. I haven't got a chance."

Zachary touched my arm gently. "You want it easy? You want everything served up to you on a silver platter?" He shook his head. "Kes will never be easy, and the person who loves him won't have it easy. But if he loves you back, it'll be worth it, because he'll love you with every part of him." He looked down. "You're lucky."

"I'm not sure about that," I said sadly. "Sometimes I think so, but at other times…"

Zachary looked at me knowingly. "Trust me: you're lucky."

I didn't have the energy to argue, so I just nodded.

The house was quiet which meant everyone had gone to bed. I prayed that Dad hadn't noticed my absence. I thought maybe I'd gotten away with it, because otherwise he'd have been waiting for me, no matter the late hour.

I crept up the stairs, cringing at every squeaking floorboard and breath of moving air; anything that might wake the monster.

With relief, I closed my bedroom door and switched on the light. I immediately saw the note lying on my pillow.

Covered for you with Mom and Dad.
You so owe me!
Jen

I flopped back on the bed, finally able to breathe easily. Jennifer was right: I definitely owed her.

Rolling over, I lay on my side and stared out the window. Just across in the next field, the colorful lights of the carnival faded one by one, until only the orange glow from a few trailer windows could be seen as the carnies settled down for the night.

It had always been so magical to me as a child—seeing the field blossom into life, like one of those desert plants that only flowers after rain.

Kes was over there. Maybe Dono had woken him by now, and he was in his own narrow cot bed.

Maybe thinking of Kes conjured him, because I heard his voice outside my window, calling softly.

I leaned across the sill and saw him standing in the moonlight. He smiled up at me, his eyes as bright as polished silver and his bare chest gleaming, all color leached away.

Before I could say a word, he started climbing up the side of the house, his fingertips digging into the board cladding, hooking around the drainpipe. He made it look as easy as walking upstairs, and then he pulled himself onto the windowsill and glided into my room.

He didn't speak, not with words, instead pushing me back onto my mattress and kissing me hard.

I pulled my sweaty tank top over my head, surprising him, I think, because he paused, his hands gripping my waist. But his hesitation didn't last. He reached behind me and released my bra, tossing it over his shoulder, then started to suck my breasts—not just the nipples, but all over, molding my soft flesh in every tender direction. I gasped and dug my fingers into the back of his neck, pulling him closer, encouraging him to use all his mouth, his lips, tongue, teeth, as his jean-clad hips settled between my knees.

I think he said something, but I couldn't hear—the pounding in my ears was too loud. Warm spikes of desire started shooting up my body, leading to a point of heat between my legs.

I could smell his sweat, harsh and spicy, and when I licked his skin, he tasted of salt.

I couldn't wait to shimmy out of my shorts when he flicked open the button. He dragged my panties down my hips, and I kicked them off.

Slowly, he leaned back on his heels, staring down at me wide-eyed. After the frenzy of the last few minutes, I felt exposed and I tried to tug the sheet over me, but Kes's weight pinned it to the mattress.

I whimpered in embarrassment and his gaze flicked upward.

"I'm just going to try some stuff," he said, his voice thick with lust.

I didn't know what 'stuff' he wanted to try, but I needed him closer. I ran my hand down his chest, my nails scraping across his stomach. I watched, fascinated, as his muscles trembled under my touch. It was some confirmation that he was feeling as much as I did. I relaxed a little and shifted my hips against him.

His eyes fluttered closed and he took a deep breath. He shook his head, seeming to center himself, and reached into his pocket. I swallowed nervously when I realized he was holding a condom. He held it in the palm of his hand, watching me with such intensity that my body reignited.

I nodded and he smiled tightly.

He unbuttoned his jeans quickly and pushed them off his hips and over his knees. He swore when his feet got tangled. I laughed a little because I'd never seen him do anything that wasn't graceful before. He shot me a furious look that shut me up.

Then he stood and slid his briefs over the curve of his ass, revealing a dip on either side where the muscles met thigh. A warm, musky scent rose from his body, making me want to lick the dips and learn the ridges of his body.

He faced away from me to roll on the condom, but it looked like his hands were shaking. I didn't know if that was nerves or adrenaline because I definitely felt both.

When he turned around, I reached out to touch him, surprised by the texture of the condom, fascinated by the heat I felt through it.

He stepped back quickly, shaking his head, a small smile tugging at his lips.

I didn't know what he meant, so he showed me instead.

Kes stretched out on the bed, the full length of his sun-warmed, sex-heated body against mine. I shivered and began to sweat, beads of perspiration forming in my armpits and the small of my back.

We kissed for the longest time, until my lips felt swollen and my body was tightly wound. Kes was panting against my neck, licking and sucking in a way that would leave bruises. I bit him, hard, and his body jerked in surprise.

"Shit, Aimee!" he gasped, holding his hand to his neck.

I grinned at him and his eyes grew wild and dark.

He retaliated by grabbing my thigh and tugging it over his hip. I gasped as his cock pushed against my entrance for the first time. His smile told me that was payback. Holding his dick firmly with one hand, he began to rub it up and down. The blunt, round head teasing and tempting my wetness, but I wasn't the only one who was being tortured.

Kes pulled back, shaking his head. "I'm going to come, I'm going to come," he gasped. "Fuck, I don't think I can … shit!"

I cupped his cheek and brought his lips back to mine.

"We're doing great," I whispered, feeling the need to reassure him.

He took a shuddering breath and closed his eyes briefly. When he opened them again, he nodded jerkily.

After that, he seemed to regain some control, and he dragged his fingers from my knee up to my thigh, pausing before tentatively stroking between my legs. I nearly leapt off the mattress as he accidentally swiped over my clit.

"Oh God!" I gasped.

He did it again, getting the same intense reaction. His eyebrows drew together, focusing all his energy on that one, tight point. Watching and feeling the way my body writhed and arched, he found a rhythm that had me making a noise I'd never heard before, a low breathy groan.

"Fuck, that's so hot!" he gasped, rubbing harder.

His surprise and pleasure in my pleasure pushed me over a threshold I didn't even know was there. Lights bloomed behind my tightly closed eyelids, and my body shook and trembled when he pulled me against his chest.

As I gradually resurfaced, my senses slowly slipping back into my body, a wave of love and gratitude flowed through me. Every part of my body felt surprising and new, as if Kes had found me sleeping and kissed me awake. Everything sparkled with a fresh clarity. An intense rush of love spilled out and I pressed my lips against his chest, reassured by the warmth, startled by the frantic pounding in his chest.

I glanced up at his beautiful face and realized that Kes was gritting his teeth, his muscles tense, his body like iron.

"Are you okay?" I said, my voice sounding hazy and drugged.

He gave a strangled laugh. "Yeah, but I really need to come. My balls are about ready to explode."

I reached out to touch his hard cock. But before I'd done more than stroke him once, he gasped and thrust into my palm, his whole body shuddering, and he cried out softly.

For half a minute, I felt the full weight of his body pressing me into the mattress. I stroked his shaggy hair, tangling my fingers in the curls at the nape of his neck, exploring his silky skin, and letting my free hand swoop over the smooth curve at the base of his spine.

"Ah, shit," he muttered, sinking onto his back and pulling off the condom. "It wasn't supposed to happen that fast. Fuckin' useless."

I smiled and stifled a yawn. Secretly, along with the pang of disappointment, I was a little relieved. It had all happened so quickly. I felt like I needed a few days to get used to everything. I hadn't changed my mind, I just needed more time. But as always, the hours were counting down to goodbye.

"Did you come?" he asked, sounding dejected.

"Either that or the world just ended and nobody told me."

His laugh held a tone of relief and pleasure.

"We've got time," I lied. "We don't have to rush."

I felt his answering grin against my lips.

I woke up to the feel of Kes's hands roaming over my body, his warm breath in my ear as he licked up my neck to my cheek. In the dawn light, I could see the tendons in his forearms flex, then lost a little of my mind as he pinched my nipple. His touch set my body on fire and I moaned, arching my head back.

His cock was nestled against my ass and his hips shifted restlessly against me, a gentle rocking motion. I reached back to touch him and he shivered.

I twisted in his arms until I was on my side, our chests pressed together. His eyes were wide and wondering, fluttering closed as we kissed. Soft kisses became hard and desperate, and my own body sparked with anticipation.

Kes's warm hand drifted from my shoulder to my breast, stroking and kneading, then pinching and teasing until I was moaning open-mouthed kisses against his throat.

I could hear him cursing softly, amazed that he could make me react so brazenly as I arched against him again.

I was stunned, too. I was only just beginning to understand my body's capacity for pleasure.

We ground against each other as dry humping turned to wet humping. Kes used his fingers again, on and around my clit, until we both came, panting and gasping.

I looked down at the trail of cum across my stomach and laughed in astonishment.

"Fuck, Aimee," Kes gasped. "You are so fucking sexy!"

And I felt sexy at that moment. Losing myself in him, I'd somehow found a little of myself. I couldn't explain it, and didn't try.

We cleaned up quickly, too aware that we were losing a race against the rolling dawn, and that our bubble of happiness was about to burst.

Kes dressed reluctantly, his gaze watching the clouds turn

pink with the rising sun.

"You'll be there today, won't you?" he asked.

And I could tell by his frown and the fact that his eyes were focused anywhere but on me that he hated to sound needy, hated to ask anything of me, need anything, want anything. I loved it.

"Where else would I be?" I said, kissing him hard.

For the rest of the week, Kes worked three shows a day, and every night he fell into my bed exhausted. Every dawn, I woke to his searching kisses, his hard body met my soft one, and we enjoyed learning about ourselves and each other. He didn't press me to go further, but I knew he wanted it. We'd come close a couple of times, but I'd chickened out.

He called it fucking, of course, but to me it was making love. We both knew that's what it was.

We spent long, languid mornings lying in the grass behind the Ghost Train; afternoons and evenings of grinding work and snatched moments.

It was the happiest time of my life.

And then Camilla decided to make her play for him.

Kes's reputation had spread across the tri-county area, and people were even coming from the city to see his show. I think Dono would have put on another performance if it weren't for Jacob Jones threatening to go lame.

"He can't do it, Grandpa," Kes said on Friday afternoon of their second week, and just two short days before they packed up and moved on. "He'll founder if we push him, and it would take months to train another horse. Hell, he's all I've ever known; I don't know if I *could* train another one."

He stroked the pony's nose, earning him a gentle head butt as Jakey searched Kes's pockets for an apple.

Dono looked tired. "Just trying to make hay while the sun shines."

Kes stared at the ground and pushed his bare feet through the red dirt.

"I could maybe put an act together without the horses. We'd need another person. Maybe Aimee could…"

"No, boy," Dono said, his voice serious. "We're only here for two more days. Pick someone else."

Kes looked mutinous, but I stroked his arm.

"Dono's right," I said, trying to hold my voice firm. "I'll help all I can, but you need someone who knows what they're doing, and … someone who'll be around all summer."

Our time was ticking away hour by hour, minute by minute. It hurt too much to watch the hours slip by toward my imminent loss. Our loss. I think Kes felt the same.

He threw me a searching look and I saw pain and resignation there.

An ugly choking feeling reached up from my gut and twisted my heart hard.

Dono cut through my self-inflicted misery.

"Ask Zach. He should be able to help out. Maybe Lucy, too, if Henry can give her time off from the Waltzers."

"You could pick someone from the audience each night," I piped up. "The part where Kes throws knives at Sorcha—get a volunteer. Then Sorcha can set up for the next section."

God, it killed me to suggest giving the bitch a role of more importance, and secretly, my favorite part was when Kes aimed sharp objects at her skanky head.

Dono nodded thoughtfully. "What do you think, Kes?"

Kes smiled tiredly. "Yeah, that'll work. Nice idea, Aimee."

I beamed with pleasure.

My good idea backfired immediately, or at least that's how it seemed, because during the final show that evening, the volunteer Kes picked was Camilla. I could thank Lauren for that. I knew she was the one who'd told Camilla about my date at Perkins with Kes, and I'd overheard them talking about how hot he was. It must be the reason they'd come back to see his show for a second time. Bitches.

Kes strode toward her, his hand held out as Camilla hammed it up and acted shocked, *Oh, little me? Will it be dangerous? I might faint!*

Vomit.

Kes's eyes seemed to glitter in the setting sun and I wondered what he was thinking, or if he even remembered her. I thought I saw him stiffen slightly when she said her name, but I couldn't be sure.

I grew increasingly uneasy. He was far more tactile with her than he'd been with any of the previous volunteers during the day, and Camilla was lapping it up.

Worse still, at the end of the show she was waiting for him, and I swear she passed him her phone number. But then Kes leaned across and whispered something in her ear—something that brought a huge smile to Camilla's face.

As soon as she left and Kes could get away from the rest of his fans, he tossed Jacob Jones' reins to me.

I stared at him coldly. "What the actual fuck, Kes? You were flirting with her in front of me. Do you know who that was? Camilla fucking Palmer—the girl who's been a bitch to me for years."

I expected him to deny it or be defensive, but instead he grinned.

"Yeah, I know who she is. Trust me?"

I sighed, his smile, as always, making my bad mood evaporate.

"Yes, but I don't trust her."

Kes winked. "After tonight, she'll never bother you again."

He was still smiling, but a shiver ran through me. There was nothing kind about the look on his face.

"What are you going to do?"

"Wait and see," he said.

Kes shook off his tiredness and went to shower, leaving me to look after the ponies. Blake and Jesse had disappeared, too. I was more than a little annoyed. It was one thing to help out, but another entirely to leave me with all the work.

At least I knew what to do for Jacob Jones and his buddies, but there's one thing that isn't cute about working with horses: you end up smelling like them.

So of course, I was sweaty and stinky when I bumped into Camilla, Lauren, and one more of those heinous bitches, caked with makeup and laughing their asses off at me.

"Oh my God! He's got you doing all the work while he plans a date with me! I think your girlfriend status has officially been revoked," she smiled wickedly.

I didn't know what to say, because I had no idea what Kes had in mind. He'd asked me to trust him, but this hurt.

Kes was nowhere to be found and Jesse and Blake had mysteriously disappeared, too. My savior, Zachary, walked me home again, telling me not to worry. Like that ever worked.

I took a shower and sat on my bed brooding.

Brooding turned to anger and anger turned to tears. Then I fell asleep with my pillow damp under my cheek.

I woke with a shock shortly after midnight when Kes

appeared through my window. He smelled like cigarettes which was weird because he didn't smoke. Camilla did. He also stunk of women's perfume.

As usual, he crawled up the mattress and yanked his t-shirt over his head, kissing my shoulders and neck.

"Get off!" I hissed, pulling away and throwing my pillow at his head.

His reactions were fast, catching the pillow before it hit him, but he rocked back on his heels looking shocked.

"Aimee?"

"I can smell her all over you, Kes! Go on, deny it!"

"I'm not going to fucking deny it," he snapped, his eyes narrowed. "Check your phone."

"What?"

"Check your fucking phone!"

Furious, I pulled it out from the back of the drawer where I kept it hidden, and immediately saw that I had six messages. I opened the first text to find a grainy photograph of Camilla with her boobs out for the camera, pouting and grinding like a Vegas stripper. I stared at the picture, then up at Kes, who was grinning broadly. I swallowed and opened the next text. It showed Blake and Jesse's hands were all over her, although you couldn't see their faces, and someone had also got a great shot of the Ferris wheel's glowing lights in the background. The next four photos were more of the same, the last one showing Jesse with his hand in Camilla's panties.

"Oh my God!" I gasped. "What … what did you do to her?"

Kes frowned. "Nothing she didn't want. Anyway, I left when Jesse was fingering her, so I don't know if they fucked."

He shrugged like he didn't care one way or another.

"What am I supposed to do with this?" I asked as I waved my phone at him, really upset.

"Whatever you like."

His voice was bored, indifferent.

"You … you want me to *blackmail* her?"

I was incredulous.

Kes laughed. "No need. I used her phone and sent the photos to her whole address book. All her friends will see this in the morning. And her parents."

I swallowed several times, seeing nothing but vindictive pleasure on his face.

"This is wrong," I whispered, afraid, because I didn't know this boy sitting on my bed.

His eyes glittered dangerously. "She would have fucked me just to hurt you. That bitch has bullied you for years. It stops now. Tonight."

I backed away from him until I was scrunched up against the headboard, my knees tight to my chest.

Kes stared at me and started to look worried.

"I did it for you, Aimee. I … I wanted to protect you, but I can't do that when I'm not fucking here! I had to do something so she'd leave you alone. Permanently. Fuck, just … talk to me or something!"

"I don't know what to say."

Wasn't that the truth.

I was appalled by what he'd done. I hated Camilla with a passion, but what Kes had planned, it was just too much. I liked Blake and Jesse—they seemed like okay guys, but they were older than us, in their twenties, and I had no idea how far they'd take things.

"How did you get her to do that?" I asked, my voice rising with disbelief.

Kes looked at the comforter and didn't answer.

"Was she drunk?"

He nodded. "She brought some stuff with her. I don't know what, but she was off her face."

"Did you kiss her?"

"Yeah," he said, without looking at me. "I had to … to make her trust me."

I put my hands over my face, hiding from his searching gaze. I felt the mattress shift under me, and Kes tried to pull my stiff body into his arms.

"I did it for you, Aimee," he said again. "I'd do anything for you."

I believed him. And that scared me.

"Just … let me hold you."

I forced my body to relax against him, allowing him to hold me, but I couldn't force the images away. I kept seeing Camilla's glazed, drunken expression, men's hands in her panties. *She wasn't stopping them*, I kept telling myself, but I knew that she'd been set up. I didn't know what to do.

Kes said he hadn't done anything more than kiss her, but

even that made my stomach turn.

He kept holding me, stroking my arms and kissing me softly, acting so sweet. It was confusing. I couldn't look at him, so I lay with my back to his chest as he tried to soothe and reassure me.

We didn't make out that night. I knew that Kes was disappointed and didn't understand my point of view at all.

He left at dawn and I was alone with my thoughts.

I couldn't get back to sleep, so I lay awake staring at the ceiling. I didn't know what to think. Kes was trying to help me, to protect me in some weird, warped way. But I was shocked by how far he'd gone, and I had the uneasy feeling that he would have let it go even further without an ounce of conscience. Maybe it had gone further.

When I heard Mom and Dad moving around downstairs, I dragged myself out of bed and into the shower. Jennifer was staying with a friend, so at least I didn't have to explain to her why I looked like a zombie. I told Mom I was tired, and Dad didn't even look up from his newspaper before leaving for the golf course.

When the phone rang, I almost jumped out of my skin. It was Erica, a friend from school.

"Oh my God! Have you heard about Camilla Palmer?"

I didn't even get a chance to answer before she was telling me all the gossip.

"You know I have her cell number because I worked on the Homecoming committee with her? Anyway, I got this text this morning and it was, wow, I don't even know what to call it! Really *steamy* photos of her making out with *two* guys. Like boobs out and everything! It's been sent from her phone so it's definitely legit! Everyone knew she was a total slut, but wow! I heard she went with two guys from the football team at the same time and honestly, I didn't think it was true because she was dating Jamie Larsen, but it looks like it's her *thing*, you know?"

Camilla's reputation was ruined. I should have been pleased, but that wasn't in the flux of emotions I was feeling.

I didn't want to go back to the carnival, but I couldn't stay away either.

When I got there, Kes was in a foul mood, and his temper was making the ponies nervous. Jacob Jones stamped his feet and twitched his ears when I approached.

I knew Kes had heard me because his whole body went rigid.

I also knew that he'd never admit he was wrong.

"Hi," I said.

He grunted, which may or may not have been a greeting.

"I know you think you were protecting me…" I began.

Kes whipped around and glared at me. "I *was* protecting you!"

I sighed and looked down. "It was too much. What you did was cruel."

He spat at my feet, his chest heaving and his face twisted with fury.

"She's a bitch and she got what she deserved. Why are you defending her?"

Good question—why was I? Because it was too much? Because he could have ruined her life? And if she ended up hurting herself because of it? But at the heart of it, I wondered how Kes could be so sweet one minute, and so vicious the next. I wondered if he'd turn on me one day. But my heart begged me to give him the benefit of the doubt.

I hated that the last 12 hours had put an ugly distance between us—it hadn't been there before he decided to take Camilla down.

Kes looked at me like I was a puzzle he couldn't solve, and I'm sure my eyes gave away my concern that I didn't know him as well as I thought I did.

And I couldn't stay away from him. How dark would those stormy eyes become before I had to run away? I hated what he'd done, but I couldn't hate him.

Our time was running out—I wouldn't waste it on anger. So in the end, there was no decision to make.

"Can you just hold me now?" I asked.

His storm-cloud eyes softened and he wrapped his arms around me.

"I love you, Kes."

It was the first time I'd said it, but far, far from being the first time I'd thought it.

Kes's face was shocked, and he pulled back to look at me. I could see him working to keep the emotion off his face, but in the end, he looked more confused than happy that I'd declared myself to him.

"I thought you hated me," he said, his forehead wrinkling as if that idea was painful. "I thought we'd broken up?"

I shook my head, surprised. "No! Why would you think that?"

"But you wouldn't do any stuff with me last night."

I gaped at him.

"Kes! We had a fight. I was upset, that's all. But it doesn't mean we have to break up. And that other stuff, well, I've got to be in the right mood, you know."

A slow smile spread across his face.

"I could get you in the right mood," he said, pressing his hips against me suggestively.

"Hmm, I think it's working."

"Yeah?" he said, sounding surprised.

I laughed. "Oh yes! I'm really wishing you had your own bedroom right now."

"Hell yeah," he sighed. "Can we go to your place?"

I shook my head. "Nope, Mom's at home. All day."

Kes looked irritated. "I can't even borrow the truck. Dono's gone into town and he won't be back until the first show."

"We could go for a ride?" I suggested.

I rather liked the idea of sitting behind him on Jacob Jones as we wandered the fields and lanes, but Kes shook his head.

"Dono would kick my ass if I took the horses out before a show."

I could hear the sound of another fantasy crashing down.

"I know!" I said, suddenly feeling excited. "Let's go on the Ferris wheel!"

"We can't do stuff up there," Kes said, his eyebrows shooting up.

I smacked his arm. "No-oh! Of course not. But we haven't gone for a ride on it yet because you've been so busy. I'd just like to."

Kes rolled his eyes. "Is this that romantic stuff that girls want to do on dates?"

I laughed, thrilled that he'd used the word 'date'.

"Maybe, but we had our first kiss up there. That's where the magic started."

His eyes softened. "Yeah. Okay, one Ferris wheel ride coming up," and he held my hand and started pulling me toward the midway.

"I didn't mean right now—the carnival isn't open," I huffed as he towed me along. "None of the rides are operating yet."

He glanced at me, his smile condescending. "Seriously, Aimee. You think Gilligan will say no to me?"

"Oh," I said, feeling silly. "I guess not."

He winked, and my happy heart flip-flopped.

Gilligan was a greasy-looking carnie that you'd cross the street to avoid. He didn't talk much either, staring cold-eyed when Kes asked him to start the wheel for us. But he didn't say no either, just jerked his head at the empty cars. I suppose that meant we could sit down.

"He doesn't talk much," I muttered, watching Gilligan operate the machinery out of the corner of my eye. "Cat got his tongue?"

Kes nodded. "Yeah, got his tongue cut out in a bar fight. We're not sure what happened to the tongue."

"You're kidding!" I squeaked.

Kes laughed loudly.

"You're full of shit, Kestrel," muttered Gilligan, throwing Kes a filthy look.

I jumped when he spoke, accidentally-on-purpose elbowing Kes in the ribs.

"That wasn't funny!" I hissed.

"Nah, but your face was," he said, rubbing his side and grinning at me.

I didn't like being teased, but I couldn't resist that grin.

Kes slipped his arm around my shoulders and I leaned against him as we were lifted into the air. I sighed, enjoying the illusion of safety that his arms around me always created.

"I love the Ferris wheel," I said, almost to myself.

Kes shrugged. "It's alright."

"You grew up with it, but to me … I can see so far. I've never been anywhere, I've never even left Minnesota, but here I can see for miles and miles. Everything looks so small. It makes me sad and happy all at the same time."

Kes was silent for a few seconds.

"I like it because it's peaceful," he said at last. "There's no privacy in the carnie. Everyone's up in your business all day long, so you have to be private in your head, you know? But up here, no one bothers me. I remember coming up here with my mom…"

I looked up at him cautiously. He'd never willingly mentioned her before.

"How old were you?"

He shrugged. "Four, maybe five. I don't remember."

"Did you grow up in the carnival?"

"Yeah. Mom's Dono's daughter."

I don't know why that surprised me, but it did. And then I wondered: did he say *is* his daughter or *was*? Nothing Kes said was ever simple.

I chewed my lip, wondering whether I could risk another question.

"What happened to her?"

Kes didn't answer and his face took on a closed look. I guess that meant the conversation was over. I sighed, wishing he'd give me more pieces of himself.

The wheel turned slowly, only the faintest breeze taking the edge off the ruthless sun. The fields around us were red from the dusty earth, or brownish yellow where sweet corn grew. I could see my house and our hickory tree; I could see the road into town, straight and boring; and the cluster of utilitarian buildings in the distance. I could see the string of lakes leading down to Amber Lake, glittering like polished glass.

But I couldn't see my future; I couldn't see which road led to Kes.

As if he sensed my sadness, he wrapped his arms around me more tightly. I wished the strength I felt in those arms would keep the world away.

"Let's do it tonight," I said. "I want to go all the way. With you."

His voice was rough when he answered. "Are you sure?"

"Yes, I've never been more sure. Make love to me tonight, Kes."

He kissed my hair lightly and I felt his chest heave.

When the ride was over, Kes thanked Gilligan, doing some complicated handshake and a promise that he "owed him".

Then without even needing to discuss it, we walked hand-in-hand to the dry grass behind the Ghost Train and lay silently in each other's arms. Enjoying the heat, enjoying the solitude, another countdown to goodbye.

Kes's shows were sold out again, and people who'd missed buying a ticket were bitching and complaining, or so Zachary cheerfully reported. The overspill meant that all parts of the carnival were reaping the rewards, and Dono was cautiously optimistic that they'd make a decent profit, if they could keep the momentum going in the next town.

It turned out that Zachary was a bit of a whizz with computers, and beefed up their online presence significantly. It all helped.

Despite his tiredness, at the end of that long difficult day, there was an unrestrained energy that I could see pulsing through Kes. I felt an echo of it in my own body. I was glad I'd waited for almost two weeks, because I finally felt ready.

"I'm going to walk Aimee home," Kes announced.

I saw the knowing smiles, and Sorcha scowled. Dono just nodded.

"Be safe," he said, giving Kes a pointed look.

The heat in my cheeks could have powered Minneapolis for a month. Kes grinned to himself as we walked through the empty midway.

"That was so embarrassing," I muttered.

Kes laughed. "He's been saying that since Con got his first pube. Dono's had to look after us all of these years, I guess two bastard kids is enough."

His voice had become bitter.

"I'm sorry," I said.

"Why? You didn't do anything."

"No, but…"

"Don't worry about it."

But I did.

Once we were home, Kes waited under the hickory tree while I let myself into the house, praying that everyone had gone to bed. I listened intently, but all I could hear was my father's rumbling snore and the quiet creak of the timbers as the house settled into sleep.

I crept upstairs and shoved a chair under the handle of my bedroom door as a makeshift lock, something I'd done since Kes started sleeping in my bed. Then I yanked open the window and nearly fainted when Kes's grinning face popped up in front of me.

I don't know how long he'd been hanging onto the sill, waiting for me to open the window. I shook my head in disbelief—always the showman.

His muscles bunched and he flipped inside, his body

unwinding from the floor in a flowing, liquid movement.

My mouth hung open as he prowled around my bed, wild, free, alive—his dangerous beauty, panther-like and predatory.

"Come here," he growled.

Here, now, in my childhood room, we were going to do it; we were going to make love. I'd give myself to Kes, and he'd give himself to me. No more waiting, no more wondering. Questions didn't belong in this place, it was only us.

I threw myself at him, literally, hearing the breath gush out of his lungs as I slammed against his body.

If his kisses were hard, mine were bruising. In an instant, he met me stroke for stroke, bite for bite, moan for breathless moan.

My hands roamed freely across his taut, tight body, feeling his muscles ripple and shiver under my touch, the hard planes of his stomach trembling.

When I rubbed the bulge of his erection firmly, he growled against my neck.

"Make love to me, Kes," I gasped.

He didn't even answer but simply pulled a condom out of his back pocket and laid it on the bedside cabinet.

His t-shirt was yanked off and fell to the floor. Mine followed as he snapped my bra free, tugging the straps over my shoulders roughly. I pressed my breasts against him and he immediately ducked his head to suckle and tease, using his teeth and tongue with all the lessons learned over the past two weeks.

"Are you wet?" he asked, his voice shaking.

I rubbed my thighs together. "I think so."

He reached down and unbuttoned my shorts, pushing them down with my panties, then running his finger over my clit, making my hips buck to meet his.

"Shit, yeah," he whispered.

With shaking hands, I fumbled as I yanked his zipper down, and then he was out of his jeans, his heavy cock bouncing slightly as he pressed me backwards onto the bed.

Surprising me with gentleness, Kes rolled me onto my back, his body hovering above mine. I think he was waiting for me to say no, to change my mind, but I was sure of this.

I nodded and licked my lips.

He reached for the condom, sliding it on with familiarity.

Then he took a deep breath and held his cock in position

with his hand. He pushed inside an inch, and I thought, *that's nice*.

As he pushed in further, I sank my teeth into his shoulder, making him arch against me so he entered with one complete thrust. Pain burned inside, and for a second I wanted him *out*, I wanted him *gone*; I didn't want this invasion.

"God, that's so good," he groaned, circling his hips cautiously.

Somehow he managed to brush against my clit, and a surge of pleasure pushed the pain to the back of my mind.

"Aimee?"

His voice quavered when he said my name.

"I'm fine," I hissed. "I'm fine."

I felt full and adult, the strange and satisfying sensation of him all around, inside, above me. I wanted to laugh and cry and scream and yell and kiss him and touch him and tell him I loved him. It was so much. So much.

His head dropped to my shoulder and it was clear that he couldn't hold himself back. Soft, desperate grunts broke from his throat.

My hips lifted to meet him and the change of angle made him frantic. Kes lost any semblance of control. His eyes flashed to mine, and for once I could see everything: I felt wanted, desired, needed; abandoned and found; washed with emotion and sensation—born again.

He cried out and dove inside me more deeply, his heart pounding furiously. Two weeks of touching and tasting, waiting and wondering was too much for both of us.

Kes grit his teeth as his body thrashed against mine, furious and unforgiving. I felt his body tense, then shudder as he came.

I had tears in my eyes from pain and pleasure. I hadn't come—it was all too new, too strange, the pain too real, but when Kes looked down at me, his lashes were wet, the same as mine.

"I love you," I said.

Kes screwed his eyes tightly shut, trying to force back the surge of emotion that he couldn't hide. And then he smiled his beautiful smile, the one reserved just for me. It was like the sun had learned how to shine again, and I was warmed.

He couldn't say the words himself, he just wouldn't allow himself to be that exposed. I was disappointed, but Kes couldn't hide what he felt, I could see it in his eyes, feel it in his touch, hear it in his voice.

But then the world intruded, as it always did.

"I'd better get rid of this," Kes mumbled.

He couldn't meet my eyes when we both looked down to the see the blood smeared along his dick.

"Wow," I said softly. "I guess we really did it."

He still couldn't look at me.

"I'm not sorry," I whispered. "Now you can never forget me."

His head whipped around and his wide eyes met mine.

"I won't … I never … I…" but he still couldn't say the words.

We kissed for the longest time, tears streaking our faces, mumbling promises to each other that were lost the moment they were spoken.

CHAPTER 7
EMPTY PROMISES

"You have to go get ready," I said sadly.

Kes sighed and rested his forehead against mine.

"This really fucking sucks."

I didn't reply because there was nothing to say.

We'd spent our last morning together retracing our steps through the carnival: the first time Mr. Albert leapt into my arms, the first time Jacob Jones accepted an apple from me. The first time we held hands, the first time we kissed,

We ate a coconut, because we'd done that on the first day we'd met, and we rode the Ferris wheel again, alone, riding through the air, trying to frame our memories in forever.

Finally, we lay on the hard earth behind the Ghost Train and held hands staring up at the sky. I begged the sun to shine forever and the Earth to stop turning; I hated the minutes speeding around my wristwatch. And then time ran out.

Kes stood up gracefully and put his hand out to heave me up. He didn't let go as we walked back to the RV.

I remember everything about that day. The way the sun bounced off the hard ground, burning my feet as I walked. The sky was a steely white, bleached and cloudless. Kes stared straight ahead, ignoring the waves and shouts from the other carnies as if he didn't hear or see, as if the world he walked in was separate. But I noticed. I felt their eyes slide over me, curious and compassionate, hard and hateful. I noticed the paint peeling from the sign above the Ghost Train, turning it into 'Ghost rain'. I wondered what ghost rain was like—wetter, colder, or gray and soft like cobwebs?

I remember the rough texture of Kes's hand, the grip of his fingers, the soothing caress of his thumb rubbing soft circles on the back of my hand. I felt the fine hairs of his forearm brush against mine. Walking side by side, I could appreciate his height and lean silhouette, his long strides making me trot to keep up. His eyes were narrowed against the sun, or maybe in thought, and I hoped he was thinking of me, of us.

I remember it all.

Sorcha was waiting when we reached the RV, tapping her chewed nails against her elbows.

"You're late," she scowled, but Kes ignored her.

He kicked off his shoes, stripped off his shirt, and sank into the deckchair so she could apply his makeup.

As the first show was mostly for kids, she toned down the recently-undead look, instead covering his face with gold paint. It was very effective, giving him an angelic quality that was the opposite of real life, and if she wasn't such a witch, I'd have told her so.

The day progressed and Kes's exhaustion deepened. By the time he prepared for his farewell show, tiredness seemed etched into his bones. The change to ultra white makeup and black-ringed eyes seemed apt now.

He grinned at me loosely, sadness shining in his silver-gray eyes.

"Last show."

"Make it a good one," I said, kissing his warm lips. "Make it great."

"Always," he said, his smile curving upward.

And it was great. He was great. I was totally enraptured with the boy-man standing in front of me. He was the ultimate performer, the showman, a man of many faces.

But when he called for a volunteer and a hundred voices yelled, "Choose me!" his eyes turned toward mine.

I shook my head, my eyes wide as he prowled toward me.

Yes, you! his eyes said.

He held out his hand toward me, and the woman sitting in the next seat gave me a little push.

"Go on, honey!" she said encouragingly. "Once in a lifetime opportunity. You'll regret it if you don't. Go on now!"

Kes pulled me into the center of the arena, and I was vaguely aware of my sneakers sinking into the sawdust, scattered to soften the percussion of the horses' hooves.

Usually Kes blindfolded his volunteers, on the grounds that

if they jerked suddenly because he was throwing sharp knives at them, he might end up injuring someone. But he didn't offer me a blindfold.

His eyes glimmered with trapped emotions as he positioned me onto the wooden frame.

He smiled his devilish smile as he aimed the first knife. I tried to keep my eyes open, fixed on his as they seemed to glow in the dusk, but I couldn't. I quivered and squeezed my eyes tightly shut, feeling the thud next to my left ear.

The *oohs* and *aahs* of the crowd became distant.

Then the knives seemed to rain down around my head, and it was all I could do to keep standing. I was almost grateful when Kes barked at me, "On your knees!"

I dropped down, feeling a sharp stone dig into my kneecap. I could have sworn that I felt the breath of the final knife streak past as it flew over my head.

Someone in the crowd screamed, and I wouldn't have been surprised to see one of my ears on the ground, but then the sound turned to one of delight and I opened an eye.

"Look behind you," Kes commanded.

I twisted around to stare at the wooden target. My mouth dropped open in awe. He'd framed me with a jagged row of knives, forming the shape of a heart. The last knife was the point at the bottom.

Stunned, emotional, and tired beyond words, I stared at the steel heart. Then I felt Kes's hand on my shoulder, and he was helping me up.

The crowd roared and cheered, and a few people whistled, but when his mouth crashed down on mine and he kissed me in front of hundreds of people, I couldn't hear any of it.

Grinning, Kes bowed to the crowd who yelled their approval, and then he handed me over to Blake, who escorted me from the ring, one hand hovering around my waist because he could see that my legs were shaking so badly, either from shock or lust. Maybe it was the same thing.

Kes took his bows and made a final circuit standing on Jacob Jones' back, before leaving the arena to loud applause.

"Are you okay?" Blake asked me, his voice halfway between amused and anxious.

"I think I'm going to pee myself," I said faintly.

He laughed with relief. "You did great. I've never seen him

get so close to a target before. I think he cut off some of your hair."

"What?" I gurgled. "He did what?"

Blake laughed again, more nervously this time. "I'm probably wrong about that. Just the angle I was standing."

"Bullshit!" I snarled.

Blake tugged me to a stop. "Take it as a compliment," he said, his smile turning harsh. "The kid knows what he's doing. You want to be a carnie's woman, well suck it up, little girl. Suck it up."

He stalked away, leaving me angry and a little afraid.

Kes was talking to Dono, his shoulders sagging with tiredness. But when he saw me, his gaze brightened.

"How'd you like the show?" he sniggered.

"You're evil!" I huffed, crossing my arms across my chest. "Brilliant, but evil mastermind."

He laughed loudly, and even Dono seemed amused.

"You did good, kid. You can have five minutes before we start the takedown. Don't make me come looking for you."

Kes scowled but didn't argue.

I expected that now: the times Kes tried to argue with Dono ended with a backhander. No one could win an argument with Dono.

Kes sighed and slung his sweaty arm around me. "Takedown's gonna be most of the night. You want to go home? I should be able to get there maybe four or five in the morning."

"I could help," I offered. "I must be able to do something."

He shook his head.

"You'd just get in the way."

I know he didn't mean to hurt me, but he did.

"Oh, well okay then. Guess I'll see you later?"

I turned to walk away, but Kes stopped me.

"You can wait in the RV if you like," he said softly. "I could pull my bed out for you. If you want. You don't have to. I mean, it'll be pretty noisy. Only if you want to…"

There'd be hell to pay if my parents decided to check my room. It was a remote possibility—neither of them seemed to care much what I did. And tonight was my last night with Kes.

I nodded. "Yes, I'd like that."

A look that could have been relief passed over his face.

"Okay, great. Um, the sheets should be pretty clean." He gave me a sly look. "I haven't used them for the last two weeks."

I grinned back at him. "Sounds good."

He pulled open the RV's door and Mr. Albert leapt down, chattering angrily, annoyed at having been cooped up, and he scampered off into the dark.

"Will he be alright?" I asked worriedly.

Kes shrugged. "Sure, but don't be surprised if you wake up to find him on the bed." He looked embarrassed. "Because, um, he does that most nights when I'm here. He's kind of pissed at me that I haven't been around so much lately."

I snickered quietly as Kes folded up the tiny kitchen table and pulled out his cot bed.

"Must be because you found someone else to sleep with!"

He grinned and hooked his arms around my waist. "Must be," he agreed, then slid his tongue into my mouth, thrusting with casual slowness, until Dono yelled for him again.

"Gotta go," he said. "But I'll see you later."

I curled up on the rough sheets that smelled like him, and stared through the open door at the stars sprinkled above the canvas buildings of the carnival.

I wondered what it would be like to sleep like this every night, to see the same stars from a different town. What it would be like to be traveling, traveling, always moving on?

As the sounds of the carnival being torn down filled my ears, tears filled my eyes, and finally, finally, I drifted to sleep.

At some point in the night, Mr. Albert came home, creeping into my arms so we were curled up together.

I vaguely remember hearing him chatter his complaints as Kes plucked him off the bed and sank down next to me. He kissed the back of my neck and we were asleep.

We were woken by the sounds of shouting.

"Where is my daughter? What have you done with her?!"

Kes was instantly awake and swearing softly.

"Fuck, I meant to get you home before now. Shit, I overslept."

I sat up, my eyes sore from lack of sleep, tears and tiredness, but my heart hammering as adrenaline surged through me.

I stumbled out of the RV behind Kes, my hand flying to my birds nest hair. I was met by my father's furious glare and the

113

cold-eyed stare of Sheriff Smith.

"Miss Andersen, are you alright?"

"Yes, yes! I'm fine," I stammered.

Dad grabbed my wrist and pulled me toward him so hard that I stumbled.

"Hey!" Kes called out.

"Keep back," the Sheriff warned.

Suddenly, Dono was walking up behind Kes, his stern presence calming him, his strong hand restraining him.

"Just two kids who want to be together, Sheriff," he said. "No harm done."

"No harm?!" shouted my father. "She's fifteen!"

"I'm sixteen, Dad!" I snapped. "I turned sixteen two weeks ago!"

He tugged on my arm again, a clear message that I should shut my mouth.

Dono's voice was cold and hard.

"My grandson is also sixteen. Whatever they did was consensual. The girl has been hanging around every day for two weeks."

I couldn't believe Dono had thrown me to the wolves like that. It hurt so bad: I was 'the girl'. I wasn't Aimee; I wasn't one of them; I was 'the girl' who'd brought trouble to their door. Maybe it was his way of defending Kes, but that didn't lessen the sting. Not yet.

"Grandpa…" Kes began, but Dono slapped him almost casually across the cheek.

"You can speak when I tell you to," he said harshly.

Kes was knocked back against the side of the RV, his cheek imprinted with Dono's hand.

No one but me seemed to care, and Sheriff Smith simply asked, "Are you here of your own choice, Miss Andersen?"

"Yes!" I gasped, shocked to my core.

He looked back to my father. "I think we should leave it there, Adam."

Dad's face was grim and he didn't reply. Instead, he turned on his heel, dragging me after him, walking so fast, I almost lost my footing.

"Kes!" I shouted, but Dad just yanked my arm so hard it felt like it was being pulled out of its socket.

I heard yelling behind me, but I couldn't tell who it was.

A number of carnies had been roused by the noise, and were there to see my humiliation as I was dragged from the field and stuffed into Dad's car.

"Do not speak," he ordered icily. "I don't want to hear anything you have to say. I'm ashamed of you."

Tears started to burn my eyes, but I wouldn't cry in front of him. I wouldn't.

Mom was waiting anxiously at the front door, but she wasn't allowed to speak to me. I was sent to my room and told to stay there. Probably until the world ended.

I could hear Jennifer's voice in the hallway, but Dad yelled at her, too, and the house fell silent except for the crash of pans and plates in the kitchen.

I felt dirty. What I had with Kes was so wonderful and special, and my own father had dragged me through the mud. I hated him for that.

I was in love. *We* were in love. What was wrong with that? Just because we were young, it didn't make it any less real. If anything it was *more* real, because we weren't jaded and we could still believe that love conquered everything.

Later, it was hard to remember that I'd ever been so idealistic, but at that moment, righteous indignation burned brightly inside me.

How *dare* my father treat me like that? Treat *Kes* like that? And call him such ugly names. I became angrier and angrier, until I felt like screaming.

It was only when I realized that my hidden cell phone was ringing that I took a breath. Fumbling and frantic, I grabbed it from the back of the drawer where I kept my bras, and then crawled under the covers so my voice would be muffled.

"Kes!"

"Jesus, Aimee! Are you okay? Did he hurt you?"

"No, I'm alright. Well, I'm locked in my room. What about you? Dono looked mad."

He started to reply, then said, "You sound really weird."

I giggled sadly. "I'm hiding under the covers in case anyone hears me."

"Oh right."

"Where are you?"

"Leaving," he said, his voice already distant.

"What?!"

"Yeah, Dono wanted me out of the way in case that asshole Sheriff came back. Look outside right now, Aimee."

I scrambled from under the covers and ran to the window.

Kes's RV was already turning out of the carnival field. I could see Dono at the wheel, and Kes leaning out the window waving at me.

"I can see you! I can see you!"

His voice went muffled and I could hear shouting in the background. "Fuck's sake! Stop the fucking car!"

There was an odd bang and the call was disconnected. I tried to call him back, but the phone rang unanswered. On my fourth try, his phone was turned off.

I watched disbelievingly as the RV disappeared toward the horizon, followed by Blake driving the truck with the horse trailer. I kept waiting for the vehicles to stop, for Kes to come running back for one last kiss, something, but all I could see was a cloud of red dust rising into the air as the boy I loved drove into the distance.

All the anger fell away and I cried and cried.

It was two days before I heard from Kes again, and when he did call, he was subdued.

"Oh, thank God you called! I've been going crazy. What happened?"

He sighed. "Dono."

"I guess he was pretty angry."

"Yeah. How about your old man?"

"Oh," I laughed thinly. "He's been okay. He's not speaking to me. That's fine because I'm not speaking to him either."

"What about your mom?"

"Well, she's feeding me, but I'm still grounded. I'm just allowed bathroom breaks."

I was trying for funny. I knew it was feeble, but if I didn't laugh, I'd cry, and I'd cried enough tears.

But Kes didn't laugh.

"I have to see you," he said, lowering his voice as if he was afraid he'd be overheard. "I can't stand this."

I was thrilled to hear him say that, and heartbroken because there was nothing we could do about it.

"Our last show is Thanksgiving. The week after, I turn 17. I'll have a full license. I'll take the truck and come see you."

"But ... won't Dono be mad?"

"Fuck him!" Kes snarled.

"Oh," I said, my voice flat. "He doesn't want you to see me."

"He's being a complete douche," Kes growled. "I can barely take a piss without him holding my dick for me."

My mind spun at the mental image that created, so I quickly batted it away.

"But if you take the truck without permission, won't he … I don't know … call the cops or something?"

Kes laughed coldly.

"Nah, he won't do that, but…"

"But what?"

"I don't know what he'd do and I don't care." Then he took a deep breath. "I'm coming for you, Aimee. Will you come with me?"

The world fell away and I was teetering on the edge.

"What?"

"Come with me!" he whispered, desperation making his voice harsh. "Fuck what everyone says. This is real, I know it is. Come with me. We can make this work, I know we can! Just say yes!"

My heart pounded in my chest, my logical, rational side fighting with desire and need.

"Please!" he begged.

Because he'd never begged me for anything before, I leapt off the cliff.

"Yes," I whispered. "I'll go with you."

And so we started to make our plans. I was terrified. I'd be leaving my family, my home; dropping out of school at sixteen for a life of uncertainty. Some days it seemed like a crazy idea, but every time I had that thought, my heart told me to shut the hell up.

Our biggest problem was money for gas. Kes said he had just about enough saved to get here—at least he thought he did. But after that, he was out. I had money that I'd saved up over the years, birthday money and from odd jobs that I'd done, but it was only $200. And that was barely enough to get us the 1700 miles back to California in Kes's gas guzzling truck. I was afraid we'd get stuck in Utah or lost in the Sierra Nevadas.

I wanted to delay until after Christmas when I'd have some more money, but Kes refused to wait. So we talked in secret every night, plotting our escape. Kes said we could save money by sleeping in the truck. I wasn't happy about it, but we didn't have any choice. I was worried that we'd freeze to death as Fall turned to Winter.

But all Kes said was, "I've got chains for the tires if it snows."

That wasn't my biggest worry, but we were young and in love and everything seemed possible.

Once, I tried to ask Kes what would happen when I got to California.

"You can be part of the show," he said confidently.

"But what if Dono sends me home?"

"He won't."

"But what if he does?"

"Then fuck him," said Kes, which seemed to be his answer to everything. "We'll go on the road on our own. Lots of carnivals would take our act. We're fucking awesome."

"What about Jacob Jones?" I asked nervously.

Kes swore again. "I don't fucking know. Jakey's my horse, so Dono can't stop me. But I don't think he'd let me take the trailer. He'd kick my ass if I tried." He sighed. "Yeah, that's not going to happen. Don't worry about it. Dono won't want me to leave the act. We'll be fine."

I wasn't so sure, but arguing with Kes was hard. Besides, I wanted him to be right.

I lived for our sneaked phone calls every night, sometimes talking till late. We had to cut that down after a while, because neither of us could afford to put more money on our phones.

At school, I went through the motions. I studied, I got good grades, but I couldn't tell you anything that I learned.

Camilla never came back. Her family made up some excuse about why boarding school was a superior form of education. I felt a twinge of guilt, but not much more. Lauren ignored me, which was just fine.

When Karl Ullen asked me to be his date for Homecoming, I almost laughed in his face. I didn't mean to be cruel, but wasn't it obvious that I was in love with another boy and not interested in anyone else? I turned him down as tactfully as I could, which wasn't saying much.

I didn't tell Kes because his jealous-o-meter was already out of control if I so much as mentioned another guy.

We had our first telephone fight about that, because he

happened to mention that Dono had him putting together a new act where Sorcha had a bigger role.

The jealousy I always felt when her name was mentioned flared up like a rocket.

"Of course I have to do the act with her!" Kes shouted.

"But why does that skank have to get a bigger role?" I yelled back.

"Because she's hot and the audiences like her," he snarled.

So *not* the right thing to say to me.

"I have to put up with you talking about all the guys you see in school!" he yelled.

"That's ridiculous! I have to go to school. I can't help that there are boys there!"

And so we tore each other apart until he slammed the phone down. Then we didn't talk to each other for two days. I broke first and called him back.

We both refused to apologize, but he managed to admit that he missed me, and I told him that I loved him.

And so we went on, plotting and scheming, ironing out the problems that we could, ignoring the ones that were too tough for us.

And then we were discovered.

It was so stupid, such a dumb way of being found out.

I was trying to be a model daughter, trying to buy Mom and Dad's peace of mind so that I'd be able to sneak away when the time came. Which meant I was being extra helpful around the house.

Mom was grateful, so to thank me, she did my laundry.

And then she put my laundry away.

In my drawer.

Where I hid my phone.

By the time I got home from school, she'd read every text, listened to every voice message that I couldn't bear to delete because I craved the sound of Kes's voice, and she knew every secret.

She called my father at work and he rushed back to sort out his wayward daughter.

Within an hour, my suitcase had been packed and I was sent to stay with Dad's sister in Michigan. I wasn't allowed to call Kes or text him. I wasn't allowed to leave a note. I was sent away in disgrace.

I couldn't sleep, refused to eat. I was desperate for news and I think my aunt took pity on me because she let me call him. I tried. I tried over and over again. I kept the same stupid message: 'the person you are trying to reach is not accepting calls right now. Please try your call again later.' I did try again: again and again and again.

I began to plague Mom and Dad with phone calls instead. Every day I asked the same question: *Is he there?*

And every day I got the same icy answer: *No.*

I paced my tiny room at night, my body starved, my brain blazing with unanswered questions. I couldn't go on like that.

So I just stopped.

Stopped talking, stopped eating, just stopped. And then I collapsed.

The doctors called it a breakdown, but the only thing that was broken was my heart.

He never came. I couldn't believe it, didn't want to believe it. I accused my Mom and Dad of lying, of hating me, of wishing that I'd never been born.

I'd lost all restraint and wasn't scared of my father anymore.

When I was finally allowed home at the start of January, Minnesota was blanketed in thick snow that glittered, promising a fresh start. It was all lies.

In the weeks that followed my month-long trip to Michigan, I learned an essential truth: sympathy has an expiration date. Friends wear out and lose interest in your broken heart. It's not their heart that's broken, and they get tired of you moping around like you've lost your reason to live, even though that's exactly what happened.

The rest of my Junior year of high school was the loneliest of my life.

My cell phone had been destroyed so I couldn't even read his old messages or listen to his voice.

I googled the shit out of 'Donohue' and 'carnival', finding only a few out-of-date newspaper articles and Zachary's old website—but the link was broken.

I tried to find Con, since I knew he was pre-med at Northwestern, but he wasn't on any student lists, and they refused to give me any information. It seemed as if he'd never been there.

I wrote to Kes at the old address he'd given me in Arcata,

but that letter was returned unopened, with 'return to sender' scrawled across the envelope.

I was grounded for a month when Dad found out.

Jennifer tried to help me. One of her college friends lived in northern California, and she persuaded them to drive out to Arcata Bay and ask around. I waited, desperate to hear the news. It amounted to a big fat zero.

The log cabins that Kes had described were empty, and Jennifer's friend didn't think that they'd been lived in for months.

So, the waiting game continued.

And then everything changed again. Dad left.

It turned out that all those 'sales conferences' were really a woman named Dee. He'd been seeing her for years. Mom wanted to blame me. She said all my drama had been the last straw. But she was so apathetic, even her blame was half-hearted. We stumbled on in misery together—all through the Spring, all through the mild warmth of May, and the blazing heat of June.

With Fourth of July out of the way, my heart began to beat again. *In just a few weeks*, I told myself.

I gazed out of window, waiting for the cloud of dust and rumbling ground that told me the carnival was coming. I was so sure that everything was going to be okay. The certainty of our love was the only thing that had kept me from breaking apart completely, from shattering like a cheap vase.

Mom said I was banned from the carnival, of course, but that wasn't going to stop me, and in the end, she didn't even try. She just shrugged her shoulders and said, "On your own head be it," as if she was some cut-rate Biblical prophet, rather than a sad, middle-aged, soon-to-be divorcée.

Before the thick dust had even settled, I ran all the way to the carnival field.

My heart was beating wildly, and I thought I'd choke on the emotions welling up inside.

"Where's Kes? Is he here?"

I ran from trailer to trailer, asking the same question, but he wasn't there. I didn't believe the first person who told me, or the second, or the third.

I couldn't, wouldn't believe that my Kes wasn't there.

But he wasn't, and no one could tell me where he'd gone. No Kes, no Dono, no Mr. Albert. No Zachary, no Blake, no Jesse, no Madame Cindy, no Ollo.

I recognized some of the other carnies, but they weren't talking. For whatever reason, they closed ranks; I wasn't one of them anymore.

And then I saw Sorcha.

She was helping to set up a hoopla booth when I found her.

"Look, I know you hate me," I began, "but please, please, where's Kes? I haven't heard from him in months. Please!"

She shrugged indifferently.

"No one's heard from him. Not since Dono died."

I thought I was going to throw up.

"What? Dono?"

"Yeah," she said, tossing her hair over her shoulder. "Guy had a heart attack; the carnival has a new owner now. Maybe Kes went to his brother."

She put her hands on her hips as I swayed on my feet.

"You really fucked him good, didn't you?"

"W-what?"

She laughed coldly.

"You got Dono so pissed he had a freakin' heart attack. Nice goin', rube. Now fuck off, I'm working."

I stumbled away from the carnival choking on my tears.

Kes was lost and alone, somewhere in the vast emptiness, and I couldn't find him, couldn't reach him, couldn't tell him that I needed him. That I loved him.

PART TWO:
ON THE ROAD

EIGHT YEARS LATER

CHAPTER 8
ENDINGS AND BEGINNINGS

I wanted to hit him. I wanted to punch his perfect white, dentally-approved teeth into the back of his throat and out the other side. I wanted to hurt him.

Because goddamn it! He was hurting me.

I think we should take a break.

"Really, Gregg—that's what you think? We should take a break?"

"Hon," he said, as if he was talking to a slightly dim pre-teen, "we've been together four years—since we were juniors in college. I don't think we should just settle for each other without…"

"*Settle?* You think you're *settling* for me?"

He backpedaled immediately, but it was already too late. It was too late as soon as he opened his big fat mouth ten minutes ago and said, 'We should talk'.

"Well, you know what, Gregg? I think you might be right."

"You do?" he said with obvious surprise.

"Yes, I don't want to *settle* for you either."

He rolled his eyes.

"You're being melodramatic, Ames."

"I guess people get like that after they've been dating for four years and they suddenly get…"

I couldn't bring myself to finish the sentence with the word 'dumped', but that's what it was.

Gregg slipped his arms through the sleeves of his linen jacket, the one I thought looked so debonair and European when I bought it for him, and made sure the lapels were lying flat.

"You know I respect you," he said seriously. "I hope this won't affect our professional relationship."

126

I shook my head in disbelief. Hell, yeah! Did the prick really think I was going be pleasant to him in the Staff Room where all the teachers met for morning coffee before the hordes descended.

"Of course," I said, with an insincere smile.

He looked relieved then winked at me. He freakin' *winked* at me!

"See you in September, Ames. Have a great summer!"

Oh, he didn't just go there!

We'd planned to spend summer vacation together visiting his parents in St. Louis and then have a long weekend in NYC doing cultural things before I headed to Minnesota to see my family. Gregg wasn't planning to go with me for that—too expensive, he said. The pay of an elementary teacher fifty miles from Boston meant that neither of us were rich, and we both had student loans to pay off. But we would have been together, and now he was waltzing away on the first day of summer vacation, leaving me high and dry.

"Wait!" I called after him. "Is there someone else?"

"No, of course not," he said soothingly.

His right eye twitched, a sure sign that he was lying.

"Really," I said, folding my arms across my chest. "Well, that's reassuring."

Then I picked up my purse and followed him out of the apartment.

"Where are you going?" he asked, his voice wary.

"Your place," I said with a bright smile. "I thought I'd pick up my things."

"Oh, you don't need to do that," he replied hastily. "I already did it," and he pointed at two cardboard boxes stacked outside my door.

Anger tightened inside me, and a headache started to throb behind my temples.

"You really have it all figured out, don't you?"

He smiled briskly. "Best to make it a clean break."

"Fine," I snapped. "I'll bring your stuff over later."

"No need," he said, patting his pocket. "I've got my toothbrush."

"What about your clothes and DVDs?" I asked.

"Ah," he said looking down. "I moved those out last week while you had that parent-teacher conference." He had the grace to look slightly ashamed. "I thought it would make things easier."

My eyes bulged. "That was Thursday. We fucked on Thursday."

He winced. "Do you have to be so crude?"

"Seriously, Gregg?! You'd already planned to break up with me, going so far as moving your stuff out, and you *still* slept with me?"

"I thought you needed comforting—you'd had a rough day."

Un-fucking-believable.

He must have seen something in my eyes because he backed away.

"You really don't want to do this, Aimee," he said, trying to sound like he was still in control. "Have a little dignity."

"Low fucking blow, Gregg!"

"Please don't use curse words," he said. "You're better than that."

I lost it. "You don't get to tell me how to behave anymore!" I screamed at him.

"I'm only trying to help you," he said, a sharp tone in his voice that usually made me cautious.

"No you fucking aren't!" I shrieked. "Breaking up with me is not *helping* me!"

"I can't do this," he said firmly. "I've tried to be nice, but you're so emotional."

"Well, what a fucking surprise," I yelled. "Because we've been together four years! Four years! We talked about getting married!"

He looked uncomfortable. "That was a mistake," he said.

I slapped him hard.

I'd never hit anyone in my whole life, but damn, it felt good!

His eyes narrowed as he rubbed his cheek. "I could have you charged with assault!"

"Oh, feel free!" I laughed wildly. "I can see the police getting a real kick out of that!"

He frowned, knowing I was right. He'd always hated being in the wrong.

"We're done here," he snapped.

He turned and marched away. I watched him for a moment, then something made me follow him. I grabbed my keys and ran down the stairs barefoot.

He crossed the street to his car and surprise, surprise, Lulu Masters, the junior high science teacher was sitting in his passenger seat.

"You cheating bastard!" I yelled, throwing the first thing I could find—which happened to be a large bag of trash—at his shiny red, environmentally friendly car.

I watched with vindictive pleasure as eggshells and banana skins rained down, and coffee grounds stuck to the windshield.

It was a lot of fun seeing Gregg lose his composure, until he finally screeched off.

Adrenaline drained away and I sighed. Four years lost to that asshole—next semester was going to be gruesome.

I trailed back to my apartment and called my best friend Mirelle.

"Chica!" she screamed down the phone. "I told you and told you that Gregg-with-two-g's was a douche."

Mirelle made me smile. I'd always thought it was kind of ridiculous that he spelled his name with two g's.

"Now we can celebrate his assholishness," she crowed. "I'll be over with margaritas, and then we're hitting the bars and gonna get you laid good!"

I laughed sadly.

"The margaritas sound great, but can we save the barhopping for another day? I really just want to wallow right now."

She clucked her tongue. "I tell you, girl, you've been wallowing for four long, sexually-frustrated years. You gotta ring in the changes!"

At one time I'd regretted telling her that my sex life with Gregg left a lot to be desired, but now her teasing was definitely helping.

An hour later, we were curled up on my sofa, knocking back margaritas like they'd ration them tomorrow and dissing men in general, which was always fun.

"So what are you going to do now?" she asked, her dark eyes sympathetic. "You're totally welcome to come visit with my folks."

Mirelle's family was huge. She had cousins and aunts and uncles all over Puerto Rico, as well as four brothers and one sister who lived in San Juan. I'd met some of them when they were visiting her in New Hampshire.

We both taught at Walker Elementary School in Concord,

and I thought I was so lucky that Gregg had managed to get a job at the same school. Now I was thinking it was a huge mistake—in more ways than one.

Mirelle never liked him, although I hadn't really understood why. She just said he was too tidy. I didn't know what that meant. I liked that he was tidy and always well dressed.

"No, chica," she said, shaking her head, "you thought he was safe."

I hung my head and picked at the frosted pink nail polish I was wearing. She was right. So right.

"Come to San Juan! We'll party till we drop! You gotta learn to loosen up!"

"I can't afford it…" I began, but Mirelle grabbed my arm and shook me.

"Yes, you freakin' can! You've been working and saving your ass off. Live a little. You've got a lifetime to pay off your student loans."

I cringed at her answer, wondering if I should remind her that the government wanted the loan repaid. Yes, they offered a lengthy repayment plan, but I certainly didn't get to pick when I would have to start repaying. Plus, being a teacher in New Hampshire, I knew that I'd need to have a Master's degree eventually. Mirelle and money weren't the best of friends. I could see why, but the girl definitely knew how to have a good time.

"Fine, I'll come. But I should see Mom, and I promised Jennifer that I'd visit with her and Dylan. I love spending time with him."

"Hell, he's a kid! You spend every day with kids. Anyway, that's what summer camp was invented for!" Mirelle bitched.

I knew she was trying to get a rise out of me. But the truth was, Mirelle spent most of her vacations looking after her nieces and nephews and assorted neighborhood kids, and she loved it.

Visiting Mom was a duty visit, and neither of us got much pleasure from it, but I loved seeing my sister. She married Brian when they graduated from college, and Dylan came along right away. I liked Brian, but the marriage hadn't lasted, mostly because of the long hours he worked as a property developer.

Despite the fact I lived halfway across the country, Jennifer and I had stayed close with phone calls two or three times a week and long, chatty emails.

"Okay, girl, but I'll be expecting you no later than the first week of August, or I'll come and kick your ass all the way to Puerto Rico. You hear me?"

I smiled for the first time that day.

"It's a date."

The air conditioning on the plane was blasting fetid vapors across my face, but not enough to distil the overpowering stench coming from my neighbor.

I was sandwiched between Mr. I've-never-used-deodorant and a guy who looked like he could have played NFL about 20 years ago. There was no escape.

I shifted uncomfortably, trying to relieve the ache in my right buttock where I was wedged into the coach seat.

I resented paying my hard earned cash to an airline who put me through so much torture.

My gut tightened as the red and brown patchwork fields of the Twin Cities swept into view. It reminded me of a time and place that hurt to remember, one that I never wanted to go back to. But here I was, all the old emotions churning through me. Damn them.

Jennifer wrinkled her nose when she picked me up at the arrivals hall.

"Wow, you need to change your deodorant, Aimee. Just saying!"

I growled at her. "You'd stink if you sat next to the swamp monster I've been wedged against for the last three hours."

She grimaced sympathetically. "Oh God, I know that feeling! I smelled of spit-up for nearly two years."

"How is my favorite nephew?"

"Excited to see his favorite aunt."

I smiled, genuinely happy at the thought of seeing the little guy.

Jennifer directed the car out of the parking lot and we headed northwest along the I-94. It helped my messy emotions that she lived in Saint Cloud, a two hour drive from Fairmont and our mother.

We were nearly at Jennifer's home when I threw my hands in the air.

"Come on, spit it out. Whatever is bugging you, just say it."

"What?" she huffed, trying to sound indignant. "I don't

know what you're talking about."

"Jen, you're so uptight, you've been practically levitating. Whatever it is, the suspense is driving me bat shit, and you know that I always get crazy coming back here—you're going to wind up with a nut job on your hands."

"Okay, fine. But before you take my head off, I really didn't know it would work out like this."

"Jen!"

"Alright, alright! I promised Dylan that we could go see the State Fair."

"Yes, so? That's not until the week before Labor Day?" I said, puzzled.

"I know, right! But it turns out that he didn't mean the State Fair—some of the other kids he plays with were going on about this awesome traveling fair that's playing in the city next week."

I started to feel nauseous.

"Jen, you know I hate fairs…"

"I know, honey, I do. But I *promised* Dylan that we'd go. I didn't know it would be while you were visiting."

"Well, no problem," I said lightly. "I'll visit Mom that day. You guys go have fun and I'll see you later."

The car was silent. Jennifer was staring straight ahead and biting her lip.

"Something else you're not telling me?" I asked, raising one eyebrow.

"Possibly," she said, her voice reluctant.

"Come on, get it over with."

"It's only because Dylan got upset…"

"And?"

"Itoldhimyoudcomewithus."

"What?!"

Jennifer's expression was guilty. "I'm sorry, Aimee, but he was crying, so I told him you'd come with us. I know I shouldn't have, but come on! He's just a little kid, and what with the divorce and everything, he's been through a lot. I couldn't say no."

"You're totally guilt-tripping me and you know it!" I snapped.

"Is it working?"

I sighed. "Fine. Yes, it's working. But you're paying for *all* the rides *and* the candy *and* hotdogs. And I plan to eat a lot. And then there'll be alcohol when we get home. Possibly for the whole week."

"You are the best sister!" she grinned at me.

"Well, you suck."

But she didn't stop smiling.

We collected Dylan from his friend's house, and it was so wonderful to see him again. I loved teaching third grade, but I couldn't help wondering if kindergarteners were where my passion really lay. Their minds were so fresh and open, everything was an adventure. I loved that about them.

"Wow! You got so big!" I laughed as Dylan hurtled toward me. "Has your mom been watering you?"

He wrapped his arms around my legs and stared up at me, puzzled. "You're supposed to water plants, Aunty Aimee, not people."

"Oh, silly me. Guess I got mixed up. Did you miss me?"

He shook his head shyly.

"Not even a little bit?" I teased, tugging on his t-shirt.

He held his thumb and finger an inch apart.

"Gee, as much as that! I must be the luckiest aunt in the whole world."

His giggles were the best sound, and helped calm the uneasy stutter in my heart as I thought about taking him to the fair.

I told myself I was being dumb and pathetic, but it didn't help. I'd avoided anything like that since … well, since the summer I turned 17.

When we were at Jennifer's house and Dylan was in bed, I told her the whole sordid story of Gregg-with-two-g's and the unfortunately named Lulu.

"You're better off without him," she said, opening a second bottle of wine and handing me a glass.

"I know, but I feel so stupid. All the signs were there and I just ignored them."

Jennifer shook her head. "You trusted him, honey. You're supposed to be able to do that in relationships. There's nothing wrong with you. He's the asshole."

I raised my glass and we clinked them together. "He's the asshole."

Jennifer had to work for the next two days, so I was in charge of Mission Entertain Dylan. We went to the Soft Play

Center in town and then swimming in the lake at Shroeder Park. It was my favorite place to take Dylan because the beach was huge and the water wasn't full of weed. It also had a fun playground that Dylan loved, grills and picnic tables, and large clean restrooms. Anyone who's ever been on a day out with kids knows that good restrooms can make or break a trip.

He fell asleep tired and happy. I'd have felt the same, if it wasn't for the twinge in my gut. I'd be glad when the trip to the fair was over and done with.

We packed up the car the next day as Jennifer talked loudly, covering her guilt for making me do this. Dylan was in high spirits because all his friends had already been to see the fair, and he was the only one who hadn't. According to the other five-year olds he knew, it would be "awesome" because the cotton candy came in 15 different colors.

Zip-a-dee-doo-dah.

Dylan chattered the whole way, which was good, because Jennifer kept throwing me worried looks that were seriously pissing me off. I would have told her so if it wasn't for the cute kid strapped into his child seat.

But after all the anxiety, once we got there I started to enjoy myself.

I breathed in the scent of frying onions and hotdogs, the sweet air around the cotton candy stall, watching the excited faces of children and the restrained excitement of adults as they moved down the midway. The scents and sounds took me back to a magical part of my childhood. *I've missed this*, I thought. The carnival had been such an important part of my life, and I'd cut it off ruthlessly—even if it was to protect my heart from further damage.

Dylan tugged on my hand, almost overwhelmed with the choices surrounding him.

First stop was the Monkey Maze which Dylan adored and went a long way to running off some of his nonstop energy. Then we headed down the midway, playing all the dumb games and trying to win stuffed elephants and toys that no one in their right mind would ever want. But that was the point, wasn't it? The fair wasn't about being sensible, it was about having as much fun as was legal.

I had a little pang when we went on the Ferris wheel, but it was so different being there with Dylan that I didn't really mind.

I couldn't help wondering if the whole thing hadn't helped me grow up a little. After all, it had been eight years. I was nearly 25—definitely time to get over it. Over him. He-who-must-not-be named. But breaking up with Gregg had left me feeling surprisingly emotional—and add that to being back in Minnesota.

In the afternoon, Dylan decided he wanted to go see the show playing at the back end of the fair. There was some motorcycle stunt rider that he wanted to see.

I wasn't very keen. I'd seen things like that on TV—those guys were nuts.

We could hear the roar of engines set against the backdrop of some heavy rock music, presumably to ramp up the drama. Jennifer winced at the volume and I raised my eyebrows.

With resigned shrugs, we paid our 15 bucks each and went inside.

We'd missed the first few minutes and had to squeeze into the middle of a row of seats, much to the annoyance of the other patrons. I didn't think we'd missed much because all I could see through a cloud of dust and fumes, was some guy in red and black leathers, using his poor motorcycle to screech around, leaving a pattern of tight circles in the dirt. Dylan told me these were called 'donuts'. Good to know.

I could see it took timing and precision, but I found it deadly dull to watch. But that was just the warm-up.

The donuts were followed by a display of wheelies: along the ground, up ramps and onto seesaws. I liked the innovation of a digital display on a large wall-mounted screen that showed the rider's hair-raising point of view. If I squinted, I could see the camera mounted on his helmet.

Then he picked some poor woman from the audience who practically threw herself at him, and he practiced screeching around her, and skidding to a halt inches from her open legs. Ugh. She had her eyes closed the whole time, not that I blamed her for that, and I think half the audience were hoping that he'd run her over, but he didn't.

He followed that with some wheelies standing on the seat, first on the back wheel and then on the front wheel, which was pretty cool, even doing it with no hands, which made me wonder how he controlled the bike.

So far it was technically stunning, but not that exciting.

Apparently things were only just getting started. Next up were the jumps, and that had me gripping my seat. Two ramps, about sixty feet apart were set up. He raced up one, flying through the air. I gasped as his feet left the footrests and he seemed to be doing a handstand on the handlebars. I was sure I was going to see a horrible crash, and watched through my fingers as he landed.

Dylan was whooping and cheering, but Jennifer looked a little queasy.

"I want to do that, Mommy!" shouted Dylan.

Jennifer threw me a horrified look, and I shrugged as if to say, *You wanted to come here.*

But then the stunt guy topped that by doing a full somersault in the air. I squeaked with nerves as he seemed to mis-time his landing, but I guess that was all part of the act.

Jennifer tugged my elbow. "Bathroom break," she mouthed.

Yeah, right. No coincidence on the timing, although, to be fair, she did look a little green.

Then two more riders entered the arena and they all jumped the ramp one after another, the guy in red and black freakin' *lying* on his bike, hands in the air.

Insane. They were all insane.

And I thought that *before* two of the riders screamed up opposite ramps, seeming sure to hit each other midair, but missing by mere inches.

I'd never seen anything like it and was relieved when it was over.

Dylan was so excited he sounded as if he'd been sniffing helium. His squeaky high-pitched yells broke through my trance.

"Aunty Aimee, they're signing programs! Can we go, can we?" And he waved the program in my face that we'd been given along with our tickets.

"Sure thing, buddy."

I was happy to do anything now it was all over.

We made our way down to the arena where the three guys were chatting to the crowds. Unsurprisingly, the most popular was the guy in red and black leather.

Apparently, he was some sort of world record holder, jumping his bike more than 180 feet by Sydney Harbor Bridge, Australia, or so the program said. I couldn't say I'd ever heard of Hawkins' Daredevils—with or without the apostrophe that was missing from their program.

He had his back to us and I could hear his deep laugh as a bunch of kids asked him questions. He was really patient with them, which I appreciated, and seemed genuinely interested as he chatted with them.

Finally, he turned to us, and my breath rushed out of my lungs. I was staring up into silver-gray eyes that still haunted my dreams.

CHAPTER 9
STORIES AND LIES

"Kes!"

He looked equally shocked, but recovered so quickly, I wondered if I'd imagined it.

"Yeah?"

"It … it's Aimee … Aimee Andersen."

He stared at me, his expression giving away nothing.

"Yeah, I remember you," he said at last, his voice grudging.

Then he leaned down to sign Dylan's program.

"What's your name, dude?" Kes asked, his voice gruff and deep.

"Dylan," he replied shyly, holding my hand tightly, half hiding behind me.

"Cool name," said Kes, his trademark smirk evident as he scrawled his signature across the program with a Sharpie.

I stood there stiffly, desperately trying to think of something to say. *Speak to him!* My head screamed, but the words were thick and gluey in my mouth.

"Can … can we talk?" I choked out.

His eyes darkened to a stormy gray. "I'm kinda busy."

"Please?" I whispered.

Dylan looked up at me, a small frown on his face.

Kes's expression softened slightly.

"Twenty minutes," he said. "Out back."

I nodded jerkily as he gunned the engine and rode away.

"Is he a friend of yours, Aunty Aimee?" Dylan asked, "Because that would be cool."

"Um, I used to know him," I answered honestly, "but I haven't seen him for a long time. He probably doesn't even remember me."

The lie lay heavily in my chest, but Dylan accepted it easily.

At that moment, Jennifer found us.

"Hey, buddy! Did you get his autograph?"

"Yes, Mommy. And he's Aunty Aimee's friend!"

Jennifer smiled at his enthusiasm, but it faltered when she saw my face.

"Aimee, are you okay? You look really pale."

I clutched her arm.

"It was Kes."

"What?"

"The guy in the red and black leathers—it's Kes!"

"Holy sh—" she started to say, then bit her tongue. "Are you sure?"

I nodded rapidly.

"Did … did you talk to him?"

"He told me to meet him out back in 20 minutes. Oh my God, Jennifer! What am I going to do?"

She stroked my arm reassuringly. "I guess you go talk to him. I'll take Dylan to get some food. Call me when you're done."

"I can't!" I gasped. "I can't do this!"

She grabbed my shoulders and gave me a small shake, letting go quickly before Dylan got too worried.

"You can and you will. You've wanted closure for eight years—well, here's your chance. Just … breathe, okay?"

She threw me another warning look and then walked away holding Dylan's hand.

I headed toward the exit, my legs feeling stiff and awkward, as if my knees wouldn't bend properly.

I wasn't sure where 'out back' meant, so I stopped to ask one of the ushers. He looked at me pityingly.

"If you want to get Mr. Hawkins' autograph, I'm afraid you've missed him. He's finished for the night, ma'am."

The name threw me until I remembered that the whole motorcycle show was 'Hawkins' Daredevils'. Kes had changed his name. But why? Later, I'd find out later.

"No, you don't understand," I managed to explain. "He told me to meet him out back."

The man sighed, his kind face crinkling in a worried frown. "You seem like a nice girl; this really isn't the place for you. Why don't you just go on home now."

I shook my head, my nerves so tight, I felt as if I would snap.

I could almost imagine pieces of me flying through the air, shattered and broken.

"I know him. His name is … was … Kestrel Donohue. I knew his grandfather and … and his brother, Falcon."

The man looked surprised. "I guess you do know him. Well, come this way."

He led me below the bleachers, the grubby underbelly of the stage above, and out to a parking area behind the stadium. A large silver RV was parked next to a trailer that held five stunt bikes.

The man knocked on the RV's door. It was all so familiar, yet different. It wasn't the same RV: this one was much newer and sleeker.

"Lady to see you, Mr. Hawkins," he said.

When the door opened, Kes was standing there, silent and stern. He definitely wasn't smiling.

"You came back. That's new."

The usher looked at me, shook his head, and walked away.

I stared at Kes. Already off balance, his odd greeting threw me even further.

"You said to meet you 'out back'. I wasn't sure what you meant, so … here I am."

I knew I was babbling, but his slate-eyed stare wasn't designed to put me at ease. After a long moment, he stepped back, allowing me to enter.

Looking at Kes felt too awkward, especially as he didn't seem the least bit pleased to see me, so I gazed around the RV's interior. It was how I imagined a yacht would look, all blond wood and polished surfaces, with a small galley kitchen designed in black and chrome.

Kes hadn't invited me to sit down, but my legs were shaking, so I plopped down on one of the small built-in sofas and looked up.

He was leaning with his shoulder propped against the door, one long leg crossed over the other and arms folded.

He was taller than I remembered, perhaps by as much as three or four inches, and much broader. Under his t-shirt his chest was well defined, and his biceps popped as he moved his arms. His hair was a shade darker than the pictures in my memory, and his face was narrower—the roundness of childhood long gone.

The dark scruff on his chin was new. My Kes hadn't needed to shave.

I finally met his eyes. Those were the same. Still silvery-gray with the curious dark blue ring around the iris. And now they were staring at me without a hint of warmth.

I licked my lips and watched his eyes drop almost reflexively before he looked up again angrily.

"What are you doing here, Aimee?"

"I came with my sister Jennifer and Dylan. You remember Jennifer?"

My voice was high pitched and falsely bright.

Kes shrugged his shoulders impatiently. "I mean, what are you doing *here?*"

"I … I wanted to see you."

"Yeah? Well, now you've seen me, you can go."

I swallowed quickly as tears started to gather behind my eyes. "You want me to go?"

He muttered something under his breath. "Yeah, that would probably be best."

"But … I don't understand!" I cried out angrily. "Why are you being so … so cold!"

His eyes closed and he ran his hands over his damp, tangled hair, the curls springing up as soon as he released them.

"Do you want a coffee or something?" he asked, opening his eyes and dropping his hands to his hips.

He seemed to have reached a conclusion to whatever internal war he'd been waging. I was allowed to stay—for now.

"Thank you," I said, managing to sound calmer although in reality my nerves felt utterly shredded.

I hadn't had time to expect anything from seeing him; I just hadn't expected *this* … this coldness.

He walked into the galley kitchen and turned to a complicated looking coffee machine.

"Black okay?" he muttered.

"Does it do lattes?"

A tiny smile quirked up the corners of his mouth.

That small sign released the stranglehold hope had on my heart.

Finally, he handed me a cup that smelled delicious, with a creamy froth on top.

"No leaf shapes in my foam?" I asked, pretending to look

disappointed.

"You should have said. I could have done a monkey riding a unicycle."

I sighed.

"When you opened the door, I half expected Mr. Albert to jump out."

His expression became somber.

"I was sorry to hear about Dono," I said, deciding to start the difficult conversation that we needed to have.

Kes's shoulders tensed.

"How did you know?"

"Sorcha told me and…"

"Sorcha?"

He sounded surprised, but then again everything about today was surprising.

"Yes, I was looking for you, but I found her—she told me about Dono. I felt so bad, like it was my fault or something."

Kes's forehead wrinkled. "Run that by me again?"

"Sorry, I'm not making much sense. I suppose because it happened after … well, you know … I'm sure the stress didn't help."

He cocked his head to one side, staring at me intently, his dark eyebrows drawn together. Then he blew out a long breath.

"Yeah, not a good time."

"No, it wasn't."

We sat there in uncomfortable silence.

"You seem to be doing well," I said at last. "Hawkins' Daredevils—the name suits you. Why did you change it?"

"Long story."

I sighed. The conversation was more painful than pulling teeth.

He cleared his throat. "Did you go to college like you wanted?"

I smiled. "Yes, I did."

He nodded slowly. "Teacher?"

"You remembered!"

He nodded again. "Yeah."

"I love it," I said. "I'm teaching third graders at a school near Boston and…"

"Boston?" Kes sounded surprised.

"Yes, it's different. I like it." *God, could I sound any lamer.*

"Married?" he asked, looking at my empty ring finger.

"No," I laughed, my cheeks flushing. "You?"

He shook his head. "No, but I'm … involved … with someone."

Of course he was. The disappointment was ridiculous, but there all the same.

"Well, that's nice. Lucky lady."

He raised one eyebrow, as if waiting for a sarcastic footnote, but I had nothing to add. Whoever had him was very lucky. I hoped she knew how special he was. Just being near him again had all the old memories flooding back, newly colored with appreciation for the man he'd become.

"So … you're back in Minnesota for the summer?"

"Not the whole summer, no. Just a quick visit. Catching up with family, you know."

"Not really," he said.

Shit. How tactless could I be?

"Um, how's Con doing? I tried to find him at Northwestern, but, well, I couldn't."

Kes was startled. "Northwestern?"

"Well, not recently, of course. But after … I just thought that he might be able to help, or something."

"Help with what?"

"Jesus, Kestrel!" I yelped, slamming my cup down onto the table. "Finding you, of course! You just disappeared and I didn't know where you were or what you were doing. I called your cell about a million times, but you never answered and then … just nothing. I was desperate! Even if you didn't want to see me, I just wanted to know that you were okay!"

His cheeks flushed with anger, and I could see that he was gripping his cup so tightly he was in danger of breaking it.

"What do you mean, even if I didn't want to see you? Of course I wanted to fucking see you! I drove all the way to Fairmont just for five minutes of your precious time!"

His voice was rising with his anger, but I was too shocked to care.

"What? When? When did you drive to see me?"

His eyes narrowed. "Seriously? You're saying you didn't know?"

"Didn't know what?"

"Fuck," he muttered. "I tried to see you, Aimee. I came for

you, just like we'd planned. I was going crazy when you wouldn't answer your phone. Then Dono found out what I was planning and threw my phone in the bay. We got in the worst fight..." he paused, the memories crowding his eyes. "I called your house so many times, but as soon as I spoke, the call was cut off. I didn't know what to think. I even wrote you but I never heard back, so I packed up everything and stole Dono's truck.

"It took me two weeks to get there from Arcata because the fucking thing broke down in the snow, and I got stuck in Rapid City for eight days while I found an auto shop that would let me use their tools to fix it."

He took a deep breath.

"Your mom answered the door. I remember that. She looked so shocked, I thought she was going to faint. But then your dad turned up." Kes scowled. "He tried to freeze me out, but I sat outside your house for two hours. I think the only reason he let me in was because he knew I wouldn't go away. He told me that you'd gone to live with your aunt in Michigan and weren't coming back." Kes stared at me coldly. "He said that you'd realized how it was a huge mistake to get involved with ... trailer trash ... and that you didn't want me to contact you. He told me that you'd thrown your phone in the garbage."

I gasped, and Kes looked away.

"I'd used up all my gas money to get to you. Your Dad had to give me three hundred bucks to fuck off. Pretty ironic, huh? At least I could get home. Dono kicked my ass about halfway to Sacramento for that stunt. But he didn't get sick until two weeks before Easter. We were getting the RV ready for the Spring circuit and ... I guess his heart just gave out. That's what the docs said."

He looked down.

"Old story now."

I didn't know what to say. I felt so betrayed by my parents. I couldn't believe they'd told Kes such horrible lies about me, that he'd come for me and they never said.

"I thought you'd changed your mind," I choked, my throat aching. "They didn't tell me. They didn't."

Kes's expression was sad. "I'm figuring that out now."

"Yes, they had sent me to Michigan, but I was only there for a month. I came back to finish school. I probably only missed you by a couple of days." I shook my head, the truth making me feel faint. "Dad smashed my phone to pieces—that's why you couldn't reach me. I would *never* have thrown it away. I wrote to you, but my letter came back, marked 'return to sender'. That's when I tried to contact Falcon, but that was a dead end, too. I couldn't find any reference to you or Dono on the web, it was a nightmare. One of Jennifer's friends lived in Redding, and she offered to drive out to Arcata Bay to try and find you, but when she got there, the log cabin was empty—abandoned, she said."

Kes shook his head. "I can't believe this. We were both looking for each other…"

"At least you knew where I was," I accused him.

"What?" he snapped.

"You gave up on me!" I shouted. "I waited for you, but one word from my dad and you left with your tail between your legs."

I knew I was being unfair, but the anger and frustration and loss was pouring out of my mouth in a flurry of ugly words.

"Just back the fuck up!" he snarled.

"No! You back up! How could you be so stupid?"

His eyes blazed. "I'm not stupid!"

"You are! You're so dumb! You're as dumb as dirt for believing my asshole father! I didn't want to live when you didn't come back." I looked down, my voice barely audible. "They called it a breakdown, but it was just my stupid heart that was broken."

The tears broke through my angry walls: eight years of being lied to by the people that should have loved me enough to tell the truth. It was too much. I turned my face away from him and sobbed into my hands.

But then I felt his arms around me, his strong safe arms, and Kes pulled me against his solid body. He murmured soothing words as if he was talking to a wounded animal. And I was wounded, but being here with him now, that small jagged part of me that had been broken for so long began to heal.

After ten minutes of bawling, a wave of embarrassment stiffened my shoulders.

"Sorry," I sniffed. "God, I must look like hell."

I dug a tissue out of my purse and wiped my eyes and nose. I was pretty sure that my mascara had run and I looked hideous.

"Better?" he asked, his voice warm with concern.

"Ugh, I feel just horrible … and I've cried all over your shirt.

I'm so sorry."

"Hey," he said, grabbing my chin gently and making me look at him. "It doesn't matter. It's been a shock. For both of us."

His fingers drifted down my cheeks, wiping the last of my tears. I felt a cold abandonment when he shifted his body away from me.

Embarrassed and awkward, I combed my fingers through my hair.

"Do you mind if I clean up this mess?" and I waved a circle around my head.

Kes gave a small smile.

"Sure, no problem. Second door on the left."

I stood up and avoided his eyes as I hurried out.

The view in his bathroom mirror was even worse than I expected. I cringed at the gruesome reflection: red, swollen eyes; disastrous hair; snotty, tear-stained cheeks; and wrinkled clothes that had a smear of ice cream across my tank top, courtesy of Dylan.

I splashed some water on my face and cleaned up as best I could. I wasn't going to win any awards, but at least I didn't look like a scary, drug-addicted psycho.

As I walked back out, I wondered where we'd go from here, if anywhere. I hoped we could be friends, at least. I still had so many questions about what he'd been doing for the last eight years.

But my questions died on my lips when I saw two tall, well muscled men who were probably in their late twenties or early thirties sprawled out in the living area. I guessed these were the other riders in Hawkins' Daredevils.

The one with dirty blond hair turned and stared at me, a mean smirk on his face.

"Who's been a naughty boy, Kestrel? The boss-lady isn't going to be happy that you've been screwing on company time."

Kes scowled. "Shut up, Tucker. It's not like that. Aimee's an old friend."

"Sure she is," the asshat laughed.

"Not bad though," said the dark haired guy who had full sleeve tattoos on both arms. "Although it looks like you had to rough her up some."

"Shut your fucking mouth, Zef," snarled Kes.

Yep, these two prizes were Kes's stunt colleagues. No

wonder the usher had warned me to stay away.

Kes held out his hand toward me. "Come on, Aimee. Let's get out of here."

But before I could do or say anything, the door opened and a stunning blonde woman walked in.

Her skin tight jeans and low cut top screamed *look at me*, and from the way the two assholes studied her, she'd got the clothes just right.

She didn't even glance up from the papers she was studying as she walked inside.

"Nice show, boys. Good door receipts. I'll have the total in a couple of hours. For the next show on Thursday I want you to…"

Then she saw me and her lips curled. "I thought we agreed that you'd keep your tramps out of the RV."

My mouth dropped open as Zef laughed and shook his head.

"She's not one of ours, Sorcha. This is all on Kes."

A frightening look of fury darkened her face, but as soon as Zef said her name, I recognized her.

Sorcha had become a blonde and artificially straightened her naturally curly hair. It looked as though it had been ironed to within an inch of its life. Her tattoos seemed a little faded and she no longer had her piercings. One other thing had changed: I guessed she must have had her assets upgraded over the years, because her tits were definitely bigger than mine, which was new.

My mouth finally connected with my brain as I stared at her. "Sorcha? You're Sorcha? I didn't recognize you as a blonde, but your manners sure haven't improved."

Kes's gaze was shuttling between us, a look of complete confusion on his face. Finally he pinned his steely eyes to mine.

"I thought you said you already talked to Sorcha?"

"I didn't say that!"

"Yeah, Aimee, you did," Kes said, his voice rising with baffled anger. "You said she told you about Dono."

Sorcha's face paled, leaving the tan as a sheen of orange over her skin.

"Oh right," I said as understanding washed over me. "But I meant years ago. The year after you … left, I went back to the carnival and Sorcha was working the hoopla booth. That's when she told me about Dono."

Kes's eyes narrowed and his gaze slowly moved to Sorcha.

She licked her lips nervously, shifting from foot to foot.

"Sorcha? You want to explain what the fuck is going on?"

Zef and Tucker were following the drama eagerly as if they'd just stumbled on a particularly riveting edition of 'Judge Judy', except that Kes looked more like an executioner than a judge.

"We can talk about this," Sorcha said tentatively, reaching out to touch his arm.

Kes jerked back as if he'd been burned.

"Now," he snapped.

"Babe, come on," she whispered, pouting a little.

"NOW!" he roared, making me jump.

"You've got this all wrong," she whined. "I knew that little bitch was no good for you. Everything was fine until she came along. We've got a good thing going, haven't we, babe?"

Kes threw his coffee cup hard, and it shattered behind her head, showering her with cold coffee and shards of china. Shocked as I was, I knew he didn't intend to hit her—the guy used to throw knives for a living. He never missed.

Sorcha yelped as brown liquid spattered all over her.

"Tell me the fucking truth for once!" Kes yelled.

"Fuck you!" she screamed. "You'd be nowhere without me! Nowhere! I took you in when you had nothing. You're a fucking illiterate circus act. I gave you everything!"

Kes grabbed hold of her arm hard enough to leave bruises and manhandled her out of the RV. She stumbled, landing on her hands and knees in the dirt.

I winced, and Tucker grinned at me. "Don't worry, sweet cheeks, they do this all the time. They get off on it. Sorcha likes it rough, if you know what I mean."

My stomach churned and I gave him a withering glare which just made him laugh.

Kes turned on him, his fists balled. "Out! Get out! Everybody get the fuck out!"

I scrambled to my feet, joining the mass exodus. Kes was freaking out and he was damn scary.

"Aimee, stay?" he whispered.

I hesitated at the door. His eyes said *please* but his lips couldn't say the words. Something else that hadn't changed.

"Okay," I said hesitantly.

I sat nervously on the edge of the sofa while Kes paced up and down the tiny living area, his hands gripping his hair as if he wanted to yank it out at the roots.

"I can't fucking believe this," he muttered to himself. "Eight years. Eight fucking years!"

He slumped into the sofa opposite me and rubbed his thumb over his eyebrow.

"Just like your parents," he laughed without humor. "You think you can trust someone, but they just screw you over."

I stayed quiet, not sure if it was safe to speak. Kes's temper had been fierce as a teenager, but he was a man now, and I didn't know what he was capable of.

He looked up at me, and I could see that the storm of anger had passed for the time being, although I was still wary of him.

"What a bitch," he said sourly.

Was I supposed to agree? Because frankly it went without saying.

At that moment, my phone rang. Lousy damn timing.

"Do you mind if I get that? It could be important."

He didn't reply, but sat slumped in his seat, staring morosely out of the window. I reached into my bag and walked a few steps away, just to be polite.

"Sorry, Jen. Things took a little longer than I was expecting."

"Is everything okay?" she asked. "It's just that Dylan's getting tired now and you know how bad tempered he gets."

"He's being a real handful, huh?"

She laughed lightly.

"Okay, no problem," I said. "I'll be there. Where are you?"

"By the cotton candy stand, where else? We're on color number four … or it might be five. I'm afraid he's going to barf on the way home."

"Something to look forward to. I'll see you there in ten minutes."

I finished the call and looked apologetically at Kes. I hated to leave him here like this. Everything seemed to be such a mess.

"You've got to go," he said, without looking at me.

"Sorry, duty calls."

"That's okay," he said heavily. "Your son needs you."

I blinked several times. "Dylan's not my son," I said at last. "He's my nephew."

Kes looked at me and frowned. "I thought … he's Jennifer's kid?"

"Yes. Wow, you really thought he was mine?"

"Yeah, you looked really close."

I smiled. "Dylan's a really great kid. I miss him so much when I go home."

Kes nodded slowly. "How long is it before you leave?"

"It's kind of open at the moment. I had some things planned, but they fell through. I want to spend time with Jennifer and Dylan, and I was going to see my mom…"

I frowned at the thought, and Kes studied me with interest.

"Are you still going to see her?" he asked.

"Hell, yes!" I snorted. "She's got some explaining to do!"

Kes's eyes narrowed. "And your father?"

I shook my head. "I haven't spoken to him for two years, and I haven't seen him in four. He and Mom split up when he had an affair. He's not really a part of my life."

"Good," Kes said coldly, "because otherwise I'd be tempted to beat the shit out of him."

From the look on his face, he wasn't joking.

I glanced at my watch. "I'm sorry, I've really got to go."

Kes stood up suddenly. "I'll walk you."

"Oh," I said, surprised. "Thanks. I'd probably get lost, so that'll be great."

He opened the RV's door and jumped out, then turned to give me his hand to help me down.

"Thank you," I muttered.

See him lurch from raw violence to sweet old fashioned values was confusing.

But he dropped my hand quickly and I decided not to make too much of it. Besides, he said he was involved with someone. A horrible thought crossed my mind.

"So, Sorcha's your manager now?"

He nodded briefly.

"And your girlfriend?" I prodded.

He shrugged. "Not really."

"Oh." *Was I relieved?* "It's just that you said you were involved, so I thought…"

I saw him glance at me out of the corner of his eye, and the penny dropped.

"She's a manager-with-benefits?"

He gave a small smile, but didn't agree or disagree.

"How come you call yourself Hawkins now?" I asked, thinking that might be a slightly safer subject to discuss.

But Kes scowled. "That's a long story."

I zipped my lips and decided that if he wanted to talk, he could choose the topic.

I think he must have picked up on my irritation because he spent the rest of the time asking questions about Boston and living in New Hampshire.

"Have you ever visited there?" I asked.

"Yeah, a few times," he said. "Not all that recently, but when I was a kid we had some bookings: Philly, Scranton, Albany, D.C. ... some other places—I don't really remember."

"You've traveled so much," I said wistfully. "I always meant to, but really I've just shuttled between Minnesota and Boston."

He was silent, but I had to say something because I could see the cotton candy stall at the end of the midway where Jennifer and Dylan were waiting. Time was running out.

"It's been really good to see you again, Kes. I'm happy things have worked out for you. I always knew you'd be a star."

He smiled, but it didn't reach his eyes.

"And you've done well," he said quietly. "You're a teacher: what you always wanted."

"Yep, guess it worked out for both of us," I said, hiding my sadness at the thought of saying goodbye to him again.

He nodded and looked down.

"Maybe we could ... talk ... or something, before you head back east?" he offered, his voice hesitant as if he thought I might say no.

"Really? That would be great!"

My voice was far too enthusiastic, and this time Kes gave me his patented Kestrel smirk and raised one eyebrow.

"Fine!" I snapped, elbowing him in the ribs. "If you hadn't asked, I would've come back to the fair to stalk you."

He laughed out loud and I saw his right cheek dimple. My heart swooped as if I'd fallen a thousand feet.

Kes was still shaking his head, very much amused.

"Give me your cell phone. I'll program my number."

I handed it over and watched while he added his details, then he called his own phone.

"Now I have your number, too."

I grinned at him, and he winked.

As we walked up to the cotton candy stall, Jennifer's eyes grew huge. I could see her totally eye-fucking Kes, and for some reason, that really pissed me off.

Then Dylan gave a happy shout.

"Aunty Aimee! We've been waiting for*ever!*"

I laughed at his annoyed expression. "I was catching up with an old friend."

Dylan squinted at Kes and audibly gasped. "Motorcycle Man!"

Kes smiled, then surprised me by dropping to the dirt on one knee so he was the same height as Dylan.

"Your Aunt Aimee has been telling me all about you," Kes exaggerated. "You sound like a cool kid."

Dylan squirmed with shyness and half hid behind Jennifer's legs. "I like your motorcycle," he murmured at last. "When I grow up I'm gonna have one just like it."

"Is that right?" Kes laughed, standing up again.

"Not unless he wants to give his mom a thousand gray hairs," Jennifer insisted. Then she smiled at Kes. "Good to see you again, Kes. It's been too long."

He looked surprised at the warmth in her voice. I suppose he'd never heard anything but small minded slurs from my family before.

"Um, thanks," he said, bemused.

Dylan seemed encouraged by his mom's ease with Kes, because then he said, "You could bring your motorcycle to my house and I could show all my friends."

"Dylan," Jennifer chided gently. "I'm sure Mr. Hawkins is far too busy…"

But Kes interrupted her. "I've got shows Thursday through Sunday, but I could come by after that."

Jennifer's mouth dropped open and she looked at me for guidance on how to answer. I beamed at her.

"Well," she said lightly, "that would be lovely. Maybe we could set something up for next week…"

"I'm free Monday," Kes said quickly.

"Great," Jennifer smiled. "I take it Aimee has your number so she can text you the directions?"

Kes grinned at her, not the least fazed by her interrogative tone. "Yeah, I just gave it to her."

"That's all settled," she said. "Now I need to get this monster home before he grows horns and a forked tail."

"Mom!" Dylan groaned, but we all saw him check his head

and butt, just in case.

And then we had that awkward moment where nobody quite knew what to say or what to do with their hands.

Or mouths, as it turned out, because Kes bent down and quickly kissed me on the cheek. But then he spoiled it by kissing Jennifer, as well, and I scowled at her while she raised her eyebrows. Finally, Kes reached down to shake Dylan's hand.

"Take good care of these ladies," he said, and Dylan nodded seriously.

Then Kes winked at me and strolled off.

Jennifer fanned her face, mouthing, *Oh my God!*

"I know, right?!" I laughed.

"He's certainly all grown up."

"Mmm-hmm!" I agreed.

Jennifer nudged me. "We'll talk later."

We drove back to Jennifer's house in silence until it was safe for adult talk.

Asleep in his child seat, Dylan was flopped like a cuddly toy, his round face ruddy from the sun, and his rose-pink lips parted.

"He is so gorgeous," I sighed.

"Are we talking about Kes or the sleeping beast in the back seat?" smiled Jennifer.

"Well, I was talking about your son, but yes, either/or."

She paused. "Are you going to tell me what was said? Because you two looked awfully cozy back there."

I blew out a breath. "Honestly, I don't know where to start. It's still a little confusing. He wasn't all that happy to see me at first, but then it turned out that he'd gone to see Mom and Dad the winter I was sent to Aunty Mon's."

"You're kidding me!"

"No, I'm not. He stole his grandpa's truck and drove all the way from California. According to Kes, Dad told him that I thought he was trailer trash."

I winced, hating to repeat the words.

Jennifer looked really angry. "That's such a vile thing to say. Sometimes I can't believe we're related to that man."

"I know. So there he was, stuck in Minnesota, no money, no job, nowhere to stay. He was only 17 years old. He had no way of getting back to Arcata: he'd spent every last penny on coming to see me." I sighed. "Dad paid him to leave."

Jennifer gripped the steering wheel tightly. "Unbelievable."

"But then things get even more strange."

"This should be good."

"The summer after it all happened, I went back to the carnival, but he wasn't there. You remember that?"

"Yes?"

"But I did find this girl he used to do his act with—Sorcha."

"The skank?" Jennifer asked.

"The very one," I laughed dryly. "Well, it turns out that either she lied and she did know where he was, or they met up again later. I'm not too clear on the details there."

"What a bitch!" Jennifer fumed.

"True, but it gets worse. When she found him … or he found her … she didn't tell Kes that I'd been looking for him. So all this time he's believed that I thought he was trash. Hence the rather frosty greeting."

"Oh my God! That poor guy! He must be pissed that she never told him. So what happened to her?"

I laughed angrily. "Ha well, she's only his manager. She walked into the RV while we were talking and Kes completely lost it. He basically threw her out—he was so mad, I thought he was going to mash her into the wall."

"So she didn't even deny it?"

"No! The evil bitch basically told him that she did it for him, and that he was better off without me!"

Jennifer shook her head. "That's some story. I don't know how they'll work together after that."

"That's not all."

"Oh my God, there's more? You should have your own freakin' spot on Jerry Springer!"

"Sorcha is his manager-with-benefits … and apparently she likes it rough."

Jennifer shook her head. "I'm afraid to ask. You mean…?"

"Yep. When we first started talking, Kes told me that he was involved with someone."

Jennifer shook her head in disbelief.

"Now you see why I'm all over the place," I added.

Jennifer scrunched her eyes together. "But he really seems into you?"

"I don't know. It's a lot to take in. Basically, he's been with Sorcha for quite a while, as far as I can tell. And he's only just found out that she lied to him all those years ago. Maybe they'll just kiss and make up."

My stomach revolted at the thought.

Jennifer shook her head. "I don't know. It may be an old lie, but from what you said he had a pretty violent reaction to it when he heard. I mean, how do you feel about Mom never telling you? I'd expect it from Dad, but Mom…"

I sucked my lips over my teeth. "Oh, believe me, Mom is going to be hearing about that. I am so angry with her, I don't even know if I'll be able to be civil."

Jennifer sighed. "Mom's a basket case. Since Dad left, she's completely lost the plot. I'm not even sure it's worth talking to her about it. You can try; just don't expect too much from her. Or anything at all."

I nodded slowly. "I know you're right, but I have to at least tell her that I know the truth. I'm not saying that running away with Kes when I was 16 would have been the smartest thing ever, but we wouldn't have had to go to such extremes if we could have just stayed in touch or seen each other."

Jennifer frowned. "Why didn't you just write to each other after Dad trashed your phone, or email, or something?"

"I did write—eventually—but I left it too late. Kes's grandpa died and…"

Jennifer gasped. "Oh my God, that poor kid!"

"I know. I'm not even sure what happened to him after. I didn't get to hear that part of the story. But by the time I wrote, he'd already moved on."

"And you hadn't swapped email addresses?"

"Kes didn't even have a computer, but that wasn't the problem."

"Then what was?"

I chewed on my decision for a few seconds. I felt disloyal giving away Kes's secrets, but maybe that was all water under the bridge now.

"Kes was … is … severely dyslexic. He never went to school, and I don't think anyone in his family ever had much time to help him, so…"

"So?"

"Kes is functionally illiterate. When I knew him before, he could read a few simple words, but he really needed specialist help, and I'm pretty certain he never got it."

Jennifer nodded, compassion softening the shocked

expression on her face.

"And does that have anything to do with the fact that you always wanted to specialize in children with special needs?"

I smiled at her. "That transparent, huh?"

"Just a little," she smiled. "Wow, that's some story."

"And I haven't even heard all of it yet."

Jennifer threw me a quick smile. "Well, he was pretty eager to drive all the way to Saint Cloud next week, so perhaps you'll hear part two then."

"I hope so."

Jennifer grinned at me. "I think you can count on it."

CHAPTER 10
GAMES PEOPLE PLAY

Over the next four days, Kes and I texted constantly. His spelling was still horrible, and autocorrect did some very strange things to some of his messages, but I usually managed to work out what he was trying to say, although sometimes it felt like code-breaking rather than communicating.

But more than that, there was something of the old ease we used to have. We didn't talk at all, and I wasn't sure what that meant, but I was too happy enjoying the soft *ching* from my phone as another message from Kes dropped in.

He didn't mention Sorcha at all, and I couldn't help torturing myself with images of them together. You know, *together* together. Ugh.

His messages were so sweet and funny, telling me about his day, and how the stunts had gone—actually, that bit wasn't cute; that bit gave me cold chills. Generally, he just told me what he was up to. I liked the idea that he was thinking about me. And I was definitely thinking about him. I sent a few selfies of me with Dylan, and he sent one back of him in his leathers and helmet.

It was so good to be able to text without worrying about who was going to catch us. Unless, of course, he was worried about Sorcha seeing my messages. Maybe that was why he didn't call me or suggest that I call him.

The thought made my stomach lurch. So, as with all important things in my life, I decided not to think about it. If I didn't think about it, it wasn't happening and wasn't real. Yes, I could be very mature.

Dylan was excited to see Kes again, too. He'd convinced himself that 'Motorcycle Man' was coming to perform stunts in our backyard. No matter how many times Jennifer told him that wasn't the case, Dylan had it in his head that Kes would turn up with the whole show.

We arranged that Kes would arrive at lunchtime so we could have a picnic under the sprawling bur oak that spread its wide branches across half the backyard. But it was barely 11AM when I heard the throaty roar of a motorcycle.

"That's him!" Dylan yelled excitedly.

"It can't be," I muttered under my breath.

But Dylan was right and I was wrong.

I walked around to the front of the house where Dylan was hopping from foot to foot, and saw Kes dismount.

He wasn't wearing the full set of leathers today, but he looked deadly and delicious in dark jeans and a black motorcycle jacket.

I couldn't tell if he was riding one of the stunt bikes or not. It didn't look like a road bike, but I was hardly an expert.

He pulled off his helmet and gloves, and grinned at Dylan, his eyes skipping quickly to me before giving my over-excited nephew his full attention.

"Hey, buddy! Have you been looking after my girls?"

My heart skipped a beat. Stupid heart. Fooled by some sweet words and an ass that looked great in denim. Besides, he'd said 'girls' as in plural, as in including Jennifer.

Dylan nodded seriously, suddenly shy.

Jennifer came out the front door grinning.

"Welcome, Kes. Come on into the house. Can I offer you something cold? A beer or a lemonade?"

"Lemonade would be great, Jennifer. Thanks."

And he kissed her on the cheek. Ah hell. It was going to be a long day.

But then he leaned down and brushed his lips just above the corner of my mouth, and it felt like he might have lingered. I hoped so. He smelled so good, spicy and something citrus, perhaps. But it wasn't the same as I remembered. He was freshly shaved, so that would make a difference. Then it clicked.

"Oh, I know why you don't smell right!" I blurted out.

His eyebrows rose. "I smell bad?"

"No, gosh, no! I didn't mean that. But you always used to smell of hay and … um … hay."

Ten seconds too late, I realized that telling a guy he smelled like a horse probably wasn't a compliment, but Kes knew exactly what I was saying.

"You mean I used to smell like Jacob Jones?"

"Ah, yes. Sorry."

He smiled, his eyes a little sad. "Don't be, he was a great horse."

Dylan's eyes got really big and his mouth formed an impressed O. "You've got a horse?"

Kes shook his head. "I used to. When I was your age my grandpa gave me a pony named Jacob Jones. To me he was Jakey, but I don't have him anymore."

Dylan's face fell. "Why not?"

Kes rubbed the back of his neck, clearly ill at ease.

"That's enough questions for now," Jennifer said quickly. "Why don't you take Kes through to the backyard and show him where we're going to have our picnic?"

Dylan took Kes's hand and towed him through the house, chattering excitedly. Kes threw me a bemused look but followed Dylan, his large shape shadowing my nephew's much smaller one.

Jennifer put her hands on her hips and shook her head at me.

"Really? You just told the man he used to smell like a horse?!"

"Oh God, just shoot me now!"

Jennifer laughed. "The look on your face—priceless!"

I groaned. "You're making it worse. But he *did* smell like a horse, and it was … nice."

"Whatever you say," Jennifer smiled.

We were interrupted by the doorbell ringing.

"I'll get it," I offered.

"No, that's fine. It'll be for me anyway. You go entertain our guest—or save him from my son, one or the other."

When I walked out to the backyard, Dylan was sitting on his swing set and Kes was pushing him. He looked up when he saw me, his eyes in shadow, so I couldn't tell what he was thinking.

I didn't have a moment to ask him either, because Jennifer hurried out looking flustered, followed by a small crowd of young mothers and their various offspring.

"Kes, I'm so sorry," she said. "It seems Dylan here took it on himself to invite all his friends to a picnic—with you as the star attraction. Dylan, what have you got to say for yourself?"

Dylan's small shoulders slumped. "I thought it would be fun."

Jennifer's eyes softened. "I understand, but you shouldn't have done it without asking me or asking Kes. I haven't got enough food prepared for everyone, and I explained to you that Kes is our lunch guest and wasn't invited here to entertain us. He's come on his day off to have a nice quiet meal, but you've told everyone he'll do a show! You need to apologize to both of us, but especially Kes."

Dylan's eyes filled with tears. "I'm sorry, Mommy. I'm sorry, Kes."

Kes broke a second before I did.

"Don't worry about it, buddy," he said. Then he turned to Jennifer. "I'll put on something for the kids. It's not a problem."

Jennifer still looked uncertain.

"But I'll need a couple of assistants," Kes smirked, looking at me and winking at Dylan.

"Are you sure? It seems such an imposition—I'm just so embarrassed."

"Nah, it's fine. It's what I do."

Jennifer shook her head. "I know, and that's why I feel so bad—you're supposed to be having a day off!"

I could have hugged my sister. She was just being herself, but she was also showing Kes that she valued him as a person and that not all my family thought he was trailer trash.

"I'd be happy to entertain Dylan's friends," Kes said sincerely.

Jennifer looked grateful. "Thank you so much. I really appreciate it."

Kes shrugged, beginning to look embarrassed. "Yeah, well, I'm a bit out of practice … so when do you want to do this? Now or later?"

"Probably best to let the kids run around and wear themselves out a bit first," I suggested. "Then they'll be more likely to sit quietly for you."

Jennifer agreed, then went to explain to the other mothers what was happening.

Kes leaned down to whisper in my ear. "It's sexy seeing you go all teacher-like."

I blushed and gave him a little push. "Shut up," was my witty response.

He laughed throatily.

It turned out that Dylan had invited about eight of his little friends along with their brothers and sisters and moms, so there were 27 of us for Kes's impromptu performance.

The kids ran around shouting and screaming and basically behaving like savages. I was used to that level of noise and mayhem now I was a veteran of grade three and several school trips. But what surprised me was how at ease Kes was with it all. Most guys his age didn't have a whole lot of experience with kids and it made them uncomfortable, but it didn't faze him at all.

He sat next to me on the grass and watched them screaming around the garden, shrieking at the top of their lungs. I pitied my sister's neighbors.

I glanced at Kes. "You haven't made a run for it yet."

He grinned. "Nah, it kind of reminds me of the carnival. Kids would get so excited and I always wondered why. It took a while before I realized that not everybody got to go on the rollercoaster before breakfast every day."

"You mean you don't now?"

He laughed. "It's not so much fun doing it by yourself."

I wondered if there was a message in that, but I wasn't going to ask.

"I bet you and Con went on all the rides when you were kids."

Kes smiled briefly. He didn't often talk about his brother.

"He was never into carnie life as much as I was—always had his nose stuck in a book. Kind of like you."

"What's he doing now?"

"Flying jets in Afghanistan for the Air Force."

My mouth hung open. "You're kidding me? I thought he went to school to be a doctor."

"Yeah, he did. But he couldn't afford med school, so he thought he'd join the Air Force for a few years and get them to foot the bill. But it turns out he's a great pilot, so he's made that his career."

"Wow, from the carnival to the Air Force! That must have been some culture shock."

"He's happy, I guess. I see him when he's stateside."

"Is he married? Kids?"

"No, but there's a German girl, Hilde, that he's been seeing for a few years."

161

I smiled. "Well, I'm happy for him."

"Yeah, he's a good guy. We're closer now, I think."

"Really? Why's that?"

Kes shrugged. "He hated the carnival, pretty much. Too chaotic, too disorganized."

"He's in a warzone! I hear they're pretty big on chaos."

He smiled at me appreciatively, then leaned back on his elbows so he was staring up at the branches of the sprawling oak. The leaves threw a patchwork of light and shade across him, hiding and revealing all at once.

"Remember that hickory tree in your garden? This kind of reminds me of it."

"Of course!" I laughed. "I nearly had a heart attack every time you ran along the branches and jumped in my window!"

Kes's eyes glowed. "That was pretty cool. My first experience of breaking into a girl's bedroom."

"But not your last, I suspect."

His smile dimmed, and I regretted my words.

But then he grinned at me and said, "You used to read all your books up in that old hickory. Do you still climb trees?"

"God, no! I'd probably kill myself. When you're a kid you never realize that falling out of trees might actually hurt. I'd probably break something. I'm amazed that you still have all your limbs attached!"

"Well, I've had a few breaks over the years."

"Really? I always thought you were indestructible."

He laughed lightly. "Not so much. I have a few scars to prove it." Then he lowered his voice. "Maybe I'll show you later."

And there it was again—that quiet tease, the suggestive comment that could mean something, or mean nothing.

So I changed the subject.

"Don't you want something to eat? All the good stuff will be gone once the kids descend like locusts."

Kes shook his head. "No, I don't eat before a show—too many possibilities for losing my lunch in public."

"Oh no! We lure you here with promises of food and you can't even eat anything!"

He smiled. "I usually skip lunch. Don't worry about it."

"I feel really bad now," I said grumpily. "I'd forgotten that you don't eat before a performance. Fine, well, if you can't eat anything, I won't either."

But then my stomach gave a very loud growl and Kes fell back on the grass laughing.

"Your gut is telling me a different story."

"Stupid stomach!" I huffed, half laughing, half embarrassed.

"Aw, no. I love your stomach. It's so soft and round."

The heat in my cheeks flooded my whole body. "Are you calling me fat?"

Kes sat up quickly. "No! I just … ah, shit…"

It seemed he never had acquired the habit of apologizing.

Jennifer interrupted our moment. "Kes, do you need anything for your, um, show?"

"Have you got a bicycle?"

Jen and I both looked surprised. "You want a bike?" she said.

Kes smiled. "I'm assuming you don't want me to use my stunt bike on your lawn—it kind of tears up the turf."

"Well, my ex-husband leaves his mountain bike here. He sometimes goes for rides with Dylan."

"Show me?"

I watched Kes and Jennifer disappear into her garage, so I headed for the picnic food to see what was on offer.

The other moms smiled at me, and a couple that I knew from previous visits came over to chat. They were all intrigued to find out more about Kes, and several of them seemed to assume that he was Jennifer's new boyfriend. God, that was so irritating.

I didn't even know how to describe him, so I simply said that we'd all known each other as kids but had lost touch, which was true enough.

Kes returned a minute later with Brian's BMX. According to Jen, it had been an early mid-life crisis gift to himself, but one that he hardly ever used.

Kes adjusted the seat to accommodate his longer legs, then left it resting against a tree. Then he levered off his boots and socks, and whipped off his t-shirt.

Every set of female eyes was focused on him, and I wasn't the only one who had to reel in my tongue.

The whip-tight body he'd had as a teenager had morphed into something amazing. You could count every muscle of his abdomen, which I did twice, because I lost count the first time.

The V-shaped ridge that disappeared into his low slung jeans was advertised by a line of dark hair pointing down from his navel. Then he stretched his arms above his head, making his muscles dance and ripple. When he rotated his hips, I wasn't the only one having a hot flash.

Obviously these were his warm-up exercises, but honestly it was the closest thing I'd ever come to watching porn.

Jennifer seemed to agree.

"Holy shit!" she whispered. "To think that you've slept with that!"

"Believe me," I hissed out of the corner of my mouth, "he was hot as a teenager, but now…"

I was lost for words, but I think Jen understood because she nodded, following his every movement from behind her sunglasses.

"He moves like a dancer," she sighed. "It's a waste having him covered up in leathers all the time."

I had to agree.

Kes wandered over smiling. He looked happy and relaxed; very different from the tense, angry man I'd met less than a week ago.

"Ready as I'll ever be," he said. "They look like a tough audience."

I laughed. "Tell me about it. Sometimes third grade is more like crowd control than teaching."

"I'll need my assistant for this show," he reminded me with a wink.

He held out his hand, and I could have sworn that I heard Jennifer sigh.

Kes strode to the center of her backyard and yelled out, "Who wants to see some magic!"

"Me!" all the kids screamed loudly.

One by one, he invited the kids to come and have coins and toys and carrot sticks appear out of their ears, out of their pockets, even out of their noses, which was really gross but funny to watch their shocked little faces. Then he did the same with the moms: conjuring up cell phones and wristwatches, and in one case a wedding ring. He winked as he passed it back to the astonished woman.

I had no idea that Kes had those skills, such magic in his hands. I wondered what else I didn't know about him.

Then he sent the kids on a scavenger hunt to find objects that he could juggle with. The kids ran around the yard, presenting him with a soccer ball, a watering can, an empty beer bottle and several other objects. He turned down the wheelbarrow that one of Dylan's friends found, much to Jennifer's relief.

Then he looked at me and grinned. "When I nod, toss me the next thing. Aim for my chest and don't throw too hard," he instructed.

Kes introduced me as his "beautiful assistant, Mademoiselle Aimee," much to Jennifer's amusement.

He started off juggling with a soccer ball and a football, telling jokes the whole time. I watched for his nod, then tossed him the watering can. Soon he was juggling four mismatched items, and then five, then six. The children's mouths were open and their eyes bright with amazement. They all laughed when Kes tossed the watering can to me and I dropped it. Yes, let's all laugh at the clumsy person. I bet they can't breathe fire.

After that, I was officially resigned as Kes's assistant and the kids all took turns at throwing odd for things to him to juggle. He never missed once, even when their throws were nearer his knees than his chest.

By now, Kes was really sweating in the formidable summer sun. But instead of looking disgusting like anyone else would, it made his smooth skin gleam, and I couldn't help following the drops of perspiration as they tracked down his broad chest, disappearing into that loose waistband.

Finally, he grabbed hold of Jen's bicycle and started showing the kids wheelies and various balancing tricks. Of course, it was slower and less sensational than his stunt riding, but I think it connected with the kids better because they all rode bikes themselves. What they couldn't do was somersault off them like Kes, or do handstands on the seat and over the handlebars. It was like watching an Olympic gymnast perform in your backyard. I had no idea he was so flexible—and my mind went straight to the gutter.

I could definitely see why he preferred not to eat before a performance.

He finished with a flourish, cartwheeling off the bike, which brought a round of applause from the adults and whoops and cheers from the kids.

I hoped that none of them tried to copy him at home, or there would be an epidemic of broken bones in the neighborhood.

Then he flopped down on the grass and let the kids jump all over him. I bet some of the moms would have liked to jump all over him, as well.

"Oh my God!" gasped one mom, her hands fanning her face. "Does he do kids' parties?"

"Forget that!" said her friend. "I want him for *my* party!"

I watched him playing with the kids, listening to each of them, making everyone feel special. I realized with a pang, but no sense of shock, that I was in danger of falling for him again. And there was no safety net for love.

There should be, because I'd fallen so far before and I was afraid that my life would fly apart again if I let it, leaving me broken.

I remembered Zachary's words from all those years ago, warning me that loving Kes would never be easy. He'd been so right, and the words were as true today as they were then. But I couldn't stop. Even now, it was too late. I was hurtling head first over the cliff, with no guarantee that Kes would be there to catch me at the end.

I saw him watching me, a slight frown on his face. I had to look away.

After that, the kids started getting sleepy, which meant they were becoming fractious, so the moms carted them off home with thanks to Jennifer, and lots of invitations for Kes to perform for them in future. He declined them all politely, explaining that he'd be touring again soon.

I was disappointed to hear that, but not surprised. That was what he did, that was his life. And seeing him perform today, it was obvious that he loved it.

I cleaned up outside while Jennifer fed Kes, and he seemed happy to inhale whatever was left over. He must have been starving after the performance he put on. I walked over to join them, carrying a coffee for each of us.

Jen had managed to take one sip before Dylan appeared in his pajamas, carrying a storybook.

"I want Kes to read me a bedtime story," he said.

Kes immediately tensed and his expression darkened with shame. I hated that look on his face.

"Maybe Kes could tell you a story instead, about when he lived in the carnival," I said gently. "Did you know he had a pet monkey?"

Dylan's eyes glowed. "I don't know anyone who has a pet monkey! Eric Sutton has two dogs, but that's not as cool as having a monkey!"

Kes's eyes flicked to mine, but I could see that he'd already shut down. Even so, he followed Dylan to his bedroom, and we could hear the soft murmur of voices.

"That was a little awkward," Jennifer said with huge understatement. "Nice save on your part."

I sighed. "I used to do that all the time when we were kids. I just sort of went onto autopilot."

Jennifer stared at me thoughtfully, but whatever she wanted to say was lost, because Kes strode out of the house. I could almost see the swirling black anger that followed him. Jen raised her eyebrows and muttered, "I'll leave you two alone."

Kes paced up and down in the backyard, his expression fierce, his eyes stormy.

"How fucking pathetic," he sneered. "The kid is five years old! Five fucking years old and he reads better than I do. I can't even read a fucking kiddy book!"

I left him to pace, hoping that letting the rage pour out of him would help, but instead it seemed to stoke the fires.

"Kes, it's fine," I said at last. "Dylan had a wonderful, magical day. You made that happen."

"I couldn't read him a fucking story! What part of that do you not understand!" he roared.

"Don't shout at me!"

His eyes tightened, but at least he stopped ranting.

"You can learn," I said quietly. "You're smart ... no, listen to me," I insisted as he began to interrupt. "You've just never had the chance, never given yourself the chance. I can teach you."

"Like you teach your third graders," he sneered.

"Yes, like that."

He scowled at me.

"Kes," I sighed, "what you did today, what you do with the stunt bikes, only a few people in the world can do that. Yes, you have problems reading, but I can give you techniques to overcome it."

He growled, a low, feral sound.

"Did you learn how to patronize when you became a teacher, or does it come naturally?"

I looked at him sadly. "Thank you for a lovely time, Kes. You really made Dylan's day. Drive safely."

I brushed past him, but he gripped my arm tightly.

"Is that it?"

"I'm not in the mood to be your emotional punching bag, oddly enough."

He released my arm, and his hand dropped to his side.

"Sorcha does all my contracts," he said quietly.

"What?" I asked, confused by the left-turn in the conversation.

"I can't read my contracts," he confessed. "I've no idea what's in them. Sorcha tells me, but…"

He didn't finish the sentence, and I stared at him, deciding if I wanted to take the bait. Who was I kidding? I'd never been able to say no to Kes.

"Are you asking me to go through your contracts with you?"

He nodded jerkily, refusing to meet my eyes. I knew how much he hated asking for help, so I didn't push him.

I sighed. "Okay, I'll take a look."

Kes was silent.

I watched him a little longer, hoping he might actually thank me, but of course he didn't.

"Does Sorcha know that you're here with me today?"

Kes's eyes glittered with vindictive delight. "Oh yeah, she knows. I made sure of that."

My heart wilted at the glee I saw on his face. This wasn't about Kes wanting to see or wanting to be with me after all. Instead, it was just a giant *screw you* to his ex-girlfriend, ex-manager, ex-whatever. But I wouldn't retract my offer to help him. It just about killed Kes to admit he needed help at all. I wouldn't make him beg.

You don't do that to people you love, do you?

And that was the truth: I'd never stopped loving him, but I was beginning to wish that I could.

CHAPTER 11
FORWARD ROLL

Kes left shortly after, but the mood was still subdued even though he'd gone.

"That looked like a painful conversation," Jennifer said.

"Yes, you could say that."

"So what are you going to do?"

I shrugged. "Help him with his contracts."

"That's not what I mean," she said. "What are you going to do about you and Kes?"

"There is no me and Kes. There's me, and there's Kes and Sorcha. It sounds like they have a pretty complicated relationship. I'm not sure I want to get in the middle of that."

"You can lie to yourself all you want," Jennifer said quietly. "But it's obvious that what you two had is still very much alive. I don't think it's as one-sided as you make out. And let's face it, Sorcha lied and cheated to get him. I'm sensing that Kes isn't a very forgiving person."

"Exactly why I don't want to get between them. If he decides to leave her, then it has to be because it's the right thing to do for him, not because he and I … because … ah, hell, I don't know, Jen. I don't know what I'm doing. I feel like I ought to just text him and say thanks for today and that I'm heading back to Boston."

"Is that what you want to do?" she asked.

"No, but it would be the sensible thing."

"I agree, but what's sensible about love?"

I didn't even try to argue with that.

I thought back to my four years with Gregg and realized that the whole relationship had been a Band-Aid to my broken heart. I felt slightly guilty that I'd used him to try and be normal, but

169

the way things had finished between us, I was finding it pretty damn hard.

I didn't text Kes that night, and I didn't hear from him either. I wondered if once he went home to Sorcha's loving arms that he'd change his mind about wanting me to help him.

I was wrong about that, too.

When I woke up the next day, there was a text from Kes.

* Contacts today? *

I assumed he meant 'contracts', so I simply texted back,

* Where? When? *

While I was brushing my teeth, he replied.

* Hear 4 *

"Yes, sir," I said, snapping a sarcastic salute to the mirror.

Well, if I was jumping whenever he called, it was my own damn fault.

Jennifer restrained herself from saying anything, which I thought was valiant of her. If the positions had been reversed, I would have told her she was making a huge mistake.

But somehow, it still felt like he was 'my Kes', and I'd help him if I could.

I borrowed Jennifer's car and arrived at the fair on time. But then it took me an age to find a parking spot and work my way through the crowds.

When I finally knocked on Kes's door, I was 20 minutes late. He wrenched the door open and scowled at me.

"Where have you been?"

I was hot and sweaty and very pissed off.

"Fighting my way to a parking spot, fighting my way through the crowds, because I couldn't wait for such a warm and gentle greeting!"

A surprised look flashed across his face and then he grinned at me, which made his dimple pop.

Darn it, why did he have to go and bring out the big guns when I was still annoyed with him?

"You look hot," he said.

I raised my eyebrow, and he winked at me. "You want a beer or a soda or something? I think there are some in the fridge."

"Just ice water, please."

He stood back and let me inside. The place looked as if it had been ransacked. Drawers had been upended, doors were hanging open, and a huge pile of paper had been heaped onto the fold-down table.

"Oh my God! What happened?"

Kes shrugged. "I was looking for contracts."

"Of course you were."

I cast a jaundiced eye over the mess and dumped my bag on the floor. I needn't have bothered wearing something cute—Kes only wanted me for my brains, not my body. How very disappointing.

"I've got another show at 6PM," Kes said, his expression relieved now he'd dumped all the work on me. "Do you think you'll be finished by then?"

I stared at him in disbelief. "Um, no! Have you seen how much paper there is here? Let alone what Sorcha might have stored on the laptop."

His face fell, and it was obvious that he hadn't thought of that.

"Do you know the password?"

Kes gave a small smile. "Kestrel."

Of course—the woman was more obsessed than me.

"I'll just have to hope she's organized," I said at last.

Kes strolled into the kitchen to get me a glass of water, and watched for ten minutes as I stacked paper together. Then he started twitching and looking impatient.

"Okay, we need some ground rules here," I said. "First, I'm doing you a favor, mister, and don't you forget it. Second, I'm not an accountant, so I'll do my best, but I suspect you'll need professional help once I've got it in some sort of order. Third, stop staring at me, you're freaking me out!"

He laughed and held out his hands.

"Fine, go ahead. No staring."

I frowned, but he just grinned at me.

"You're still staring."

He winked, completely unabashed.

"What do you normally do when you've got some downtime?" I asked.

"Play on the X-Box with Tucker or Zef, work out, go for a run, or if Sorcha's around, we fu—"

He stopped suddenly and I cringed. "By the love of all that's holy, please don't finish that sentence."

He had the grace to look abashed, but only slightly.

"Fine, go for a run, or go do your workout. I'll be here for hours … possibly days," I mumbled to myself.

In the end, he opted for a run, and I got stuck into the paperwork, resentful that I was spending my vacation like this. Balancing my checking account and trying to ignore my credit card statement was usually as financially minded as I got.

The first thing I did was to make sure that I had every piece of paper in front of me. I checked all the drawers and cabinets, and even had a quick look in the bedrooms. I could tell which rooms belonged to Zef and Tucker, or the twin pits of depravity as I would call them from now on. Kes's room was much more tidy, and I knew it was his because the shirt that he'd been wearing at Dylan's impromptu party was lying on the end of his bed.

I couldn't find any more documents, so I stacked everything together and began to go through it piece by piece.

I laid out four piles in front of me: anything to do with money including bills, credit card receipts, invoices and bank statements; anything to do with public appearances and contracts; fan mail (of which there was a ton, and nobody seemed to have done anything about it); and miscellaneous.

Looking at his private documents left me with an uneasy feeling—even more so when his bank statements told me that Kes was loaded.

But then I found something that really made me sit up. After some hesitation, I placed the piece of paper on the miscellaneous pile. It was a certificate from Guinness World Records saying that Kes's motorcycle stunt in Sydney was the longest jump *ever* in its category. I'd read about the record in the 'Hawkins' Daredevil's program before I knew that was Kes, but seeing the certificate made it real. I wondered what else I was going to find.

Now I knew the name he went by, I decided to Google him. But getting into his laptop wasn't straightforward. I tried 'Kestrel', 'Kes', 'Kestrel Hawkins' and even 'Kestrel Donohue' without any luck. Frustrated, I wracked my brain, and finally tried 'K35tr3l'. Bingo! It occurred to me that the combination of alphas and numerics, while more difficult to hack, would make it really tricky for Kes. Or maybe I was being paranoid.

Then I decided that being paranoid didn't mean everyone, Sorcha, wasn't out to get him. She'd lied to him once; who was to say she would do it again? I changed his password to 'Mr. Alb3rt'.

When I saw that Kes's name brought up over 500,000 Google hits, I began to realize how far his fame had spread.

A warm feeling filled me: despite his problems, and his very apparent learning disability, Kes had done really well for himself. He'd always shone so brightly, and now he was a star. I was proud of him, if that wasn't too patronizing. I scowled at the thought; he'd accused me of that last night. I was slightly afraid he was right.

While I was online, I tracked down the names of four Financial Advisory firms who were used to dealing with performers, spoke to three of them, and made an appointment for Kes with one that had offices on the west coast as well as in Minnesota. Looking through the pile of papers, it was obvious that he needed more help than I could give him.

But I had an uneasy feeling, too. The money in Kes's bank account, while substantial, didn't seem to be as much as it should be, given his intense touring schedule. And it was also hard to see which offers had been accepted and which had been turned down, and the reasons for that. I needed to talk to Kes.

He came in from his run, hot and sweaty and very distracting. I thought I should get a medal when I managed to focus on my work, and not his glistening body.

"How's it going?" he asked.

"Hmm."

"Is that a good *hmm*, or a bad *hmm*?"

"Not sure yet."

He smiled and leaned down to squeeze my shoulders. "Okay. I'll go get ready for the show."

I nodded, still slightly distracted by the spicy scent coming from his body, but managed to keep my mind on the paperwork. Just about.

But when Tucker and Zef strolled into the trailer, the atmosphere cooled by several degrees.

"Hello again, sweet cheeks," Tucker said, his eyes flicking to the piles of paper. "What are you doing?"

"Riding a unicycle," I replied.

"Huh?"

I looked up at him, irritated. "What does it look like I'm doing?"

"It looks like you're sticking your nose where it doesn't belong," Zef said, his voice threatening.

Kes came out of his bedroom, his face serious.

"Back off, Zef. I asked Aimee to come here."

Zef and Tucker exchanged a look, but immediately stepped back, eventually going into their rooms to prepare for the show.

I'd really liked to have gone and watched them—the show, I mean, not watch them getting changed, although I'd make an exception in Kes's case—in fact, I'd rather do anything than be stuck in a trailer with a scavenger hunt in paper.

An hour later, the three of them trooped back, trailing clouds of testosterone and all in better moods.

"I take it the show went well?" I asked, stretching my aching back.

"As always," Tucker said with a wink. "And I have a couple of phone numbers of ladies who might get lucky tonight."

"What? Get lucky when you *don't* call them?" I said.

Tucker just laughed, taking my bitchy comment in good humor, which kind of surprised me.

"Oh sweet cheeks, no woman has ever been left unsatisfied by me. I can prove it if you want."

Kes frowned. "Aimee's off limits."

Tucker grinned at him. "You don't say? Wow, I'd never have guessed that. Why don't you just piss on her to mark your territory?"

"Yuk! That is totally disgusting. There'll be no pissing on anyone!" I yelped.

Kes gave Tucker a push, and then there was a lot of macho posturing which meant thumping into furniture.

Zef watched them tolerantly. "Careful, kids. The teacher will give you detention if you're not careful."

Tucker winked at me. "She can give me detention anytime she likes."

At which point, Kes got him in a headlock and ran him into a kitchen cabinet.

"Cut that out, Kestrel!" he whimpered. "I was just messing with her."

"Off. Limits!" Kes growled.

"Sheesh, you used to be fun," Tucker complained, rubbing his head.

Kes ignored him. "Aimee, have you finished with this?" and he swept his arm over the piles of papers.

"Yes and no. I haven't finished, but I do need to talk to you about it."

He sighed, and I could see that he didn't relish the fact. "Okay, you want me to call for takeout?"

"Sure, anything except sushi."

"Pizza okay?"

I should have guessed. "Yes, pizza's fine."

Kes looked at the guys. "You in or out?"

"Out," they both said.

Then there was a line for the shower and the rather heady smell of three sweaty sets of leathers dumped in the living room. I tried to ignore it, but in the end I ordered them to clean up. They took it pretty well. Perhaps they were used to Sorcha ordering them around. The thought was not a pleasant one.

Kes was last in the shower because the guys were eager to get going, heading out to score—according to them—and weren't planning on getting in till late, if at all, which meant Kes and I would be alone.

I was looking forward to that, but really I wasn't in the best frame of mind. My head ached from staring at paper all afternoon.

But when Kes strolled barefoot into the living room, wearing only a pair of jeans, my headache was miraculously forgotten.

"Well, what do you think?" he asked.

Now *there* was a loaded question.

"You mean about all of this?" I said, waving my hand at the neat stacks of paper.

Kes smirked at me. "Unless you want to discuss anything else?"

"Oh, Mr. Hawkins, or is it Mr. Donohue? If you're giving me carte blanche to ask questions, we could be here all night."

"Suits me," he said slyly.

I looked down. "Don't tease," I said quietly. "It's not fair."

Kes didn't answer. I sat staring at my hands, at the papers, at the floor—at anything, except him.

"What if I'm not teasing?" he said at last.

"You have a girlfriend…" I began.

"No, I don't," he replied firmly.

"Fine. Friend-with-benefits, or manager-with-benefits. Whatever you want to call it, you have Sorcha."

He sighed. "It's not like that with her."

"I think it is."

"We were never exclusive. We both saw other people. It was just … easy."

He was quiet then, and the awkward silence was only interrupted by the pizza delivery guy knocking on the door.

Kes answered the door and handed the man some folded bills, muttering at him to keep the change.

I opened the box and took a slice. I'd lost my appetite along with the conversation, but my stomach insisted on being fed, and it grumbled and griped until I ate something.

"Do you want a drink?" Kes asked, breaking the stillness.

"Do you have any wine?"

One glass wouldn't hurt before I drove back to Jennifer's.

"No, I've got beer or juice."

I sighed. I wasn't much of a beer drinker, but it would do.

"Sure, I'll have a beer," I replied. "Um, I've made you an appointment with an accountant tomorrow…"

He turned to look at me, his face blank.

"You don't have to—I can cancel it…"

He was frowning as he answered. "No. I'll talk to them."

Then he walked to the fridge and flipped the cap off a bottle of beer before handing it to me. It was a small gesture, but one that I appreciated. Gregg wouldn't have noticed if I'd opened it with my teeth while dancing a cancan, if there was pizza on the table.

"Thanks," I said quietly.

Then I noticed that Kes was drinking water.

"You not having a beer? I thought you'd be kicking back after a show."

He gave me a small smile. "No, I don't drink."

"Really? Not at all?"

He shook his head.

"Why not?"

"It's a long story."

I huffed in frustration. "That's all you ever say: *it's a long story*. I've been hearing that since I was ten."

He frowned, but didn't answer.

Sighing with frustration, I took a sip of beer and ate some more pizza.

Then he said, "Our mom used to drink. Like, a lot."

I froze with a slice of pizza halfway to my mouth. I glanced up to look at Kes who was watching me seriously. I replaced the pizza back in the box and wiped my hands.

"I didn't know that."

He shrugged. "I don't tell people. It's ancient history, but that's the reason."

"Okay," I said slowly. "Thank you for telling me."

He nodded and looked away.

A tiny piece of the puzzle that was Kes slotted into place. But there was a reason I'd gone into teaching: I was greedy for information, to learn, to understand, and now I wanted to know more.

"I won't tell anyone," I said at last.

"I know."

He stood up, his eyes fixed on mine. Without giving me time to react, he leaned down and brushed his lips over mine.

Then he kissed me again, more firmly, his hand cupping the back of my head so I couldn't move away.

Bad, bad idea, I told myself as my lips began to respond.

Then I gripped his arms, pulling him down to me as all the old feelings swirled around. The lust, the passion, the amazing chemistry was all still there. But this time I was kissing a man, not a boy.

I felt the scratch of his scruff against my chin, and the hard muscles of his arms as I held on tightly. The weight of his body pushed me back on the sofa until he was almost lying on top of me.

"Kes…" I began, my voice hoarse and breathless.

"No talking," he said, his voice a soft growl.

Then he scooped me into his arms, surprising me with the swiftness of his movement, and then we were heading to his bedroom.

I really wasn't that sort of girl; I really, really wasn't. I didn't keep condoms in my purse; I didn't sleep with guys on the first date, or even the second, or the third. I didn't allow myself to get swept up in emotion—because emotions were messy and difficult, and the last time I'd let that happen, I'd been prepared to run away in a snowy winter with a boy who didn't even have enough money to buy gas to get us to the next town. Definitely not.

But Kes wasn't just any guy—he never had been. He was *my Kes.*

For once, I told my mind to take a vacation and let my body dictate the terms. My body said, *Yes, we're doing this.*

He dropped me down on the bed and started crowding me immediately, his kisses determined and insistent, his hands squeezing my breasts, my hips, my ass too hard.

"Kes, you're hurting me," I cried out.

He stopped and rolled onto this back, panting.

"You used to be gentle," I said, tears forming.

He leaned up on one elbow and stared at me.

"I remember," he said softly. "I remember, Aimee."

Then he trailed a finger down across my cheek and kissed my shoulder, his lips caressing my skin.

He looked up again, his silvery eyes locked on mine. I felt as if he was asking permission to continue, so I nodded quickly, and he smiled.

This time, he lay on his back, pulling me into his arms, letting me control the movements. My knees rested on either side of his hips and my hands were planted on his firm chest.

He ran a warm hand up my thigh, stroking the flesh lightly.

"Cute skirt," he said, as his fingers inched upward.

"So you did notice?"

He laughed gently. "Hell, yeah! It was all I could do not to leap on you when I saw you standing at my door."

I shook my head at him. "You're very confusing—I thought you weren't interested."

"I'm interested," he said seriously.

And to show that he meant the words, his hands moved under my skirt to cup my ass.

"I've always been interested in you, Aimee."

I leaned down to kiss him, and he opened his mouth, his tongue making lazy thrusts that moved with the rocking of his hips beneath me.

I could feel that he was aroused, and a bolt of pleasure shot through me. I moaned softly, and he took this as encouragement to pull my tank top over my head, and crane his neck upward to kiss and nuzzle my breasts.

When he reached behind me to release my bra, I didn't even try to resist him. I *wanted* his hands on me. I *wanted* to lie with him skin to skin. I wanted every part of him, the way it used to be, but more than that, too.

I pushed on his shoulders so he lay flat, then crawled down his body, kissing his cheeks and his chin, his neck and the solid curve of his shoulder. I swirled my tongue in the soft dip at the base of his throat and licked a salty line down his firm chest, pausing to tease and tug at his nipples.

"That feels good," he sighed.

When I reached his stomach, I felt the hard muscles tremble under my touch, and when I dipped my tongue into his bellybutton, his hips jerked upward.

"Fuck, Aimee! You're killing me!"

But his touch was still gentle as he rubbed his hands down my bare back, his fingers drifting to the waistband of my skirt and upward again.

"This feels familiar," I smiled, "but different, you know?"

"Yeah," he agreed happily. "It was always different with you."

I took his words at face value, not wanting to analyze them too closely.

When I reached the button on his jeans, his hips rocked upward again, and I could feel the solid warmth underneath me.

Carefully, I pulled down his zipper to find that he'd been going commando all this time.

I nearly melted.

His cock was hot to my touch, the silky skin stretched tightly over the length.

He sighed as my hands stroked up and down, and his eyelids fluttered.

I watched his face as my mouth closed over his tip, and he breathed in deeply through his nose, the nostrils flaring.

He arched up again, then gently cupped the back of my head to encourage me to go further.

"Shit, that's good," he said rolling his hips.

I was briefly reminded of some of the warm-up exercises that he'd done at Jennifer's, when he'd rotated his hips to loosen his muscles.

I moved back from him quickly, watching him blink as I shimmied out of my skirt and panties.

His pupils dilated and he licked his lips, a small, pleased smile curving his lips. Then he reached into his bedside drawer and pulled out a condom.

He shucked his jeans quickly and rolled the condom down his straining shaft, a small frown of concentration creasing his forehead.

He lay back and smiled up at me, his expression warm, almost loving. I crawled back over him, but then he pulled my hips toward his face, clearly planning on returning my oral favors.

I resisted and he looked up at me.

"I'm not … not ready for that," I said, a blush of embarrassment making me want to hide.

"Whatever you want, Aimee," he said, his voice soft, dreamy, as he kissed my breasts instead.

His tongue played in the valley of my cleavage and his fingers danced around my nipples, then trailed over my shoulders.

When his left hand stroked my thigh, I opened up for him, allowing him to skim a gentle finger over my clit.

I moaned softly and his strokes became firmer and more precise.

We'd had so little time when we were teenagers, but every touch was something he seemed to have memorized. Or maybe it was like riding a bike. The thought made me giggle, and he smiled up at me.

"Did I find a ticklish spot?"

"Sort of!" I gasped.

I was so close to coming that I could have smacked the smile off of his face when he moved his hand away.

"I want to feel you come on my cock," he whispered. "Play nice."

He grasped himself with one hand, angling his cock away from his body, and I lowered myself down.

Tears came to my eyes, but it wasn't from pain; it was from a pleasure so complete that it didn't seem possible. Memories, so many memories, smiles and laughter, talk of love, tears, so many tears, and the years and years of being apart. It was almost too much.

My body began to respond quickly and Kes swore under his breath.

I climaxed fast, so fast that I felt like I couldn't breathe.

Gasping for breath, I fell onto his chest.

Kes rolled quickly so I was pinned beneath him, barely aware that we'd moved. He rolled his hips, and I groaned so loudly, I'm sure people outside could have heard me.

And then he proceeded to expertly pound me into the wall of his bedroom with hard, certain strokes, the muscles of his back and ass flexing in a pattern that built and built, rendering me liquid and useless beneath him.

With a final surge of speed, he thrust into me hard, ruthlessly chasing his own release with an intensity that was animalistic.

When he came, his neck tensed and his teeth were tightly clenched, but his silvery-gray eyes were fixed on mine, open and unclouded, for once hiding nothing. And I saw wonder, desire, pleasure, and I saw love. I was sure I saw love.

Then he took a breath, but instead of collapsing onto me, he rolled to the side so I wasn't crushed by 200 pounds of solid muscle.

I dropped a soft kiss onto his chest and was about to tell him how amazing it was, and how unexpected to have two orgasms in the same evening, when his bedroom door burst open, and a furious Sorcha tried to burn me into atoms with her raging eyes.

I squealed and hurried to cover myself.

"You've made your point, Kestrel," she sneered. "We'll talk when you've gotten rid of your little friend."

I thought he'd say something to defend me. I expected it, waited for it, but instead he laughed—a lazy, pleased expression on his face.

Sorcha slammed the door shut, and a cold fear speared icy fingers through my blood.

"Did you know she'd come here and find us like this?" I asked, desperate for him to tell me it was a ridiculous idea.

When Kes didn't reply, that was answer enough.

I leapt out of bed and began to dress hurriedly.

"I can't believe you'd use me like this. I'm so stupid!"

My words were gasped and quiet.

Kes just rolled his eyes.

"Jesus, Aimee. We're not kids. Everyone uses everyone!"

I turned to stare at him, hurt almost beyond words.

"If you really believe that, then I feel sorry for you. Goodbye, Kes."

And I left.

CHAPTER 12
STANDING ON THE EDGE

I had to pull over after I'd driven a short way. I was crying too hard to be safe.

When I finally managed to pull myself together, or at least enough to steer the car without going off the road, I was left with a list of unanswered questions and an ache in my soul. How had I misread him so badly? He'd been so sweet with Dylan, so cruel with me. I thought we'd made progress, I thought we'd stopped blaming each other for all the hurt when we were teenagers. Apparently not.

Turning into Jennifer's driveway, I was relieved that she hadn't waited up, although she'd left the porch light on. It felt like the lamp from a lighthouse: *Land ho! Watch out for the rocks!*

Alone in the guestroom, I pulled open the curtains and watched the stars. After Kes had left the last time, I'd spent hours staring at the night sky, finding relief in the thought that he was somewhere, looking up, like me.

With a soft swish, I yanked the curtains together and undressed in darkness.

Sleep was slow and reluctant, and anger and hurt gnawed away at me.

The next morning, I pleaded a headache. Jennifer saw my blotchy face and whispered, "Talk later?"

I nodded and gave her a watery smile.

When I finally managed to drag myself out of bed, I was surprised to see that I had a missed call from Kes. He hadn't left a voice message, but he had sent a text.

* Call me *

I laughed incredulously. Really? And then I realized that I'd changed his laptop's password but hadn't told him what it was.

Well, he was the smart one who didn't need help from anybody—let him figure it out.

I puttered around and had a long, leisurely bath, something that was a luxury in a house where a small child constantly wanted you to play with him. I was thinking about taking a walk into town to meet Jennifer and Dylan for an ice cream at the local Dairy Queen when I heard the sound of a motorcycle engine.

My stomach clenched, although whether it was from fear or anticipation, I couldn't tell. They seemed to be the same thing around a certain carnival stuntman.

When I opened the door, Kes was striding up the driveway, his face dark and furious. I folded my arms across my body and lifted my chin, refusing to be cowed.

"You didn't answer your phone," he snapped. "I sent you a text!"

I looked at him as calmly as possible, drawing on my two years' experience from quelling eight-year olds, praying it would work on Kes, and enunciated clearly.

"That is because I did not want to talk to you."

He frowned, seeming surprised by my answer. Good grief! Was he really that dense?

"So, you just fucked me and left?" he growled, his eyes narrowing.

My jaw dropped. Yep, he really was that dense.

"Let me see," I said, checking off points on my fingers, as my voice rose with anger. "You had me doing your paperwork all afternoon; then you screwed me in your bedroom; you *planned* that your girlfriend would find us, just to make a point; *then* you tell me that you were using me—no harm no foul. Does that sum it up for you?"

"You said you didn't mind taking a look at the paperwork."

"Oh my God!" I screamed. "You wanted your girlfriend to catch us fucking so you could have some sort of revenge on her! What is wrong with you?!"

His furious expression cleared a little and he leaned toward me. "She's not my girlfriend. I told you that."

I glared at him. "You *used* me! You *hurt* me!"

He shook his head impatiently. "You've got it all wrong!"

I snorted in disbelief. "Unbelievable! Just unbelievable!" Tiresome tears started to fight their way through my anger. "Just go, Kes," I said wearily.

I tried to close the door, but he blocked it with his boot.

"Aimee…" he seemed at a loss for words, but at least he didn't look angry anymore.

He scratched his eyebrow with his thumb, his eyes crinkling with frustration.

"Can we talk … or something?"

"No, I don't think we can talk … or anything else."

I tried to close the door again, but he pushed it further open.

I gave up, stomping into the kitchen and leaving Kes by the door. I heard it close, and then his boots thudded through the hallway.

Finding it hard to be in the same room with him, powerfully attracted to a man who, by his own acknowledgment, had used me, I walked into the backyard, afraid I couldn't trust myself to stay strong.

I sat on the deck and stared out at the bur oak. The sky was white with heat today and the leaves looked black against the searing light.

Kes sat down next to me, close enough that I could smell a faint scent of soap, but far enough away so that no part of us was touching.

"Why are you here, Kes?"

"You changed the password."

I gave a small, hollow laugh. "Couldn't you figure it out?"

"Yeah, I did. Eventually. But Sorcha couldn't—she was pretty mad."

I couldn't help turning my head to look at him; he was smiling, his expression smug.

"I bet she was," I said tiredly.

"She threw the laptop at my head."

"Good."

"I ducked."

"Pity."

He laughed, but it was a bloodless, anemic laugh.

Then he sat quietly, but his restless fingers drummed against the wooden boards until I felt like screaming.

"Aimee, I meant it when I said that you'd got it wrong. I did want Sorcha to see us, but not for the reason that you think. If

184

she'd told me eight years ago that she'd talked to you, I wouldn't have given up and I'd have come back for you. I'd never have been with her in the first place. That's why I wanted her to see us—I wanted her to know that she hadn't won."

I stared at my feet. The coral pink polish made my toes look like small seashells in the grass.

"It's not a war, Kes," I argued, even more confused after the explanation he'd just given. "You could have just told Sorcha. You still used me, and that really hurts."

He sighed with frustration. "When we fucked, that wasn't me using you. It didn't feel like that, did it?" he asked, a small note of uncertainty creeping into his tone.

"No," I replied honestly. "And that's the problem. I trusted you, but it wasn't warranted."

His boot kicked at a dandelion.

"You don't trust me?"

I shrugged. "I don't know you. Not anymore."

"You do. You know me better than anyone."

I shook my head. "You've been with Sorcha for … I don't even know how long … but a lot longer than we ever had."

He was quiet for a moment. "I told you about … not being able to read … the second time I ever saw you. It took her *two years* to figure it out."

"Is that supposed to make me feel better?"

"Yes!" he snapped. "You know things about me that she'll never know."

"Kes, oddly enough, it doesn't reassure me that you spent all these years with Sorcha and never let her in. You're supposed to trust people when you have a relationship with them."

I was echoing Jennifer's words, but then my mind flew to Gregg, and I lost the thread of what I was saying. It probably didn't matter anyway.

"She thought I changed my name to Hawkins to sound more theatrical." Kes's laugh was hollow.

I bit back a sigh. He never addressed anything directly—I had to keep up with the quick leaps his mind made, if I wanted to understand this bewildering man.

"She liked it," he continued. "She said it was easier to market. She liked the whole 'bird of prey' theme," he grimaced.

I listened earnestly, my body bending toward his, even as I tried to fight it. As if to acknowledge my closeness, Kes's voice dropped to a whisper.

"Hawkins is my father's name."

I glanced up in time to see a muscle tic in his jaw.

"You've never mentioned your father before."

Kes looked down. "When Dono died … it was sudden. One moment we were talking about the Spring circuit and the next second he was dead. If Bev—Madame Cindy—hadn't been there, I'd have fallen apart. She took care of … of the police and the paramedics and everything. Con was in Germany, and it took him three days to get home. Bev even arranged the funeral. It was really something—carnies came from England, Ireland and all over the world to give Dono a good send-off."

He smiled sadly at the memory.

"But I was a 17 year-old kid, and they wanted to send me to a foster home until they could contact my dad. Bev would have taken me, but they said she wasn't a suitable candidate with her 'itinerant lifestyle', for fuck's sake. Con tried, too, and if we'd had more time, he'd have been able to swing it for me to go to Germany with him, but because he was in the Air Force, he had to go through the proper channels, and that takes time."

I held my breath as the story unfolded.

"When they got hold of my father, it was too *inconvenient* for him to take me. Having a carnie for a son was … he tried to throw money at the problem…" and at the word 'problem' Kes scowled. "He said if I went into care until I was 18, he'd help me when I got out. Fuck that! I decided to leave. So I joined the first carnival that would take me, but that wasn't good enough for dear ole Dad. He didn't care about me, but he cared what people thought about him, about doing 'the right thing'—or his version of it. So he sent his people to bring me back. It wasn't hard to track me down, because I was doing the same act, and using the name 'Donohue'.

"I spent one night in a group home, and I broke out. I knew I couldn't use my real name after that, so I went by 'Smith' for a year. I hooked up with a guy who needed some cheap labor to maintain his stunt bikes, and I fit the bill."

"Wow," I said softly.

"Yeah," Kes said, his face grim. "When I turned 18, I started using Dad's surname just to piss him off. He hates that he has a son who works in a carnival. He likes Con okay, being a pilot and a hero, but me … I'm an embarrassment."

I could hear a faint edge of bitterness in his voice.

"Why is he so bothered about what you do?" I asked, puzzled. "Why does he even care? He's had nothing to do with you all these years?"

Kes glanced at me then sighed. "He's in politics, so he has to look good in public."

My eyes grew wide. "Oh!"

"Yeah."

We stared at each other for a long, long moment. The air around us seemed to warp and shiver as if time stood still, but didn't like being locked up tightly.

Kes glanced away first.

"I make mistakes and I move on. That's what I do, that's what I've always done. I leave, and other people leave. You're the first person in my whole life who stayed. And then you were taken away. But now you're here again … and you're trying to leave me. That fucking hurts, too."

I'd rarely heard such raw emotion in his voice. I don't think I'd ever heard him admit to feeling pain before. But it was exhausting being ripped apart just so that he'd reveal a tiny piece of himself.

"Thank you for telling me all of that," I said. "It helps me understand so much better. But it's still not right to use people—Sorcha. You couldn't even apologize to me and…"

He sprang to his feet, his face twisted in an ugly snarl.

"I won't apologize!" he shouted. "You'll *never* hear me say sorry because it doesn't mean anything! I learned that from my mom. She was always sorry: sorry for forgetting to feed us, sorry for leaving us alone for a whole weekend, sorry for getting knocked up in the first place, sorry we'd ever been born. So if that's what you're waiting to hear, you'll wait a long fucking time!"

And then he stamped through the house and was on his bike before I caught up with him.

The engine was already growling when I tightened my arms around him.

"Kes," I said softly. "Kes."

He leaned his head against my shoulder, his breath ragged and unsteady.

"Come inside," I said soothingly, and held out my hand.

After a moment, he nodded brusquely and dismounted in

one graceful, fluid movement. I took his hand, feeling the tremor in his fingers as I touched him.

He followed me without further argument. Maybe he felt as drained as I did. My brain was still processing everything that he'd told me, and a good chunk of it I needed to file away to examine later.

But right now, this closed-off, complex man had opened himself to me. I felt deeply inadequate, having no clue what to do other than hold him.

"I never stopped loving you, Kes," I said quietly. "But when I couldn't find you, I had to let you go. Having you in my life again, it's magical."

He smiled softly. "Magical?"

"Yes," I laughed quietly. "A little bit of fairy dust, just like Ollo used to say. I always suspected that the carnival was a magical place and, well, here you are. Please … just don't do anything like that to me again. Okay?"

Kes looked down. "Ollo said that?"

"Oh yes, he was very wise," I smiled.

"Yeah, he's a good guy." Kes sat up straighter, a questioning looking on his face. "I'm going to be catching up with Ollo soon."

"Really?"

"Yeah, and Zachary. You remember him?"

"Oh gosh, yes!"

"They helped me after … you know. They're still doing the circuit, and I always book a few shows with their outfit during the summer." He frowned. "And I'm supposed to be leaving at the end of the week."

I sighed. "We always seem to be on a timetable, don't we?"

"Not necessarily," he said, his expression clearing. "Come with me."

I stared at him, not sure I'd heard him right.

"Come with me, Aimee. Do the circuit for this summer."

"That's crazy!"

"Why?"

"I can't!"

"Why not? You said you had nothing else to do. Look at you—you were so bored, you're doing my freakin' paperwork for fun."

"You bastard!" I yelled as he grinned at me. "That was to

help you out. I hated every second of it!"

"Come with me," he said persuasively, leaning across and brushing his lips over my neck. "Come with me—we'll travel together. See everything, just like you've always dreamed. Together."

So, so tempting.

"What about Tucker and Zef?"

"What about them?"

"Well, what would they think about this idea? The RV is their home, too."

"They'll be cool," said Kes. "Anyway, they'll be driving the rig, so you won't see that much of them."

I wasn't so sure. But even with the thought of the two clowns being around, I was tempted.

"You're crazy," I said again, my voice weak and unconvincing.

Kes laughed lightly.

"Aimee, I jump a motorcycle off high ramps for a living. Of course I'm crazy."

"I'm not sure this is right," I said hesitantly.

"It's right for us," he whispered, as he covered my throat with warm, heavy kisses.

I pushed him off and stood up.

"I can't think when you're doing that."

He leaned back on his elbows and grinned at me.

"If you can think when I'm doing that, I'm not doing it right."

I couldn't help smiling at his logic.

"Come on," he said, "just for the summer."

I frowned, a little piece of ice piercing my heart at his words. That's all we'd ever had, a few weeks in the summer. Would it be the same thing all over again, risking my heart again?

Kes's smile faded and he looked down.

"I don't even know how it would work," I whispered. "Sorcha would be there and…"

He shook his head quickly. "No, I'm done with her. I met with that accountant you contacted. He's not sure if she's been skimming for years or she's just shit at being a manager. Either way, my contract with her is worthless. She won't be doing the circuit."

He looked at me challengingly.

"Any more reasons you can think of why you shouldn't do this?"

I laughed disbelievingly. "Yes, only about a hundred!"

Kes pulled a face. "Such as?"

"What would I do? Where would I sleep? How would I...?"

"What do you mean, where would you sleep? You'd be with me. I'm not asking you to come and read me bedtime stories."

"Oh, that's clear then," I said flatly. "I'd be your new fuck-buddy for the summer. Glad we got that cleared up."

"You drive me nuts, Aimee!" he yelled. "Of course I want to fucking sleep with you! I want to have you every possible way. I get hard just thinking about the look on your face when you come. When I woke up this morning and my sheets smelled like you, it took me about 30 seconds to come all over my hand. Fuck's sake!"

"I'm not your sex toy! I'm a person! I have feelings!"

"I care about you!" he roared. "Christ!" He took a deep breath. "I'm trying here, Aimee. Maybe I don't say it pretty enough for you. But this is me, trying."

"I'm sorry," I said quietly. "You can be a little overwhelming."

He looked up, his mute eyes begging me to give him a chance.

"Okay," I said, my voice shaky. "Let's try."

He didn't smile. His eyes searched my face, looking for any hesitation or reluctance.

I had reservations, of course I did. But I would give this thing between us a chance.

He nodded, then held out his hand to me. I took it, and he pulled me in, wrapping his arms around me. "Let's try," he said.

"You're nuts! Completely and utterly bat shit crazy!"

"Yep," I said, grinning at Jennifer's face.

"Seriously, Aimee! This morning you looked as if your world had ended—again—and now you're telling me that you're going on the road with him."

"Yes," I smiled happily. "For the whole summer."

She shook her head disbelievingly, her hands on her hips. "And then what? I know you, Aimee, you go all in. You even tried to make it work with Gregg-with-two-g's for years longer than you should have because you're not a quitter. So I'm asking you: what happens at the end of the summer when you have to go back to Boston and Kes carries on traveling?"

Ah, she'd found the weak point in my plan.

"I don't know," I shrugged, trying to seem carefree rather than careless with my happiness.

Jennifer's face was strained.

"Kes will break your heart again. How can you not know this?"

"You don't know that."

She bit her lip and didn't answer.

"I have to try, Jen," I said. "You were the one who said I needed closure."

"Yes, closure! Not re-opening old wounds. You're not the love 'em and leave 'em type, Aimee. So when you have to say goodbye *again* in seven weeks…"

"I know," I said breathlessly. "I mean … I don't know what I mean. Part of me thinks this is a huge mistake, but…"

"You still love him."

"I love the boy he was. I could love the man, too. I don't know, and that's why I have to find out."

"Oh, Aimee," she said sadly, pulling me into a tight hug. "Please be careful."

"Too late," I whispered.

Kes had two more shows to do before he'd fulfilled all of his commitments in the Twin Cities. I spent the time with Jennifer and Dylan, including a whole day at the water park with lots of screaming children, which felt like work, except I was wearing a bikini, which made it feel very odd.

Dylan was buzzing with excitement when I told him that I'd be traveling with the carnival. He wanted to come with me, and threw an almighty tantrum when Jennifer firmly said that he couldn't. And then he got it into his head that I'd be riding a stunt bike like Kes. Jennifer laughed her ass off about that. I felt like showing her my fire-breathing skills, but thought better of it on the grounds that I hadn't done it in over a decade, and I wanted to have sex with Kes at least once more before I died a horrible, flaming death.

Jen was resigned to my leaving, simply reminding me that whatever happened, she was my sister and she loved me—even if I was a "crazy, sexually-stunted idiot, being led around by my libido." I think those were her exact words.

"By the way," she asked, "are you still going to go see Mom?"

I hesitated.

"She'd really like to see you, Aimee. She'll be hurt if you don't go."

"Fine," I huffed. "I'll go this afternoon. Can I borrow your car, or are you and Dylan coming with me?"

She rolled her eyes, smiled, then shook her head in defeat.

Dylan was excited about going to see his grandma. I took that as a good sign. My relationship with my mother was more complicated. There were good things to remember, many of them, but since she chose to blame me for Dad leaving, the good times were all in the past.

Every time I visited now, the house looked smaller and shabbier. The first part was in my imagination, but the latter was true.

As Jen's car neared our old home, I could see that the white boards outside that had always been kept pristine, were peeling and weathered. Weeds pushed up through the driveway, and the whole place felt sad and neglected.

The hickory tree was still standing proudly, taller now, its thick branches brushing against my old window with every shift of the faint breeze: *tap, tap*, just like someone else who'd tapped at my window. I smiled, remembering hiding in that tree with my books, and the many, many times that Kes had climbed it so he could jump in through my bedroom window.

Mom seemed happy to see us, making a huge fuss of Dylan. Maybe she was a good grandma.

It was too hot to be inside, and too hot to sit in the sun. So we sat in the shade of my hickory tree, drinking homemade lemonade, and watching Dylan dash in and out of the sprinkler, his happy shrieks making me smile.

"So, what are your plans for the rest of the summer, Aimee?" Mom asked, oh so innocently.

Note my sarcastic voice: she knew I'd broken up with Gregg-with-two-g's, and was fishing for information.

"Funny you should ask that, Mom," I said, as Jennifer closed her eyes in despair. "I'm running away to join the carnival."

"I don't think that's funny," she said crossly.

"It's not meant to be," I replied calmly. "Although you might be amused to hear that I took Dylan to the fair outside Minneapolis last week. We bumped into an old friend of mine. Maybe you remember Kes?" And I stared at her.

She shifted uneasily in her seat, but chose to comment on how hot the weather was instead.

"He told me everything," I said quietly. "That he came here, begging to see me. You never even told me. How could you do that, Mom? How could you not tell me?"

"You were such a difficult teenager, Aimee. How am I supposed to remember every little drama?"

Then she excused herself to go and rub more sunscreen onto Dylan's back and arms.

"What did you expect?" Jennifer asked gently. "She's the queen of denial."

"I want her to admit she lied!" I snapped.

"Why?" Jennifer pressed. "It's obvious that you know what happened, and it's also obvious that she's not going to admit she was wrong. She's weak, Aimee. She always has been. It took me years to figure that out. Don't ask her to give you more than she's able."

I looked at her thoughtfully. "When did you get to be so wise?"

Jennifer smiled. "I think it comes with being a mom—you spend a lot of time seeing things from someone else's point of view."

I nodded, accepting the excuses she made for our mother. And it helped. Despite the way Mom had lied to me—for years—I found myself forgiving her. Just a little. I seemed to be doing that a lot lately.

We spent the rest of the afternoon talking about more neutral topics, most of which centered around Jen's job and Dylan, which I didn't mind. Mom warmed up enough to ask me how I liked my school, and what I thought of living on the east coast. It wasn't a completely awful afternoon.

When we prepared to leave, and Jennifer was getting Dylan situated in the car, I was left alone on the porch with Mom.

"I'm going on the road with Kes," I said. "Just for the summer. I don't know if we can have a relationship. It's been a long time and we're both adults now. But I wanted you to know that's what we're doing."

Mom's face was stiff. "Do you want me to be happy about

that, Aimee? That you'll be living in a *trailer*, performing like a seal in public?"

I shook my head sadly. "I'd like you to be happy that I'm happy. But no, I don't expect anything from you. Bye, Mom."

I kissed her on the cheek and climbed into the car.

Jennifer saw me swipe a traitorous tear from my cheek, and she squeezed my fingers.

"Proud of you, kiddo," she whispered.

I was upstairs packing when I heard the rumble of a large vehicle coming up Jennifer's road.

"Motorcycle Man!" yelled Dylan, and he shot into the front yard, hopping from foot to foot as Kes maneuvered the huge RV to the curb.

It looked even larger on the small suburban street than when I'd seen it at the fair. This would be my home for the next seven weeks. With Kes. I gave a silent squeal, feeling like the girl who'd just got asked to the school dance by the captain of the football team.

Kes stood out front talking to Dylan, his face creased with a wide smile, his eyes hidden by Aviator shades—real ones, these days. When he saw me, the look on his face made me feel like I'd won the lottery, and when his eyes dropped to my suitcase, his smile became even bigger.

I realized then that he thought I'd change my mind. That little hint of his uncertainty opened the gateway to my heart another inch. Damn him.

He strode forwards, and I thought he was going to really kiss me, but he hesitated at the last second, simply offering a feather light touch of lips across my cheek.

Then he scooped up my suitcase like it weighed nothing, and carried it to the RV as if he was taking it hostage—which was probably close to the truth.

Dylan jumped inside, and Kes gave him the tour. Dylan was bouncing on his toes, so happy and excited that I couldn't help being caught up in it. I remembered this feeling, the innocent childlike belief that magic could happen because your house had wheels.

And it was magical: it felt like we were stepping into an unknown world, like Columbus, like Neil Armstrong.

And Kes … it should have been business as usual for him,

but he seemed almost as excited as Dylan.

Jennifer wrapped her arm around my waist.

"If my son runs away to join the circus, I'm totally blaming you," she whispered.

"What if your sister runs away to join the circus?" I whispered back.

"Totally blaming him," she said, jerking her chin at Kes.

Jennifer offered to make Kes a cup of coffee before we left, but I could tell he was itching to be on the road, his need for movement almost compulsive.

"I'll call you," I said, hugging her and Dylan tightly.

"You'd better!" she said, sniffing a few times.

"Ready?" asked Kes, holding out his hand.

"Ready as I'll ever be!"

His grin widened and he winked at me. "This way, princess," and he ushered me inside.

I plopped down into the enormous captain's chair, staring at a dashboard that looked like it belonged on the Starship Enterprise.

Kes pushed a button and the engine roared into life.

"I can't believe you're here," he grinned at me.

"Neither can I!"

His smile dimmed. "I've waited a long time for this," he said.

Then he leaned across, gripping the back of my head as he kissed me thoroughly.

I felt dizzy and immensely turned on by the time he released me. What a great start to my vacation. I looked up in time to see Dylan's disgusted expression and Jennifer shaking her head, a huge smile on her face.

As Kes pulled out into the street, I rolled down the window and waved wildly, watching until they were out of sight.

"Where are we going?" I asked excitedly as Kes punched a new destination into the GPS.

"Anywhere you want, Aimee," he answered, a huge grin on his face.

I pinched his arm lightly. "Really, where?"

"Cedar Rapids, Iowa. Then Olathe, Kansas; Amarillo, Colorado, Salt Lake City, Reno, and finishing up in California."

"Oh, wow! That's so exciting!"

Kes grinned at me. "Take us about five hours to reach Cedar Rapids today. I thought we could stop for lunch in Mason City."

"Sounds perfect."

"You ever been to either of those places?" he asked, raising an eyebrow.

"Nope. Still sounds perfect."

He laughed happily.

We passed through the outskirts of Minneapolis, and I watched in the wing mirrors as the city faded into the distance, the road ahead opening out to a patchwork of fields and lakes. My heart was light, as if I might do something corny like break into song. Kes kept glancing at me, and each time he caught my eye, he grinned and winked.

We headed steadily south, passing through Owatonna and Albert Lea. But instead of stopping at Mason City as he'd suggested, Kes turned west toward Clear Lake. I had to close my eyes as Kes expertly weaved the enormous RV through impossibly narrow streets, until he stopped alongside a small lake.

"Picnic?" he offered.

"Wonderful."

After the air conditioning in the RV, the heat was bordering on brutal. But Kes had picked the perfect spot at a pretty lakeside café, under spiraling oak trees.

"This seems fancy," I said, smiling at the beautiful setting and linen covered tables.

"What did you think it would be?" Kes asked. "Greasy truck stops and fast food?"

I cringed, realizing that was *exactly* what I'd expected.

"Well, yeah, usually," he admitted with a grin, "but I wanted something better than that for you."

"You don't have to treat me differently," I said gently, "or spoil me."

"Yes, I do," he replied quickly.

I threw him a glance, but that closed expression was back.

I sighed. Obviously our whole experience in communicating would be a work in progress.

When the waitress came to take our orders, Kes asked for a ham and cheese sub, and I chose a tuna salad.

It was peaceful sitting by the lake, and I realized how unusual it was to see Kes like this. He was always in motion, but for now, he seemed to be at peace. I was happy to think that I might have had a hand in that.

"Will we see Ollo and Zachary tonight?"

He smiled. "Yep, they've been there for a few days, and Tucker and Zef got there last night."

Oh. I'd put them out of my mind. I didn't care for either of them much. I was pretty sure it was mutual.

"'Zef' is a strange name … almost as strange as 'Kestrel'," I said, raising one eyebrow.

Kes smiled. "Yeah, except his name is really Joseph, but he prefers Zef."

"What's their story? How did you meet them?"

Kes shrugged. "They were on the circuit. Tucker was already doing some stunt riding. He was with this rinky-dink wall of death act, real boring shit."

"I'm hesitating to ask, but … *wall of death?*"

Kes grinned. "Where you have a drum—something that looks like an empty silo or tube shape—and the audience stands at the top looking down. Then you get one or two riders using the centripetal force to hold them up."

"And that's boring?"

"Hell, yeah," he said, looking disgusted. "Anyway, Tucker was looking for a change, so we set up our own act. We found Zef drifting in Idaho. He'd just got out of prison and…"

"Wait! Back up! Zef just got out of prison! What did he do?"

Kes shrugged. "I never asked."

"Oh," I said faintly. "How long have you all been together?"

"With Tucker for three years, and Zef for about 14 months."

When Kes asked me to come with him, I hadn't really thought through the implications of traveling with two single men—and now I was finding out that one was an ex-con. Not only that, but the guys had a well-established routine and also slept in the same RV as us. It was going to take some getting used to all around.

"What about Sorcha?" I asked, my curiosity getting the better of me.

Kes scowled. "Does it matter?"

I took a moment to think about that. Did it matter? "I guess not, but I'd like to know."

Kes fiddled with his water glass, and for a moment I thought he wasn't going to answer. But then he looked up at me and spoke firmly.

"She traveled with us sometimes. Mostly, she flew on ahead

to set things up, especially for the bigger gigs, like in Santa Fe or LA."

Then I had a horrible thought: had Sorcha lost her home because of me?

"And when you were on your winter break?"

He shrugged, looking irritated.

"Mostly I was traveling overseas."

"Kes, I'm asking if Sorcha has lost her home … because of what's happened?"

He pulled a face. "Nah, she's got an apartment in Sacramento."

"But on the road … she lived with you?"

This time his answer was reluctant.

"Yeah."

"Oh. How long were you … together?"

He blew out a breath. "Seven years. Give or take."

I couldn't lie—it was a kick in the gut. But I was going to have to move past it. Somehow.

"Thank you for telling me."

He nodded curtly. I took the hint: topic closed.

"What about you?" he said stiffly. "You must have dated since…"

Case not closed—apparently it was my turn now.

"I didn't date in High School. No one could compare to this hot carnie boy I used to know."

Kes looked very pleased with himself when I said that. But I wasn't blowing smoke: it was all true.

"When I went to college, I thought I should, I don't know, at least try to enjoy the college experience and go on dates. You know, try and move on." I paused, glancing up at his somber expression. "It was casual until my Senior year."

"What happened Senior year?"

"I met Gregg-with-two-g's."

"Who?"

"Some douche who strung me along for four years then cheated on me."

Kes scowled. "He cheated on you?!"

"I appreciate your outrage. That's pretty much how I felt when I found out."

Kes looked positively vicious, and I shivered.

"Which brings me to here and now," I said as cheerfully as I could manage.

Kes raised his eyebrows, gazing at me with surprise.

"You've only had one boyfriend ... since us?"

"I know you think that Gregg was an asshole for cheating on me, but I've recently come to the understanding that I wasn't fair on him either."

"You mean you cheated on him, too?" Kes sounded stunned.

"Well," I said, dropping my eyes, "it occured to me that all the years I was with Gregg, I was in love with the memory of someone else."

Kes studied me closely, then he leaned forward and kissed me with all the intensity of which he was so capable.

A red-faced waitress coughed discreetly as she dropped the check onto our table, then backed away muttering an apology.

"We'll finish that later," Kes said decisively.

I took a long drink from my glass of ice water, trying to cool myself from a heat that had nothing to do with the midday sun.

"What do Zach and Ollo do these days?" I said after I'd gathered my scattered wits.

"Zach is the carnival director on the circuit where we're going—Mr. Health & Safety." Kes grinned at me. "Ollo is old-school: he calls himself a roustabout. He's done pretty much everything at one time or another. He's Zach's right-hand man."

"I'm excited to see them again."

Kes grinned. "They're just about shittin' a brick to see you!"

I blinked at him. "Really? You told them I was coming?"

Kes rolled his eyes. "Of course I freakin' told them you were coming!"

I smiled happily. Kes was already on his feet and paying the bill. It was only then that I realized we hadn't discussed money. I wasn't going to be a kept woman; I wanted to pay my way.

"I'll leave the tip," I told Kes.

"Already taken care of," he growled.

"Okay, I'll get the next meal."

The look in his eyes told me that might be trickier than it sounded. A part of me rather liked that he was taking charge. And the part of me that was a career woman with her own apartment, who was used to making her own decisions, was really kind of pissed—even though I was a teacher making crap money, and with loans to pay back.

It was going to be an exciting seven weeks.

The GPS announced the Cedar Rapids carnival site was just 40 miles away. I bounced in my seat like an overly excited toddler when I saw the first poster. Kes grinned and we were both in ridiculously high spirits, infected with the thrill of a new adventure. I felt young and carefree and daring to be in love.

CHAPTER 13
ALONG FOR THE RIDE

"Oooh! I want cotton candy!" I shouted. "I haven't had that in forever! And a hotdog—don't hold back on the onions. I shall breathe my onion breath all over you!"

"Babe, you're turning me on!" Kes grinned, wiggling his eyebrows.

"Shut up! That's disgusting!"

He laughed happily.

"And don't call me 'babe', that's sexist," I teased, pretending to be offended.

Kes didn't miss a beat.

"Babe."

"Baby."

"Babealicious!"

"Baby face."

And then he started singing in a ridiculous falsetto, "Baby! My sweet baby!"

"Oh my God! Did you just quote 'Dirty Dancing' at me?"

"No," he snorted.

"Yes, you did!"

"No way! That's Mickey and Sylvia, 'Love is Strange'."

"It sure is, because you just quoted from one of *the* great chick flicks of all time!"

Kes shifted uncomfortably on his seat. "Did not."

"Did, too!" Then I laughed. "Oh my God! Are we eight?"

Kes muttered something under his breath, but I didn't try very hard to hear him.

"I have something here," I said, "that will impress you."

"You impress me all the time. Babe."

"Ugh, you did not just go there!"

He winked at me, showing his cute dimple, so I had to ignore him.

"I stayed up very late compiling a road trip playlist of songs about carnivals."

Kes rolled his eyes.

"Don't roll your eyes until you've heard it."

"Fine, I'll just guess. 'The Carny' by Nick Cave."

"Maybe," I huffed.

"And I bet at the top of the list is 'Carnival' by The Cardigans."

"Possibly."

"If you've got 'Quando o Carnaval Chegar' on your list, we'll have to rethink our relationship," he said.

I cocked my head on one side. "Is that what we have? A relationship?"

Kes looked taken aback. "Well, yeah." Then he hesitated, "What would you call it?"

"Well, at the moment, I'd say it's two old friends catching a ride together to go see the carnival."

Kes nodded. "Okay," he said. "Works for me."

"Just so you know," I sniffed, "that's the wrong answer. We're totally in a relationship."

Kes grinned. "Good. So we're both clear on that."

I couldn't help thinking that I'd been played.

"We going to hear that playlist now?" he asked.

"Oh, look! We're nearly there!"

He laughed and flicked the turn signal, slowing as we inched through the narrow entrance to the carnival field.

I stared out of the window eagerly, trying to make sense of the scene of organized chaos. Kes knew exactly where he was going and circled the perimeter until he pulled up next to a huge sixteen-wheeler with 'Hawkins Daredevils' emblazoned on the side. That missing apostrophe still really bothered me.

"Wow! That's your rig?"

Kes smiled. "What, did you think we borrowed some planks of wood and a couple of sticks to make the ramps when we got here?"

"No! I'm just impressed." I was silent for a moment. "I Googled you."

Kes's expression was wary. "Yeah?"

"You've got a Guinness World Record."

He grinned. "Oh, yeah! Sydney was epic. I landed so hard, my balls cracked the casing on the fuel tank."

"Oh my God! Seriously?"

"Yeah, it was fucking painful—it felt as if I was pissing around corners for weeks."

I shook my head, laughing.

"And I looked you up on You Tube."

"And?"

"Some of the stunts you do, they're amazing. They scare the hell out of me, but they're amazing." I turned to look at him. "You're amazing."

I couldn't see his eyes behind his sunglasses, but his lips pulled into a pleased smile. "You know, you said the same thing to me when we were kids, almost the exact same words."

"It's always been true."

I was about to say something else when Kes's door was yanked open and Zachary stood there grinning at him.

"Jeez, Kes! It's good to see you, man!"

Kes leapt out of the RV in a single lithe movement, and Zachary swept him into a bone-crunching man-hug.

Then he turned, a huge smile on his face.

"Holy shit, Aimee Andersen! He told us you were coming, but I didn't believe it!"

He jogged around the cab and opened my door, holding out his hand to help me down the steps like some nineteenth-century gentleman.

"Gosh, Zach! It's so good to see you!" and then I hugged the ever-living crap out of him.

"Hey! Save some of the good stuff for me," came Ollo's voice from behind him.

Seeing his face again, the shock of jet black hair, his quick eyes and wrinkled face, I wanted to cry. He'd always been so kind to me.

"Ollo! You haven't changed a bit!" and I hugged the little man until he squeaked.

Kes was grinning like a loon, and as soon as I released Ollo, he got down on his knees and embraced his old friend.

I was somewhat surprised when Ollo leapt on his back and put a painful-looking armlock on Kes, forcing him face down in the dirt.

"Ow! Jesus, watch it, Ollo! You'll break my fuckin' arm!"

Ollo was relentless. "You owe me five bucks, you lousy stinkin' cheat! You welched on our bet!"

Zachary laughed at my worried expression.

"They do this—it's kind of their thing."

"Really?"

"Yeah, they take turns seeing who can be the biggest cheat at poker."

"They cheat?"

"It's almost a matter of honor who can get away with the most. I'm talking cards up sleeves, cards in pockets, counting cards, the works—bunch of grifters! One year, Ollo made Kes and the guys play naked."

"Um, okay, because?"

"So they couldn't hide cards. It was the strangest game of poker I've ever seen."

"Huh," grunted Ollo, who was now sitting on Kes, yanking his arm at an awkward angle. "Tucker still managed to hide his cards."

"Ugh, I don't want to know!" I shrieked.

"Anyway," Zachary continued, his tone conversational as Kes thrashed around, coughing in a cloud of dust, "I've always suspected it was just a ploy to see who had the biggest dick."

My eyes automatically drifted to Kes, and Zachary saw me.

"And in case you're wondering, it's Ollo," Zach laughed.

Ollo turned to wink at me, and Kes just looked pissed, although it may have been because Ollo was mashing his face into the dirt at the time.

"Let me up, you short-assed little shit!"

Ollo shook his head, but then Kes bucked his whole body and Ollo went flying off.

When Kes stood up and dusted himself down, he rubbed his arm, wincing slightly. Ollo was lying several feet away, winded.

Zachary laughed. "Boys will be boys."

I shook my head in disbelief—it was like having playground duty, except the kids fighting weren't eight years old, even if they acted like it.

Ollo sat up, puffing slightly from the exertion and scowling at Kes.

"Is Mr. Albert in your trailer?" I asked Ollo. "I was expecting him to come running out. I wonder if he'll remember me?"

Kes stiffened and Ollo looked at me sadly.

"I guess Kestrel didn't tell you."

"Tell me what?" I asked, my eyes skating between them.

"When Dono died, Mr. Albert wasn't far behind him. Died of a broken heart is my opinion. Losing Dono like that, it was too much. And he was pretty old for a monkey. Little guy must have been nearly forty."

"Oh," I said, wishing I could think of something more adequate to say. "That's awful. Poor thing."

I'd really loved that little fella—I remembered the way he'd snuggle against me and wind his tiny hands into my hair.

Ollo shook his head. "I can never understand people who say animals have no souls. You only have to look in their eyes to know that they do. Human beings can be so goddamn arrogant."

He turned away, and I think it was because he had tears in his eyes. I know that I did. I felt so bad that I hadn't asked Kes about Mr. Albert or any of the other animals that had meant so much to him—his other family, in many ways.

"I'm sorry. I didn't even ask you," I said to Kes, walking up and wrapping my arms around his waist tightly. "I know how much Mr. Albert meant to you."

I felt Kes's lips in my hair, but he didn't speak.

I pulled back to look up at him. "What … what happened to Jacob Jones and the other ponies?"

He sighed. "They got sold. Dono had debts, so … Jakey went to a kid in Arcata. Her dad had promised her a pony for her birthday. He got a good crib, nice life, I guess. Better food than he ever had on the road. I saw him once. He'd gotten fat." Kes gave a small smile.

"And the others?"

He shrugged. "Sold."

Sadness and memories drifted in the air, and we were all silent.

I wasn't sorry when we were interrupted by the appearance of Zef and Tucker. They greeted Kes warmly, and Tucker smiled at me and winked, but Zef stonily ignored me.

This was going to be cozy, considering I'd be practically living with the guy for the next seven weeks. I think Kes noticed, but he didn't say anything. Instead, he hooked his arm about my neck and pulled my head toward him so he could kiss my forehead, his gesture casually possessive. Then he stood upright.

"Gonna go check on the ramps. I'll catch you later," he said, as he strolled away with Ollo on one side, Tucker and Zef on the other, a lopsided entourage.

If Kes hadn't made it so clear that I was surplus to requirements, I'd have gone with him. I wanted to learn about his life. But we were both new at this, so I decided not to crowd him. Besides, Zef was throwing me such dirty looks, it was definitely best to leave them to it. For now.

But I must have looked a little forlorn, because Zachary took pity on me.

"Don't worry about it," he said, following the guys with his eyes. "Sorcha never had much interest in the technical side of things, so Kes is just doing what he's always done."

"That's what bothers me," I admitted.

Zach realized that his wording could be construed in more ways than one.

"Sorry," he said wincing. "That was tactless. I'm really glad you're here, Aimee. It's good to see Kes so happy."

"Oh! Does he seem different to you?" I asked, surprised.

"Yeah, definitely," Zach said, nodding briskly. "He tolerated Sorcha, but he never really cared about her. They used each other for … comfort. Sorcha always wanted more, but Kes was never willing to give it. He can be pretty stubborn—I guess he'd call it normal, we'd call it single-minded."

"I've noticed," I said firmly.

We stood uncomfortably for a second.

"Let me show you around," Zachary said, changing the subject. "We're not opening until tomorrow afternoon, and some more acts are arriving this evening. It'll be crazy later, but we've got some time now."

The midway was clearly laid out, and most of the booths and stalls had already been erected.

A huge, skeletal Ferris wheel marked the back end of the midway, with the arena for Kes's show, as well as the other rides fanning out around it.

"Two other acts are sharing the arena," Zachary explained. "There's a family of rodeo riders and a clown troupe. You'll meet them later."

As we strolled along the midway, Zachary waved at the stallholders and show people.

"Sid over there in the red jumpsuit, he's got a game called 'Drown the Clown'. It's your old fashioned dunk tank, where visitors have to throw a ball at the target to knock him in the water. The kicker is that the more they miss, the more he insults them. He used to be a stand-up comedian, so he's pretty good at heckling the hecklers. The worse they are, the better he is."

"Remind me not to get on his bad side," I laughed.

"Yeah, it can be pretty ripe at times, so he saves his best lines for evenings. But even then, we have to watch out for people waiting for him after the show. You know, wanting to fight him. But anyone who tries it, we throw them out. Besides, Sid used to be a professional boxer. His fight name was The Troll."

"I'm not going to ask."

Zachary smiled broadly.

"He says he makes good money doing this—and he gets to make people laugh. Better than getting beat up, I guess."

I gazed around me, eyes wide at the canvas city unfolding in front of me, our backdrop, the wide Iowan sky.

"It's so much bigger than Dono's carnival," I sighed. "It's amazing. Even when you can see it all being set up—I still find it magical."

Zachary's smile matched my own.

"I love this life," he said, his eyes sweeping across the scene in front of us. "We turn an empty field into a stage. But it's not easy making the magic happen. We all work 12- or 16-hour days. But in return for the hard work, I get a family, I get space. It's definitely not a 9 to 5 job—not like teaching."

He smiled at me slyly, then ducked as I tried to smack him.

"Kes told you that I'm a teacher?"

Zachary grinned at me. "Yeah, he told me. Still sounds like a pretty easy gig."

"Huh! You try wrangling a bunch of eight-year olds all day, planning their lessons and marking their work every evening, not to mention parent-teacher conferences, and writing IEPs for every child, reading schemes, phonetics, prefixes, suffixes, phonemes, multiplication tables..."

I was making myself feel queasy, but Zach put his hands over his ears and yelled at me to stop.

"I'll take your word for it, Miss Andersen," Zach laughed. "Just don't make me stand in the corner."

"Lame! Like I haven't heard that before."

"Yeah, sorry. We get all the stereotypes here, too," he said seriously. "People still think we're dirty, thieving carnies, but traveling shows aren't like that. We've all had to clean up. People think that carnies live in trailers and have nothing. Most of us have homes to go back to, although not all. It's hardest on families. If you're single or," he said, side-eyeing me, "traveling with your other half, you live where you work and it's an exciting life. Maybe we are all misfits, who knows? But we create a community when we're on the road."

"There doesn't seem like much privacy," I said, glancing behind me to the muddle of RVs and trailers.

Zachary shrugged.

"We make it as private as possible, and the living area is separated from the public. When Kes is with us, we park the motorhomes so that they face each other and create a kind of courtyard. We have cookouts and invite friends."

"Very homey," I said, wondering how that fit with my image of a bunch of single guys living together.

Zachary guessed what I was thinking.

"It can get pretty wild at times, drinking and gambling. And we're all on top of each other, so that's an explosive mix. I'm the manager for the whole show, so it's my job to calm things down. Not just with Kes's crew," he said, jabbing his thumb in the direction that they'd gone, "but with everyone here."

"So who owns it? I'm assuming someone does?"

Zach smiled. "Yeah, an old carnie family called the Reynolds. They have the rodeo act that you'll see later. But Old Man Reynolds retired two years ago. It's his children and grandchildren who have the act, but they're happy to have me manage everything." He laughed. "Most carnies are allergic to paperwork, so I come in handy. So yeah, it's their carnival, but we're all family." He smiled. "I guess I've got sawdust in my blood after all these years."

"You're making yourself sound ancient!" I laughed. "You're only, what, 30? Anyway, what's your story, Zach? One summer, you just appeared with Dono."

He smiled sadly. "Same story as most people who end up on the road: family didn't want me. Didn't have any place to go. Dono caught me trying to steal a mark's wallet because I was hungry and needed money to buy food. But you can't scam a scamp. He kicked the shit out of me, then brought me over to his boys and fed me."

"Why didn't your family want you? Sorry, I shouldn't ask."

Zachary looked at me evenly. "I told them I was gay."

Sadness touched his eyes, but he brushed it away. I wanted to hug him and tell him I knew what it felt like to be rejected by your family, but I didn't think he'd want that.

"Oh, I see," I said quietly. "Sorry, it's none of my business."

"Don't be. I have a good life. I'm happy."

"But don't you find it lonely?" I couldn't help asking.

Zach shook his head. "I'm surrounded by people the whole time."

"That's not the same though, is it? It must be hard meeting someone when you're always traveling."

The truth of those words hit me. Maybe it explained why Kes had stuck with Sorcha for so long.

"Guys like Tucker and Zef, they're happy to score with any woman who's going to get a thrill out of banging a rough roustabout." He shrugged. "That's just how it is."

"And you?"

"Sometimes I'll meet someone, hook up for a couple of days." He shrugged. "It's easier to meet other gay men nearer the cities. There's usually a gay bar I can find if I want company."

"Don't you want to meet someone, fall in love, the whole fairytale?"

A fleeting look of pain passed over Zachary's face.

"Oh," I said, my voice softening with understanding. "You already have. Who?"

His eyes wandered across the carnival field then back to mine.

"Can't you guess?" he said, his voice husky. "You love him, too."

A shocked gasp escaped me, and I lowered my voice. "You're in love with Kes?"

Zachary gave a pained smile. "Ever since I met him."

"Does he know?"

Zach looked down. "Yeah, he knows."

I was silent.

We walked further down the midway, but I didn't see what was in front of me, I was trying to digest Zachary's bombshell.

He sighed. "Is this going to be weird for you, Aimee?"

I smiled up at him sadly. "No, not really. Even when we were teenagers, he was the one everyone wanted. I can't compete with that."

Zachary frowned at me. "You're not competing with anyone."

I shrugged. It had always felt like it.

"I can see how much he loves being on the road," I said. "And I can see what performing means to him. He draws people in, even when he doesn't want to—he can't help it. I suppose that's charisma, or star quality, or whatever you want to call it. He's extraordinary ... and I'm just me. I'm here for the summer. I won't ask for more than that."

Because even if I did, even if I begged for more, I knew that I wouldn't get it. I'd learned to be happy with scraps.

"So, tell me more about your empire," I smiled, trying to dispel the air of gloom that had settled over us.

"My empire? Does that make me Darth Vader?"

"Ooh, you must be older than I thought with that 'Star Wars' reference."

"Well, okay, Miss Teacher-girl. Pin back your ears and learn some lessons in carnie lore—although Ollo would do it better. He's been with carnivals and traveling fairs his whole life."

"Really? How old is he anyway?"

"No one knows, and I'm not dumb enough to ask. He's got some great stories, though. He says in the old days, they used to sleep on the ground under the trucks. Although a lot of guys still do when it's hot."

"I remember," I said. "Kes used to do that all the time."

"No one does this for the money, that's for sure," said Zachary. "Hell, not everyone even earns minimum wage, but it's still better than saying, 'You want fries with that?' Some kids come for the summer and live off of Ramen Noodles, saving their money for when they go back to their lives. Some use what they earn to pay their way through college. I've got one Psych Major who swears he learns more here than he ever does in a classroom."

I couldn't help laughing—and I suspected he was right.

"I've seen 41 states," Zach continued, his face relaxed, "and I plan on seeing the others one day. It's more than the paycheck. We get to see America. Ollo says that we're adventurers, not tourists."

I smiled. "I like that. It's sort of how I felt when Kes asked me to come with him: like I was about to discover a new world."

Zachary leaned down to whisper in my ear.

"Your wish is my command. Welcome to my empire," and he gave a villainous cackle.

I pushed him away and laughed.

"Anyway," I said, "it must be like trying to wrangle kindergarteners to get everyone set up."

Zachary shook his head. "It looks chaotic, but it's not. We've got a pretty slick system. Everywhere we go, the midway is laid out the same. Al, the ride foreman, it's his job to place the rides in the best positions. You want visitors to see them from as far away as possible, especially in flatter country like northern Iowa. So the tall rides like the helter-skelter and Ferris wheel go at the end of the midway. That's how you draw people down the middle and encourage them to spend as much as possible on the way to the big attractions.

"But that's not the only reason. It can take up to 36 hours to get everything up and running and ready for those damn inspections. We get them up fast, and we can do the takedown even faster. The rides are always first to leave the lot, so they can be put up first at the next site. Last to move out are the house trailers and sleeping quarters. It also gives the wives and kids the chance for a few hours sleep before we start putting up the show in a new location.

"Right now, there are about 150 carnies on site, and more will come in the next 24 hours because it's such a big event."

I looked at Zach, evaluating. "Because of Kes?"

Zach smiled. "He's a huge draw, definitely. He could earn ten times as much money sticking to the cities, but he does this for the nostalgia, I think, and to help us out. Because he pulls the crowds, it means all the guys have got a chance to make good money during the season. Kes is a carnie at heart and he's loyal. He'd do anything for the people he cares about."

I smiled softly. "I know.

"So, Carnival 101. There are times we do what's called a Circus jump. That's when we close on Sunday and open on Monday or Tuesday. Basically, we go 24 to 48 hours with no sleep and we work our asses off. You'll see—we've got a few of those on this tour. So here's a tip for the future: never visit a show that opens on Monday. Let everyone else find out which bolts they didn't tighten on the Ferris wheel."

"Good tip," I breathed, cringing as Zach laughed at my

horrified expression.

"Weather is our biggest problem: could be the heat, and trying to get enough water pipes laid for everyone; sometimes it's the rain, and the trailers getting bogged down and the shows being rained out. Then the rides need to be maintained: we carry spares of most things, but sometimes we have to order in specialist pieces. And, don't ask me why, but carnival rides have unusual tire sizes, so it can be a pain in the ass to find replacements in a hurry. Thank God for the internet! You can order just about anything."

"It's some family," I said, looking around me.

Zachary nodded, more serious now he was in work mode.

"It's our home, so I'm careful about who can come along for the ride. I do criminal records checks for all the staff, even if they're just seasonal. Gotta be careful with so many kids around, if you know what I mean."

I was a teacher, so I knew exactly what he meant. The hoops we had to jump through to allow adults to help out in school could be crazy, but we always took it seriously.

"But it's not just casual labor," Zach explained. "You've got to have people who know what they're doing for the big rides. It takes about six hours to set up the Ferris wheel, and I need a crew of seven to erect the roller coaster. It's got 300 pieces and takes eight hours. The track sections are lifted into place by hand and held together by steel pins. Some pieces weigh more than 300 pounds. It can get dangerous.

"When we're not operating rides or getting visitors to try the games, we still have to make sure that the concession stands have hot dogs and cotton candy, that the generators have fuel, as well as ordinary things like cook food for the family or do the laundry."

"Do you think the attitude to carnies has shifted?" I questioned, "or are people still like my parents were?"

Zach shrugged.

"Both, I guess. There are places where we get treated like dirt. But other places we're welcomed year after year. For some small towns, the carnival is the highlight of their summer—hell, the whole year."

"I totally get that," I sighed. "I only felt alive for those two weeks each summer. I used to get so excited when the trucks rolled past my house."

Zachary smiled. "I thought that was because it meant Kes was coming."

I laughed. "That, too. But the first time, oh it was wonderful! I was so impatient to see it all go up. But my parents were very disapproving: to hear them talk, it was Sodom and Gomorrah come to Fairmont. I would never have been allowed near the carnival if it weren't for the fact that it was my birthday and I got to choose how we spent the day. I chose the carnival."

Zachary frowned. "We always hit Fairmont in the summer."

"Yes?"

"So it must be your birthday soon?"

"Oh that. I never celebrate it."

I could see the puzzlement on Zach's face. "Why not?"

I shrugged.

"Well, as we seem to be swapping sad stories … after Kes left, I never felt like celebrating my birthday again. I associated it with being miserable, I guess."

Zach put his arm around my shoulders, giving me a hug.

"It'll be different this year, Aimee."

I gazed around me, almost needing to pinch myself to believe that I was really here. The setting sun glinted off the Ferris wheel's steel frame, and the sounds softened around us as pink-tinged clouds turned Camelot into a blaze of color.

"Welcome home," said Zachary.

"Stop it!" I said, swatting his shoulder. "You'll make my mascara run."

"I knew I had it in me to make a woman cry," he teased. "Come on, let's get back to our lord and master before he accuses me of running off with you."

He held out his arm and I took it, laughing, as we strolled back along the midway. He introduced me to everyone as, "Aimee, Kes's friend."

"Why are you doing that?" I asked, when he'd done it for about the fourth time.

He shrugged, looking a little uncomfortable.

"Wait! Did Kes put you up to this?"

Zach cleared his throat and looked away.

"Zachary! Tell me!"

"He just wanted everyone to know that you were protected."

My mind flew back to the first time I'd met Kes. Dono had implied the same thing when he met my Mom.

"What does that mean? That I'm 'protected'? Who am I protected from?"

Zach sighed. "It's an old carnie thing. Back in the day when it was a real *them* and *us* mentality, some townspeople were good to us, so they were protected. That meant no grifting, no scams—they were safe—and all the carnies respected that."

"Okay, I'm confused. You've just been telling me how traveling shows have cleaned up their acts."

"We have. Kes is putting the word out that you're one of us."

"You look shifty. What aren't you telling me?"

"Jesus, Aimee! Do you work for the FBI?"

"I teach third grade—we train the FBI. Spill."

Zachary grimaced. "He didn't want any of the guys hitting on you, okay?"

I started to laugh. "Are you serious? Kes has put out the word that I'm, what, untouchable?"

"Don't laugh," smiled Zach. "He takes it very seriously."

"Oh my God! I think I just fell through a crack in time. What century does he think we're in?!"

"You should be flattered," Zach whispered, a huge grin on his face. "He never told anyone that Sorcha was protected."

My mood soured. "Yes, well, she looked like she wrestled grizzly bears in her spare time and sharpened her nails on unsuspecting lumberjacks. I'm not surprised she didn't need protecting."

Zachary laughed. "It's going to be a wild ride."

I gave his arm a squeeze. "Yes, it is."

When we arrived back at the sleeping quarters, a large bonfire was blazing away. A group of carnies who'd just arrived came to see Zach, so he excused himself to get them situated. Tucker and Zef were chatting to a couple of the women I recognized from my brief tour. Tucker gestured for me to come over, but no one else looked welcoming, so I just waved and pointed to the RV, heading inside.

Kes was standing in the living area talking to a scary-looking man with a bald head and tattoos spiraling down his neck. Kes grinned but didn't introduce me, and the man stared coldly.

Feeling unwelcome with Tucker and co, feeling unwelcome in the living room, I retreated to the bedroom, deciding to unpack my case for something to do. Kes's bed filled most of the room and the cabinets were all tiny. The largest storage area seemed to be under the bed, with a narrow closet for hanging a few clothes.

But when I opened the closet door, several sparkly dresses were hanging in the space. For a happy moment, I thought Kes had bought them for me, but then I realized that these were Sorcha's.

I was furious. Kes hadn't even bothered to empty the closet of her clothes.

He chose that moment to walk in the door.

"You're an asshole!" I snapped.

"I walk in the door and that makes me an asshole?"

I flung open the closet door, cracking it against the bed, and gestured wildly with my arms.

"No. *That* makes you an asshole!"

I would have stormed out of the room, but that would have meant crawling across the bed and tackling 200 pounds of pissed stuntman. As that didn't seem like a sensible option, I simply stood with my hands on my hips, waiting for an explanation.

"Oh," he said flatly.

He grabbed the clothes from the hangers, piled them into his arms and stomped out, leaving me speechless and furious.

I followed him as far as the RV's door, then watched open mouthed as he tossed the pile onto the bonfire. A ragged cheer sounded from all around, and for a moment Kes's eyes glittered in the firelight, the flames throwing weird shadows across his sharp cheekbones, his expression dark and devilish.

Then he prowled toward the RV, his eyes fixed on mine, and a look on his face that told me a storm was about to hit. I backed away and he slammed the door behind him, muting the laughs and catcalls that followed.

He didn't even speak as he grabbed my hand and towed me into the bedroom, physically lifting me from my feet and tossing me onto the bed.

Then he ripped off his t-shirt and pinned me to the bed with his body, the heat pouring from his skin and through my thin blouse, heating my blood and burning my flesh.

When he kissed me with a bruising thoroughness, I thought I was going to pass out from lack of oxygen. Then he sat back on his heels, his eyes black in the unlit interior, and stared at me.

"She's history. We're not discussing this again."

I pushed myself into a sitting position. "Don't tell me what to do!"

"My place. My rules."

"Fuck that!" I yelped. "I'm not some serf you can order around! Right now I'm pissed enough to…"

His lips were on mine, then on my cheek, trailing down my neck.

"You're not pissed," he whispered. "You're turned on. I know that because I want you so badly I could come in my pants right now."

I snorted with laughter. "Wouldn't be the first time, Kestrel."

He smirked at me. "I know. That's why I said it. Fuck's sake, Aimee, I only want you. The clothes are gone."

"Okay, fine, but there was no need to go all caveman."

"I kind of got the impression that you liked that?"

"Not with an audience!" I coughed. "Not with a bunch of strangers watching!"

Kes shook his head. "They're not strangers; they're family."

"Your family, maybe. But they're strangers to me."

He shook his head again. "You don't get it. You're with me—that makes them your family, too."

A warm feeling spread me through at the idea that Kes wanted them to think of me as family. But he wasn't off the hook either.

"And what's with this notion of me being 'protected'?"

He shrugged. "That's just the way it is."

I huffed with frustration. A huff that turned into a moan as he kissed my neck then flicked his tongue across my breastbone, dripping down into my cleavage.

I gripped his biceps then pulled him closer, sliding my hands over his satiny skin.

The feel of his erection digging into my hip made me pause.

"We can't," I whispered.

"Why not?" he mumbled as his hand disappeared up my t-shirt.

"Because everyone saw us come in here—they'll all know what we're up to."

"So?"

"So! I've only just met them—it's embarrassing!"

Kes chuckled. "No secrets between carnies, Aimee. We all live too close to each other for that. Cut one, we all bleed."

"How sweet. But I don't want my new family to know that we're in here *fucking*, five minutes after I met them."

"They won't care," he said, squeezing my nipples hard enough to make me gasp.

"I care," I said, as my voice wobbled unconvincingly. "And there are kids out there, Kes! We can't give them the wrong impression."

This time he laughed loudly.

"I never knew you were such a prude!"

"I am not!"

"Jesus, Aimee! These are carnie kids. They live in trailers and RVs like us. They've heard their parents fucking a thousand times. They've seen the stallion take the mare when she's in heat, and believe me, once you've seen that, *every* guy has performance anxiety."

I laughed a little when he said that, but he wasn't finished.

"Do you remember when we were kids and you asked me how I knew that Madame Cindy was Dono's girlfriend? I *heard* them. I knew what sex was before I could say the word. These carnie kids are just like that. We're not doing anything wrong, we're not hurting anyone."

His tone had started off light and amused, but had become more serious and insistent as he'd gone on.

"Maybe I am prudish," I said quietly. "It was the way I was brought up. I just happen to think that *making love* is a private thing between two people: not a public display of your testosterone, unless you're doing it to make that stallion blush."

He sighed and shifted onto his back. "Did I imagine you rubbing my cock while we were laying in the field at the carnival when we were kids?"

I didn't answer, but fiddled with the hem of my t-shirt.

"You want to wait until everyone has their backs turned, pretending that they don't know what we're doing *in the privacy of our own home?*"

"Yes, exactly."

He turned his head to smile at me. "My funny girl."

I smiled back, and he reached out to wind his long fingers around mine. He brought my knuckles to his lips and kissed them one at a time.

It was the sweetest gesture, and I fell a little more under his spell.

"Come on," he said quietly, tugging me to my feet. "Let's go get something to eat, and you can meet some more of your new family."

Smiling, brimful of happiness, I followed him out of the RV. A cheer went up and someone yelled, "Four minutes and 23 seconds. Is that a record, Kestrel?"

He shot me an annoyed look as if to say, *I told you so!*

I couldn't help laughing, which probably didn't help.

CHAPTER 14
PLAYING NICE

We sat around the bonfire, roasting hotdogs on sticks, and from all the RVs, delicious cooking smells filled the air. Women came to our bonfire with armfuls of food: salads, cold pasta, baskets of bread, huge bags of homemade cookies. Bottles of beer were opened and loaded plates were passed around. Someone played a guitar, and the offerings poured in.

I was surprised how traditional the roles seemed to be. Zachary said it was about physical strength: guys were stronger when it came to wrestling the large pieces of machinery into place for the rides, but I thought it was more than that.

I'd so often thought of carnie folk as following an alternative lifestyle, and they were, but it had its own set of rules, too.

Everyone wanted to see Kes. All the men wanted to shake his hand, all the women wanted to kiss his cheek. Each time, he stood and greeted them by name, with a laugh and a smile for everyone and a hug for the chosen few. Each time Kes would introduce me and simply say, "This is Aimee."

I smiled and waved, a little embarrassed to become the focus of so much attention. I saw people throwing me searching looks. They weren't unfriendly, just questioning. No one mentioned Sorcha—at least not in front of me.

The older carnies wanted to talk about Dono and the good ole days; the younger ones wanted to talk about Kes Hawkins, stunt rider. I had a sense of the old world meeting the new, and finding some synergy in the carnival's magical alchemy.

The carnie children played around the bonfire, daring each other to get as close to the flames as possible until one of the mothers put a stop to it. Then they had to find another game to play.

There were about 15 kids of different ages, and all seemed happy—excited to be on the road for their summer vacation. Zachary said that most of the families traveled part-time. During school, the moms stayed home with the kids, while the fathers moved with the carnival; during vacation time, they could be together again. As Zach said, it was a hard life.

Zachary squeezed into a place next to me and passed me a s'mores.

"I think I love you," I sighed, leaning against him and licking cautiously at the sizzling, sugary goodness.

I had a nice little buzz going from a couple of bottles of beer, as well. Kes stuck to water, but nobody commented on that.

Zachary smiled and whispered in my ear. "Don't look now, but I think I'm making Kes jealous."

"Don't be silly," I said, but when I glanced at Kes out of the corner of my eye, he didn't look very happy, scowling in Zachary's direction.

"Oh my God!" I giggled. "I think you're right. Do you think he'll lock me in the trailer if I kiss you?"

"Are you drunk, Aimee?" Zachary laughed, a faint blush blossoming in his cheeks.

"It's possible," I said. "Just feeling a little overwhelmed with all of this," and I waved my s'mores at the people seated around the fire. "I had no idea Kes was so … so…"

I was lost for words, but Zachary understood.

"Dono's father was Irish, and he came from a long line of traveling men, restless souls. Kes is the equivalent of carnie royalty. Times are changing, but we like our traditions, and quite a few of the senior members remember the old ways."

"I get it," I said. "It's nice being part of something. That's why I like teaching. I like being part of the faculty, part of the team. I like having my classroom and my kids, teaching them the way I want, you know? Well, apart from having to follow the curriculum, which is a giant pain in the ass. But, it's being part of something that's important."

Zachary smiled and risked putting his arm around me.

Not long after that, the party split into two: the families went back to their own trailers and motorhomes, while the young and single stayed around the bonfire, drinking and laughing.

I think I was unconsciously delaying the moment when we'd go to bed. This would be the consequence of my hasty decision to travel with Kes, and I hadn't really thought through what it meant. Of course he'd assume that sex would be on tap, but I was nervous after what happened last time. Yep, really dumb time to realize that.

I was sure he'd sleep in the rig if I asked him to, but I didn't want that either. Hence the beer—and the delay. God, I was being so pathetic, I was annoying myself!

After a while, Kes came and put his hand on my shoulder. When I turned to look at him, he didn't say anything, he just stared fixedly into my eyes. My breath hitched, and I didn't argue when he pulled me to my feet.

I vaguely remembered Zachary saying goodnight and drifting away.

Kes left the RV's door open, and I guessed that was to allow the sultry air to circulate, but it made me hyper aware that anyone could hear … whatever it was we were going to do. And the look on Kes's face didn't leave much guesswork.

He closed the door to our compact bedroom and stood silently, staring at me.

"Kes, I…" but I didn't know what I wanted to say.

He cocked his head to one side, listening intently, his eyes fierce and glowing.

Then he took a step closer so our bodies were almost pressed together in the tiny space, but it was the feather light touch of his fingers drifting down my bare arms that made me shiver in the humid air.

His head lowered, his lips seeking out mine. The kiss, if you can even call it that, was the merest breath across my skin. I reached upwards, threading my fingers through his crazy curls, and pulling him against me more firmly, kissing him with abandon.

I heard his soft gasp of surprise and then his lips were at my ear, whispering.

"Are you being a cavewoman, Aimee? Are you going to ravish me now?"

And then he laughed gently, his arms snaking around my waist as my teeth grazed his neck.

"Shut up and kiss me!" I snarled.

So he did.

He returned my bossiness tenfold, taking charge of my body in a way that left me breathless. He seemed to be on a mission to kiss every part of me. My t-shirt was tossed away, my bra gone in a second. I kicked off my flip-flops, shucked my shorts and tried to wrestle Kes's jeans from his long legs. He laughed and stepped away, pushing them down in one long smooth movement. I didn't even get the chance to see if he was wearing briefs.

His cock was already hard, bobbing as he walked toward me.

As a question about underwear, some silly joke, formed on my lips, he turned me around, sweeping my long hair over one shoulder so he could kiss the back of my neck, my shoulder blades, the curve of my spine, the soft flesh of my ass. And then he bit me, hard, and I squealed.

"What the hell, Kes?"

"I thought you'd be mad if I left a hickey where everyone could see it," he teased, "because apparently no one is supposed to know that we're having hot, dirty sexy in here."

"That hurt!" I complained, rubbing my ass.

He batted my hands away and soothed the bite with his tongue and lips. Then he ran a gentle finger between my ass cheeks and blew a warm breath that made me tingle. When he ran his finger down the seam, I squirmed slightly. He immediately changed direction and rested one hand on my hip, reaching around to cup my mound with the other as the weight of his body pressed me forward.

I had to prop my hands up on the bed to keep from falling face first into the sheets. But then his weight was gone and he was picking me up and moving me onto the mattress.

He knelt on the floor at my feet, and pushed my knees apart.

"Oh, I'm not sure…"

He paused, one hand resting on my ankle.

"Why not?"

"I've never really liked it before. It's too … impersonal."

Kes's eyes widened in surprise. "You think this is *im*personal?"

"I can't see you when you're down there. I can't touch you. Well, I can reach your head, but…"

"Let me," he said, "and you'll change your mind."

"Pretty confident of yourself, aren't you?"

He shrugged. "Not really. I just can't think of anything more personal than using my tongue to stroke your clit, the scent of you hot and aroused, seeing your face, feeling you writhe against me until you're begging me to stop but praying for me to keep going, watching as you come on my face."

My cheeks flamed at his casually dirty words.

When he said it like that, I felt really dumb. I realized that I was parroting something Gregg had always said because he didn't like going down on me.

Kes didn't wait for me to reply. Instead, he grazed the insides of my thighs with his rough beard and didn't stop. Kissing became touching, and touching became tasting, and he was so right: there was nothing impersonal about what he was doing. I felt like he was touching my core and turning my skin inside out. The soft probing of his tongue was different from his nimble, callused fingers; a world away from the blunt width of his dick. I jerked and snapped against him until he had to hold me firmly with his hands, concentrating his mouth and teeth and tongue to bring me to a gasping orgasm.

I was still somewhere in the stratosphere when I heard a condom packet being ripped open, and then I felt him enter, shocking me into awareness, slamming me back to earth.

I felt the tremor in his strong arms as he tried to control what he was feeling.

"It's okay," I whispered, circling my legs around his waist and gripping him inside and out. "It's okay. Just … feel me."

He groaned and murmured something, the words too indistinct to reach me. Then he pulled out slowly, so only the tip was still inside. I could feel the rapid rise and fall of his stomach as his body hovered over mine, then he hooked his hands under my shoulders and used the leverage to crash into me, hard and determined, climbing deeper and deeper inside.

His eyes blazed down and his focus was thrilling and disturbing, his irises black and fathomless. I wanted to look away; I wanted to close my eyes, but I couldn't. I watched every second of his drive for release, the soft parting of his lips, the look of wonder and surprise that replaced the hard determination. His shaft stroked against sensitive nerve endings, and my short, gasping whimpers seemed to spur him on. I came again, but he pushed through my orgasm, until I was almost begging him to stop—everything was too sensitive. Then his cock thickened inside me, and his body tightened everywhere.

His climax was silent, the explosion in his body apparent only to me. Only me.

When his body relaxed against mine, his large frame covering me, I felt a warmth that had nothing to do with the sweat that glued our bodies together. I felt all the things I'd told myself I shouldn't feel with a man who was always traveling, never stopping, never still.

The whole night was a wordless, desperate need to keep touching. Touching, arousing, caressing, moving, floating, tensing and softening. It was a conversation with our bodies: pauses and questions, answers and responses. Question: *If I touch you like this?* Answer: *Yes, I'll fall a little further.*

I felt safe and protected. I felt like I belonged.

The light was a sheen of white across my eyelids and I shifted in the bed, feeling a trickle of sweat down my back. I was too warm and the rattle of the generator outside was an annoyance. And then I felt Kes's breath on my neck as he spoke.

"I've dreamed of this so many times, I can't believe it's real—that you're real. You were always there, just out of reach, and I'd wake up and find my bed empty. But now you're here."

His voice was gruff from sleep and an emotion that came from deep inside him. Maybe because written words scared him, he measured his spoken words so carefully. He rarely spoke without thinking, so each barb, each slight, was weighed and evaluated before released with stinging accuracy. But now his words hit another target, and the walls around my heart were breeched.

Part of me didn't want to fall for Kes again: he was too difficult, too dangerous, too unrestrained and wild. Since that summer, I'd looked for safe; appreciated it. *What the hell was I doing here?*

He didn't speak again, I suppose because he'd said everything he needed to. Instead, I felt the press of his erection against my ass, his hands kneading my breasts and pinching the nipples.

Despite the fact that we'd made love all night, never sleeping for more than an hour before my hands found his beautiful body, or his legs tangled with mine, I wanted him again.

His hands left me for a moment, and I heard the telltale rip of another condom packet and the rustle of the sheets as he moved on the bed. Then he entered me slowly from behind, our spooning even more intimate, and his hands crept back to cup my breasts again, his arms enclosing me as he gathered me against his chest, then the slow push and pull, the slide of his thick cock in and out of me.

It wasn't the hardest fuck or the deepest, which was just as well given the soreness of my well-used body, but it had an intimacy that took my breath away.

My arousal spiraled higher, his hands working me as if they'd known this his whole life. I called out softly and his hips moved faster, sweat making our bodies slick. Then he shuddered and buried his face in my hair, coming silently and deeply.

When he pulled out carefully, he rolled onto his back and I turned around so I was nestled against his gleaming chest.

"Better than my dreams," he whispered.

I smiled and kissed his glowing skin.

But the morning sounds were all around us, and reluctantly we had to leave our cocoon.

Tucker and Zef had been banging around in the kitchen and were now outside, calling loudly to the other carnies.

"I have to get up," Kes yawned. "Gotta do an equipment check and a run-through before the show."

"Will you be safe?" I asked, stroking his firm chest and tweaking the few dark hairs that grew there. "You didn't get much sleep last night."

A low laugh rumbled out of his chest. "You can keep me awake like that any time you like."

I tugged a little harder and he opened one eye.

"I'll be fine, Aimee."

He dropped a quick kiss into my hair, rolled to the edge of the bed and walked to the door.

"Kes!" I squealed. "Put some dang clothes on before you leave this room!"

He threw a cheeky grin over his shoulder, showcasing his dimple, before he strode butt naked from the room.

I heard the shower run and he returned two minutes later, droplets of water on his chest and dripping from his hair, and *thank you*, a towel draped loosely around his waist.

"That must have been the fastest shower in history," I muttered.

"Habit," he smiled. "You can have longer. We're hooked up to water, so we don't need to worry about the tank running out."

Then he dropped the towel, and I was surprised to see that

he was semi-erect. I think he was surprised, too.

"Well, damn," he said, staring down. "It's you, lying in my bed looking like every fantasy I've ever had."

"You've fantasized about this?" And I let my hand drift down under the sheets.

I wasn't really planning on doing anything more than tease him, because I was tired and sore, but the heated darkness in his eyes taught me never to taunt the man about sex. His cock thickened, twitching with intent, but then Tucker banged on the side of the RV.

"Kes! Get your ass out here. We've got H&S on site!"

Kes groaned. "Gotta get to work. Will you hold that thought?"

I grinned at him. "I'll hold something."

"Ah, shit!"

He turned his back deliberately and dug through the detritus of our hasty strip show from the night before, found his jeans and pulled a clean pair of briefs from his drawer.

"Not going commando today?" I queried.

He laughed, a deep contented sound. "Not when I'll be changing into my leathers later. They chafe."

I snorted loudly, and he winked at me before strolling from the room, a happy and satisfied man.

I was feeling those emotions, as well. *Definitely* satisfied. God, I hadn't had sex like that in … well, ever. As a teenager, Kes and I hadn't been granted the time to get to know each other's bodies the way we'd done last night. The other guys I'd dated had been nice, nothing special, and Gregg—it was okay. I mean he tried; he wasn't a completely selfish lover, but I suppose there's not a lot you can do when the woman you're with just isn't that into you.

Hindsight is brutally clear, and I was seeing everything with 20/20 vision.

I peeked through the tiny curtains that framed our bedroom window, squinting at the bright light of an intolerant sun. I had a slight headache, which could have been from lack of sleep or the two, maybe three beers, that I'd had the night before.

I needed a long, hot shower, and as Kes had said water wasn't an issue, I decided to indulge myself.

The guys were nowhere to be seen, so I slipped into Kes's t-shirt from the day before and slunk through the RV to the shower. I hated having to share a bathroom, especially with three guys. I tried not to think about it too hard. It couldn't be any worse, surely, than the gross communal showers I'd had to endure in college.

The bathroom was messy, but not dirty, so that was something. All I had to do was pick up two wet towels and hang them on the small rail, before stepping into the shower cubicle.

I winced as the hot water hit stubble burn on my face, neck, chest, stomach, between my legs … ah, hell, just about everywhere.

I'd only been in there long enough to lather my hair before someone banged on the door.

"Hurry up! I need to take a piss!"

I couldn't tell if it was Zef or Tucker yelling at me.

"Five minutes!" I shouted back.

But whoever it was ignored me and the door was flung open.

I squealed, and Zef's grumpy voice came through the glass shower door.

"Relax, Yoko. Nothing I haven't seen before."

"Get the fuck out, Zef!" I screamed.

But he just used the toilet, and flushed.

I don't think he even washed his hands.

I was furious. Furious and humiliated. And very determined to lock the door in future and let the bastard piss his pants.

I finished my shower quickly and pulled on shorts and a tank top, even though my body was still damp.

When I stomped into the living room, Zef was sitting on one of the sofas drinking coffee, relaxed as anything.

"What is your problem?" I snapped. "And why did you call me Yoko?"

He placed the coffee cup on the table with great deliberation and stared at me.

"I don't like you," he said bluntly.

My mouth dropped open. "What did I ever do to you?!"

"You've fucked up our boy out there," he said calmly. "And if he's fucked, we're all fucked."

"I don't know what you're talking about!"

"Oh believe me, I'm more than happy to explain," he grunted, his voice dripping with sarcasm. "He's out there yawning his head off, distracted, completely unfocussed. He's been fucking all night when he should have been sleeping. Have you any idea how dangerous his stunts are? There's a reason he's one of the best in the world—because he's focused, dedicated. Or maybe you hadn't grasped that, with your small town mentality and middleclass horizons. He only has to be off his game the smallest fraction, and a broken leg is the best case scenario."

"But I…"

"I'm not finished," he snarled. "And I'll call you Yoko because you've already split up the gang. Sorcha managed the whole show. She fucked him, kept him happy, managed his bookings, even washed his damn clothes—that poor bitch did everything, and got nothing back. A free ride and some pocket money to keep her quiet. You come along, and nothing is getting done. Tucker and I haven't got a fucking clue what's happening after this summer or whether we'll even have a gig to go to because Kes needs a manager. Thanks to you, we don't have one."

Then he stood up to walk out.

"Don't you dare!" I yelled at him. "Don't you dare put all that on me then walk out like a coward without giving me a chance to say anything!"

He turned, folding his arms across his broad chest, his hazel eyes darkening with fury.

"This should be good," he muttered.

"You have no idea what Kes and I have been through to get here," I yelled. "I've known him since we were ten years old. I've loved him all that time, and I am *not* throwing away our second chance because Sorcha held him hostage by playing on his weaknesses, his reading…"

I ground to a halt, afraid I was giving away Kes's secrets. But Zef just glared at me.

"You mean because he can't read? Yeah, I figured that out. I look out for my friends, but *you* … I don't know you."

"No, you don't! But you decided I was the bad guy anyway! I can tell you just from one afternoon of looking at Kes's paperwork that she was taking a lot more than *pocket money!* And for reasons that I haven't worked out—yet—she turned down some very lucrative bookings that could have made all three of you rich. My guess is that she wanted to keep you on a short leash, but especially Kes."

"You can't prove any of that," he sneered, although I could

see the confusion on his face.

"Maybe not, but Kes has passed all his paperwork to a forensic accountant, and he's come up with enough questions to…"

I forced myself to stop my furious defense. If Kes chose to make public what Sorcha had done, that was up to him, not me. Besides, anything I said would just taste like sour grapes.

"What questions?" scowled Zef.

"Forget it," I said tiredly. "Just do what you have to do to keep Kes safe … and stay the fuck out of my way."

I turned and walked into the bedroom, thumping the door shut behind me. But Zef followed, slamming the door open again.

"What questions?" he shouted.

"None of your fucking business!" I yelled back.

He prowled into the room, his eyes narrowed and his lips peeled back from his teeth.

"Tell me what the fuck you found out," he growled.

As well as angry, now I was scared. I didn't like being cornered by this hulking brute, with his full sleeve tattoos.

When I saw Kes's shadow behind him, I breathed a sigh of relief. Zef turned just in time to see Kes's fist coming, and he crashed back onto our bed, narrowly avoiding knocking me over.

Kes was panting with fury, shaking out his hand, but looking as if he was going after Zef again.

"Someone had better tell me what the fuck's going on!"

Zef sat up rubbing his jaw. "Ask that bitch," he said.

Kes hit him again.

"Enough!" I snapped.

Kes took a breath, but kept his fists raised. Then Tucker came running up, out of breath, a worried frown on his face.

"What's going on?"

"That's what I'd like to know," Kes said tightly.

I could feel the situation about to explode again, so I knew I had to be calm even though I was still shaking.

"I'm fine," I said, with as much control in my voice as I could muster. "Zef and I had a slight difference of opinion, but there are things we need to talk about. All of us. Kes, can we reconvene in the living room? Family conference?"

"Family conference?"

"Yes, you keep telling me we're all one family, so let's try and act like it."

"If it's anything like my family, we'll all get drunk and beat the shit out of each other," Tucker added cheerfully.

I threw him a look that should have reduced him to a pile of ash, but he just grinned at me.

"Please," I said quietly, gazing at Kes.

He looked like he was going to argue, but Tucker laid a hand on his shoulder and murmured something I couldn't hear. Kes shrugged him off but stepped back out of the room, although still keeping a wary eye on Zef who was dripping blood onto the sheets.

Zef threw me a look full of hate, then stumbled into the bathroom.

I gave up trying to be Zen like the butterfly, and stalked into the living area.

"Was he hitting on you?" Kes growled, grabbing my arm immediately.

"No, nothing like that."

"Then what?"

"Let's just wait till Zef is here."

"Fuck's sake, Aimee! I hear you yelling at each other and he's got you cornered in our bedroom. I mean, what the fuck?!"

"I'm fine," I said again. "Zef didn't touch me—just a difference of opinion. But let's wait until he's here so we don't have to say it all twice."

Kes was fuming, and when Zef walked into the room, I thought they were going to go for round two.

"You sit over there," I said pointing at Kes. "Don't punch anyone. And you," I said pointing at Zef, "don't be an asshole to anyone. And you," I turned to Tucker, "um … don't flirt with anyone."

"Don't tell me what to do!" snapped Kes.

"Fine. Fine. Sit where you like—just no more punching, please?"

He didn't reply, but slumped onto the sofa, as requested.

"Okay," I said quietly, as Zef leaned against a kitchen cabinet, eyeing me coldly while Tucker smirked in the opposite corner. "It's come to my attention that there are some concerns about who's managing Hawkins' Daredevils … now Sorcha is out of the picture."

"It's not going to be you!" hissed Zef.

"Why not her?" Kes growled at him.

"No, not me," I said firmly, and Kes scowled. "With the best will in the world, I don't know enough about the business to be helpful. But I do have a suggestion."

"This should be good," Zef muttered, and I wanted to throttle him.

So did Kes, if the murderous look he was giving him was anything to go by.

"I suggest that you ask Zachary to be your interim manager. He knows the business and knows which bookings you should go for. What he doesn't know, he'll have an idea of where to go to find out. It sounds like he's pretty busy running the carnival, but I'm sure he'd help out on a short term basis. Either way, it'll give you time to find a new manager, set up some meetings for when you're back in California. That'll give you five or six weeks to figure things out."

"Makes sense to me," said Tucker with his usual, charming smile.

Zef grunted, which could mean anything, and Kes just looked surly.

"Or not," I said tiredly. "Maybe your accountant could find an interim manager."

Kes stood up suddenly and walked away, jumping out of the RV and stalking off through the fairground.

"Don't worry," said Tucker with a smile. "He's going to find Zach."

"How do you know?"

He grinned. "Masculine intuition. Nice catch, sweet cheeks."

Then he strolled out and followed Kes, leaving me alone with Zef.

"You could have fucked me," he said.

I pulled a disgusted face. "I wouldn't let you fuck me with someone else's dick on the end of a ten-foot pole."

To my surprise, Zef cracked a grin. "I meant, you could have fucked me over. If you'd told Kes I'd come on to you, I'd be out on my ear and chewing my food with dentures."

"Oh," I said, cautiously pleased that we were communicating rather than shouting at each other.

"I thought you got rid of Sorcha so you could take over, tell the boy what to do."

231

I frowned and shook my head, wondering where he'd gotten that absurd idea.

"Like I said, I know nothing about this business. Besides, I'm only here for the summer."

Zef looked puzzled. "Just the summer?"

"Yes, I already have a job, thank you very much. I'm not looking for another one."

"Oh right. Teacher, isn't it?"

I nodded curtly.

He stood up and lurched toward me. I scrunched back against the sofa, but Zef just held out his hand.

"Truce?" he said.

"I was never fighting you."

He smiled again. "I see that now."

I took his meaty hand, and he shook mine gently. Then he stepped out of the RV and disappeared.

I blew out a breath. So much for this being a vacation. Right now I'd opt for extra playground duty with my third-graders. But then the pleasant ache between my legs reminded me that this road trip still had a lot of pluses.

Kes didn't come back, so I spent the next hour puttering around and tidying up. I yanked the bloody sheets off our bed and shoved them into the washing machine. It was one of those neat little washer-dryers, but it was such a lovely day, it made sense to hang the sheets outside. I just needed a clothes line.

I wandered over to an RV a couple of trailers down from us and knocked on the open door.

"Come on in," called a friendly voice.

I stuck my head around the door and saw a woman with blonde curly hair sitting with a young child on her knee.

"Oh hey, you must be Aimee. We didn't get to meet last night. I'm Tonya, and this is Brody."

"Hi, Tonya. It's lovely to meet you. Hello, Brody."

Tonya gave me a genuine smile, but her little boy hid his head.

"What can I do for y'all?"

"I was wondering if you had a spare clothes line? I'm sure Kes must have some around, but he's meeting with the Health & Safety rep," I elaborated, not entirely truthfully, "so I didn't want to bother him."

"Yeah, I've got some. If you could just hang on to Brody for a moment…"

She passed me the boy who gave a small wail, but at least didn't try to fight me. I propped him on my hip, and he fastened his small fingers into the strap of my tank top.

"Oh, he likes you," smiled Tonya. "You got kids?"

"No, but I have a nephew that I adore. He's five now."

Tonya nodded. "You're a natural. Ah, here it is," and she passed me a length of twine. "You can string it up between trailers—no one will mind."

"Thanks. I'll do that."

"Oh hey, I'm going into town in about an hour if you want a ride?"

I smiled, really pleased by her offer. It would be good to have a break from all of the testosterone—now there was a sentence I never thought I'd say.

I waved and agreed to meet her later.

I felt very domestic hanging out the sheets, channeling my inner homemaker. All I needed was a white picket fence and a dog.

I checked the fridge in the RV and, surprise, surprise, it was full of junk food, white bread that had a shelf-life of about a hundred years, and a lot of beers and sodas. So I sat down and made a shopping list. I decided my contribution to the summer could be to buy groceries.

I was very pleased with my list of nourishing, healthy food, but of course there was still something I needed to add: *candy*. A lot.

Tonya honked her horn, and I scrawled a quick note for Kes to tell him where I'd gone. Then I screwed it up, feeling stupid. He had a hard enough time with printed words—I doubted he'd be able to read my scribble. I decided to send him a text instead.

There were four trucks all heading into town. I jumped in with Tonya who said that she was pleased to have the company. Then she introduced me to her oldest son, Liam, who was seven, and explained that her boyfriend traveled with the carnie nine months of the year. She'd just driven them from El Dorado, Kansas, to join him.

"It's hard when he's away, on the road. We miss him, but school's got to come first. You'll understand when you have kids of your own."

"Not planning on that for a long time," I laughed nervously.

"Pity," she said with a smile. "Kes is awesome with kids."

"Yes," I admitted. "My nephew adores him, and he was great when I saw him at the fair. He was signing autographs and talking to all the children for ages."

"Hmm, sounds like someone is getting broody!"

"Not at all," I said adamantly.

Wisely, she changed the subject.

Tonya drove us to a large supermarket on the outskirts of town and all the carnie vehicles parked together. I was one of the youngest in the group, but they were all really friendly.

I couldn't say the same for the staff in the supermarket. As soon as we walked inside, I felt the stares. It wasn't that anybody said anything directly, but they were definitely watching us. Maybe it was just because we were strangers, but it felt like more than that.

When the security guard started following me around the store, my hackles rose and I turned to say something, but Tonya grabbed my arm.

"Don't. I know it sucks, but it's best not to go looking for trouble. We'll just do what we gotta do and get out of here."

"Fine," I said stiffly, grabbing a shopping cart and throwing an angry look at the security guard still trailing us around the store.

The cashier was just plain rude, eyeing us like we were trash, and snapping her gum in my face. It made me want to pull off her false eyelashes and shove them up her nostrils, but Tonya's advice was ringing in my ears, so I restrained myself.

I was fuming when I left the store, resentful that I'd paid good money to be treated like that. If we'd known of anywhere else to shop nearby, I would have told them to stuff it. Or words to that effect.

"I know, honey," Tonya said, her voice bitter. "You get used to it. The only way you can fight it is by being better than they are, you know what I'm sayin'?"

I took a deep breath. "You're right, but just … ugh! Did you see that girl who rang us up? I could have smacked her. Next time I'll send my secret weapon to buy the groceries."

Tonya looked puzzled. "You've lost me, hon."

"I'll send Kes. Women just melt when they see him. She'll be too busy staring at his ass to worry about what I might be hiding under the broccoli."

Tonya gurgled and nearly choked on a laugh.

"That'll definitely work. My Brett has a nice ass but your Kes, oh boy, he has a *great* ass."

"I know," I said smugly.

CHAPTER 15
DAY BY DAY

Arriving back at the carnival, just a few hours from opening, anticipation was in the air, and we were all excited.

The other ladies hurried off to their respective homes, and I went back to the RV to unload groceries. Tucker was there and he leapt to his feet, helping me with the bags.

"Wow! Real food," he said, holding up a bag of fresh vegetables and studying them as if he'd never seen anything like it before. "What's this?" he asked, poking the broccoli head.

I stared at him in amazement. "It's broccoli," I replied, bemused.

"Oh, okay. Can you put it on pizza?"

"Yes," I said quickly. "It goes great with pizza. You want some for lunch?"

Tucker smiled happily. "Cool!"

Lesson learned: if I wanted the boys to eat vegetables, put them on pizza.

"Where's Kes?" I asked, as I stuffed a bag of pasta into one of the cabinets.

"Aw, ain't that sweet?" he said, with a corny accent.

"What?"

"Can't be out of his sight for more than five minutes. What's the matter, sweet cheeks, you afraid to be alone with me?"

"Don't push your luck, Tucker, or I'll smack you upside the head with my broccoli. Not that I could do much damage by hitting you in the head—you've already landed on it too many times."

"You're immune to my charm, but I'll grow on you," he promised.

"You make yourself sound like fungus," I snarked, but he

just laughed and I couldn't help giggling, as well.

But when Kes strode inside, the look on his face wasn't amused. He grabbed my arm and pulled me toward the bedroom.

"Hey!" I yelped, tugging free.

Tucker slipped silently from the room. Smart guy.

"What's with you?" I snapped, rubbing my arm.

"What the fuck was that ambush this morning?" he shouted.

"Don't yell at me! I'm not your servant!"

His eyes narrowed and his nostrils flared, but I could see him controlling his anger.

"Thank you," I said, more calmly. "I didn't ambush you. I was responding to a situation that should never have happened…"

"No, it shouldn't!" he interrupted, his voice rising again.

"Because *you* shouldn't have put me in that position," I said firmly.

"What?"

"The Daredevils is your business, Kes, but the moment you told Sorcha to go, you didn't think about what came next."

"I asked you to look at my contracts!" he shouted.

"God, yes! Like I could forget that afternoon!" I took a deep breath, forcing myself to speak more quietly. "And I found you an accountant to manage your finances, but Kes, I'm not a business manager. I have no idea what your work entails. You'll have to…"

"You know I can't!" he yelled. "I can't do that fucking shit!"

He was getting really worked up, so I tried to stay calm. But he was a lot more scary than my eight-year olds who were generally smaller than I was. Kes towered over me, but it was the hurt I heard in his voice that kept me from flinching at his anger.

"We can figure this out," I said softly. "I'll try to help—we could look at your emails together and I can help with your fan mail, but as for the rest…" I shook my head. "I'm really sorry that you felt boxed in earlier, but Zef needed to know that I wasn't some sort of Yoko Ono trying to break you guys apart. I was trying to … I don't know, stop it from flaring up like it did. But as for running your business, honestly I don't know where to start. That's why I suggested Zachary could…"

"I don't want Zach managing me," he said firmly."

I blinked a couple of times. "Oh well, okay. I thought he'd

do a good job and…"

"It's not that," Kes said, rubbing his thumb across his eyebrows.

"Is it because of the way Zach feels about you?"

Kes looked up, surprised. "He told you about that?"

"Yes. I take it it's a problem for you?"

Kes sighed and slumped onto the sofa. "Yeah, but not in the way you mean. Yeah, I know about Zach. It's one of the reasons I don't travel with him all of the time. I keep hoping he'll meet someone, not be…"

"Hung up on you?"

Kes looked embarrassed. "It's sounds arrogant, but yeah."

"Oh," I said softly. "I hadn't thought of that—it's actually really sweet of you."

Kes raised his eyebrows. "Sweet?"

I waved the comment away.

"Let him do it for now. You're already on this tour with him so it won't make any difference to how often you see each other. And you can spend the next month or so looking for a manager."

"You sure you don't want to do it?"

I shook my head. "I wouldn't know where to start."

"You'd figure it out—you're smart."

"Thank you for that. But what about when I go back to Boston? You'll be at square one again. No, you need a professional."

"Fine!" he snapped. "Maybe I could just impose on your precious time for a few minutes and get Zach into my emails and shit!"

"Why are you yelling at me again! I'm trying to help you!"

He swore softly and left me standing in the RV, annoyed and upset.

He didn't come back at lunchtime either. Zef ate his pizza in silence and Tucker kept up a stream of bad jokes. I felt too tense to eat more than a few bites.

At 2 o'clock, the carnival was ready to open. The boys went off to prep for the first show, and I decided to take a walk along the midway.

There was already a line of what looked like hundreds of people waiting at the arch. Unlike everyone else, I didn't have a particular role, so I could just be one of the visitors for the day.

I watched as they poured inside, everyone excited and ready for a good time. I wandered along, not quite lost in the crowds, because every now and then the carnies would look across and give me a wave. Their quick eyes missed nothing.

I bought myself a cotton candy, for old time sake, but found that my taste buds had outgrown the sickly confection. The thought made me wistful.

"Do you want to know the future, dearie? Madame Sylva will tell you your fortune."

I looked over my shoulder to see a woman dressed like an old fashioned gypsy, sitting outside a brightly-decorated booth. I was surprised by her English accent, and her words made me giggle. Her face was deeply wrinkled, the color of a walnut, and her hands were curled into claws and wracked with arthritis. She must have been at least a hundred.

"I don't need my fortune told," I said, smiling at her. "I keep a schedule on my cell phone."

She wheezed out a hoarse laugh. "That won't tell you what you need to know. Cross my palm with silver, and learn what the Fates have in store for you."

I decided to humor her, so I pulled out a few dollars as well as a handful of quarters.

"Thank you, dearie. I like to use the traditional words: you've got to respect the classics."

She winked, beckoning me into her small tent. The heat was stifling—just being here was making my head swim.

Madame Sylva gestured to a chair, then eased herself behind a small table, waving her hands over a crystal ball.

"Ah, I see! This is about your traveling man," she declared. "He was born to wander, this one, born to fly."

She was a poet, I'd give her that much. But honestly! How gullible did she think I was? It was obvious that being Kes's new girlfriend had made me high profile in this small world.

"Do you know Madame Cindy by any chance?"

A rasping laugh rattled out of her chest.

"She's my daughter, dearie."

"Oh! I had no idea. How is she?"

Madame Sylva shook her head sadly. "Living in California. In a *house*."

She spat out the last word as if it was dirty, but her eyes twinkled.

Then she sighed heavily as she peered in the misty crystal. "He's a hard man to love."

Madame Sylva had definitely got that bit right.

"And you're at a crossroads. You're wondering which way to go—toward safety, or toward love."

She peered up at me. "Personally, I'd always go for love, but love isn't safe—it cuts and burns." She shrugged. "Difficult choice."

I laughed a little, but it wasn't easy to feel the humor when her words had me rattled.

She patted my hand kindly.

"That which is broken can still be mended, if your glue is strong enough."

Her riddles were giving me a headache.

"Thank you, Madame Sylva," I said, standing up quickly. "It's been fascinating."

She smiled. "You're welcome. Now, don't forget to keep the Ferris wheel close to your heart."

I shook my head, waving as I left. Nice woman, but nutty as a fruitcake.

Then she popped her head out of the tent and called after me.

"Don't be too hard on yourself, dearie. Or him," and she ducked back inside.

I was glad to be out of her stifling tent, but it definitely added to the atmosphere of the whole experience. I had to admit she put on a good show. Except for that nonsense about keeping the Ferris wheel close to my heart. I couldn't help feeling that she'd been sipping at the cup of loony juice.

The crowds had increased by the time I staggered back out, despite the pressing heat of the afternoon sun. The soft drink vendors and ice cream concessions had long lines in front of them. All the carnies were working and I was feeling like I didn't really belong. I didn't have friends here—they were all Kes's friends—even Zachary. And Kes hadn't texted me, so I guessed he was still mad after part two of the day's debacle. I was aware I'd stepped on his toes by interfering with his business, but honestly, Zef hadn't given me much choice. I hoped Kes would understand once I'd explained.

I decided to head back to the RV and take a nap before Kes's show.

I was walking past Sid and his 'Drown the Clown' show, moving more easily because the crowds were thinner here, when he yelled at me.

"Hey, you! Hey, girlie! All by yourself—don't you have any friends?"

I stared at him, mortified. It was a little too close to what I'd been thinking, but then I caught his wink.

"Hey, I'm talking to you!"

"Oh, I heard you," I said blandly. "It's just that you're confusing me with someone who gives a damn."

He sniggered, and I could see the message flashing in his eyes: *Game on!*

"I thought you were a nice girl, but if you're going to be two faced, at least make one of them pretty," he snarked.

"Oh really?" I said, pretending to yawn. "I would like to see things from your point of view … but I can't seem to get my head that far up my ass—it's not as big as yours."

The people around me tittered, and several stopped to listen.

"You're cute," grinned Sid. "I'll have to put you on my to-do list!"

I placed one hand on my hip and stared back.

"You couldn't handle me, even if I came with instructions."

"Don't be hasty," he said with a leer. "Let's try having sex before we rush into dating."

Several parents ushered their children away, but the crowd around us still grew.

"Why don't you dunk that clown, honey?" a woman in the crowd encouraged me.

"Yes, he needs to wash his mouth out!" shouted another.

I definitely agreed, so I handed a couple of dollars to his assistant who was smiling broadly, and I rolled up my metaphorical sleeves as I was handed a baseball.

I went through my first dollars quickly, missing four times in a row, which only had Sid taunting me loudly. I was determined to duck that quick-tongued asshat.

"Aw," said Sid, as I handed over a few more bills. "How can I miss you if you won't go away?

Soon, I had an even bigger audience. Sid jeered and laughed at me, and I was surrounded by people giving me unhelpful advice.

Growling a little, sweating in the harsh sun, I threw yet

another ball at the target … and missed.

"I love the sound you make when you shut up," he laughed.

"I would love to insult you," I said evenly, "but I'm afraid I wouldn't do as well as nature did."

"You're not funny, but your life, now that's a joke," Sid shot back, as I missed again.

"You're the one who's about to get dunked!" I snapped, missing for a gazillionth time.

Sid cackled. "You're standing here talking to me! Why don't you check eBay and see if they have a life for sale?"

I gritted my teeth, and tried to remember some of the cool insults my third-graders yelled at each other in the playground. "Ooh! I've got a good one: somewhere out there is a bunch of trees, tirelessly producing oxygen so you can breathe. I think you owe them all an apology."

One of my kids had thought up that joke after a lesson in photosynthesis.

People around me laughed, and I bought another four shots, determined to stop Sid's mouth with a big drink of water.

"Honey, you're proof that God has a sense of humor," he snorted, as I wound up to take another shot.

Ugh, he was good!

I tried again—and missed. I was actually getting kind of pissed at myself for being such a girly thrower.

"Well, If you spoke your mind, you'd be speechless," I sniped, handing over my final dollar for balls to throw.

"Well I could agree with you, but then we'd both be wrong," said Sid.

Oh, I was never going to win against him.

"If you're going be a smartass, first you have to be smart. Otherwise you're just an ass. Oh wait, too late!" I laughed, impressed that I'd thought of a great comeback.

The crowd had built up a lot in the last five minutes as Sid and I continued to trade insults across a large tank of cold water. *Jeez, my life!*

"Still can't dunk me!" he crowed.

Damn!

When the last of my throws had come and gone, I was in such a lather and dripping with sweat, that I'd definitely lost my cool. I pulled off my sneaker and flung it at him.

Miracle of miracles, I hit the target! Sid was dunked at last!

The audience were laughing at him, laughing at me, and couldn't wait to try their luck.

His assistant passed me my soggy sneaker and winked at me.

"Nice work! You've really got the rubes going with all those misses!"

I didn't want to tell her that I hadn't missed on purpose—my aim really was that bad. But everyone was happy. Sid tried to kiss me, but I dodged out of his dripping arms and headed off down the midway, stopping once or twice to chat to people.

I had half an hour before Kes's first show, so I decided to go say hi to the ponies used in the rodeo act. Animals didn't lose their temper or make bad jokes at your expense.

They snickered softly when they saw me and trotted over to see if I had any apples.

"Sorry," I said, stroking their noses and patting their necks. "I'll definitely drop by with apples next time. I don't suppose any of you like broccoli?"

A woman with short dark hair and a friendly smile strolled over.

"Hi! You must be Aimee. I'm Rhonda Reynolds."

"Oh! You own the carnival!"

She smiled. "Myself and my husband Dan, but Zachary is really the one in charge. I saw you this morning at the supermarket, but I didn't get a chance to introduce myself. Did I hear you offering broccoli to my horses?"

"Oh sorry," I laughed. "Just trying to find someone around here who'll eat vegetables. I had to tell Tucker that broccoli goes great with pizza."

She laughed loudly. "That's a good one! You should try giving them son-of-a-gun stew."

"Son of a what?!"

She grinned at me. "It's a big ole stewpot with pieces of beef or pork or whatever meat you've got. Then I throw in a ton of vegetables and stew it all up so no one knows what son-of-a-gun is what. That way, my kids will eat vegetables and hardly know they're doing it."

"That's brilliant! I'll have to try that."

She smiled. "So how are you enjoying traveling with the carnival?"

"Oh, I'm absolutely loving it. I just had a very interesting run in with Sid."

Rhonda sniggered. "Yeah, I heard about that."

"You did? I was only just there!"

"Oh, you'll learn. News like that spreads fast. Sid said he hasn't had so much fun in a long time."

I was pleased that I'd been able to hold my own with a guy who used to be a stand-up comedian—even if I was a lousy shot.

"It must have been a big decision for you to give up your work and your life back east," Rhonda said as she stroked the horses. "I remember when I told my parents that I was going to follow Dan on the rodeo circuit and that his father owned a carnival, you'd have thought I'd told them I was joining a cult." She laughed sadly. "But in a way they weren't wrong. This life, well, you've seen for yourself. We don't always get treated so well because we're outside of the norms, different from other folk and how they live their lives."

"Yes, I've definitely seen that," I agreed. "It must be hard. But no, I haven't given up my whole life—I have a job waiting for me in Boston at the end of the summer."

Rhonda looked surprised. "You do?"

"Well, yes!" I laughed. "I teach third grade at a school just over the border in New Hampshire. I've been there for two years now. I love it."

Rhonda seemed confused, but she nodded slowly.

"And you're going back there, after the summer? I just thought that…" she hesitated. "Oh well, that sounds great. Just great." Then she smiled again. "Well, better get ready for the show. We're on right before Kes. Catch you later, Aimee!"

I headed back to the RV, wondering if I should ask Rhonda for her recipe for son-of-a-gun stew, or whether I should just give it a try.

But when I got back to the RV, I was pleasantly surprised to see that Kes had a smile on his face. He scooped me off my feet and twirled me around, kissing me soundly.

"What's that for?" I asked breathlessly.

"Do I need a reason?"

"Definitely not."

He laughed and kissed me again.

"Cheryl, Sid's assistant told me how much you helped them with the act. Sid was really pleased. He wanted to know if you'd do it every day?"

I was astonished. "Really?"

"Yeah, he says you got the marks going."

Kes looked so proud of me, and I sunned myself in the warmth of his praise.

"Well, it wasn't planned. I just tried to keep up with the insults. I guess teaching has a wide spectrum of applications. Who knew?"

His smile faded a little, but then he kissed me again.

"I have to go get ready now, but you'll come see the show?"

"I wouldn't miss it," I smiled, glad his sulk was over.

While the guys were all at the arena, I boiled up a huge pot of pasta, put it in a dish with a bunch of vegetables, smothered it in cheese and shoved it in the fridge ready to cook for dinner later. I also had my secret weapon in completing the battle of winning over Zef: homemade apple pie. Well, homemade in that I bought a frozen pie crust at the store and added a can of apple pie filling.

No one would know the difference. Yeah, I'd keep telling myself that.

I schlepped on over to the arena to watch the rest of the rodeo show. Rhonda's family did a fast and furious comedy rodeo that had the audience laughing and cheering, but to my critical eye, it lacked the drama of the act Kes and his brother used to do.

There was a short break between the shows while the two bike ramps were put into place.

The crowd had tripled in size, and there wasn't a single empty seat in the bleachers. A rustle of anticipation rippled around as the start time came and went.

And then, against the backdrop of that vast open sky, tinged pink as the sun sank, Kes roared into the arena in a cloud of dust and exhaust fumes.

He looked lean and dangerous in his red and black leathers, painted flames dancing over the top of his helmet. The crowd went nuts, screaming and stamping their feet. He skidded the bike to a halt, then pulled it up onto its back wheel. If it had been a horse, it would have been pawing at the sky. I shivered and said a quick prayer. *Keep him safe tonight.*

When I saw the show in Minneapolis, I didn't know who was performing those perilous jumps. It was bad enough watching a complete stranger do them, but so much worse now that I knew it was Kes.

I spent most of the hour watching between my fingers. To be honest, I was relieved when it was over.

Why couldn't I have fallen for a guy who worked in an office? Then the biggest thing I'd have to worry about would be paper cuts.

Once the show was over, Kes spent more than half-an-hour going around and signing autographs.

I hung around to watch the clown act, which was pretty funny, but I was glad to be sitting near the back. I dreaded all that audience participation stuff. Then I got to see Rhonda's second show, then Kes was on again.

It hadn't got any easier to watch. I wondered how the hell I was going to last through seven weeks of this.

I slunk back to the RV to finish up making dinner while the guys were signing more programs. Then I prepared my game face for when Kes walked in.

Tucker and Zef arrived back first, buzzed on adrenaline. They were like bear cubs, horsing around and banging into furniture as they wrestled. I suggested they take themselves outside: okay, I may have yelled, but they just laughed at me. I'm not sure they'd have done what I asked if they hadn't smelled the apple pie baking in the oven. I swear, they both drooled.

They showered quickly and flopped down on the grass outside, beers in hand. That was two out of my three guys satisfied.

Kes arrived back shortly after—hot, sweaty and tired.

He'd already peeled off his leathers and left them in the bike trailer, so he was strolling across the grass in his underwear. I guessed that was normal behavior for all of the guys. Sweat had turned his dark hair jet black, droplets glistening in the setting sun on his chest and back. He looked dark, deadly and delicious.

"Hey," he said softly, the shadows darkening his eyes and highlighting his cheekbones. "What did you think?"

"Amazing, as usual," I said honestly, kissing his soft lips. "But it scares the crap out of me. I had to watch most of it through my fingers."

He laughed lightly. "I've done it a thousand times, more. I'm fine."

"Doesn't stop me from worrying," I said.

His beautiful lips curved upwards and he kissed me back.

I ran my hands over his firm ass, and against my hip, I could feel he was getting hard.

"Hold that thought," I said, nipping his earlobe. "Dinner is nearly ready and you need to shower."

"Hmm, you in my kitchen and food on the table. I think I like this scenario."

I swatted his delectable ass with a dish towel as he danced out of reach.

We ate our meal outside. And even though I thought I'd made enough for two days, there was nothing left at the end. They inhaled the food as if they hadn't eaten for a week.

I was definitely going to have to rethink how often I bought groceries.

I was surprised but pleased when Kes and Zef cleaned up, and Tucker rolled his sleeves up to his elbows and washed the dishes. They were happy to have me cook, but I wasn't completely taken for granted. Thank God. Because I'd had enough drama in that direction for one day.

Zef and Tucker stayed up talking and drinking beer, but Kes made it obvious that he was hungry for more than food.

In the end, he just scooped me up and carried me inside. Then he made sweet, sweet love to me for hours. Then he fucked me hard.

Perfect end to a not-so-perfect day.

We got into a rhythm over the next week, not just me and Kes, but with all the other carnies, as well. I made myself useful sparring for 20 minutes or so with Sid if things were a little slow. I started a reading group for the kids, letting them choose the books we read. Adventure stories were popular, so I stocked up in town at one of the thrift stores that had some used paperbacks.

Several of the parents told me they appreciated my help, and I enjoyed it. Kes was pleased that I was making an effort to fit into the life.

I did chores, too, but no more than my share, bearing in mind that the guys had rehearsals and maintenance of the ramps and motorcycles to do every day.

I knew a lot more about the bikes they used now. These were sports bikes, light weight and powerful, with a few adjustments that made them more durable for the hard wear and tear they received during the act. They had frame sliders that protected the fairings from damage when the bikes were sliding, as well as lots of adaptations that the guys had developed. It was definitely a whole new vocabulary, and one with which Kes was far more fluent than me.

It didn't make watching the stunts any less frightening, but at least I knew more about the safety precautions. It helped. No, I was lying—it was still utterly terrifying.

My self-appointed job was keeping everyone fed. My son-of-a-gun stew was a big hit. I even confided to Rhonda that it was 90% vegetables, which she thought was hilarious. Zach and Ollo ate with us most nights, too. Zach had a way of calming everyone down, and Ollo's quick eyes missed nothing. I picked up a lot about the business end of things from those conversations. I also spent half an hour every evening going through Kes's fan mail and emails with him. Or I tried to: he had the attention span of a gnat. I wasn't sure how much of it was an inability to concentrate, or whether it was more that he was reluctant to remind me that reading often defeated him. Probably a bit of both.

I enjoyed having my makeshift family around me. But I had to do grocery shopping every other day, because there wasn't much storage space for fresh food, and I needed to keep up with the boys' huge appetites.

Keeping up with Kes's sexual appetite was something else. I swear I lost weight from our athletic love-making.

But there was a downside to the carnie life. It was the lack of privacy that I found wearing. Communal living was definitely a taste that I wasn't acquiring as much as I thought I would. It was a noisy, bickering, watchful family that rigorously policed itself, but was unapproachable and wary of outsiders. It seemed even more remarkable to me that Kes had let me in.

Everyone knew everyone else's business: and I mean everything. If Kes and I had words before breakfast, which was quite often because I wouldn't let him get away with being The Man, then I'd have comments about it as I walked around the living quarters an hour later.

Our sex life seemed to be of great interest to everyone, and I hated that. Other women slyly commented that they'd heard us inside the RV. Well, they couldn't have heard Kes, because he was never loud, not even when he came. Embarrassingly, it must be my gasps and screams that they were hearing, unless it was the sound of me being thoroughly pounded. Yeah, not at all embarrassing.

Surprisingly, Zef and Tucker were more circumspect about their comments, certainly around me, but I think Kes came in for his share of ribbing. But what guy cares if everyone knows he's getting laid … a lot?

I complained quietly to Zachary one morning when the guys were working on the bikes.

"I don't know how you stand it sometimes," I moaned. "If I sneeze, a hundred people yell 'Bless you!'."

Zach smiled. "It can take some getting used to, but on the whole people mean well."

"I know," I sighed. "Everyone's been really nice. I just wish they weren't so *vocal* about things."

Zach frowned. "Not sure I'm understanding you."

I sucked my teeth and looked around.

"I won't tell anyone, Aimee," he said, sounding a little hurt.

"I know that, but…"

"But what?"

My cheeks flushed red. "Everyone is always making these little digs about our sex life. It's so embarrassing. I'm sorry, I shouldn't talk to you about this."

"Believe me," he teased, "I'm intrigued. You straight guys are weird."

"Shut up!" I laughed. "It just feels like everyone's talking about me. I know they aren't, but…"

"They are," he said.

"What?"

He winked at me.

"Zach, what!"

"It's nothing bad. They're just not used to anyone being quite so, um, how should I put this … you guys do it *a lot*. Everyone's impressed."

I thought I was going to faint. "Please tell me you're joking!"

He shook his head, grinning. "Come on, Aimee! If it's not Kes hauling you off to have his wicked way with you, then you're giving him these scorching looks across the bonfire. Hell, it makes *me* want to go take a cold shower, which is interesting seeing as you're a girl and I'm gay."

I started to deny it, but what was the point.

"I'm so embarrassed," I muttered.

"Don't be," he laughed. "All the guys are jealous. Kes gets laid like clockwork, and his girlfriend is hotter than hell."

I gulped. "You think I'm hot? I thought I was, you know, average?"

Zachary laughed. "No, you're cute. But somehow, when you and Kes are together, there's this incredible sexual tension in the air. Hell, it makes everyone horny. I think there'll be a lot of kids born in about nine months time after this tour."

"Oh," I said faintly.

Zach grinned at me. "They're all very grateful to you," he whispered, hooking my arm through his. "And just so you know, you're not the only one who's getting lucky every night."

My eyes widened at the smug smile on his face.

"Zach! Who?!"

"Just someone."

"Tell me!"

"Okay, but we're keeping it on the down low for now."

I narrowed my eyes at him. "Seriously? After you just got through telling me that my sex life is public discussion topic numero uno?"

Zachary had the grace to look a little sheepish.

"I know. In fact, I should thank you. You and Kes have taken the heat off of me. The King of the Carnival and his beautiful bride." Zach's smile faded. "I'm cautious because that's the result of experience over hope, if you know what I mean."

I nodded. "I can understand that. So, who's the lucky guy?"

Zach's smile was a thousand megawatts. "His name is Luke, and he was taken on as a roustabout for this season. He's hot, well, not as hot as Kes, of course."

"Of course not," I grinned. "Well, I'm really happy for you."

"Yeah, it's just for the summer, but it makes a change to be traveling with someone." Zachary smiled. "And how about you? Apart from the gossip about your exciting sex life…"

"Do you want me to say shut up again?"

Zachary gave me a quick hug. "Seriously, how are things going for you—and Kes?"

"Good, mostly, I think. It's been quite a baptism of fire. I mean, all those years when we didn't see each other, but within a week of meeting up again, we're living together for all intents and purposes. It's a little disorientating. In a good way, but it's going to be awful when it's over."

Zach looked thoughtful.

"Does it have to be over?"

"Well, yes," I laughed sadly. "Unless we want to cripple ourselves financially by commuting from coast to coast on weekends. Or seeing each other three or four times a year for holidays. Long distance relationships don't work. It just wears you both down. I'd rather we ended on a high."

Zach sighed. "It's none of my business, but I get the impression Kes is hoping that it won't be the end."

I felt tears prick my eyes. "I don't want it to end either, Zach, but how can we do anything else? Even if I moved to California, he's traveling all the time. Am I supposed to give up my job, my career, to go and ... what? Be his housekeeper?"

I shook my head.

"No, I need more than that. And even if I was content to live off of him, what if he got bored of me? I'd be stuck."

"He loves you, Aimee," Zachary chided gently. "More than anything—he loves you."

"Maybe. For now. It's shiny and new, but..."

"I think you're wrong, but it's your life. He told me that he asked you to be his manager."

"Oh, come on! I don't know diddlysquat about any of that! I'd be useless."

"I could teach you."

I was silent, wondering if what he suggested were possible.

"Do you know why I got into teaching?" I asked quietly.

Zach shook his head.

"To help children like Kes. I know that you're aware of his issues with reading. He never got a chance to learn past his dyslexia. He doesn't believe he can be helped, but he can, if he'd just give himself some time. I spent every summer trying to help him and encourage him when we were kids. He'd make a little progress, and then by the next year, we'd be almost back to square one. I decided then that I wanted to know how to help people like him."

Zachary was silent, but he wrapped me in a big hug and held me gently.

"You'll work it out, Aimee."

I wasn't sure he was right.

CHAPTER 16
WILD ROVER

"I'm really sorry about your birthday," Kes said, as he stood gulping down scalding black coffee.

My birthday had fallen on a jump day, which meant that everyone had spent the night before taking down the show. The guys had worked solidly packing up the bleachers and ramps, and stowing it all in trailers.

Now dawn was breaking, and we were about to start the 400 mile drive from Kansas City to Amarillo. I'd caught a couple of hours sleep, so while I drove the RV, Kes was going to take a nap. I'd had a little practice, but I was still nervous about driving such a large vehicle. Zef promised that all I had to do was follow him in the rig. He even agreed he wouldn't go over 55 the whole way. I was prepared to try.

"I don't care about my birthday," I said to Kes, wrapping my arms around his solid warmth and peering up at him. "Really I don't. I haven't celebrated it in years. Well, my friend Mirelle made me go clubbing with her last year, but that's all."

"I didn't even know you liked dancing," Kes said bitterly. "It's fucking unfair that we've missed out on so much."

I didn't say anything, because there was nothing to say.

Kes shook his head, then he reached into his jeans pocket and pulled out a small box.

"What is it?" I asked, startled.

"Well, here's the thing: you have to open it to find out," he teased.

The box was covered in black velvet, the texture soft and smooth under my fingers as I stroked it lovingly.

Kes leaned down and whispered in my ear. "It's just a box: the good stuff is inside."

I grinned up at him. "Well, who'd have thought?!"

When I opened the box, my breath was stolen away.

Inside, a delicate gold chain lay nestling in black silk, but it was the miniature Ferris wheel with a tiny diamond at the center that brought tears to my eyes.

I stared at it, and it was several seconds before I could speak.

"Kes, it's beautiful! Thank you! I've never … it's gorgeous!"

"You like it?" he asked anxiously.

"I love it. I absolutely love it!"

Kes lifted it from the box and I moved my hair out of the way as he fastened it around me, smiling to myself as he kissed the back of my neck gently.

"Now, wherever you go, you'll always have the carnival with you."

"Thank you. I love it … and I love you."

I hadn't allowed myself to say those words, hadn't wanted them out in the open, although they'd been implied every day. I couldn't hold them in any longer.

Kes's arms tightened around me and I turned, taking in his beautiful face, softened now with what surely must be love, even though he couldn't or wouldn't say the words back to me.

Then he kissed me sweetly, his eyes silver in the pale light.

We held each other for too brief a moment.

"We have to get going," he sighed.

"I know. Zef is trying not to look impatient, but it's not working."

Kes laughed quietly. "Yeah, I see that." Then he rubbed my arms and looked at me fiercely. "Promise you won't take it off."

His gaze was intimidating, almost angry.

"I promise," I whispered.

He smiled and the tension drained from his body as he straightened up.

"Just remember to leave plenty of space between you and Zef when you're driving," he said in a more normal voice. "When he makes the turn for the truck stop, he'll swing out to take it. Follow his line and go slow. Okay?"

He looked a little worried.

"I'll be fine. I'm looking forward to it," I lied. "Try to get some rest, and I'll wake you when we get to Oklahoma City."

He kissed me again, then helped me up into the driver's seat and made sure my seatbelt was in place. He could be such a gentleman. A complete asshole at other times, but right now, all the boxes were checked.

I touched my beautiful new necklace as Kes winked at me and waved to Zef.

When I pushed the button to start the powerful engine, the throaty roar had my nerves twanging. I eased off the handbrake as the RV bumped and shuddered over the ridges and ruts of the carnival field.

The 24-Hour Man—the guy who went ahead to post arrows so we could find the right field on arrival—had left as soon as the takedown started the night before, but otherwise we were among the first to leave because putting up the bleachers was a ton of work. The only others ahead of us were the ones who dismantled the Ferris wheel and helter-skelter, and Al the foreman, who turned out to be the scary-looking tattooed guy that I'd met on my first day. I still thought he was scary.

As I inched through the arch at the exit to the field, I felt a sudden desire to squeeze my eyes shut, but I managed to keep a close eye on the wing mirrors and gripped the steering wheel until my knuckles were white.

I began to relax a little once we hit the I-35: a nice, wide highway—lots of space. Zef was true to his word, sticking to the limit, and when we had to face the spaghetti loop-road around Emporia before we headed south again, he dropped to a snail's pace, so at least I felt in control of the RV. That was the most nerve wracking moment. Although the road around Wichita gave me a few anxious moments, the rest of it was pretty easy.

Finally, we pulled into the Five Star Truck Stop just north of Oklahoma City, and I parked next to Zef, gratefully unclamping my hands from the wheel. I stretched my neck and back to get the cricks out.

Kes appeared behind me rubbing his eyes and looking deliciously rumpled as he tugged a t-shirt over his head.

"Everything okay?"

"Nope, died in a pile-up back in Kansas. This is Heaven."

He laughed, his voice still rough from sleep.

"I've got you, got the carnival—works for me."

His words gave me a jolt of happiness and a pinch of pain. Was life really so simple for him?

Kes rested his hands on my shoulders and kissed my hair, his breath minty. But then Zef banged on the door, dark circles

254

prominent beneath his eyes.

"You look like shit," laughed Kes, who was annoyingly chipper after his nap.

Zef gave him the finger and ambled into the diner with Tucker, who'd also managed to get some sleep during the drive.

We all loaded up on greasy food, then I went to lie down while Kes took over driving.

I was about to head for the bedroom when Kes turned and grinned at me. "Works out pretty good having a co-driver," and he winked.

Maybe Sorcha had never driven the RV. I wouldn't ask him about that—just hearing her name sent him into a foul mood. But maybe if Zachary happened to know…

My phone rang, and I couldn't help smiling when I saw that Mirelle was calling.

"Hey, chica!" she yelled. "Happy freakin' birthday! What are you doing right now? I hope it's that super-hot, bike-riding boy of yours!"

"I wish! I've just driven 25,000 pounds of RV 200 miles. Kes is driving now, so I'm going to take a nap."

"Shut up! You're *sleeping* for your 25th birthday?!" Mirelle's tone was disgusted.

"For now. It's a jump day, so the guys were up all night doing the takedown," I yawned. "But Kes says he'll make it up to me later. I'm going to hold him to that."

Mirelle snorted. "I bet that's not all you'll be holding!"

I shook my head as I smiled to myself: she didn't change.

I snuggled down into the sheets that smelled of Kes, and listened to Mirelle telling me about her vacation. She'd completely forgiven me for ditching her when I'd told her about Kes. She said she wanted to meet him, but I couldn't see how that would happen.

When we finished our catch up, I lay back and tried to sleep. But I kept thinking about what Kes had said: that Heaven for him was me and the carnival.

I tossed and turned for more than an hour, finally passing out as we crossed the border into Texas, my dreams confused and wearying.

I woke up as we bumped across the carnival field hours later. I felt better than I had at lunchtime, but still a little rough around the edges.

Everywhere, the crazy carnival routine was swinging into action, and already the ground plan for the midway was set up. As I squinted into the sun, I could see the helter-skelter rising into the air alongside the pin of the Ferris wheel at the back end of the field.

Kes was out of the RV and talking with Zef and Tucker by the rig, so I decided to leave them to it. I knew from experience that they wouldn't stop now until the bleachers were operational and the ramps were in place.

I'd make some of my famous broccoli pizzas later, then they could eat whenever they wanted.

In the meantime, I went to see if Madame Sylva had arrived. I often helped her to set up. Her small booth was one of the easiest, but it was still more than she could manage alone, although she did enjoy decorating it with colorful scarves.

She was standing waiting for me when I found her in the midway.

Her eyes went straight to my necklace.

"Ah," she croaked happily. "You've got your Ferris wheel close to your heart."

"Oh yes, it's beautiful, isn't it?"

Her intense gaze made me uncomfortable, so I got busy hauling on the guy ropes to erect the tent, then hammering the pegs into place. Hers was one of the simplest booths, once Ollo had taught me what to do, and I was proud of being able to manage by myself. With the tent up, I carried in her small table and two chairs.

Madame Sylva was already poring over her crystal ball.

"Ah, I see," she whispered. "You've made your decision."

I frowned at her. "What decision?"

She shook her head. "Never mind me, dearie. These Circus jump days are too much for an old bird. I think I'll go and have forty winks."

Then she waved and tottered off toward her small caravan.

I didn't have time to worry about her words, there were plenty of other people who could use a spare pair of hands.

Finally, as the sun sank in the Texan sky, most of the midway was finished, although the large mechanical rides would take longer. Zachary was pleased and flopped down on a deckchair outside our RV.

"Everything okay?"

"Yep," he smiled tiredly. "Getting there. We'll finish by three, maybe four in the morning. Everyone will get some sleep."

"Oh, that's good. Kes and the guys should be taking a break soon. How about a slice of broccoli pizza and a beer?"

"Will you get mad if I pick the broccoli off?"

"Yep."

He pulled a face. "Broccoli pizza and beer sounds great."

I'd learned from experience that one pizza each wasn't enough, and the guys inhaled food like a pack of wolves. The scent of melted cheese must have made its way to the arena, because they came loping out of the twilight, their eyes fixed on the food.

Zachary finished his meal and stood up.

"Gotta get back to it. H&S inspection scheduled for 9.30AM," he said, waving at Kes who saluted him with a slice of pizza.

Kes didn't even sit down to eat, scarfing a whole pizza, before giving me a cheesy kiss and heading back.

"Don't wait up," he called over his shoulder. "It's going to be a late one."

I cleaned up and fell into bed, totally exhausted, knowing that I had it easier than most people in the carnival.

It was only a couple of hours before dawn when I felt the mattress shift beneath me.

"Did you finish?" I asked, rolling over sleepily as Kes pulled me into his arms.

"Yeah, we did," he whispered against my hair. "Go back to sleep, beautiful."

When I woke three hours later, the Texas light was bright, the sun already blazing overhead. Kes was still curled around me, his left arm holding my boob firmly. Typical.

Trying not to disturb him, I managed to extricate myself. I stood up soundlessly and watched him as he slept. He looked younger and sweeter in sleep, the energy that fizzed under his skin absent; the hard edges and single-minded focus that made him the top of his dangerous profession were softened for now.

His hair had grown longer, curling across his forehead and at the nape of his neck, making me want to wrap it around my fingers. The sheet had slipped from his shoulders, so it was draped in a tangle around his legs and hips, one foot sticking out at the bottom, a vulnerability that wedged my heart wide open.

Even in rest, he looked powerful, the muscles ridged along his chest and stomach, his biceps hard, his thighs and calves firm to the touch.

And I knew, under the sheet, his cock was like steel. I'd felt it against my ass as I'd climbed out of bed. I'd been tempted to touch and taste, but right now he needed sleep more than he needed sex. I wouldn't be selfish.

I took one last look, fixing the beautiful picture in my mind, and then headed to the kitchen.

When I glanced at my watch, I knew I could only give Kes and the boys another hour in bed before they had to be ready for the townies to inspect the site.

The thought made me pause. For the first time, townies were *them*, which meant that I was *us*, one of the carnies. A small smile crossed my face.

As it happened, I didn't need to wake Kes, the scent of grilling bacon did it just fine. Then Tucker and Zef came stumbling in.

Bleary-eyed, they swallowed down forkfuls of eggs, bacon, fried tomatoes and toast, washed down with pints of OJ. I was on a mission to get fruit or vegetables into every meal. I don't think they even noticed: food was fuel.

Through the window, we saw Zachary heading our way with two men in suits and hardhats. The H&S men were on time, which was a good sign. Zach hated it when he had to chase down the local officials, because it delayed everything, sometimes for hours. That had happened when we got to Kansas, and I could see how much it added to everyone's stress.

The guys drank down a last mouthful of coffee, then headed out. But Kes turned back, pulling me into his arms and kissing me thoroughly.

"Go!" I laughed. "You have important people to talk to."

"No one more important than you," he murmured against my lips. "You had a shit birthday, but I'm going to make it up to you."

"What did you have in mind?" I asked, rubbing against the front of his jeans and waking his dick in the process.

"Yeah, I'll make it up to you … behind the bleachers, at the bottom of the field after dark, in our bedroom, several times…"

I laughed happily. "Sounds like a great birthday. I can't wait."

I think Kes took that literally, because he started pulling me back to the bedroom.

"Health and Safety!" I giggled.

"Condoms," he replied, which made me laugh even harder.

But then Zachary was at the door, giving Kes a stern look.

"Kestrel! Get your cute ass down here!"

Kes turned and gave him a withering stare. "Don't ever call my ass cute, man!"

"But it is cute!" I joined in as Zach winked at me.

Kes muttered something under his breath, then jumped out of the RV, accidentally-on-purpose shoulder-barging Zachary along the way.

I didn't see the guys again till just before their show, and I spent most of the day hanging out with Rhonda and her kids. Kes found me talking to their horses.

"I've been looking for you."

"Any particular reason?" I asked.

He shrugged, a self-conscious gesture that had me smiling to myself.

"Do you ever miss this?" I questioned. "The horses, I mean."

"Yeah, I do."

"But you never went back to it after…"

He shook his head.

"Why not?"

Kes sighed. "No money, for one thing. Horses cost money: feed, transport, veterinarian bills. I could have joined someone else's act, but they all seemed kind of lame. You know, girly circus shit."

"What about Cirque du Soleil? They wanted you."

"They wouldn't take me till I was 18, and I needed to work. When my father…" and he pulled a face, "when he brought me back after I ran away the first time, I knew I had to stay clear of anything familiar. I was good with engines, so…" He gestured loosely. "But yeah, I miss being around animals."

One of the horses nuzzled Kes's shoulder, and he stroked her velvety nose.

"Rhonda lets me take a ride sometimes. And I helped teach her kids some stuff."

"Really?"

"Yeah, a few tricks, jumps, things like that. I guess you never lose the knack."

Then his phone vibrated in his pocket. He squinted at the screen, and I could see his lips moving as he made sense of the words. It was painful to watch.

"Zach wants me," he said. "We'd better get going. Come see the show later?"

"Always," I said.

He grinned and draped his arm around my shoulders as we walked back toward the arena.

I was surprised to see a woman in a pant suit sitting in one of our deckchairs outside the RV. Another man was with her, and Zachary was hovering by the pair of them, looking uncomfortable.

"Ah, here he is!" said the woman, running her eyes across Kes in a proprietary way that made my hackles rise. "Shelly Lendl—great to meet you."

Kes gave her his trademark smirk, but raised his eyebrows at Zach.

"Ms Lendl is a journalist," Zachary explained, although he needn't have bothered. Her colleague with the large, professional camera bag was a giant clue.

"How can we help you, Ms Lendl?" I asked politely, my hand around Kes's waist.

Her eyes slid to me, a curiously icy sensation. "And you are?"

"Very interested in journalists," I smiled, my expression bland. "Who did you say that you work for?"

Her plump glossy lips tightened a fraction. "I'm freelance." Then she focused on Kes again. "I'd really like to interview you, Mr. Hawkins. Readers will be fascinated to know why a record-breaking stuntman is traveling with a smalltime funfair."

Kes's expression didn't change, but the sudden stiffness in his body told me he wasn't impressed by Ms Lendl.

"I'm just about to go get ready for my show," he said, taking a step toward the RV.

"Super! I'll have Josh here take some shots now and while you're doing your show, too. We can talk after."

I could tell what Kes was thinking. This woman had rubbed him the wrong way by describing the carnival as a 'smalltime funfair'. It wasn't so much what she'd said, as the sneer in her voice when she said it. But at the same time, he recognized the value of publicity.

His eyes flicked to Zach's, and he nodded minutely.

"Great!" said Zachary, visibly relieved. "We'll set that up for later."

Inside the RV, Kes spoke quietly. "What do you think?"

"No reason she shouldn't be legit, except that she's a bitch."

Kes smiled at me and winked.

"But just to be on the safe side," I continued, "I'm going to look her up. Go get ready for the show and I'll let you know what I find out."

One quick search brought up everything I needed to know about Shelly Lendl—and she was exactly what she said she was.

Kes came up behind me while I sat at the laptop. "Anything?"

I was momentarily distracted by the fact he was bare-chested and barefoot, wearing just a pair of ripped jeans.

"She's definitely a journalist, but the tabloid kind. Most of her stories have been sold to 'TMZ' and some to 'Us Weekly'. She seems to have more articles on the size of Kim Kardashian's ass than anything else." I gave Kes a pointed look. "No ass pictures, even if yours is cute."

He grinned. "You think I should talk to her?"

"You must have done Press interviews before?"

"Yeah, when I got the world record thing, but it was casual. I don't think it was of much interest except to gear-heads and grease monkeys."

"Well, I don't see why you shouldn't talk to her. Just be careful. Talk about your work, but probably best to steer her away from personal topics."

Kes didn't look happy at the thought of that. "Other than telling her it's none of her fucking business?"

"Probably best to avoid that. Just say, 'I'm happy to discuss my work, but not my private life'. Okay?"

He nodded.

"And then smile. She'll be putty in your hands."

Kes laughed and shook his head. "Got it."

"And don't walk around in your underwear."

He leaned down to kiss my throat. "You love it when I do that."

"Ah, you've noticed my ogling."

"It was pretty obvious."

"Darn it! I thought I was being discreet."

He laughed, a low down sexy rumble in his chest. "Last time I did it, you licked my chest. Then I bent you over the bed and fucked you."

My cheeks heated up at the memory. "Fair point," I breathed.

He turned to leave, shooting a scorching look over his shoulder. "Hold that thought."

I watched him from the window as he padded across the grass to the rig, ready to leather-up.

The reporter tried to follow him, but Zach cut her off, explaining that Kes needed to get in the zone before a show. She frowned, but didn't argue. I noticed that the photographer took some shots of Kes in his ripped jeans.

The show was great, which meant I had to watch most of it between my fingers, as usual. I thought it would get easier, seeing Kes fling himself fifty feet in the air, and pounding down a narrow ramp on the far side of the jump, but it didn't. If anything, it got worse. It almost seemed like a game of Russian roulette to me, and as much as I hated the feeling in my gut, I couldn't help thinking that eventually, one day, the odds would be against him and something would go wrong.

Afterward, Kes was relaxed and happy. He showered quickly, then sat outside with a glass of ice water to talk to Ms Lendl.

I hovered in the background, listening to her questions, which were bland enough. Clearly, she'd done her homework, and had the basics of what Kes did. I was impressed, and I ended up learning quite a bit from her, annoying as that was.

But then her questions took a more personal turn.

"I can't help wondering," she asked, "why someone with your talents is traveling with a smalltime fair?"

I could tell that Kes was pissed, but he hid it well.

"The Reynolds family are friends, so I'm happy to work for their carnival," he said.

"What does your own family think of your choices?" she asked, digging a little more.

"I'm happy to talk about my work," he said, crisply repeating the phrase I'd given him, "but I won't talk about private matters."

She didn't bat an eye.

"And your preference to stay smalltime, is that anything to do with the fact that you're illiterate?"

I took a sharp intake of breath as Kes's expression darkened.

"Who told you that?" he said, almost growling at her.

"So, it's true?"

I decided to step in before Kes gave her a story about how he lost his temper and punched the cameraman who was in his face, recording Kes's brooding anger.

"I don't know where you got your information," I laughed lightly, "but dyslexia is hardly the same as being illiterate. Goodness, you don't want to give your readers the wrong impression when between ten and fifteen percent of adults in the US suffer with the same issue."

Ms Lendl was thrown by my sudden interruption and scowled at me, but she recovered her poise quickly. More importantly, I'd given Kes enough time to shut down his explosive temper.

"Dyslexia?" she jeered. "Isn't that just a convenient cover for someone who never learned to read or write?"

"I don't think there's anything convenient about dyslexia," I said, with a cool smile.

"And I suppose you're an expert on the subject?" she asked nastily.

"Well, as a trained educator specializing in dyslexia, I've certainly studied it and worked with a number of dyslexic children."

"I see," she said tightly. "So you're saying that there is no problem with illiteracy and children who travel with fairs?"

"No more than in the general population," I stated calmly. "We even have our own book group for children here at the carnival. You can come and meet some of them if you like."

"That won't be necessary," she said forcefully. "Because it's Mr. Hawkins' illiteracy that I'm interested in."

What a bitch! The gloves were coming off.

"As I explained earlier, that is factually incorrect, but I'm sure Mr. Hawkins' lawyer would be happy to discuss it with you more fully."

She stood up and tried to smooth out the wrinkles in her expensive clothes.

"Well, thank you for your time, Mr. Hawkins," she said, completely ignoring me. "You have my card. I'll be in touch."

She offered her hand, but Kes simply stood staring at her, arms folded across his chest, and Ms Lendl huffed softly, before marching away.

"Where the hell did she get her information?" I fumed.

Kes looked at me thoughtfully. "Sorcha."

"You think she'd set you up like that?"

"Yeah, I do. She used to say that it would be a great 'human interest story'—illiterate and successful." He shrugged. "Said we could make a ton of money out of selling that shit."

I was shocked. "I think you will have to talk to a lawyer, Kes."

He pulled a face. "What's the point? She didn't say anything that wasn't true."

"You are *not* illiterate!" I said firmly. "You're dyslexic, but you're perfectly capable of reading and writing."

"Sure," he said sharply. "So long as it's simple enough for a five-year old to understand."

I took a deep breath—it was an old argument. But there was something else important that I needed to discuss.

"Kes, did you ever mention your father to Sorcha?"

His quick brain followed my train of thought immediately.

"She knows his name is Hawkins, but I didn't tell her anything else about him. I don't think."

Suddenly, he looked unsure.

"What if this journalist starts digging?"

Kes shrugged. "If she outs my old man, I don't really give a shit. It'll be more embarrassing for him than me."

"So there's nothing that you're worried about her finding out?"

He swore softly under his breath. "I need to speak to Con."

"What's wrong?"

But Kes deliberately ignored me, striding away already dialing his brother's number, leaving me standing.

To say I was upset would be an understatement. Kes was hiding something from me. I thought we were past all secrets.

I was wrong.

But what was so bad that he couldn't tell me? Hell, for all I knew he could be married, have a child or children stashed away. No, not that—Zachary would have told me. But would he? It was clear that his loyalties were with Kes and not me.

I felt like screaming as my brain went haywire trying to think of the multitude of possibilities.

The ugly thoughts reminded me of the last time I saw Gregg

and the lies he'd told me, maybe for months. I didn't like the comparison at all.

Kes was gone for nearly an hour, finally returning quiet and subdued. It wasn't like him at all. Usually, energy crackled from him, to the point that he seemed to vibrate even when he was sitting still. But now, he was quiet, silent, sitting by himself and staring into the distance.

I put down my book and walked across, sitting down on the grass next to him—close, but not touching.

"Do you want to talk about it?" I asked gently.

"Nothing to talk about," he muttered.

"Did Con...?"

But he stopped me immediately. "I said there's nothing to talk about."

I didn't want another argument, so I let it drop. I stood up and returned to the deckchair and my book. But inside, I was begging him to share what was upsetting him. If it hurt him, it hurt me. I wanted to help him, but he wouldn't let me in.

Zachary wandered over, looked at Kes and shrugged at me sympathetically.

"Wanna make S'mores?" Zach suggested with a kind smile.

"Sounds perfect," I agreed, feigning a lightness I definitely didn't feel.

Zach built a small bonfire, and I threw some blankets onto the ground, stretching out, watching the flames leap and dance.

Eventually, Kes came to join us and wrapped his arms around me. He didn't explain where he'd been, what he'd said to his brother, or what had him so rattled.

I fell into a sort of trance as I stared at the fire, Kes's fingers moving rhythmically as he stroked my hair. I was tired enough to go to bed, but too comfortable to move.

I smiled when Ollo came toward us, ambling along with a skinny guy that I'd seen around, but didn't know. The new guy was carrying a guitar, so it looked like it would be campfire songs tonight. I didn't mind; it would be nice to fall asleep listening to that, as long as things didn't get too rowdy, in which case I'd send Kes to kick some asses.

It was the expression on Zachary's face that made me sit up. A huge, beaming smile broke out as soon as he saw the new guy.

"Everyone, this is Luke," he said casually, as if it didn't matter.

We could all tell that it did.

Luke ducked his head, smiling shyly, and plopped down next to Zachary. I glanced at Kes and saw that he looked pleased, but not surprised.

Ollo was clattering around in our kitchen and suddenly appeared with a large white box in his hands.

"Make a wish, birthday girl," he said, placing the box in front of me.

"What?"

I opened the lid to find a beautifully decorated birthday cake with my name on it.

Luke started playing *Happy Birthday* on his guitar and everyone sang along with him. To my surprise and delight, Tonya and the boys, and Rhonda and her family walked out of the shadows carrying flashlights, and joined in.

"Oh wow! You guys! This is amazing! Thank you so much!"

Kes grinned and raised his eyebrows.

"You knew about this!" I accused him.

He shrugged, but he wasn't fooling me.

"Thank you," I whispered, and kissed him full on the lips, my hurt at his earlier behavior dissipated for now. Instead, a flurry of emotions washed through me, and the word 'family' rattled around in my tired brain.

"Where on earth did you get the cake?" I asked him.

"A shop in town. Ordered it on the internet myself," Kes said proudly. "Zach picked it up for me this afternoon."

I sniffed and rubbed my eyes.

"Happy tears?" Kes whispered.

I nodded, my heart too full to risk a word.

He slung his arm around me so that I was snuggled into his chest again, and he took my hand and held it, gently rubbing his fingers over my knuckles. Zachary was smiling, taking a bunch of photographs on his phone, then passed me the cake to cut into slices so it could be handed around.

The icing was too sweet, the cake itself too dry, the sprinkles that decorated it were too hard—it was the best birthday cake I'd ever had.

"It's perfect," I said to Kes, my mouth smeared with icing.

Who'd have thought I'd be celebrating my 25th birthday in a dusty Texas field with a bunch of carnies? I'd been so safe with my dreams over the last eight years, refusing to allow such color into my life again.

Kes laughed and kissed the sugar right off my lips.

Then Ollo walked up, two burning torches in his hands.

"For old time's sake?" he grinned, holding out a torch to Kes.

"Hell, I haven't done this in years," he laughed. "Okay, but if I can't kiss my girl tonight because my mouth is burned, I'm going to kick your ass!"

"You can try," snickered Ollo.

Kes took the torch and a quick sip of lighter fuel, then he and Ollo put on a demonstration of fire-breathing that had the other carnies shouting with delight.

His face was dark, and the flames threw unholy shadows across him, the effect almost demonic. A shiver passed through me. My man could hold an audience, there was no doubt of that.

Then he turned and grinned at me. "Want to try, Aimee?"

Zachary looked at me in surprise. "You can breathe fire?"

"Yeah, she can," Kes said proudly, but I shook my head.

"I did it once, but no, I can't do it anymore."

"Sure you can," Kes encouraged, but I shook my head. "No, definitely not."

Kes covered his disappointment, but I could feel it all the same. He leaned backwards so his upper back was parallel to the ground, then swallowed the torch, putting out the flames with his mouth. I couldn't help wincing, even though I'd seen him do the same thing many times when we were kids.

He dropped down and pulled me against him again, the whiff of smoke and fuel clinging to his skin.

Then Luke began playing another song, his voice surprisingly sweet as he sang.

> *I've been a wild rover for many a year,*
> *And I've spent all my money on whiskey and beer.*
> *And now I'm returning with gold in great store,*
> *And I never will play the wild rover no more.*
>
> *And it's no, nay, never!*
> *No nay never no more.*
> *I will play the wild rover,*
> *No never no more.*

I knew that it was an old Irish folk song, and when I'd heard it before, it was sung in a wild, rousing way. But Luke played it as a lullaby, full of longing and sadness, and although the rover was coming home, to me the words sounded like an ending, not a beginning.

My emotions were very close to the surface that night, and the song brought tears to my eyes.

Kes stood gracefully and helped me to my feet. He didn't even need to ask if I wanted to go, he knew me so well.

I thanked everyone for coming, then let Kes lead me back to the RV, leaving the others to enjoy the rest of the party.

I washed my face and brushed my teeth, but I was surprised when Kes stepped into the tiny space behind me.

"Shower?" he asked, running his fingers down my arms then tilting my chin up so he could kiss my mouth.

"Together?" I asked, my breath rushing out.

He nodded, a smile hovering on his lips.

Nearly a month of communal living had made me far less uptight about what people might or might not hear, but Kes and I hadn't showered together before.

I found that I wanted to very much.

I smiled up at him, and with a grin, he flicked the lock on the door.

The bathroom was soon filled with steam, and I stripped off my clothes as Kes did the same. Then he smoothed his hands over my hair and tied it up so it wouldn't get wet. I never washed my hair at night—and I loved that he cared enough to notice that fact.

When he moved back, I wasn't surprised to see that he was fully erect. I met his eyes, dark and intense, and the hazy light seemed to make them gleam.

When I stepped into the small cubicle, Kes squeezed in behind me. The cold tiles on my ass made me gasp, but his hot body warmed my front as he pulled me against him, with the heat of the water wonderfully soothing as it poured over us.

There wasn't much we could do in such a small space, but it was deliciously erotic to feel his hands on my breasts and between my legs, washing my back and my neck and trying to keep the spray off my hair.

Then it was my turn to run my fingers over his hard body, washing his back and the muscles of his chest, the ridges of his flat stomach. I crouched down to soap his legs, kissing his dick as it twitched next to my mouth.

Kes hissed. "I'm so close to coming right now."

"I don't mind."

"I do. Let's go to bed."

Without waiting for me to answer, he turned off the water and wrapped me in a towel, not bothering with one for himself.

Once we were in our room, I dumped the towel on a chair and crawled up the bed, dead tired.

But not too tired for Kes to make love to me.

He used my towel to dry himself off a little, but water still trickled from his hair and down his chest when he was finished. He leaned against the headboard and patted the space next to him.

I bent down to kiss his stomach, then worked my way up his chest, until his lips were sealed against mine, and his tongue was touching and tasting, sensually dipping into my mouth.

I sighed against him and he gathered me up so I was straddling his thighs, his thick cock rubbing against me hard enough to make me gasp. Kes plucked a condom from the small bedside cabinet and rolled it on quickly, the tendons on his neck standing out as he touched himself.

Then he angled his cock away from his body so I could sink down onto him as he braced his knees against my back.

We stared at each other, chests heaving, eyes locked together—intense, sensuous, intimate.

As his long, strong fingers reached out to stroke and caress my breasts, I felt as though he was trying to communicate through his body—maybe because he was mistrustful of words, because words made lies and he'd been lied to enough. Maybe because when he looked at words on a page, they warped and twisted and taunted him. I don't know. I did know that I felt his love. Whether he wanted to say the words or not, I felt his love.

Our bodies moved together, desire washing through our tiredness, a slow, desperate climb as we continued to stare into each other's eyes, our shared breaths, faster, gasping together, until Kes clenched his teeth and hissed against my throat, his entire body shuddering. I flew off the cliff, falling, until I crashed against his body, gasping air into my lungs.

"I love you!" I panted. "So much, Kes. My Kes."

He formed sounds that had no words as his lips sent soft

prayers against my throat.

A tiny piece of my heart crumbled because I needed to hear the words, just once.

Please, I prayed, *Please say it, just once—say that you love me, because then I can believe it.*

But the words never came, and inevitably our bodies separated from each other again.

It's enough, I told myself. *This intensity. Because I can feel his love, and that's enough.*

We fell asleep, the sounds of Luke's guitar and soft laughter in the background. Kes's family; my family; our family.

For now.

CHAPTER 17
CAROUSEL

From Texas, we headed north to Colorado, then west to Salt Lake City and Reno. My final stop was in Bishop, California where we were pitching up for the Eastern Sierra Tri-County Fair, 60 miles from Fresno.

It was a big gig for the carnies, and we all knew that it was Kes's pulling power that brought us here. But he never once mentioned it, preferring in many ways not to acknowledge that he was the star attraction.

For the last few days, things had been tense between us. Kes had been irritated—to say the least—when Gregg texted to thank me for an email I'd sent him. Of course, Kes heard the message arrive and asked who it was from. It didn't occur to me to lie, but then he demanded to know why I'd emailed Gregg in the first place, and I had to admit that I'd sent the class files on each child because my third-graders would be Gregg's new class. I was just being professional, but Kes made it sound like we'd been emailing each other regularly, which was *not* the case. I couldn't give a damn about Gregg-with-two-g's. But the result was still a huge fight. Kes saw it as a betrayal. Nothing I could say made it better as far as he was concerned.

"He doesn't want you to go," Zach said to me the morning after we arrived in Bishop.

"Well, he didn't say anything like that to me," I muttered. "He was mad that I'd emailed Gregg. But I *had* to do that. I'm being professional, that's all. I don't want anything to do with the asshole, but it's not my choice. And I'd do exactly the same with any other colleague."

Zachary sighed and looked away.

"He's going to miss you."

271

My heart wrenched. I could barely admit to myself how bad things were going to be when we finally said goodbye. Maybe the current coolness between us would be a good thing. Ease us into the separation a little. My sigh matched Zachary's—I was lying to myself. It was going to be painful and awful.

"He thought you'd change your mind," Zachary said quietly. "He still hopes you will."

"I'm going to miss all of you," I said.

Zachary put his arm around me. "And we'll miss you … but it's not us that you're in love with."

I leaned my head on his shoulder.

"Love isn't enough."

He was quiet for a moment. "Then what is?"

"Feel free to ask an easy question!" I said sarcastically.

"I'm serious, Aimee. If love isn't enough, then what is?"

"Fine! I'll tell you: having enough food to eat, having a roof over your head, having a means to earn money. You need all of that before love has a chance. Love doesn't feed you or keep you warm—it withers and dies when you have to get *practical*."

"But if you have all those things *without* love, what's the point?"

"Ugh! I didn't say I had all the answers. I'm just trying to be sensible. I have a job that I love. I have a life back in Boston."

"And you don't here?"

"No, not really: I have Kes's life."

Zachary looked down.

"You must know that he earns enough to support you both?"

"I went to school for four years to earn my bachelor's in teaching. I'm starting a master's program. What about that? Doesn't that matter at all? Because it matters to me!"

Zachary nodded slowly. "You should really be having this conversation with Kestrel."

"I know," I acknowledged, my voice becoming hoarse with unshed tears. "But at the moment we're just snapping and snarling at each other the whole time."

"That's because you need to *talk*."

"I'm dreading it."

"So is Kes."

I nodded because I knew Zachary was right. Kes and I were running out of time again, and I hated it. All the old feelings came rushing back; that horrible sensation of not being in control of my life. It was standing at the edge of a cliff, your vision blurring, because the ground is rushing toward you. But it was stupid, because I *was* in control of my life. And my life was back in Boston, teaching, not being a glorified Kes-groupie.

I knew now that he kept secrets from me. Over the last few weeks, I'd tried to bring up his concerns about what Shelly Lendl might find out, but each time he'd shut me down. I kept hoping that he'd talk to me, confide in me. When he didn't—couldn't or wouldn't—that confirmed my decision. I needed some distance between us; I needed to leave.

The tension between us had built to an unbearable level. Zef and Tucker had taken to avoiding the RV, and not even tempting them with apple pie worked anymore. The other carnies were eyeing Kes like he was an unexploded bomb, and looking at me like I was to blame for the inevitable detonation. Which I was.

In the end we had a stupid fight. About the apple pie. Too hot, too cold, I don't even remember.

I stamped off toward the end of the field, and Kes roared off on one of his bikes. We were really handling this so well.

It was Zef who came to find me.

"What do you want?" I barked when I heard his quiet footsteps behind me.

"Thought you might want some company."

I laughed bitterly.

"It's so ironic: I'm in the middle nowhere, surrounded by nothingness, and I can't get any space!"

"Okay, I'll go. But one of you needs to get their shit together."

"Thank you, Oprah."

"I'm not joking, Aimee," Zef said firmly. "When Kes is like this, he's going to make a mistake. He'll get hurt and it'll be on you."

"Oh, that is so unfair!" I yelled. "You know I don't want anything to happen to Kes! I'd do anything to keep him safe!"

"Anything?" he asked harshly. "Doesn't look like it from where I'm standing."

"Don't worry, Zef," I said nastily. "Two days from now and I won't be your problem anymore."

He sighed. "So you're really going?"

"It was only ever supposed to be a summer vacation," I murmured, half to myself.

"Yeah? Well, life happens while you're making other plans."

I laughed a little at that, but felt even sadder when he left me alone, as I'd so graciously requested.

I thought about a lot of things as I sat watching the shadows lengthen across the spiky grass. I thought about how I felt when I was 16 and Kes disappeared from my life. I thought about what it was like through the empty years, meeting Gregg, my teaching, my life in Boston. I thought about what it meant to me, meeting Kes again in the most unexpected way. I thought about the last seven weeks, the way he'd made love to me, fucked me, kissed me.

I touched the tiny Ferris wheel necklace that I never took off. I thought about Kes's volcanic temper and his life with Sorcha. I thought about the secrets he was keeping from me. I weighed up everything, or tried to. I imagined what it would mean, to stay with him, with all those uncertainties between us, with no real role for me, and no means of earning a living if I traveled with him. I pondered the possibility of him coming back to Boston with me, and immediately dismissed that fantasy. Kes wasn't born to stand still, and if it came to a relationship with me, I was holding him back.

With Zachary managing him, or a new manager taking him on, the sky was the limit. And what could I offer? My heart told me to stay; my head said I was a fool, and that I wouldn't survive the ice that would inevitably form in Kes's eyes one day when he looked at me.

I thought of how callously he'd turned on Sorcha, throwing her out of his life after seven years—and all because she'd loved him too much to tell him the truth. I still wasn't clear how much she'd used Kes as well, but when she'd omitted to tell him that I was looking for him, it was because she wanted him for herself. She always had. After seven years, he'd left her with nothing but regrets—at least that's how I thought she must feel. I didn't owe that bitch anything, but I couldn't help thinking, if he could treat her like that after all those years, would I be next?

I thought about the friendship the carnies had shown me, and I thought about their piecemeal lives: traveling and moving on, traveling, always traveling. I thought about the families left behind, meeting up for a few weeks a year.

And I thought about Kes. The way his eyes darkened when he was angry or turned on, the way they seemed silver at dawn or in twilight. I thought about his smile when he looked at me, the way his gaze brightened when he turned around to see me watching him.

I thought about the anger in his expression when I displeased him, the simmering violence when anyone mentioned Sorcha. I thought about the fact that he'd never ever told me that he loved me, that he needed me, that he didn't want me to go.

I thought about all these things, for hours, until the sun had sunk, and stars appeared—cold, dead suns, that still sparkled in the night sky.

For the first time during the whole summer, I'd missed Kes's show.

In the end, I did the only thing that made sense. I couldn't wait two more days, not with this painful distance growing between us. Better to get it over and done with. That's what I told myself.

I went back to the RV and packed my clothes, stuffing everything into my suitcase. And that's where Kes found me.

"You missed the show."

"I'm sorry."

He stared at my suitcase, his gaze going cold.

"What are you doing?"

"I'm going home, Kes."

"Back to Boston."

"Yes."

"Back to … Gregg?"

I turned to glare at him. "No! I'm going back to my job, to my work. I have commitments to the school, to my pupils. I've told you that!"

He took a deep breath, his chest rising and falling rapidly.

"Just like that."

"No, not just like that. I like being a teacher. I want my pupils to experience the joy of learning. I want…"

"Life's out there!" he yelled suddenly, waving his hands in a sweeping circle. "Not in those books you're always reading!"

I shook my head, disappointed that after all this time, he still didn't understand. He still didn't understand *me*.

"You're so wrong, Kes," I cried out. "There's magic in

books, in the worlds writers create. How do you think I learned about magic in the first place? Because I didn't learn it from my parents—I learned that there's a world out there from books."

"Then you should have opened your eyes and looked!" he shouted. "What we have … what I thought we had … doesn't that mean anything?"

"Yes! Of course it does! But I have responsibilities!"

Kes shook his head furiously. "When you were 12 you climbed trees and learned how to breathe fire! What happened to that girl?"

I looked at him sadly, the gulf widening between us, and when I replied, my voice was a whisper.

"I grew up."

He clenched his teeth. "Do you know what I dream about? My dream would be to die looking at the lights on the Ferris wheel. When I get old, when my body has given up, that's what I want to see. And in that dream, you're standing next to me."

Tears rose in my eyes. I'd been trying to get closer to him my whole life. Was he finally letting me in, just as I was leaving?

"Do you love me?" I asked, my voice barely more than a whisper.

"You know I do."

"You've got to say the words, Kes."

"Why? What difference does it make? Words don't mean anything!"

"They do to me."

His hand grabbed a glass from beside his bed, and he smashed it against the wall.

I ducked, crying out as my hands flew to cover my eyes as I was showered by tiny shards raining down on me. When I dared to look at Kes, he seemed shocked by his own actions.

"You say you love me…"

"I do!" I choked out.

"You love me? Why can't you love *this*? Why isn't it enough?"

Kes gestured hopelessly with his hands.

"Aimee, this is all of me. Stay. Please."

He was asking me to stay—he was begging me.

"Then tell me what you're hiding. Give me something! If you want me to be with you, Kes, you have to let me in."

I could see the war of indecision on his face, and I dared to hope. But then the gates slammed, and he stared at me, his eyes cool and shuttered.

My heart began to splinter.

"Kes," I whispered. "If we don't have trust, where can we possibly go from here?"

"Why should I trust you?" he ground out. "You're leaving me, just like everyone else in my life that ever said they loved me. It's just words. If you loved me, you'd stay."

"If you trusted me, you'd tell me the truth."

A flash of pain crossed his face. "Just … stay!"

And then I broke him.

"I can't. I have to go back to my job…"

He growled in pain and frustration.

"You want to leave so badly, find your own fucking ride!"

He left, slamming the RV door behind him.

My hands shook as I dialed Zachary's number. When he answered, I could hardly speak from hurt, from pain, because if I let go now, I'd shatter. The air swirled around me in hot, ugly colors, and my body shuddered.

"Will you take me to the airport?" I gasped. "I have to leave. I have to go now. Please, Zach, please!"

"Oh, Aimee."

And then I couldn't speak anymore.

I dropped my phone and fell to the floor, rocking myself as sickening pain lanced through me. It was too much, too much.

Only the sound of my aching sobs broke through the silence. He didn't come back. My Kes was gone.

The RV was still silent when the headlights from Zach's truck shined through the window.

Ollo was with him. We hugged, and he stroked my hair, but I couldn't speak. He simply watched sadly as I curled into the passenger seat of the truck and Zachary tossed my suitcase in the back. I hid my face from both of them, and I couldn't bring myself to wave goodbye to Ollo.

As Zachary drove into the darkness, the lights from the carnival disappeared and streetlights took their place, flickering past my eyes the nearer we got to the airport.

"Aimee, are you sure?" Zachary asked, one more time.

I shook my head.

"It's not too late to come back."

"It is. He hates me."

"Kes could never hate you."

"You didn't see him, Zach."

"Come back with me," he pleaded.

"No," I said, my voice low. "I'm going back east. I have to. I can't stay…"

He hugged me tightly. "If you ever need anything, Aimee, anything … just ask, okay?"

"There is one thing you could do for me…"

"Name it."

"Look after him. Look after Kes."

He sighed and kissed my cheek. "You didn't need to ask that."

As I waited for my flight, bathed in the too bright lights of Fresno Airport, I felt sick and cold.

"What have I done?" I asked myself. "What have I done?"

END OF BOOK I

NOTE FROM THE AUTHOR

You can read the conclusion of Kestrel and Aimee's story in *The Traveling Woman*.

38160115R00165

Made in the USA
Charleston, SC
30 January 2015